COLUMBELLA

COLUMBELLA

BY PHYLLIS A. WHITNEY

DOUBLEDAY & COMPANY, INC.
Garden City, New York

All of the characters in this book
are fictitious, and any resemblance
to actual persons, living or dead,
is purely coincidental.

When I collect background material for a book in a place which is new to me, I usually turn first to the local public library for help. This was especially true in the Virgin Islands. Blanche Souffront and June Lindquist of the St. Thomas Library not only assisted me by putting books on island history at my disposal, but also provided a number of introductions which enabled me to meet local residents. I want to take this opportunity to thank them for aid so generously given.

I am particularly grateful to Joanne Reese, a young page at the library, who was my friend and companion on trips around the island.

Others to whom I owe my gratitude are Donald and Emily Plantz, who were most understanding of a writer's problems, and generous with introductions and assistance. Howard Blaine of the Department of Commerce saw to it that I toured St. Thomas more than once. Mrs. Joseph Green invited me into beautiful Louisenhoj House—which set my imagination to "building" a fictional house of my own on a hilltop above Charlotte Amalie.

The graceful oval room in the plantation house of "Whim," in St. Croix, helped me to build my own "Caprice." And when I later found a handful of Caribbean columbellas and a black and white murex shell at Seashells Unlimited in New York, I brought them home and let them haunt me for a while until I was launched in my story of a woman bent on destruction—who liked to call herself "Columbella."

COLUMBELLA

I

I had come softly along the upper gallery so as not to waken the members of a household which was still strange to me. After all that had happened since my arrival, I was wide awake and torn between the feeling that I wanted to stay and engage myself in this strange combat and the wish to turn back to emptiness, to lethargy and a suspension of all pain.

The high gallery on which I stood looked out over the town and the lovely harbor of Charlotte Amalie, with the dark islands and little peninsulas floating on a moonlit sea. The moon was bright, but for all its beauty and the way it turned the rooftops to silver, it seemed a chill illumination.

Below the gallery a flamboyant tree spread its branches, shadowing the wide, paved terrace that had formed a stage for ugly drama only a few hours before. From where I stood I could see the tops of a thick planting of tropical forest that seemed to entice me to enter its tangle of dark undergrowth, even while its lush vegetation repelled me at the same time. I did not understand why, just as I did not understand what it was about the man, Kingdon Drew, which gave me so strong an impulse to advance and flee at one and the same time. He had made it clear that he neither approved of me nor welcomed my presence, yet I had felt a quickening in me at the first sight of him, and my sympathies were too readily engaged, for all that I was scornful and bitterly amused by my own reactions.

Why it must be this man, I did not know—though I understood the cause well enough. I could almost hear my mother's voice chiding me: "Do stop dreaming, Jessica. You are twenty-eight years old and it is ridiculous to find yourself bemused by flame trees and a moonlit tropical night." But my mother's voice had been silent for two months. I could dream if I liked—and if I was brave enough to dream.

At that moment I was shaken and far from brave. I had been in the house for only a short time yet I had already encountered hostility that dismayed me by its vigor. I was here because two women —my aunt, Janet Foster, and the formidable Mrs. Maud Hampden—had connived to bring me here. I had been gently bullied and overruled until I found it easier to drift with the tide of their persuasion than to summon the energy to swim against them.

For the past seven years I had deliberately cut myself off from a large area of living. I had tried as far as it was possible to give myself to my work as a teacher and counselor in a small private school for girls, to concern myself with the problems of young students and with the care of my mother, who had been an invalid for years. I had made large claims to myself—true enough in part—about the satisfactions of such a life. Of course there were satisfactions. But I'd turned a deaf ear to those mocking inner voices that accused me of stepping aside from any real involvement with life. Now and then wry laughter would rise in me and I would turn futilely in my trap trying to find a way to silence my own accusers, but mostly I had learned to guard my sensitivities, to dull, to blunt, to avoid. Now the need was gone and suddenly I had the alarming feeling that a driving impulse to be alive was about to come storming in upon me like a tidal wave that would wash me out to sea.

Two months ago Helen Abbott, my mother, had died suddenly and left me alone and free of my bondage. I had loved her a great deal, and sometimes I had hated her. It was because of her, ironically enough, that Maud Hampden had brought me to this house and engaged me for what seemed an impossible task.

Where I now stood on this high mountain spine of the island a wind seemed always to blow with a great rushing of sound through the trees. On the terrace below me the shadow of the flamboyant stirred in the moonlight as though something moved beneath its branches. I could hear my mother's voice, "Fanciful, fanciful!" but I did not need to listen any more. I was free and perhaps I could learn how to be a whole woman for the first time in my life. But not heedlessly, recklessly, simply because those life forces in me which had been so long submerged and sublimated were too suddenly set free.

Three weeks ago I had turned in my resignation to the school where I had taught in a small lakeshore suburb of Chicago, and I had come to the Virgin Islands. For three quiet weeks I had immersed myself in St. Thomas. In August the wintertime crowds were absent and I could find quiet stretches of beach where I might lie in the sun, letting it sap my energy and lull me into emptiness. I had not wanted to waken, or to think. There were too many questions I was afraid to face. Had I thrown my life away for so many years that it was now too late to repair the damage? If I had stood and fought seven years ago, would a marriage with Paul have brought me what I wanted? If I was to be honest with myself, I had to admit that Paul was a very small part of what had frightened me. However bitter-tasting self-knowledge might be, I must eventually face my own destructive self-doubts. I must not forever excuse myself, or be panicked into a thoughtless snatching at what I had missed.

Often enough my mother had told me that I was born to spinsterhood and the service of others. She said this in her teasing way, being realistic according to her lights. Men frightened me, she used to say —she who was never afraid of any man! How could I not believe her when I was too young to know any better? But now, though I was no longer a child, and though Helen was gone, I had not yet learned how to still her teasing voice.

Perhaps I had not tried very hard. I had drowsed in the sun and postponed any testing of myself with new encounters that might bring demands I would not know how to meet. It seemed safer that way.

Until Aunt Janet began to worry about me. She was my father's older sister and when she lived in the States she knew my mother well and liked her not at all. My aunt was a plump, hearty woman, with a frank liking for food and men. Probably in that order. Not that she tried to be anything but her age, or that she was in the least like Helen. My mother thrived on that adulation she could so easily win from men younger than herself, though once she had it she would turn fecklessly toward some new source of admiration. She acquired, tired of, threw away. Aunt Janet wanted only to give, and give generously. She felt that a healthy interest in men was vital and the men she knew responded to her cheerful enjoyment of their company. She had been twice a widow and it would not have surprised me to see her marry again. Some years ago she had taken over a handsome old Danish house in Charlotte Amalie and turned it efficiently into a small, successful hotel.

By contrast, my mother had never had an efficient thought in her head—except perhaps when it came to charming admirers. In recent years I had noticed that she no longer put on her glasses when she looked at herself in a mirror—so the effect must have remained gently blurred and undisturbing as she grew older. Not that she had lost her beauty or her ability to trouble young men with longings she had no intention of satisfying with more than kind words and a touch of the hand. I learned very early what she was doing, yet somehow I never stopped loving her.

There was a great deal about my mother to love—her gaiety and sweetness, her interest in the problems of others that made us all open our hearts and talk to her, not realizing at first to what deadly and yet innocent use the things she learned might later be put. Even her helplessness was sometimes endearing and held me to her. Before he died, my professor father had warned me that I must look after her because she could not look after herself—she did not even know who "herself" was. I had kept my promise to him. That, at least, I had done.

But here in St. Thomas I could lie on the sand, walk the waterfront, climb the hills in a state of suspension that postponed any coming to grips with the fact that I had no life of my own. However much I had avoided facing this in the past, sooner or later I must now accept it, do something about it before the wasted years slipped away and it was too late. But cautiously—always I reminded myself of that—and not because the look in a man's eyes set the blood thudding in my veins.

Aunt Janet worried about me increasingly. "Are you going back to that school to teach?" she would prod. "For goodness' sakes, isn't it time to get out of your rut and be a woman as well as a teacher? A job is important—but it's only a part of your life."

I did not want to go back. When my aunt had written me after the funeral, asking me to stay with her as long as I liked, I'd packed my bags and come. I had managed that bit of action, at least, I thought wryly. I suppose I had some vague notion that in a new place I would at once take on a new coloration. I would be so different from my old self that no one would guess I was that nice but rather timid schoolteacher who was really known by only a few young girls, and considered remote, wrapped in her work, her devotion to her mother, by everyone else.

Of course the change in scene had brought no change in me. I had not flung myself gaily into island life, in spite of Aunt Janet's attempts to introduce me to her friends. I slipped out of the way when guests gathered at the hotel, and wandered off alone, holding back from the moment when sensation would return. I suppose I dreamed of becoming someone new, without being in the least willing to work at it.

Aunt Janet had ended all this the day before. She pried me out of my hiding place and plunged me into the frightening conflict in which I now found myself. For several days she had been plotting behind my back. She was often on the telephone to Hampden House —that square white structure with the sloping roofs that stands high on its cliff above Charlotte Amalie, managing somehow to look overbearing and ominous. She had gone up the mountain to talk to Maud Hampden, and, finally, she brought Maud herself down to talk to me, leaving us alone so that I could turn to no one for assistance.

We sat in the cool, shadowy parlor of the hotel, with its grass rugs, its woven Hong Kong fan chairs and pearl-inlaid tables from old China. When Aunt Janet left us, I sat in one of those chairs, feeling dwarfed by the huge fan that exploded behind me in a regal spread.

Maud Hampden—I quickly called her "Maud" to myself, since that was how Aunt Janet spoke of her and the name came easily—knew better than to trust such a chair. She sat on the chintz sofa with its flower print that was no more flamboyant than the trees of St. Thomas which bear that name. She was probably in her seventies, a woman of medium height, thin—lean rather than slim—and turned a bit leathery by much tolerance for the sun. She wore her gray hair short and let it blow to untidiness in island winds. Her brown print dress was sleeveless and her bare arms showed the stringiness of thin old age. Her hands seemed those of a capable woman in spite of ridged blue veins, and they made one think in contrast of Helen's hands, so smooth of skin and pampered.

Maud Hampden's eyes were her one handsome feature, and wide set, gray-blue, they studied me so attentively that I was flattered into giving her an equal attention. She was a woman clearly accustomed to command and she reduced me without effort to the position of a sophomore facing the school principal. In my three weeks of nothingness I had even forgotten my teacher's useful poise, which could often hide uncertainty about myself and enable me to meet strange parents without betraying concern.

Troubling with no preliminaries, Maud Hampden's first words cut through the chitchat of convention. She had given me a confident handshake that crunched my bones and waved me into my chair, though she did this forthrightly and without offense.

"I like the way you look," she said at once.

I could think of no reply, and she smiled at me reassuringly, a warm smile that showed me how handsome she must have been in her younger years.

"Of course you're wondering what on earth I mean by that. I'll tell you. First of all, you're young and that will put you closer to Leila in age than the rest of us. You seem friendly in a reserved way, and not at all frightening. I like gray eyes that look at me directly, and I like the way you wear your nice brown hair."

To escape fuss, I wear my hair simply in a straight, smooth bob that swings to the line of my jaw. I have been caught by the turn of fashion's pendulum, so that I'm now in style again, though I suspected that Maud Hampden had little interest in style. On this she promptly surprised me, continuing in her straightforward, assured manner.

"You dress quietly too. I like that blue linen you're wearing. You haven't rushed off to the shops to get yourself up in tropical prints like a tourist."

I had no way of knowing that she compared me with Leila's mother, Catherine Drew—to what she regarded as my advantage.

"Janet tells me you have a way with young girls," she said. "She tells me you've a knack for dealing with problem children."

This was pure hearsay on Aunt Janet's part. She could not really know, except by letters I had written her about my experiences at school.

"My work has been with young people—mainly girls," I admitted, still wondering what this was all about.

Maud Hampden nodded her gray head vigorously. "Exactly. And I understand that you want to find yourself a new position and not return to your former school."

"I've burned my bridges," I said. "But I haven't got around to looking for a new place yet."

"Good. Then you're in the market, so to speak. I want you to come up the mountain to Hampden House and try your hand with my granddaughter. I can't promise you anything for sure, but if this should work out, I might be able to offer you private employment with us for the next several years."

"But—what would I be doing? How old is your granddaughter?"

"Leila is fourteen. Oh, you wouldn't be a governess in the old-fashioned sense. You'd be more a friend and counselor, with some tutoring thrown in. We still have a school problem here in the Islands, you know. Leila's father is from Colorado and he honestly believes she should be sent home to his sister's in Denver. You can help me convince him that this won't be necessary. There's time enough for her to leave St. Thomas when she's older. You can supplement what schooling she receives here and help prepare her for college."

By this time I was recovering my scattered wits. Her plan sounded doubtful to me. There was something oddly urgent behind Mrs.

Hampden's invitation. Surely I was a very thin reed for anyone to clutch with such vigorous intent—unless in final desperation. And I wanted to deal with no one else's desperate problems. I had enough of my own.

"Why don't you want her to leave the island?" I asked.

Surprisingly, the old woman's face seemed to crumple in upon itself and the look of autocracy gave way to something sad and rather touching.

"I suppose I'm selfish," she said. "Leila is all I have left. I don't want her to go away. I want her here with me, where I can watch over her as I've done since she was born. But this must be for her good, as well as for mine. Leila doesn't want to be sent away. She's fighting her father with all her might. You could offer an answer for her, though she may not accept you, even so."

This was an honest admission, and I liked Maud Hampden the better for it. Until now she had seemed well able to order her universe and I had resisted her ordering mine. I'd had too much of being ordered in my life. But this gently affecting aspect of her character engaged my sympathy.

"You spoke of a problem," I said. "Can you tell me about it?"

She did not hesitate. "It's mother trouble," she admitted, and left it there, her clear, fine eyes watching me intently.

Warmth crept all too readily into my cheeks, and to the very roots of my hair. Obviously Aunt Janet and Maud Hampden had been talking about my own mother problem, and I hated the idea that my secrets had been displayed to a stranger.

With a movement that seemed clumsily abrupt I left the dwarfing fan chair and walked through the French doors which opened onto the veranda. The hotel stood upon its own rise of hill and from there I could look over the sloping lawn with its tropical shrubbery and down a long flight of stone steps that led toward the center of town. Beyond, harbor waters lay still and blue within the arms made by Flag Hill and Hassel Island, and only small puffs of isolated cloud floated in the sky. The sun was bright yet not so hot as I had expected it to be in August. Trade winds played across these islands and even in summer the heat was not unbearable. As I stood with my back to Maud Hampden I could feel my brief spurt of anger dying and lethargy creeping back. I wanted to do nothing, be nothing. I certainly did not want to cope with the difficulties of a fourteen-year-old girl who was having trouble with her mother. That was not for me. Never again.

Behind me Maud Hampden's voice was kind. "I don't blame you

for feeling annoyed. We've talked about you, of course—Janet and I. Your aunt is concerned. She feels that you have something to work out too, and the quicker you begin, the better it will be for you. Your need and mine happen to coincide. It could very well be that you will prove my answer to a troublesome problem and it may, in part, be the answer to your own."

"I'd like to know what the problem is," I said stiffly, resisting her very kindness, shrinking from this display of my own weakness.

She raised her hands in her lap and then let them fall in a gesture that seemed touchingly helpless in so sure a woman. "No," she said, "I can't tell you that. You must come and see for yourself. You can do us no good unless your own emotions are engaged. If I tried to explain you might refuse to come at all. The situation isn't a pleasant one. Perhaps we can make a bargain, you and I."

I waited in silence.

"Come for a week," she said. "A trial week. See what you make of our troubles. Come to us without prejudice and see whether my granddaughter's problems have anything to say to you. Then you can decide. If you stay I'll see that your salary is more than you received in the States."

There was no way in which to oppose this woman, or so I believed. She would not accept the no I wanted to give. Whatever objection I might find, she would simply raise another argument that would put still greater pressure upon me, and I lacked the strength to resist her. After all, what could a week matter? Perhaps, if the thing worked out, I would have found an answer to my own necessity to make a living, and with very little effort on my part. Besides, I knew very well that I must snap out of this senseless lying on the sand and stupefying my brain with heat before I found myself unable to take action of any kind. I did not want to act—but I must.

"When do you wish me to come?" I asked.

Mrs. Hampden stood up as briskly and confidently as though the outcome had never for a moment been in doubt. "This evening after dinner will be fine. I'll go home at once and have a room prepared for you. You can settle yourself in the house tonight and begin with Leila tomorrow morning. Do thank Janet for me, and tell her I've run along."

I had a feeling that she meant to make a precipitous escape before I could change my mind. A little out of breath, and with a sense of being rushed headlong into something I knew nothing about, I went with her to the steps. She held out her hand and I felt again her dry, autocratic clasp.

"At least I should identify my household for you," she said. "So you'll know who they are when you meet them. My two daughters, Edith and Catherine, live with me at present. Edith is the elder and has no children of her own. She is married to Alex Stair, who owns a fine little import shop downtown—and an older shop in St. Croix, where they used to live near Christiansted. I was ill for a time last year and they moved here so that Edith could take charge of this house and look after me. Catherine—my youngest child—is Leila's mother. There was a boy in between—Roger. He died in Korea." Underlying pain touched her voice.

"And Leila's father?" I asked.

"King builds houses here in the Islands. Often he designs them too. Kingdon Drew. I'll send him for you this evening. Of course you must understand that he won't want you to come. In fact, none of them will like anything about this idea of mine. Not at first. But I'm counting on you to convince them that this is the best possible plan, for Leila's sake."

I found her highhanded conclusions about my ability alarming.

"What if I feel that your plan for your granddaughter is wrong? What if I side with the rest of the family?"

"Then you'll tell me so. Perhaps I'll listen and perhaps I won't. But we'll face that when the time comes. I expect, naturally, that you'll agree with me. Good-by for now, my dear. And don't look so stricken. I know even more about you than you think. And I've seen you for myself. I'm inclined to have confidence, not only in your capability, but in your natural instinct for kindness as well."

That I had shown any such instinct, I doubted, and found myself wondering if she was a woman who saw only what she wanted to see.

When she had shaken hands with me I watched her go down the steps toward town, and all the questions that lay in wait rushed upon me, tearing through the self-protective walls that Maud Hampden had breeched. Not questions about the household at the top of the mountain, but about myself—all those questions I had for so long been afraid to face.

II

Aunt Janet had kept out of sight while Maud Hampden was there, but she appeared with such alacrity the moment Maud was gone that I felt sure she had not missed much of the interview.

Dropping into one of the fan chairs with no thought of the fact that it did not flatter her to be so framed, she folded plump arms and surveyed me in a proprietary manner. Her hair was naturally curly, and its damp, graying tendrils coiled childishly about a face that was anything but childish. Aunt Janet's eyes were like my father's—but a great deal wiser. It had taken a certain innocence on my father's part to remain in love with Helen.

"I'm glad you've accepted Maud's offer," she said. "This is a way to get yourself into the swim of things again. But at the same time I have a few . . . qualms."

I smiled at her wryly. "I gather that Mrs. Hampden has too. But since she wouldn't tell me what they are, perhaps you'd better. Are they qualms about me, or guilt about what the two of you are plotting?"

"It's that woman—Catherine," Aunt Janet admitted. "Leila's mother. It's a good thing you're not the sort to antagonize people, because she can be nasty. She's a good example of what can happen when a girl is allowed to grow up without sensible restraint."

Having met Maud, I felt a little surprised. "Mrs. Hampden looks like a woman who would run her family as she wished."

My aunt shook her head. "Everything went out of hand because of the first Roger—her husband. By the time he got himself drowned in a sailboat, Catherine, their daughter, was almost uncontrollable. Goodness knows, there was a scandal or two when Catherine's father was alive and she was still a young girl, no older than Leila. Now she seems to be running hell-bent for disaster, and I don't like it one bit."

"What sort of scandals?" I asked.

Aunt Janet pursed her lips. "Oh, there was a time when they sent her away to a school in the States. She lasted long enough to snitch a sapphire bracelet from her roommate, who should never have brought such a thing to school in the first place. Maud flew over to bring Catherine home and the whole thing was hushed up. Roger thought it an hilarious prank. He didn't want his darling off at school anyway, and he bought her diamond earrings to make up for the whole thing when she got home."

"This doesn't sound very appealing," I said, "but while a bracelet might be a temptation to a schoolgirl, I suppose she has grown up by now."

"I'm afraid she's merely graduated into taking more important property. Such as other women's husbands. And she's wildly extravagant. Maud and King have been frantic about her spending—trips to Europe and South America and all around the Caribbean. I'm afraid she's become a devotee of the rich international set—the jet set, I guess they call it. Anyhow, she's already run through the fortune her father left her."

"If her husband stands for all this," I said, "I suppose there's no more strength in him than there was in her father?"

Aunt Janet grinned and gave me a quick appraising look. "I wouldn't say that. King's made of good stuff, for all his frustrations. If I were as young as you are, and as pretty as you—"

I returned her look with a frown that was only half pretense. "You've been trying to throw me at one man after another ever since I came here. If you're now going to fling me at a married man—"

"He's not so very married," Aunt Janet mused. "It's only the child who keeps him there. Maud says he and Catherine haven't shared the same bedroom for years."

I couldn't help smiling because my aunt was irrepressible. "You are a very immoral woman," I told her. "You have a one-track mind and I do wish you'd find a more likely subject for your matchmaking than I'm willing to be."

She sat silent in the big fan chair, the overt appraisal gone from her eyes, and I knew her thoughts were taking a graver, uneasier turn. When she spoke again the words came abruptly.

"King has tried more than once to get away. He's a man of pride and self-respect, and his wife is destroying him."

"Then why doesn't he leave?"

"I've told you—because of the child. Though I think there's more here than meets the eye."

I wanted to hear no more. The personal problems of Leila's parents were not mine to solve. Their existence simply meant that the girl's own difficulties—whatever they were—might be all the more troublesome as a result.

Aunt Janet was studying me rather as Maud Hampden had done—though her thoughts, obviously, took a different course.

"Catherine is supposed to be a beauty, but I can never see her kind of looks. You're the one who could be stunning if you put your mind to it. Gray eyes with all those dark lashes. That cleft in your chin."

I laughed delightedly, and was startled by the sound. I had not done much laughing lately. "Do go on," I urged.

"If I looked like you I'd have sense enough to know it!" she snapped. "You've elegant features and a fine, clear skin. To say nothing of that tall, slim figure that you know how to dress. What you don't have is any belief in yourself." She broke off as if she had thought of something that worried her. "Catherine will detest you, of course. She'll stand for no one around with feminine appeal."

I still felt like laughing. "I don't think she'll need to worry about my fatal appeal. Tell me about the Hampdens—who are they?"

"The family goes way back to early days in the Islands," Aunt Janet said. "As Maud's family does too. There were big sugar estates on both sides. The Danes were smart about bringing in help from other islands during their ownership—of whatever nationality. That's how the Hampdens came in, since they were British way back. The Hampden money—what's left of it—all came from St. Croix sugar and rum, though most of that trade has died out by now. Some of the mills are still standing, as well as the old plantation house the first Hampden built. Roger was born there. Maud went to it as his bride, and all three of her children were born there too. Now it belongs to Catherine, to whom her father left it."

My aunt fell silent, suddenly thoughtful and troubled again.

"You don't really want me to go to Hampden House, do you?" I said.

At once she pretended recovery and flashed me an indignant look. "Of course I want you to go. I just want you to be careful while you're there."

"Careful of what?"

"I'm not sure. I don't really know. Maud tells me very little. But something is going on. There's something wrong up there that makes me uneasy. I've felt it on recent visits. I suppose it's Catherine I'm fearful about. She's just come home from another swing around the Caribbean—staying at the best hotels, having herself a time. On what? Whose money is she spending now? I think they're running scared up there and I don't like it. So watch yourself, dear. Do what you can for the child, but keep out of Catherine's way. And don't go falling for Kingdon Drew—at least not under Catherine's nose."

The about-faces Aunt Janet could manage often confused me, and I could only smile in bewilderment.

"Just a minute ago you were singing his praises and telling me he wasn't so very married."

"Of course he's married—whether he likes it or not. But that doesn't make him any less attractive. It wouldn't be pleasant to have Catherine down on you. She's a taker, you know—and what she takes she keeps. Just watch your step and you'll be all right. Besides, there's always auntie to run home to if things get too thick for you up there."

I did not want to come running back to the safety Aunt Janet offered me. If this effort was to do me any good, it must be a real effort. While my aunt knew a great deal about bedding people down comfortably, feeding them well, keeping them happy, I sometimes suspected that she knew very little about more complex human needs and she often found herself disturbed when food, sleep, and love-making did not solve everything.

I avoided further discussion by going off to pack. Her talk had left me more than a little uneasy and I wanted to be rid of apprehension. I wanted to be able to make judgments of my own by the time Kingdon Drew came to take me up the hill.

When my brief packing was done I went for a walk along one of Charlotte Amalie's narrow, flower-rimmed streets and found a place where I could climb stone steps and stand in the open, to look up at the high green ridge of the mountain where Hampden House rose from amidst its own thick shrubbery. Again I had the strange sense of a house that held itself apart. Square and strong, it ruled its area of hillside, its many windows aglitter with light, but somehow cold on that sunny mountaintop—cold and oddly sinister. My apprehension grew in the face of my own fancies and went with me into the evening.

After dinner I sat on the hotel veranda, waiting apart from the guests, my suitcase beside me. Twilight lay softly upon St. Thomas, and though it would not last for long, I could still watch the approach to the hotel. Whenever I saw a man turn up the flight of long stone steps that led from the lower level of town, I stiffened, wondering if it was Kingdon Drew. My aunt's words had done nothing to allay the doubts I already had about this commitment, and I found myself awaiting his arrival with both concern and curiosity.

I guessed the man was he the moment he started the climb. Halfway up he paused and let his eyes travel the length of the veranda, to rest upon me and my suitcase. At once he came upward with purpose. As he crossed the street above the steps, approaching the hotel grounds, a brown-skinned man greeted him and he stopped to shake hands and talk for a moment, so that I had an opportunity to study Leila's father before I came face to face with him.

He was hatless and wore a light suit with a jacket—a concession to the evening hour, undoubtedly, in a place where men dressed informally by day. He was probably in his late thirties, tall, forceful, rather overwhelming. The sort of man who used to alarm me at first glance. But even though I distrusted this sort of vitality, I recognized that such distrust might grow from the fact that it challenged something in me I did not want aroused. Aunt Janet's words flashed uncomfortably through my mind and I wished she had not planted this particular awareness in me, preventing me from being entirely casual.

Not that active, vital men were likely to be interested in me. They quickly put me down as shy and hardly worth the trouble it would take to crack me out of my shell. In fact, Paul had told me that very thing, feeling that he was the perceptive exception. But that was before he met Helen. So I had kept my blinders in place when such men went by, and had almost ceased to know they existed. My mother had doted on them, and had a way with them that wasn't mine. Now she was gone and something had happened to both my blinders and my protective coloration, so that I began badly with Kingdon Drew, quickly ill at ease and all too sharply aware of him —when what I wanted to be was poised and cool and indifferent.

He came up the veranda steps and introduced himself without cordiality. I rose to shake hands with him and he gave me a direct look, frank and measuring, apparently finding little about me to approve.

"You're very young," he said curtly. "I suppose I expected someone twice your age. Do you think Leila will pay any attention to you?"

He meant to antagonize me, and he succeeded. So abrupt a dismissal of my worth stiffened my spine and reminded me that I had, after all, dealt with difficult children and their parents before.

"I don't know Leila," I told him. "I'm not any more sure than you are that I will be right for this position. I've been talked into it, I think, but since I've promised Mrs. Hampden that I'll come for a week, I would like to keep my promise."

Perhaps my candor surprised him, for a faint smile twitched one corner of his mouth.

"At least you're forthright about it," he said. "Though I doubt that Mrs. Hampden has told you all you may have to deal with when you come to the house." The timbre of his voice hardened and I suspected he might be given to harshness when he disliked or distrusted.

At least I answered him with more spirit than I'd been able to summon for some weeks. "Mrs. Hampden feels that I should make up my own mind about Leila's problem."

For an oddly tense moment we studied each other. He was a ruggedly built man, and I had to look up at him, for all that I am fairly tall. His eyes were a very dark brown, with heavy brows slashed above, emphasizing the angular, marked bone structure of his face. His hair was as dark as his eyes and rose in a curious thick ridge over the right temple. The healthy outdoor look of the Islands marked his skin, though there were deep creases running down each cheek—not smile creases, but lines which living had somehow pressed into his face.

I was the first to break the challenge of the appraisal which passed between us. I was into this now, and consequently less afraid.

"Mrs. Hampden has already told me that you don't want me at the house. In fact, she has warned me that everyone in the family may be against my coming."

"Yet you're still willing to come?"

"To come, yes. Perhaps not to stay. There's a stake in this for me too. If I can be useful, Mrs. Hampden suggests that the position may become permanent for the next few years. I'd like to stay in St. Thomas for a while if it's possible."

"Years!" The word sounded derisive. With a quick, strong movement that suggested energy suppressed, he leaned to pick up my suitcase. "That's not likely with my wife opposed to your staying. Catherine will want no interference with her daughter."

I sensed his antagonism as he spoke of his wife. Here, as I had been warned, was a broken marriage, and that usually meant an unhappy position for any child involved. I reminded myself that in spite of the hints that had been dropped against Catherine Drew by Mrs. Hampden and Aunt Janet, I must not take sides. If I was to be of any real use to Leila, it could only be from a position of objectivity

—not as a partisan interfering with her loyalties, whatever they might be.

"Come along, if you're ready," Kingdon Drew said. "You'll know the worst about us soon enough, and when you do you'll run for your life."

Like a rabbit? I thought, and found myself stiffening again. His casual assumption that I could neither handle nor endure the situation into which I was being thrust aroused resentment in me, stirred a semblance of long-buried pride.

"Why are you so determined to frighten me?" I asked.

He had taken a few steps down the veranda, but now he turned and looked at me with a sudden awareness that had not existed in him before. There seemed a certain gentling of his expression and manner.

"You might as well know that I'll accept no interference with my plans for Leila. If you come I won't make things easy for you. I don't care for anything about Mrs. Hampden's scheme. At the end of the week, if not before, I'll expect to send you away gladly. Nevertheless I like courage and I appreciate your willingness—even though I think it's foolhardiness—to make an attempt at the impossible."

Something in me leaped away in alarm from his slight softening toward me. I had no confidence in what he credited as my courage. That quality had gone too long untried in me, and I had no wish for him to guess that I might indeed run like a scared rabbit at my first testing. I did not want him to be kind to me in any way. I could best dislike and distrust his type of man when he remained in character and showed me no gentleness or consideration. It was safer to detest than to be drawn unwittingly into liking.

Fortunately, Aunt Janet joined us just then to say good-by to me with added instructions about keeping in close touch, and to banter a bit with Kingdon Drew. He responded with teasing, affectionate flattery, and I sensed again his softer side.

When we left the hotel we walked down the flight of stone steps common to Charlotte Amalie's steep hills and over to a side street where Kingdon Drew had parked his car. By the time we started up the thousand-foot rise of the mountain, darkness had fallen. Looking back I could see that the waterfront wore its evening necklace of gold and that ships riding at anchor in the harbor were alight like individual gems. Above them Flag Hill, guarding the bay, thrusting its black peak into the sky. The windows of tightly clustered houses were luminous, and once a voice reached me, singing in a garden to the strum of a guitar.

The streets we followed pitched steeply upward as we rose above the rooftops and began a zigzag course, climbing higher at each angled turn until we reached the skyline drive that ran along the central ridge, linking the string of hills. Up here brush-covered slopes dropped away on either hand and now and then a house appeared, set back from the road.

For the most part we were silent as we drove, though for me it was a silence of awareness. I was mindful not only of the excitement and beauty of my surroundings, but also of the man beside me, and in this too there was a stirring of excitement. Again I sensed in him an energy held in check, a drive suppressed—a man who rode with a tight rein upon himself. Aunt Janet had succeeded all too well in planting an awareness of him in me, and something long asleep was wakening of its own accord. What would it be like to see such energy released, to have the drive I sensed in him turn in my direction?

I closed my mind fiercely to my own betraying response. What sort of fool must I be even to glance in so futile a direction?

As we followed the high drive the furious bleating of a horn pressed hard and steadily sounded suddenly behind us, breaking in upon my unwelcome thoughts. In these islands driving is still on the left-hand side of the road, though most cars have an American drive. From my place on the right I could look back along the center of the road and see the headlights of a car advancing upon us at high speed. The man beside me swore under his breath and turned the car onto the left rim of the road. The top was down on the long white car overtaking us, and as it swept into the path of our own headlights I glimpsed a woman at the wheel, driving intently and skillfully, her long blond hair blowing back from her head. A man sat beside her, and in the back seat were two other figures. Then the car had swooped by with a mocking wave of hands on the part of the three who were not driving.

I glanced in astonishment at Kingdon Drew. "Is that the way people drive on this road—" I began, and stopped as I saw the tense, furious line of his jaw and the way his hands gripped the wheel as he swung back onto the road. He did not answer and I was silent, aware of the dark anger that possessed him. I knew now that the blond driver of the car must be his wife, Catherine.

A short distance farther on, a private driveway opened and we turned into it, bouncing over the open rails of a cattle guard, meant, I had learned, to keep roving donkeys off private property. The drive wound up a further rise of hill beneath royal palms and ended in a flat open space at the top, with garages on our left and the great white stone house that commanded the hilltop on our right. In this open space was parked a small red convertible, as well as the white car that had passed us on the road. The occupants were not in sight, but I could hear the sound of voices as Kingdon Drew opened the car door for me. An island man came toward us from the garage area, and at Mr. Drew's gesture he reached into the back seat for my suitcase.

"You might as well see what you're in for," Kingdon Drew said to me, and started off around the side of the house.

I hurried to keep up with him, my heart thumping, both because of his fury and because the madly reckless driver who had passed us on the road must surely be his wife.

My host flung open an ornate iron gate and went angrily through without waiting for me. He halted at the edge of a huge flagstone terrace that stretched almost the width of the house. On the hill-side curve ran a low stone wall, along which beach torches had been placed. Tall metal staves with their heads alive and flaming il-lumined the entire terrace in a wavering dance of light and shadow. But it was the actors who held my attention.

The four from the car could now be identified, though their backs were to me. The central figure was the woman with shoulder-length blond hair who had driven the white car. She was enveloped in a curious sand-colored beach robe rather like the burnoose of some Arab tribesman. It covered her to her bare, thong-sandaled feet, and its hood fell back upon her shoulders beneath the flow of hair.

The two young men wore wet swim trunks and sweat shirts. Their muscled, tanned legs were bare, their feet in sneakers. The older was perhaps twenty-four and fair-haired. The dark-haired younger boy could be no more than seventeen or eighteen and was slighter in build than the other. The fourth person was a young girl—undoubtedly my charge, Leila—though I had no time to study her at that moment because all attention was focused upon the woman.

With a careless gesture she dropped the enveloping robe to the terrace, revealing the briefest of ruffled green swimsuits, wet and glistening in the torchlight. Her body had the firm, supple beauty of carefully sustained youth, her tanned skin smooth and glowing. Her thick, pale hair was held back from her face by a green bandeau. I had never seen anyone so arrestingly alive, though I had yet to see her face.

She ended her advance very close to the fair-haired man, and with a tantalizing gesture she marched her two forefingers up his chest to his chin, then stood on tiptoe to kiss him swiftly and lightly on the mouth.

"Thanks for taking us to the beach, Steve darling," she said.

He laughed aloud, not at all abashed by her action, and I turned with a feeling of distress to look at the girl. She was watching every move the two made with a sort of worshiping attention that alerted and warned me. I had been told to watch for a problem. A "mother problem" had seemed to indicate conflict, but this child was regarding her mother with admiration and affection. For the young man she had the dazzled look of a teen-age crush, though he paid her no attention. While Leila's eyes shone with excitement, there was, as well, something about her that seemed young and awkward and touchingly lacking in confidence. She wore a terry-cloth beach coat that left her long young legs bare, but she huddled into the garment self-consciously, clutching it tightly at the throat.

The sight moved me to unwanted memory and an unexpected twinge of hurt. Just so could I remember standing by in my early teens while my mother—so utterly pretty and sure of herself, so greatly adored—reduced me to clumsiness by sheer weight of comparison.

At the woman's tantalizing gesture, the younger, dark-haired boy made a sound of disapproval, and she threw him a laughing glance.

"Don't growl, Mike. Don't be cross with me! Steve and I understand each other. You should be more like your brother."

Kingdon Drew had halted just in front of me, watching the scene in restrained fury. Now he strode across the terrace. The woman heard him and turned, so that I saw her strange little cat's face for the first time. An immediate, uneasy recognition seized me. Her forehead was broad and from it her face tapered to the point of an inverted triangle made by the tip of her chin. Even by torchlight I could catch the greenish glint of her eyes, the shine of perfect teeth as she smiled in mockery at the man who came toward her across the terrace.

Where or under what circumstances I had seen her before I could not remember, but I sensed strongly that she had made some unfavorable impression upon me then, as now.

There was no time to search my memory, for Kingdon Drew swung her about with a grip upon her bare shoulder that must have hurt.

"I've said there was to be no more after-dark swimming down at Magens Bay," he told her angrily. "If you go down there, you're to be home before dark."

The woman gave a cry of pain as she wrenched her shoulder from his grasp. Yet mockery did not leave her eyes or her lips. "I'll do as I please," she said. "You know I love to swim at night. And it's not the dark you object to—is it?"

Kingdon Drew turned on the man. "You'd better go," he said. And then to the younger boy, "You too!"

Mike, however, was paying no attention. His grave look had focused wholly upon the young girl, and for the first time I gave her my full attention.

Her short hair, a soft light brown, had blown into untidy wisps about her face. Her excitement had evaporated and she stood very still, staring at nothing, her expression blank. It was as if, unable to bear what was happening, she had withdrawn from the scene and hidden inside herself, closing all her outer windows against the world. The younger boy went to her, paying no attention to King's order to leave. He took her gently by the arm and shook her once or twice.

"Snap out of it, Leila," he said. "Don't do that!"

The girl came painfully to life. She flung a look of deep dislike at her father as she ran up the terrace steps and into the house, the bang of a screen door echoing behind her. The older boy had already walked toward the gate near which I stood, and Mike followed him, grim and unsmiling. Clearly Steve was eager to be away and he paid no attention to me as he went past. Mike saw me, however, as he followed his brother, and something lighted in his eyes —as if he knew who I was and why I was there, even though he did not pause to speak. A moment later I heard a car door slam and knew they must be leaving in the red convertible.

For the first time Catherine Drew saw me. She turned to stare at me directly and there was quick recognition in her eyes. I had been right. I had seen her before and she had remembered too. She claimed no acquaintance, but turned on me a flash of warning so clear that it was as if she had spoken aloud, as if she had said, "Go away. Mind your own business. Say nothing." Yet I could not remember where I had seen her. When she was sure she had impressed her meaning upon me, she picked up the burnoose from the flagstones and flung it about her.

"Don't ever touch me like that again," she said to her husband, and went unhurriedly across the terrace and into the house.

He stood looking after her—a man somehow drained and left impotent to act. Unexpectedly, and with a rush of feeling, I found myself allied on his side. The fact that he had lost his temper and behaved badly, perhaps unreasonably, made no difference, for the truth of what I had seen had rushed home to me. There was something wholly wrong about the woman who was his wife. Even the child's look of dislike for her father stemmed from an outer source —the mother—and I knew there was wrong there, too, passed from mother to daughter. Here was a man driven into a corner and all my natural instincts to aid, to support, to defend, had come awake and involved me. Whether I liked it or not I had stepped across my own carefully ruled lines and taken sides. Whether I liked it or not I was more than a little drawn to this man.

Kingdon Drew had forgotten me. By an effort he pulled himself together, suppressing the last vestige of his anger before he followed his wife into the house. The very set of his shoulders bespoke defeat —a painful sight in a strong man, and one I knew he would not willingly reveal if he had remembered I was there.

I stood uncertainly near the gate gazing at the lighted windows of the house, seeing for the first time at close hand the long galleries framed in lacy wrought-iron arches that ran all across the house and around two sides, hinting more of Spain than of Denmark. In their semicircle about the empty terrace torch flames flared wildly in the breeze, their myriad images dancing in the glass of French doors beyond the galleries. It was a beautiful house and it withheld itself from me with a certain disdain that made me know more than ever that I was not welcome.

Before I could wonder what I must do to make my presence known, a woman came out through double doors and stood at the head of the terrace steps looking down at me. She was taller than Catherine Drew, and older, but the family resemblance was clear. She was perhaps in her early forties, and rather large of bone, so that the silk of her pongee frock stretched wide over her hips. As I moved toward her across the flagstones I saw that her hair was a dull auburn, unconvincing in color and worn too tightly curled about her head. Her eyes were a blue that lacked warmth, and as I neared her they regarded me without welcome.

"I am Edith Stair," she said and came down the steps toward me. "Good evening, Miss Abbott. I'm sorry no one has taken care of you. My mother isn't feeling well this evening and she has gone to bed early."

She gave me a boneless handshake, very different from her mother's, and led me into the house. The central room was spacious —actually a wide hall that ran straight through, with rooms opening upon it on either side. At this end double glass doors gave on the terrace, while at the other a front door opened on the driveway.

It was a room of austere beauty, comfortably but sparsely furnished to effect that cool, uncluttered look so necessary in the tropics. The ceiling was lofty, giving one a sense of space and grandeur. From the center of an elaborate plaster rosette hung a crystal chandelier, while carved plaster cornices decorated the far reaches of the ceiling. In contrast to white overhead, the golden-brown parquetry of the floor gleamed warm in lamplight, and I could imagine the room as one in which great balls might once have been held. Yet it did not look to be a loved and warmly lived-in room.

Most of the furniture had that simplicity of design which belongs to the countries of Scandinavia, fluid of line, and built of smooth, light woods. There were several framed pictures on the walls, and near the foot of curving stairs in one corner of the room hung a Chagall print of red poppies and green leaves in a tall vase, looking as if its blooms had just been brought in from out-of-doors.

"This is a large house," Edith Stair said as we climbed to the landing, "but the rooms are large too, so we sometimes find ourselves room poor. Here and there we've partitioned them into something smaller. My husband and I had our own house in St. Croix, where I much prefer to live. But it has been necessary for us to move here so I could take over management of the house, due to my mother's poor health."

Aunt Janet had said something of the same sort and I could not resist a question. "Mrs. Drew is too busy, I imagine?"

"Catherine!" There was so much suppressed feeling in the way Edith Stair spoke her sister's name that I was startled. Perhaps sensing her own self-betrayal, she went on quickly, "Since Alex and I now live here, the house is more crowded, so I must apologize for the small space we can give you. Perhaps you won't be too uncomfortable for the week of your visit."

The week of my visit? It could easily be that she was right. The scene I had just witnessed on the terrace and my own intense and partisan reaction to it had left me shaken and more doubtful than ever. Where was the cool objectivity I had meant to retain in order to be of real use?

The upstairs hallway was narrower than the great main hall below, and heavily dark with mahogany. When my guide pushed ajar the door of a room near the head of the stairs, I saw that it must once have been part of a larger room which had been partitioned.

"Leila is next to you," Mrs. Stair said. "This little room is sometimes used by my sister Catherine. As a child it belonged to her when she visited here, and she still fancies it. We've had little time to get ready for you, so if you don't mind I'll come in and see if everything is right." She made a small fluttering movement with her hands that seemed in contrast to her manner of authority.

The floor was dark and well polished, with a large circular straw rug of lacy design in its center. There was a single bed and a comfortable armchair, with a reading lamp beside it on a small table. My suitcase awaited me near the foot of the bed.

Looking about her with the eye of an accustomed housekeeper, Mrs. Stair at once saw something she did not like. With a purposeful movement she went to a high chest of drawers, took something from its top and turned about to hold out an object to me in some annoyance. On her palm, more than covering it, rested a large, grotesque seashell. It was bigger than a man's fist and completely mailed in prickly spikes. The tip of its nose at the apex was pink, shading back in creamy, star-pointed whorls for an inch or two. After that the whorls sprouted into sharp black spikes that covered the rest of the body, thickening into longer spikes as they ran out to an upcurling tail. Cutting between the rows of spikes ran circular black and white and brown bands, while within its aperture the shell was oyster-white. It was arresting, rather beautiful, yet somehow ugly at the same time.

"A fine specimen of the murex family," Mrs. Stair said in admiration. "But it doesn't belong here. My husband collects shells, you know. He is an expert and I often help him in his work. I can't think why Catherine should have this murex here. Alex doesn't like his shells scattered around the house. But no matter—I'll ask about it tomorrow."

She replaced the shell on the bureau and went to the door of a small closet that had evidently been a modern addition to the room.

"Perhaps you won't need much space for these few days," she said, emphasizing again the expected brevity of my stay. When she opened the door to look inside she once more found something she did not approve, for she drew out a pale green negligee with a quick gesture of distaste, sniffing at the sweetish flower scent that clung to the silk. As she did so, something dropped from a pocket and skittered across the floor in my direction.

I bent to pick it up and found in my hand a curious golden locket on a chain of fine gold links. So unusual was the locket that I could not resist looking at it before I gave it back. It was made in the form of a small shell, perhaps an inch and a half long, its spires and whorls and ridges all clearly marked in the gold.

"How lovely," I said as I gave chain and locket to Edith Stair.

The woman dropped the negligee on a chair and took the golden bauble from me. "This is a real shell—unusually large for a columbella. Quite rare, since they're tiny shells as a rule. Of course it has been gilded over to make the locket. Catherine is careless with her possessions. I'll take care of this."

Her fingers clasped convulsively about the shell, as though she might like to crush it. Again she glanced about the room.

"Do you think you have everything you'll need? There's a bathroom just across the hall. I suppose you know about our water shortage in St. Thomas?"

She seemed anxious now to get away and I was equally willing to have her go. I told her that I knew about the water problem, that I had everything I would need for tonight. At the door she paused with her hand on the knob and fixed me with her cool look. Only her hands betrayed an inner perturbation with one of their quick, spasmodic motions as she touched the doorknob, withdrew from it, and touched it again.

"My mother has told me why you are here," she said. "I consider it only fair to warn you that your time is likely to be wasted. Mother has a tendency to believe she can make happen whatever she wishes, simply by insisting upon it repeatedly. The rest of us—that is, my husband and Mr. Drew and myself—feel that she is wrong in trying to keep Leila at home."

The omission was obvious. "What does Leila's mother think?" I asked.

The woman's shoulders lifted in a shrug. "My sister is unpredictable. The rest of us feel that it will be far better if Leila is sent to her aunt in Colorado."

"Perhaps it will seem that way to me too," I told her quietly. "But since Mrs. Hampden has asked me to come here, this is something I will have to find out for myself. If I'm able."

"If you are able," Mrs. Stair repeated. She opened the door, said "Good night," and went off abruptly, the shell locket dangling from her fingers. She had obviously made up her mind to distrust me, and there seemed little I could do about the fact.

Once I was alone, the small room closed in about me, yet at the same time it offered scant security. When I examined the door I found that it lacked bolt or key—which of course was common enough practice in a family house. But there were as well two nearly ceiling-high glass doors which opened upon the gallery that ran about this corner room, and these doors were open to the night outside, or to anyone who chose to look in from the hillside.

I am not, as a rule, nervous about such matters, but this house, with its air of long-accustomed arrogance, had seemed hostile to me from my first glimpse of it, and overbearing on its mountaintop. "Fanciful," I told myself, using my mother's favorite word for my imaginings, but I could not shake the feeling. It had often seemed to me that old houses took on characteristics, just as the people who lived in them did. This was a house that dated back to long before the United States' purchase of the Virgin Islands from Denmark, and I continued to have the feeling that it did not care for upstarts from the States and was inimical to my presence.

Even though I must cut off the breeze, I pulled long bamboo-printed draperies across the French doors and turned on another lamp. On the bureau were the same small glass bowls of candle wax that were in every room at Aunt Janet's. Even in calm weather the electric power could fail without warning and leave one dependent on candles. But at least I had no need to light these tonight as I went about the unpacking of my suitcase.

I had been wise to bring only a few things with me, leaving the rest at my aunt's. That I would not stay here long was becoming evident. As I put my things away I noticed the green negligee lying across the chair where Mrs. Stair had let it fall. When I picked it up, the scent of perfume reached me again, familiar, tantalizing—yet an odor I could not place. For some reason I did not care for the soft feeling of the material in my hands and I hung it away on a hook in the closet as far as possible from the few dresses I had brought with me.

While I finished my unpacking, remembrance of my arrival returned disturbingly to mind. I thought of how the girl, Leila, had looked when she stood blank and withdrawn, stiff with resistance to what was happening around her. I recalled with distress the anger in Kingdon Drew as he crossed the terrace to swing Catherine away from the blond young man she had kissed, and his following look of defeat that had seemed to me a shattering thing in such a man. I remembered all too clearly Catherine Drew's triangular little cat face, with its pointed chin and greenish eyes that seemed so familiar to me, though I had been unable to place where I had seen her.

I unzipped the blue linen sheath which Mrs. Hampden had approved, stepped out of it, and got ready for bed. I was anything but sleepy, and I decided to sit up for a while and read the book I had brought along. Yet when I settled into a chair, with the lamp adjusted to light my pages, I saw nothing of the scene described in print. The face of Catherine Drew came persistently between the page and my eyes and I saw only her tilted chin and the insolent green mockery of her look.

Quite suddenly I knew where and under what circumstances I had seen Leila's mother before. The recollection was no more reassuring than anything else I had met in this house to which Maud Hampden had summoned me, and to which Kingdon Drew had so reluctantly brought me.

I could no longer endure being shut in this small room. I slipped into my robe and came outside, to steal along the gallery to this place overlooking garden and hillside and harbor. Here I could stand thinking back over that strange glimpse I'd had of Catherine Drew. Already the house and its occupants had set themselves against me and I had been made to feel utterly alone and on guard. Through no choice of my own, Leila's mother was already my enemy. There was every reason for the moonlight to seem chill.

III

The harbor of St. Thomas is well sheltered on one side by the reaching arm of Flag Hill, and on the other by the long mound of Hassel Island. There is a narrow channel between Hassel and St. Thomas which opens into further water space between Hassel and Water Island beyond. It was on Water Island that I had first seen Catherine Drew.

During my early days in Charlotte Amalie, Aunt Janet had sent me via taxi, ferry, and bus on a visit to friends at the Water Isle Hotel. I took my bathing suit and swam dutifully in Honeymoon Bay. I ate the buffet lunch served hot on the beach and I suppose I talked to those who tried to be kind to me. But all the while I had my eye on that part of the beach that stretched in a long empty curve around the bay. As soon as I could escape after lunch I had set off by myself, wading through shallow water or leaving my footprints in clean wet sand. I had felt comfortably vacant, empty of emotion, as sun-somnolent as I wanted to be. I had in mind going a long way off from swimmers and voices, to cover myself with lotion and lie in a place where I would be wholly alone, where only sand and sun and sea would keep me company.

Following on my right hand as I splashed through ripples of water were gnarled sea-grape trees rimming the beach, their huge triangular leaves clustered to throw patches of shade. Beyond rose the steep, wooded hillside. I was alone quickly enough and I liked it that way. Not until I was nearly ready to choose my stretch of sand for sun bathing did I hear voices again. I can remember feeling faintly annoyed, as though the beach belonged to me. Now I would have to go farther along to find a place that would be wholly mine.

I glanced toward the sea grapes in mild annoyance and caught a glimpse of scarlet amidst the green. A man and woman were there, the woman in a swimsuit of red denim briefs and bra, the man in dark navy trunks. The man's back was toward me, and I hardly noticed him because it was the woman who caught my eye. I could not see her hair, hidden beneath a tight-fitting white cap that cupped her face with its strap. But I saw clearly enough a small triangle of face that reminded me of a cat, with green cat's eyes focused on the man before her. I made no attempt to conceal my presence and as I drew near, the man pulled her to him. In that instant she looked past his shoulder and saw me. At once she stepped back, arresting him with a hand upon his arm, whispering something. Warning him perhaps not to look around.

For what seemed an age they stood frozen there within the green arms of the sea grapes. I had no real interest in them. Having no man of my own to walk a beach with me and kiss me in the warmth of a Caribbean sun, I walked carelessly by and put the two as quickly from my mind as possible. I found my patch of lonely sand where I lay so long in the sun that a friend of my aunt's came to counsel me against such exposure. When I walked back along the beach the two by the sea grapes were gone, and I gave them not another thought—until that moment when I saw Catherine Drew on the terrace at Hampden House. Her face was the one I had glimpsed over the shoulder of the man on the beach.

The realization had added to my increasing sense of disquiet. I knew the man with her had not been Kingdon Drew, but someone of a slighter, less sturdy build. Nor had he been as young as Steve or Mike. There had been a touch of gray in his hair, I seemed to remember. In any event, I told myself, it was not my affair. It was even possible that I had misunderstood that moment on the sand and there had really been no loverlike gesture between them. Nevertheless, Catherine, in that brief moment when she had seen me on the terrace, had remembered my face, had recognized me before I had placed her, and had shown her hostility clearly.

As I stood tonight on the gallery looking out upon moonlight and indigo shadows, an enveloping loneliness crept upon me—such loneliness as I had been holding off ever since my mother's death. By keeping myself remote from all the true reasons for living, by emptying my mind, numbing myself, refusing to feel because I knew that to feel was to live, I had held off the truth I could hold away no longer. No one needed me for anything. My mother, who had depended on me for more than she had ever realized or accepted, was gone. My bondage to her had not been entirely unwilling, as I must admit if I was honest. Having no one upon whom I might spend my love, I had given it to a woman who was physically helpless and could not do without me. I had given it to the young girls in my school. Not always to the healthy, well-balanced, cheerful girls—but more often to the misfits, the uncertain ones, those who lacked a goal and were filled with fears. Like myself? Like myself when everything else was taken from me?

I turned my back on that lush tropical view—so different from my more austere view of Lake Michigan at home—and stole back to my room. There I sat for a long while, trying to face myself, and what I had been willing to do to myself. It must not be like that. It must not be too late!

A sound from the upper hallway outside my room roused me from this tasting of dregs and brought me to my door, to listen with my ear against the panel. It was late, but I had heard a voice spoken in challenge—a voice that spoke Catherine's name. I opened the door a thin crack, to find that a lamp burned on a table across the hall, so that Edith's tall figure was clearly visible where she stood near the head of the stairs. She wore a long, shapeless cotton wrapper and her reddish hair was done up in plastic rollers, her face shiny with cream. All her attention was fixed upon someone coming toward her up the stairs and, as I watched, Catherine ran up into my range of vision. She had changed from her swimsuit, but she was dressed for evening, not for bed. Near the top of the steps she paused breathlessly, looking at her sister, keyed up and tense, as if she expected some outburst from Edith—perhaps even asked for it.

It came almost at once, but low-voiced now, so that sleepers would not be wakened. I could not have heard the words had I not been so close and the house so silent.

"I can go to King with this at any time," Edith said. "I have only to tell him what you are up to and—"

"And there will be a lovely explosion," Catherine whispered. "You will be blown sky-high along with the rest of us. Besides—you needn't be afraid. I told you I'd leave him alone."

"I don't trust you," Edith said. "You're a cheat and a liar and you always have been."

Catherine's back was toward me and I could not see her face, but I could see the yellowish pallor of Edith's as she looked down at her sister, and I caught the faint tremor of excitement that seemed to lift Catherine's shoulders in an exquisite shiver.

"In a day or two I'm going to Caprice," Catherine said. "And you know what that means, Edith. You do know, don't you, dear?"

The woman on the top step caught at the newel post. "Oh, when will you stop—when?"

The younger woman laughed softly and ran past her sister and on toward a room at the front of the house. Edith Stair stood aside and let her go. But when she turned I saw her face—and something more; something frightening. There was no mistaking the hatred Edith felt toward her younger sister.

I closed my door softly, turned out my lamp, and went to bed.

For a time I lay awake, puzzling over the scene I'd just witnessed, unable to find an answer to its meaning. Catherine had some hold over her sister, but I knew too little to guess what it might be. I had only an increasing sense of something evil loose in this house, reaching out wickedly to touch all our lives. Mine too, if I remained.

When I fell asleep at last, it was to toss restlessly, to dream and rouse and dream again. Near morning I went soundly asleep, and awakened late, to find myself more rested than I had any right to expect.

Bright sunlight blazed beyond the printed bamboo fronds of my draperies and the morning was already warm. I got out of bed to fling the draperies wide and let in the daylight and the view. One of my gallery doors looked north over the driveway area and beyond to Magens Bay on the Atlantic Ocean shore of the island. Again I could see small islands and the shore line, with a bright emerald-green trim wherever there were shallows, shading into deep blue beyond where the ocean took over. The indented oblong of the bay looked inviting with its rim of white beach—lonely and surrounded by thick forest.

The second door of my corner room opened upon that ridge of hills that extended to the east until they ended in a steep drop to an inland valley where bright, small houses clustered in a village at its heart.

Though I felt a great deal better with morning warmth and light to give me new courage, the night's events had left their mark on me and I could not remain the uninvolved young woman whom Maud Hampden had interviewed yesterday. There was in me a new eagerness to see Kingdon Drew again, as well as a queerly anticipatory feeling about confronting his wife. If I had not known myself so well, I might have thought this feeling a desire for battle. But I had never thought of myself as the battling sort, and I could not understand my own reactions. True, I had been disturbed by Catherine Drew's behavior on the terrace last night, and by her treatment of her sister later on the stairs, but such matters were not my problem, nor in any sense what I had been brought here to solve. They were not my business, that beach scene notwithstanding.

When I crossed the hall to the bathroom I saw no one, and no one when I returned from a shower that trickled cautiously, trained to no abandoned waste of water. No one had told me about meals or when I might be expected for breakfast, but just as I finished dressing, there was a firm rap upon my door and a voice called, "Hurry up and open, please!"

I ran to obey, and Leila Drew came brightly into the room, carrying a large breakfast tray. "Do clear off the table," she said breezily. "This is heavy. Our cook had a look at you last night. She says you're too thin and we must fatten you up."

Again I hurried to do her bidding, both pleased and astonished by this transformation. Gone was the frozen girl of the terrace—the awkward, self-conscious, worshiping girl. Here was a long-legged, graceful teen-ager in blue Bermudas and a nautical white middy with a blue tie that matched her shorts. I watched in delighted discovery as she set down the tray and busied herself pouring my coffee, pausing to pilfer a slice of banana, unwrapping the hot toast from its protective napkin.

This girl looked not at all like her mother. The stamp of her father was in her face—the wide cheekbones and wide-set brown eyes —and that very fact drew me to her. Though there was a touch of the triangle to her face, the chin rounded, blunting the point, lessening the possible look of Catherine. The smile on her softly turned lips was a little shy, for all her breezy manner and the efficient way she was managing my breakfast. One thing I liked especially was the way she wore her shining brown hair. Last night it had been all ends. But this morning it was brushed in a smooth cap that shaped her head and left the tips of her ears exposed. Across her forehead a few bangs slanted diagonally, well above her eyes. Here was a fresh grace and sweetness that one day might turn to beauty. I warmed to Leila Drew.

As I drank coffee that had been perfectly brewed and bit into hot buttered toast, Leila moved about the room, sometimes talking to me over her shoulder, sometimes poking unself-consciously into my belongings with the engaging manner of a child. This was what it was to be fourteen—sometimes older and sometimes younger than one's chronological age.

"I wanted to catch you alone," she told me, picking up my bathrobe and slipping it onto a hanger. "I wanted to see what my new keeper is like. Gran says if I behave myself and am nice to you, you'll help me stay where I want to be—right in St. Thomas. Dad wants to send me off to Colorado with an aunt I don't even know. Though of course Cathy says Gran is being foolish to bring you here. Cathy thinks you'll make everything worse."

This was moving faster than I was ready to go. I returned her smile and put a question of my own. "What do you think?"

She went to the bureau and picked up the big spiky shell, ignoring my question. "Isn't this an ugly monster? Isn't it wicked?"

" 'Monster' is a good word for it," I said. "But I'm not sure things can be wicked. Only people."

She considered that seriously for a moment, as though I had said something profound. Then she came to sit on the end of the bed, swinging her crossed legs, the shell cupped in her hands. A slight frown puckered her forehead and her smile faded.

"Don't you think it's possible for people to leave wickedness around sometimes—so that *things* soak it up?"

"I'll have to think about that," I admitted, intrigued by her imaginative flight, wondering if this was what I felt about the house itself.

"Cathy thinks there's a sort of wickedness about this shell," she went on. "That's why she asked Uncle Alex to give it to her. I think if she'd lived a long time ago Cathy would have been a witch. Or an obeah woman at least." Then, without transition, "That's papaya you're eating. Have you ever eaten papaya before?"

I said I had not, and scooped another spoonful of fruit. Leila turned to examining her face frankly and critically in the mirror. She did not seem to like what she saw.

"Cathy's hair is naturally curly. It does anything she wants. That's why she can wear it long and put it up in all sorts of styles. But this is all I've found to do with mine, and even this way it doesn't stay put very long. It's wispy and it blows."

"The way you wear your hair is one of the first things I noticed this morning," I said. "I like it. It suits you."

She turned from the mirror, pleased. "And I like yours. That shiny dark brown bob sort of thing that comes just to the line of your jaw and swings against your cheek when you move."

"Thank you," I said, as pleased as she. "But in case you're interested, I'm not sure I like papaya."

"That's all right. You have to get used to it. Lemon helps, but I forgot the lemon."

In her next round of the room she went to the closet and pulled open the door to peer inside. At once she reached into a corner and brought out the green negligee that Edith had found there last night. She held the folds to her face as if it were her mother she touched, and I sensed a dangerous devotion in her as I watched. Even love could be extreme.

"Don't you adore her perfume?" she asked, sniffing approvingly. "It's water lily. She never wears anything else. Uncle Alex orders it for her especially from abroad. Cathy loves things to be different and special."

"I noticed a gold locket in the shape of a shell in the pocket of that gown last night," I said. "It seemed rather special."

Leila looked up from nuzzling the robe. "That must have been the columbella. It's a dove shell, if you want the easier name. Cathy used to pick them up on beaches when she was little and she even started calling herself Columbella. She's never liked the name Catherine. That's why I have to call her Cathy."

As I, in my own time, had been taught to call my mother Helen. Because there were women who did not want to be called by the name of Mother. I could remember envying girls I knew who could use that wonderfully affectionate American word, "Mommy." A word that was never permitted to me.

Experimentally, Leila slipped her arms into the sleeves of the gown and pulled it around her. At once she began to clown a little, as if she made fun of herself. Her natural young grace fell away and all last night's awkwardness was back, so that she tripped over the hem and kicked it away with a clumsy gesture.

"I'll never be able to wear clothes the way Cathy wears them!" she mourned as she snatched off the negligee and hung it back in the closet.

"Why should you want to?" I asked.

"Why shouldn't I?" She returned to her comfortable perch at the foot of the bed. "Did you see Steve O'Neill last night? Did you see the way he looks at her?"

I had seen. I had also seen the way Leila looked at Steve.

"Isn't he good-looking?" she went on. "And he has so much fun. He's not gloomy and spoilsport like his brother Mike."

"It was Mike I liked best," I admitted.

She threw me a look that dismissed such lack of discernment. "Of course Cathy can do anything she likes with Steve. He's devoted to her. I'll never be anything but a silly kid to him. I know that." She sighed deeply, woefully.

"I expect you'll recover," I said.

She flung me a look of denial and clasped her hands about her knees, studying me as I poured more coffee. "Why are you here anyway? If you came to St. Thomas on vacation from your school-work, why should you take on a summer tutoring job—or whatever it is you're supposed to do for me?"

I answered her as honestly as I could. "I didn't come to this house just for you. I came for myself as well. Because I need to find something to keep me busy, fill my time. My mother died two months ago. She was an invalid due to a fall she had years ago, and she couldn't get around very well. I've taken care of her and taught in a school besides. When she died I felt a letdown. This is something to pick me up—providing you like me and I like you."

Leila's brown eyes—so much like her father's with that wide-set space between strongly marked brows—regarded me with a sympathy I had not expected.

"Nobody told me that," she said. "Were you very close—you and your mother? Did you love her very much?"

I gave her look for look. "Sometimes I did," I said dryly.

A flicker of something I could not read crossed Leila's face and she looked away from me.

"I think no one ever loves another person all the time," I said gently. "We can't expect that of ourselves, or from anyone else."

I was playing this by ear, but I sensed a response in the girl, though she said nothing. If there was response, then her seeming adulation for Catherine Drew was not without its moments of questioning, of wondering—perhaps of seeing her mother more clearly than she wanted to see her. Leila had in her a warmth that was generous and appealing—a quality that seemed lacking in her mother, but which might well exist behind those banked fires I had sensed in her father. I found myself increasingly drawn to her.

Someone knocked on the door and she sprang off the bed to open it. Catherine Drew stepped past her daughter into the room, looking about with an air of distaste. She wore pale green capris that stretched tightly over her girlishly flat stomach, rounded her hips, and hugged her thighs neatly with scarcely a wrinkle. A bit of sleeveless white piqué tied in a bow between her breasts left her tanned midriff bare. Her hair was held in place by that open bandeau that let it flow to her shoulders, and her bare feet were thrust into brown leather sandals. She looked as long-legged as her daughter, and more supple and slender. Still—in the morning light that poured in from the gallery she did not look so strikingly young as she had last night by torchlight. The sun had etched faint lines about her eyes, and her skin had a dry, taut look, as though she had begun to weather a little, like her mother, Maud Hampden.

When she had given the room a look of repudiation, as though it had been spoiled for her by my presence, she allowed her greenish gaze to focus on me. I had never before met a grown person so openly hostile toward me as this woman seemed, and her first words shocked me.

"How did King happen to find you, Miss Abbott? How did you manage to get yourself this job, if you can call it that?"

It was as if she meant to follow the threat of her look last night with more direct action. She intended to have me gone at all costs.

Leila saved me from the blank silence that was all I had to offer.

"Oh, Cathy!" she cried. "You know it was Gran who found her. We all know Miss Abbott is here to counteract your dreadful influence on me."

The two looked at each other and laughed softly in mutual amusement. They were clearly in complete rapport, yet while I sensed that there was love on one side, I was not at all sure what lay on the other.

"Dad doesn't even want her here," Leila added. "It's all going to be very uncomfortable for Miss Abbott, I'm sure, so we might as well be kind for the few days she'll be here. I brought up her breakfast tray because no one else remembered."

It was uncomfortable to be talked about in this open manner, as though I were not present, and I tried to get back into the scene.

"That was thoughtful of you," I said to Leila, but she broke in as though she had not heard me, her attention upon her mother.

"Aunt Edith has a headache this morning, so she stayed in bed for a while. What did you do to her last night, Cathy?"

Catherine grimaced and shrugged. Remembering the meeting I had seen on the stairs, I could imagine the effect it might have had on Edith, whatever its import had been.

"I think Aunt Edith's being sneaky about something," Leila said. "Maybe you'd better watch out, Cathy. Maybe if you—if you wouldn't —I mean about Steve—"

"That is none of your business, darling," said Catherine coolly. "Don't try to mother me!"

Leila's fair skin flushed miserably, but Catherine went lightly on, ignoring her discomfort.

"I'm driving downtown in a little while. Alex has a new shipment of dresses in and I thought we might pick out something to wear for the buffet party next week. Would you like to come along?"

This time I gave Leila no time to answer. Catherine Drew's high-handed intention to whisk my pupil out from under my nose must be dealt with quickly.

"I don't suppose your mother will mind if we get to some of that schoolwork first," I said to Leila. "Your grandmother suggested that we make a start this morning and I think that is what we must do."

"Don't be silly!" Leila could be as rude as her mother. "Of course I'll come with you, Cathy. Wait till I go and change from shorts."

Catherine's eyes flicked a triumphant look in my direction and then returned to her daughter. "Why bother?" she asked.

Leila glanced down at herself and then at Catherine in her tight-fitting capris. "You mean you're going downtown dressed like that? But Gran said—"

Her mother shrugged. "Gran, Gran, Gran! And Edith, and Alex, and King! And now Miss Abbott! If you want to come with me, then come!" She turned to me. "You'll find we're very old-fashioned in St. Thomas. Virgin Islanders don't do this, and they don't do that. Downtown we wear dresses—all that sort of thing. But I'm a rebel— even if they do mix me up with the tourists. I'm a rebel about these lessons too. They can wait."

I made a last attempt to stand my ground. "Why not go shopping this afternoon? If I'm to be of any help to your daughter, Mrs. Drew—"

I knew I sounded stiff, but the woman had that effect on me. In any event she would not listen, interrupting my words at once.

"You can't be of use! Not at all. We all know that, really. Leila doesn't need lessons, or coaching. We know you're here so Maudie can block what King wants to do. But perhaps I have some plans of my own." As she looked about the room her glance fell upon the spiked black shell lying on the bed where Leila had dropped it. She picked it up and placed it beside my breakfast tray. "Sorry to deprive you of our company, Miss Jessica Abbott. But My Lady Murex can stay and keep an eye on you, Jessica. I've never known anyone with that name before. It fits you somehow. Don't you think so, Leila?"

Leila had the grace to look ashamed at the clear mockery in her mother's voice. "If we're going just as we are, then let's start before Gran stops us," she said, and went out of the room without a backward glance for me or her mother.

Catherine Drew laughed—that hushed, almost silvery sound that made my skin creep. Then she gave the black spikes of the shell what was an almost caressing tap, and followed her daughter with a last flick of her fingers in farewell to me.

When they had gone I sat for a while staring helplessly at the big shell. I had a feeling that it was, indeed, watching me, its incongruous pink nose pointed in my direction. Disliking its eyeing look, I picked it up and turned it over in my hands. By contrast to the spiked exterior, the inner curve was smooth as china, cool to the touch, dead white in color, and speckled here and there with dots of black or brown. It made a smooth, cool white cave in which a sea animal had once lived. But the armor the creature had worn pricked my fingers and I set the shell on the breakfast tray, feeling that I'd had enough of its unfriendly company. I felt, in fact, defeated on every hand.

There was no further doubt about the need to set myself in opposition to Catherine Drew at every turn if I was to stay in this house. My feeling of being allied on King's side had only increased during this first encounter with his wife. Yet if the family could not deal with her or block her influence upon Leila, how was I, a stranger and an outsider, to be of any use? I liked the child. She had not been rude to me until her mother appeared. I had been drawn to her—as I had earlier been drawn in sympathy to her father.

Tread carefully! I warned myself. Following a course that was more emotional than thoughtful could pitch me into a hornets' nest of trouble—and I wanted none of that. A week, undoubtedly, would be all I could endure in this house.

Picking up the tray, with the big shell resting beside the sugar bowl, I carried it out my door and down the stairs. Since I had lost my pupil for the time being, I might as well make my presence, and perhaps some of my doubts, known to whomever I could find about the house.

There was just one person I had in mind.

IV

I bore the tray to the landing and down to the living area I had seen last night. The big hall was empty, shaded from the morning sun, cool and dim, with the red blossoms of the Chagall print glowing near the foot of the stairs. Even by daylight the room looked a bit unfurnished to my northern eyes, more accustomed to thick rugs and warm upholstery than to the austere sight of bare wood. Yet there was beauty and dignity here, though perhaps too neatly impersonal, as of a room not lived in carelessly and lovingly. Its echoing reaches seemed to reject me. A handsome room—but cold.

Setting my tray upon a coffee table and wandering toward the terrace, I glimpsed on my right a large dining room, mahogany-dark, while on the left a door stood open upon a smaller room that seemed to be an office. As I glanced in I saw Kingdon Drew standing before a large desk, studying a glossy print he held in his hands. I stepped into the doorway, suddenly expectant.

He did not see me at once and I could watch him for a moment, as I had done last evening. He seemed dispirited and the creases down his cheeks had deepened gravely so that I felt an odd desire to make him smile.

"You forgot me completely last night," I said. "Though since you're a reluctant host, I suppose I can't blame you."

He glanced at me, unamused. "I'm sorry. I understand Edith brought you in. Has someone seen to your breakfast this morning?"

"Your daughter took care of that," I said.

This at least interested him and he drew up a chair for me. "Now that you've met her, how do you feel about her?"

"I like her very much," I told him readily. "She's an attractive girl with a great deal of warmth and quick intelligence."

He nodded sober agreement. "There are times when she is all those things. Are you telling me that she means to go along with this game her grandmother is playing?"

"I don't know," I admitted. "I've lost her for the moment. We were to begin looking over her books and studies this morning, but she has gone shopping with her mother."

"And you let her go?" His look challenged me. "Of what use are you as a teacher if you can't set down rules and hold to them?"

I sensed again his desire to antagonize me, but I would not be angry with him. I knew more about him today—and more about his wife.

"This is my first morning here," I said mildly. "There's plenty of time to set up ground rules. First I need to make Leila's acquaintance. I've already begun to do this. I think she doesn't dislike me—so we've made a start."

He fell to studying the glossy photograph in his hands, as if he waited for me to go, but there was a perverse desire in me to reach him, to let him know that I was on his side whether he wished it or not, and I stayed in my chair, watching him in silence until my look began to nettle him.

"Well?" he said. "What is it you see?"

I could not tell him exactly, but I managed an answer of sorts. "I see what I've seen a good many other times as a teacher—a troubled father. It makes me want to help."

I turned away from the quick awareness in his eyes and left my chair to move about the room. It had been set up as a workroom and equipped with the tools of his trade. Several blueprints lay flat on a desk, while others were rolled and stored on a high shelf. A drawing table stood where the light was best, with plans upon it emerging on transparent vellum. Near at hand were pencils, T squares, ruling triangles, and an architect's scale. All about the walls hung framed photographs of modern homes set in island backgrounds, and one contrasting picture—a handsome photograph of snow-covered peaks that caught my eye.

"The Rocky Mountains?" I asked.

"Yes—Colorado. My home state. I grew up in Denver."

As I moved on from one to another of the pictures I was sharply aware of the man behind me. He watched me now, as I had watched him, and the knowledge gave me an odd feeling of both uncertainty and exhilaration.

"These are homes you've designed?" I asked, stopping before the picture of a low-roofed house with a veranda cantilevered over a steep hillside.

"Yes—houses are my business. I like what I can do with them here where I'm free of the restrictions of a northern climate. That house you're looking at isn't far from here."

There seemed something in his tone that gave special significance to the house and I wondered what lay behind the apparently casual words. For whom had this house been built?

"Nevertheless," he went on, "I'd like to have lived in a time when houses like this one were built."

He handed me the glossy print he held, and I found that it pictured a large, gracefully built house belonging to a far older day.

"That's the Hampden family home in St. Croix," he said. "Both Edith and Catherine grew up there. Catherine's great-great-grandfather built it for his bride and called it Caprice."

Caprice! The word rang an echo of warning in my mind. That was the name Catherine had spoken to Edith last night on the stairs.

"What a lovely house, and what a lovely name for a house," I said.

"It's the sort of name you'll find in St. Croix. Old places abound there with names like Whim and Fancy, Rest, Hope—and Upper Love and Lower Love. I like them all. But I'm afraid Caprice is too apt a name at present. It's a caprice to keep up the place."

"Is that the sugar estate Aunt Janet has told me about?"

"It used to be. The old mill is pretty much a ruin now, though I've been trying to save it from complete disintegration. The house ought to be turned into a museum before it falls to ruin too—but there's a problem there. It belongs to Catherine and I've been trying to manage it for her, and save something for Leila's sake. Though I'm afraid it's hopeless and a more sensible course must be taken to preserve it."

There was so warm an interest in his voice that I sensed how thoroughly this man from Colorado had fallen in love with a plantation house on a Caribbean island. Clearly he meant it when he said he would like to build houses like this one, though no one could afford to build or own such mansions any more.

Abruptly he glanced at the clock on his desk as though anxious to be off. "I'd better get to the office, if you'll excuse me. I've a senator coming to see me this morning, and senators don't like to be kept waiting, even in our easygoing town. I don't know what you mean to do with your time since you've lost your pupil, but you'll need to find ways to amuse yourself, since Catherine won't leave Leila to you if she can help it. She has already told me so."

"And she has told me," I said as we left his office for the living area of the house.

He looked at me questioningly and I shook my head.

"Oh, not in so many words. But with hints and looks and her claim that there's nothing I can do for her daughter."

"That's her method," he said shortly. "You'll have to deal with some fairly ingenious opposition if you stay. Good morning, Miss Abbott."

I watched the long stride with which he walked the length of the main hall to the front door. When he moved it was often with what seemed an explosion of energy, as if too much of the time he held back and must release himself in motion when it was possible. I watched him and was stirred again, as I did not want to be.

When he had gone I stepped to the open doors of the terrace and saw that a man stood outside on the lower gallery with his back to me. My swift sense of recognition was startling. He was not in bathing trunks today, but wore a blue shirt and gray slacks—a tall man, leanly built. The back of his head—the hair dark with a flecking of gray—the straight column of his neck, these were familiar to me. I knew immediately that this was the man I had seen with Catherine Drew that afternoon on Water Island.

He heard my step upon the parquet floor and turned about. As he did so my sense of certainty was shaken. Viewed from the front, his black hair seemed scarcely gray at all, and he wore a blunt-pointed black beard, glossy and carefully groomed. A mustache framed his mouth, dividing around it to grow into the beard, leaving his rather thin lips visible, so that I could see the faint smile he wore as he studied me. His face was lean, almost ascetic in its bone structure, his eyes pale blue and curiously luminous.

"Good morning," he said. "I'm Alex Stair. And you, of course, are the teacher—Miss Abbott?"

"A teacher without a pupil, I'm afraid," I told him.

He saw my tray on the coffee table and put his finger to a nearby bell. "At least I can show you the room in which you'll work when you recapture your pupil. I understand that I'm to give up my study for a few hours every morning."

"I'm sorry if we must disturb you," I said, feeling my way cautiously. I could not throw off the arresting sense of recognition that had first gripped me, even though the effect had lessened the moment he turned about. If he had been the man at the beach, there might be a very real source of trouble between Edith and her sister.

"It doesn't matter," he assured me pleasantly enough. "I usually go to the shop in the morning. Though I'm not one to be bound by exact hours."

In answer to the bell a maid came in from another part of the house—a pretty brown-skinned girl whom he called Noreen. As she picked up the tray Alex Stair saw the shell and reached for it.

"Strange company for breakfast!" he said to me.

I noted his hands as he held the shell—long-fingered and lean as the rest of him, the nails tapered and well kept. He thumped a smooth space between the spikes with a knuckle and the shell gave off a hollow ring.

"Mrs. Drew left it upstairs—to keep an eye on me," I told him.

I had the impression of a thin, tightly drawn smile that showed briefly in response to my words.

"Catherine fancies herself as a caster of spells," he said. "But she is really an amateur. Come along and I'll show you where you'll conduct your lessons. If there are to be any lessons."

I followed him to a door that opened near the foot of the stairs, and went into a room that was the larger counterpart of the bedroom I occupied just above. Here warm-hued terra-cotta tiles covered the floor, with lacy straw rugs from the island of Dominica scattered here and there. A worktable was drawn below a pair of north windows, and books had been spilled across it, with pencils and paper set out, ready for use. At the far end of the room stood a handsome desk of polished mahogany, with a red leather armchair beyond.

There were touches of brass on the desk, a parchment-shaded lamp, a handsome African carving of a man's head done in some reddish wood. With its dark velvet backing toward me, a picture in a silver frame occupied a central position and I wondered if it held Edith's likeness. Somehow Alex Stair seemed an unlikely husband for the gaunt and dour Edith.

The man stood waiting almost expectantly for me to view the room, and when I turned to look about, I understood. The entire inside wall had been lined with bookshelves, but they held no books. Instead, every foot of space boasted a display of shells. There must have been hundreds set attractively on view—shells of all sizes, from huge conchs and tritons to those so tiny they were placed in shallow containers to prevent their scattering.

As I looked about at the array he set the murex on a corner of the desk. "Beauty with a flaw," he mused. "There's an ugliness about the thing that intrigues me. It's fitting enough. Perfection goes against nature. Good and evil complement each other and often exist quite comfortably side by side, don't you think? If we're realistic enough to accept the fact, that is. And it's probably as true in man as it is in nature."

I could not help but think of Catherine, and I wondered if his thoughts took the same course.

"When the flaw takes over," I said, "it's not very comfortable for those who must live with it. That murex, for instance—once I've admired it, I don't want it around all the time."

There was a ring of appreciation in his laugh. "Some of us have a greater acceptance of the flaw—in others, as well as in ourselves. Perhaps we're the more comfortable ones. Your moralist—but never mind! It's too early in the morning for discussions of good and evil. At least the murex has a noble history. In Roman times dye for the robes of emperors and senators came from murex shells."

I remembered my history. "Royal Tyrian purple! But what happened to it after the fall of Rome?"

"It became holy as well as royal and went into robes for the cardinals of the Christian Church. But I'll admit there are more pleasing shells than this one."

For some reason his seemingly idle discussion made me as uncomfortable as did the shell. It was as if in his talk of good and evil, in his reference to the flaws of beauty, the man spoke in symbols that carried a deeper significance—perhaps a hint of warning, meant for me? Or was I being fanciful again?

He gestured toward the shelves, inviting me, and I stepped close to one of the displays. At random I picked up a scallop shell, admiring the fan of delicate ridges.

"Scallops always have a classic look," I said.

He seemed indifferent to its beauty. "Scallops and limpets and cockles are simple shells. Open-faced, like some people. The more involuted types interest me more. They're not to be read at a glance."

Again I had that uneasy sense of a deeper meaning and knew that he watched me intently with his pale, luminous eyes.

He moved on, showing me other shells and naming them—volutes, cones, augers with long slender spires. When I found a small olive shell with a sheen to its beautiful black and yellow markings, he seemed pleased by my interest and gave it to me. Yet never did I feel easy and comfortable with him. He seemed as involuted as his favorite shells.

"It must require a great deal of work to take care of a collection like this," I said.

Again he made a slight shrug. "Some of it is rather unpleasant work. My wife does a great deal of the preparation. And of course the whole family dives and dredges for me. Steve and Mike O'Neill, who were here last night, own a boat and I do a good business with them. The best of our finds I keep for myself and send the rest to dealers in the States. Shells are a bigger business than you might think these days."

From a tray I picked up a shell that was no more than half an inch in length and studied its brown and cream speckling.

"That's a columbella," he said. "Last Christmas I had one of the rare larger columbellas gilded and hung on a gold chain as a gift for Catherine. She plays a little game of calling herself Columbella when she's feeling whimsical. It was a beautiful shell—without a flaw."

"I've seen it," I told him. "But for me the gilt seemed to flaw it. I suppose I like natural things to be the way nature made them."

"Perhaps that was the intent—the secret joke," he said.

His beard was like a mask over part of his face, the man hidden behind it. The look in his pale eyes made me increasingly uneasy. Smiling to himself, as though he enjoyed what he called the "secret joke," he walked to his desk and picked up the picture in the silver frame, handing it to me without comment.

Instead of Edith's dour expression, I was startled to find a man's face looking out at me. This was not a photograph, but a pencil sketch, and the subject wore a kerchief knotted about his head, a single loop of gold in one ear. His brows were heavy and black, the nose saturnine, with a prominent beak, the nostrils faintly flared. His mouth was drawn thin, the lips barely curved, suggesting a hint of cruelty, and the beard was thick and black and pointed. The face was Alex Stair's done with the wicked, subtle humor of good caricature.

"Leila did that sketch," he said. "Sometimes the child shows more perception than her mother."

What did he mean by that? I wondered, looking from the pirate face in the sketch to the rather urbane visage of the man himself. "Why did she see you as a pirate?"

"It's a legitimate heritage." He replaced the picture on the desk. "Tradition has it that a pirate ancestor retired from his risky existence and married the daughter of a Caribbean ex-governor, fathering a family of twelve children. I'm supposed to be descended from one of the twelve. There's no great honor attached—they were a rapscallion lot and hardly in a class with the Hampdens."

There seemed a bitterness behind his wry manner and I sensed that here was a man who might well be resentful of the very wealth he had married into. Perhaps that was what Edith meant to him—

position and wealth. Perhaps these were the answer to what seemed the enigma of their marriage.

"You're from St. Croix?" I asked. "I believe Mrs. Hampden said you had a dress shop over there."

"It was my mother's originally. She managed to send me abroad for a dab of education after my father died. When I came home she was ill and I took over the shop. Apparently I've a flair for catering to the tastes of women travelers who like the special and unusual. I've done well enough with the business, though I find I can accomplish more with my second shop here in St. Thomas."

When he spoke of shells or of his shops, there seemed a quickening of interest in the man. Now he replaced the pirate sketch on the desk and went to a large, weather-beaten chest bound with corroded bands of iron—a chest that might have belonged to old Blackbeard himself.

"Let me show you some better examples of Leila's talent," he said. "If you want to reach the girl, perhaps this is the way."

He took a huge iron key from a hook nearby and fitted it into the massive lock. The key grated as it turned and he lifted the creaking lid.

"This is the real thing," he said of the chest. "I found it in the remains of a sunken ship off the rocky coast near the Hampden plantation house, Caprice, and I had it brought up. The lock and key are imitations of the original, but the rest is as it was. Leila has taken it over for her own use."

He drew a manila folder from the chest and spread it open on a table for me to see. Here were paintings done in lovely tempera colors—portraits of shells. Leila's representation was both imaginative and factual. The shells themselves had been reproduced with painstaking care and detail, but the groupings had been placed in odd circumstances, revealing a sense of the incongruous. A great conch shell, pink-lipped, sat on the cushion of an elegant French chair, seeming a little surprised to find itself there. An arrangement of cream and pink shells rested against a background the color of wet sand, with the small, delicate white bones of a fish nearby—reminding me of something by Georgia O'Keeffe. In another painting columbellas lay scattered carelessly across folds of sand-colored cloth that looked like the Arab burnoose Catherine Drew had worn on the terrace last night.

The fact that Leila had done these paintings excited me and I found myself eager to learn how she felt about her talent—what she wanted to do with it.

"These are beautifully done," I said. "Thank you for showing them to me. A talent like this is something to build on."

Alex picked up the paintings and laid them back in the chest. When he had closed the lid and hung up the key he turned to regard me a bit skeptically.

"It's possible that you're getting into something deeper than you realize, Miss Abbott. Perhaps a psychological struggle that you might better avoid."

Here was the warning again—less veiled this time—and the clear desire to discourage me, perhaps even to frighten me. I was ready enough to be alarmed by this time, but I did not like a deliberate intent to frighten.

"Mrs. Hampden told me that everyone would be against my coming here," I admitted. "I'd like to understand why. Tutoring a young girl seems a simple enough thing."

"Now that you've met us all, you don't really believe that's why you've been brought here, do you—to be a tutor?"

"Frankly, I don't know why I'm here!" I felt increasingly exasperated. "When I talked to Mrs. Hampden yesterday she seemed to have some definite plan in mind. But so far I don't know what it is. At least you might tell me why you don't want me here."

"I?" He shrugged elaborately. "Count me out. I'm not involved and don't want to be."

At once I caught him up with his own words. "Then as an uninvolved person, perhaps you can help me to understand objectively what is happening in this house, and why Mrs. Hampden wants me here, and Mr. Drew doesn't."

His lean-fingered hands moved absently about his desk until they found a cone shell with a patterned texture like brown and white fabric. He sat for a moment playing with the shell, reading its surface with a touch of sensitive fingers—the restless gesture of a man who might have troubling thoughts. That urbane poise which seemed a part of Alex Stair's nature had, perhaps, its own flaw.

At length he answered me. "Mrs. Hampden is afraid of the past. She's afraid of reliving history. When she was young Catherine was sent away to school with disastrous results. I expect Maud's fear of Leila being in trouble away from home is at the base of her concern."

I did not tell him that Aunt Janet had informed me of that school disaster, but I could see no connection when it came to Leila.

"Isn't that an extreme precaution for keeping her here?" I asked. "The girl doesn't seem at all like her mother."

"Perhaps she's not," he said guardedly, "at least not very often. It will be amusing to see what will happen if you are given a chance to step into the middle of this fray."

"Amusing seems hardly the right word," I said tartly.

He set down the shell that had occupied his hands. "Then, since I can't warn you away, I might as well join you," he said. "Perhaps I can help you recover your pupil. But now, if you'll excuse me, I'll be on my way downtown. Stay here as long as you like, Miss Abbott. Feel yourself at home."

This last seemed a sardonic parting shot. When he had gone I returned to the desk and picked up the framed pirate sketch. Had he or had he not been the man I had seen on the beach with Catherine Drew? About one thing I was afraid he might be entirely right. I was into something far beyond my depth, something thoroughly unsettling. And I had had more than enough of being unsettled.

I was still studying the picture when Edith Stair came into the room carrying a big wooden tray with wet shells scattered across its surface. She paused to glance in my direction, frowning.

"Oh, here you are. Where is the child?"

"Leila has gone out with her mother," I said. "Your husband has been showing me his study and his shell collection."

She carried the tray to the long table and set it down next to the untouched schoolbooks. This morning she wore a yellow print dress that seemed too bright for her sallow skin and the artificial auburn of her hair. Over it she had put on a short-sleeved brown cotton smock with yellow sunflowers for pockets. By daylight the bones of her face seemed more prominent, her eyes more deeply hollowed. She looked as though she had slept badly.

"What have you there?" she asked, noting the framed picture in my hands.

I gave it to her and she stared at the subtly wicked pirate face. Evidently she had not seen it until now, for she slapped the frame indignantly down on the desk.

"The girl should be sent away! She's completely out of control. This is impertinent, wicked!"

"Your husband seemed amused by it," I said. "It doesn't appear to offend him."

Her hands made a nervous motion of clasping and unclasping. "Catherine is ruining the girl. She teaches her nothing—except not to listen to Mother or to me. The sooner King sends her to Denver, the better."

There was more than spite in her words. I suspected that Edith too was engaged in the tug of war that seemed to be raging about Leila. I liked the thought of it less and less. With such a struggle, something always gave, often with serious hurt to those who participated. Even though my sympathies were increasingly on the side of a young girl caught in this fray, I did not see how I might affect the outcome in any positive way.

Edith turned to her tray of shells, her hands moving among the array, as though, in these at least, she found something that appealed to her. She saw that I was watching and picked up a grayish-white shell to show me. A wentletrap, she said, her interest clearly less aesthetic than her husband's.

"Sometimes it's difficult to get the animal out of a shell like this. Alex dislikes the cleaning and preparing, so I take all that off his hands. Shells have more life and gloss when the creature hasn't been allowed to decay and dry up inside. Beach shells are usually dead shells and they lack the sheen of those we get from underwater ledges, or from deep water by dredging with wire baskets."

I had not heard her so voluble before. Interest and animation had come over the woman as she talked about the work of preparing shells for her husband's collection, and her devotion to the task suggested a possessive devotion to her husband.

"There's nothing of importance in this lot, but we can never tell what to expect," she went on.

"Does your sister enjoy diving for shells?" I asked, looking for a casual way to draw Catherine's name into our talk.

Edith looked at me as if I had said something nerve-shattering. Her hands fumbled as she took a soft cloth from a drawer and began to dry a shell, rubbing it to a high gloss, then setting it aside to await her husband's attention. She seemed to be trying to calm herself, to find words to answer me.

"Catherine has no interest in Alex's shells," she said at last. "No interest at all!"

I prodded her no further, but moved idly about the room, picking up a shell here and there with no purpose in mind. There was nothing for me to do until my charge returned, and apparently there was no telling when that would be.

When she had polished the last shell Edith Stair turned to me abruptly. "Mother wants to see you this morning. Since you're free, we might as well go upstairs to her now. I hope you've thought over what I said to you last night."

I regarded her curiously. "You mean have I thought about your feeling that any effort I make with Leila is useless? Why do you feel that way?"

Clearly she did not mean to answer. Her lips tightened and she thrust her hands stiffly into the sunflower pockets of her smock as she walked to the door. It was up to me to follow or not, as I pleased.

V

For a moment longer I stood looking at the tray of shells. Then I picked up my little olive shell and went out of the room. Edith waited for me at the foot of the stairs and I followed her to the upper hall.

In a deck chair on the gallery just outside her corner room, Maud Hampden lay motionless, looking like a woman who had spent herself and must now renew her energies. The sun had risen sufficiently so that the overhang of the roof offered an edging of shade and her chair was set well out of the morning glare. On a table beside her a pitcher of fruit juice stood frosty and cool, but the glass nearby was untouched. Maud's hand, holding a palm-leaf fan, drooped listlessly toward the floor.

The deck chair faced away from me, so that she did not see me at once, and I paused beside the fanciful wrought-iron railing. A breeze stroked through palm trees in the garden, rustling stiff fronds and stirring the scarlet bloom of a flamboyant that reached its leafy spread over the flagstone terrace.

This was the first time I had seen the view by daylight from the heights of Hampden House and in spite of my concern, my growing uneasiness, I was once more held. True, I had grown up at the water's edge, but Lake Michigan stretched flat and unmarked clear to invisible shores, so that my eye was accustomed to flat vistas and gray-blue waters. Here the harbor shone with sunlight, sometimes blue, sometimes emerald green, with the Caribbean beyond a far deeper blue. Beyond the mound of Hassel Island on my right, and Flag Hill's steep peak on the left, other islands marked the sea, and there was no city murk to obscure their outlines. The air was vibrantly clear, intensifying and brightening already vivid colors. I would never get enough of this, I thought, after long gray Chicago winters.

Maud Hampden dropped her palm-leaf fan on the floor with an arresting clatter and as I went toward her chair she held out her hand to me in greeting.

"You're falling in love with St. Thomas, aren't you, Jessica? I may call you that? I've known your aunt for so long that you're Jessica to me."

Her handclasp was affectionate and somehow reassuring. After the hostility I had met in this house, it was comforting to be greeted with the warmth of genuine liking.

"Of course to both questions," I said, and drew a cane chair into the sunlight, having no use for shade.

Edith hovered uncertainly and her mother gestured her into a chair beside my own. "Do sit down, dear. I want to talk to Jessica, but I want you to hear what I have to say."

When her daughter had obeyed, the old lady lay quiet once more, studying me with her fine gray-blue eyes that had somehow retained their memory of youth. Morning light was not kind to her. It yellowed her graying hair and made her skin seem creased and leathery, giving me a glimpse of how Catherine might look in later years when the sun had worked long enough on the golden tan of her skin.

"Tell me—you've had a visit with Leila?" Maud Hampden asked.

"She brought me a breakfast tray this morning," I said. "We were beginning to get acquainted when her mother took her away to town."

"I know," Maud said. "I saw them leaving. Did you bring up the subject of her lessons?"

"Mrs. Drew seems to think that Leila has no special need for tutoring."

The old woman picked up the fan and stirred the air before her face in a manner that disposed of Catherine's opinions. "Pour some fruit juice for Jessica, if you please, Edith. Of course the child needs schoolwork—but later. Lessons are only a subterfuge at present. The important thing is to make friends with my granddaughter, and if possible get her away from her mother's company whenever you can."

I took the frosted glass of juice Edith poured for me and sipped it, savoring the cool sharp tang of lime. "I'm no trained psychologist, you know," I said. "Even though my father's subject as a professor was psychology, I am merely a teacher."

"Nonsense!" Mrs. Hampden flipped her fan at me. "You're intelligent and you have an aptitude. Janet says your subject is social studies and that takes in the world, so your view is a broad one. But what I want is mainly someone with a liking for young people, with some experience in dealing with them, and a lot of good common sense. You qualify. Leila can't fail to like you, and she needs an older friend who isn't family. Lessons can wait."

Edith poured juice for herself, and when she had taken a long, thirsty drink she clicked her tongue disapprovingly against her teeth.

"This whole plan is ridiculous! No one is going to stop Catherine while Leila is here. You're grasping at last straws, Mother, and I'm sure Miss Abbott must realize the fact."

I smiled faintly. "Last straws and feeble reeds!" I agreed. "But what do you mean? Stop Mrs. Drew from what?"

Mrs. Hampden fanned a bit too quickly, and her daughter stared at her hands until she could endure the sight of them no longer and thrust them into the sunflower pockets of her brown smock.

At length the old woman began to speak, musing aloud more gently than I would have expected. "As a child Catherine was gay and charming, even though she was strong-willed. Strong-willed like me. She had a certain dryad quality. A pixy quality that held us all."

"I remember my sister!" Edith broke in impatiently. "Catherine was about as pixy as a goblin. She was a wicked little child, really."

Maud shook her head. "No child is wicked. She was her father's beautiful darling—and perhaps that was the trouble."

The old woman closed her eyes, remembering, and she did not see the look on the face of her elder daughter—who must never have been anyone's beautiful darling.

"You let her grow up believing no one else mattered," said Edith bitterly. "Now she destroys everything she touches. If only we could send *her* away!"

Maud moved in her chair, tapped her fan on its arm. "Please, Edith—let's leave ourselves a little pride. Jessica will think—"

"Miss Abbott is hardly an ordinary visitor." Edith spoke with more spirit than I would have expected. "If she stays here, she'd better know exactly what she's up against."

Maud closed her eyes and let her untidy, windblown gray head fall back against the chair's cushions. "I keep forgetting that pride is an old-fashioned quality these days—pride of name and family. There was a time when such things mattered to all of us. When I was young."

Edith tightened her lips and subsided. She reached for her empty glass and rolled the frosty tube between her hands, as though she could be still only if she occupied her fingers—or hid them.

Before I could find anything to say, we heard the sound of a car in the driveway on the far side of the house. Maud and Edith listened intently, then exchanged a look.

"That's not Catherine's car," Edith said.

Maud held out a hand and her daughter helped her from the chair. Once on her feet, she seemed more like the determined woman I had met the day before. She walked with certainty around the gallery and Edith and I followed, to stand beside her at the railing that over-looked the garages and open parking areas.

The same red convertible that I had seen last night had drawn up to the door. As we watched, Mike O'Neill got out and came around the car. Without waiting for him to help her, Leila put out her long slim legs in their blue Bermudas, sliding from the seat.

"It's the other boy—Steve—that she has the crush on," Edith mut-tered beside me.

Leila said, "Thanks, Mike," and gave him a wave of her hand as he got back in the car. As he drove away she turned toward the house, holding a package under one arm, and looked up to see us watching her from the gallery above.

"Hello, darling!" Maud called. "Did you get your dress for the party?"

Leila stared at us, her expression quickly wary. I knew how we must look to her—three adults all rushing to the rear of the house at the sound of a car, to watch her, to see who she came home with and how, to challenge and question.

"Come up and show us, Leila," her grandmother called with a hint of command in her voice.

The girl regarded us coolly for a moment before she gave in with a shrug. "All right, Gran," she said and disappeared into the house.

We were back in our chairs by the time she joined us, bringing her package with her. "Is Cathy home yet?" she asked at once, as if that were the thing of most interest to her at the moment.

"No, she's not," said Edith. "Why didn't she bring you home? Where did she go? Where did you meet Mike?"

"Oh, let me alone!" Leila cried, dropping cross-legged to the floor near her grandmother's chair. "What is this—a third degree?"

"Where is Steve?" Maud asked, ignoring Leila's petulance. "Did Catherine go off with him?"

Leila bent her head and began to unwrap the parcel she carried. "I suppose he was around somewhere," she said carelessly—too carelessly. "He usually is—when he's not out in his boat. I ran into Mike downtown and he said he'd bring me home. Cathy had some-thing she wanted to do. She didn't say what."

It was all a little rushed and glib, as if she might have rehearsed it ahead of time. Nevertheless, I hoped the other two would not chal-lenge her openly in front of me.

Perhaps Edith meant to, but some sense of reason halted Maud Hampden and she let one attack go for another that was safer.

"You know I want no one from this house going downtown dressed in those—those pants!" she said. "If you're off to the beach, or out in a boat, that's different. But in the stores—I won't have it!" She turned to me. "We continentals, as they like to call us, are here on sufferance, really. Local Virgin Islanders have standards and it's our obligation to meet them. They should be our standards too. This is one I approve. Back in the States daytime dress has become entirely too lax."

Leila cheered up a little at this familiar turn of criticism, paying no attention to it as she displayed the contents of her parcel. In either hand she held up a dress—each a duplicate of the other. At sight of flame color as bright as the flamboyant blossoms, Maud gasped.

"Cathy thought it would be fun if we dressed alike for your buffet party next week, Aunt Edith. It's a darling dress, really. Cathy tried hers on and it looked wonderful. I hope mine looks all right on me —I think I can still get into the same size she wears. Shall I put it on for you—have a dress rehearsal?"

Waiting for no invitation, she sprang up and dropped the bright frock over her blouse and shorts, wriggling ingenuously into it. Over her other clothes it was a doubly tight squeeze, but she managed it. Then she came to me to be zipped up the back. The dress was of fine imported cotton, with a sheen of silk in the weave. Sleeveless, it began at a demurely rounded neck and clung in a slim sheath that emphasized the promise of Leila's young figure, even over the bunchy middy beneath. At the bottom it flared into bands of deep ruffles just at the knee.

Delighted with herself, feeling undoubtedly as spectacular as she looked, Leila whirled herself about the gallery, her ruffles swishing, wholly pleased with herself, unaware of the detracting inch or two of Bermuda shorts showing beneath.

"Doesn't Cathy have a marvelous taste in clothes?" she challenged us.

I could sense stormy disapproval gathering in Maud and Edith, and I tried quickly to counter it.

"But is it your taste?" I asked.

Leila faltered in her whirling and came to a halt in front of me. The smooth cap of her brown hair had blown into feathers on the drive up the hill, and her ruffled bangs fluffed baby-fine across her forehead. She ran her fingers through their brown fringe and fixed me with a defiant look.

"Why don't you say what you mean? Do you mean that the dress doesn't become me?"

"It becomes you," I said softly. "You look beautiful in it. But you look like someone else."

She relaxed a little and gave me a disarmingly sweet smile. "I want to look like someone else," she said and returned to her whirling.

I knew how she felt. I knew so very well how she felt, having always wanted to look like someone else myself. Maud cleared her throat, about to express obvious exasperation, and I leaned toward her.

"Please don't," I whispered. "Just don't say anything right now."

Edith snorted rudely, but it was not Edith who worried me. Leila was undoubtedly accustomed to disapproval from her aunt and would not mind. I sensed that it was her grandmother whose opinion mattered, even though the old woman and the young girl were in conflict much of the time.

Once more an uneasy moment was halted by the sound of a car coming up the hill to the driveway, followed shortly by the slam of a door.

"That's Cathy now!" Leila cried. I saw her face briefly before she dashed around the gallery to call to her mother—saw the look of relief in it, of happiness. Because of Steve? Because Catherine had not stayed longer with Steve?

We heard her calling, "Look at me, look at me!" and then she came back to us, keyed to an excitement that seemed out of proportion to the mere fact of her mother's coming home.

A few moments later Catherine joined us on the gallery, sleek in her tight-fitting green pants, with much of the upper part of her revealing smooth, tanned skin. She gave Edith a look of mockery, and bent to drop a kiss on her mother's cheek.

"Don't scold, Maudie old dear. I didn't have time to change." Then she turned to me. "So you're still here?" she said, and I felt once more the almost abrasive quality of her look. This woman wanted to hurt me, wanted intensely to have me gone.

"Of course Jessica is here," Maud said. "And here she is going to stay."

Leila broke in impatiently. "How do I look, Cathy?" she demanded, looking as glowing and beautiful as it was possible to look in a dress that was so wrong for her sweetness and youth. Though of course they were the last qualities in the world she wanted to be guilty of possessing.

Catherine regarded her daughter and for an instant it seemed to me that she felt surprise. "You look stunning, darling," she said. "We'll be perfect as twins. Give me mine and I'll try it on."

Catherine did not make the mistake of putting the dress on over other clothes. She unzipped herself from the tight trousers, untied the piqué band, and stood unself-consciously in briefs and strapless bra while Leila helped her with the dress.

I knew what was coming. I knew it before it happened. I was prepared for it in my very bones. I had been there so many times myself that I could hardly bear to look at Catherine as she pulled the dress over her head and sleeked it down about her hips. This time it was Leila who joyfully did the zipping, and was as foolishly unprepared for what was about to happen as anyone could be.

Catherine did no whirling and flouncing. She stood perfectly still so that we could admire her and there was not one of us on that gallery who did not recognize that the dress was made for her. Her blond hair danced above the flame that enveloped her and she was a figure of such loveliness in her red and gold that I ached a little as I looked at her. The aching was not wholly for Leila; some of it was for myself. Not that Helen had been anything like Catherine. She had been more innocent than Catherine in all that she did, yet somehow the effect had been the same—the result as devastating to me. I wanted to turn away so that I need not see Leila's hurt, but I could not escape the moment.

An air of painful self-consciousness had come over the girl. The natural, touching grace of youth gave way under our eyes to awkwardness. Even her expression of wounded puzzlement made her cease to be pretty. Catherine knew very well what she was doing. I thought of Kingdon Drew married to her. I understood his frustration and anger with an anger of my own.

Yet the damage to Leila was immediate and there was nothing any of us could do to lessen it. Edith probably did not understand or care, but when I looked at Maud I found her eyes fixed upon me in sorrowful awareness. Maud Hampden understood very well and she knew not only what Leila was feeling, but how I felt as well. I turned quickly from her look, lest I make her a promise. I wanted to promise nothing, but only to escape my own too immediate hurt. I had been through all this before—I could not bear to live it again through Leila. The parallel was even more hurtful than I had expected, so that I felt a little ill from the experience.

Catherine did not leave the matter there. "Do come here a minute," she said to her daughter. "Something's wrong with the way that skirt hangs on you. Of course the Bermudas don't help, but there's more that's wrong. Can you tuck your tummy in at least? I suppose you'll lose some of that baby fat eventually, but it makes you look ungainly around the middle. I wonder what we can do?"

She plucked idly at the goods, pinching it up here and there, all charming amiability, all practical, sympathetic suggestions—now that Leila was no longer a vision; a *young* vision and perhaps to be feared.

Once more Edith surprised me. "Leila looked all right until you started fixing things," she said bitterly.

Catherine glanced at her over Leila's shoulder, her greenish eyes narrowing. "Can I help it if you don't see what's wrong? What would you know about a dress like this?"—and she went back to plucking at folds of cloth.

Edith too had been through this before, I thought—when she was younger, perhaps, with a sister who eclipsed her at every turn. So she was not wholly insensitive now, though I felt she did not truly care about Leila. Quite suddenly I was warned, watching her. If I did not take care, there went I, soured and disgruntled, old before my time, hating and resenting, not only because of what one woman had done to me, but because of what I had *not* done for myself. I had to be free of this haunting. I had to get away and start anew. Regardless of my sympathy for Leila—and for her father—I could not bear any more. I must make my own way in a different world.

It was Leila who stopped what Catherine was doing. She snatched her ruffles from her mother's hands and stepped out of reach. "Never mind!" she said crossly. "It doesn't matter. You can't make me look the way you do anyway. Leave me alone."

Catherine smiled and shrugged, turning herself about so that she could be unzipped. Then she let Leila help her pull the dress over her head. But as it came off, Catherine gave a sharp cry of pain and clapped a hand to her face. When she brought it away there was blood on her fingers from a long pin scratch across her chin. She closed her eyes and thick dark lashes lay upon her cheeks as though they had been painted there. Her bright mouth was pinched with pain and she seemed to shiver all over her exposed body.

Leila sprang to support her with a strong young arm, all contrition and sympathy. "Oh, Cathy—I've scratched you! I'm sorry. Don't worry, darling. It's not a bad scratch, really—come along and I'll put something on it."

Catherine went with her almost meekly, not stopping to put on her clothes, and I could only look after them in astonishment.

"I wonder how much of that is an act?" Edith said dryly.

"You know it's not an act." Maud leaned back in her chair and reached for her palm-leaf fan. "It's that threshold-of-pain thing. Dr. Prentice says it's Catherine's misfortune to suffer more than the rest of us when it comes to pain. You know she nearly died when Leila was born—simply because she can't stand pain. She said she'd never have another child."

"A promise she's managed to keep," Edith said. "I'd better go and see that Leila doesn't kill her with iodine."

With Edith gone, Maud Hampden lay in her chair, her eyes closed, fanning herself listlessly. I thought she had forgotten my presence, but as I moved away she tapped the fan on her chair arm.

"Come, sit where I can see you, Jessica. There are a number of facts you need to know about us before you make up your mind."

I had already made up my mind—I must get away. Everything about this situation was wrong for me. Nevertheless, I could not refuse to listen, and I drew up one of the cane chairs and sat down again.

"Edith is right in feeling that I must forget about pride and give you more of the picture," Maud Hampden said. "Except that she believes telling you will frighten you off. Somehow I don't think you're made of such flimsy stuff."

She could hardly be more wrong about me, but it seemed pointless to confess to my fearfulness. I too was afraid of pain, but of a different sort.

"My son Roger was everything I could have hoped for in a boy," Maud went on. "He was sound clear through. I believe there are such things as good and evil in human beings, even if that concept seems old-fashioned today—like my notions about pride. I can't accept all this excusing of the wrongdoer because of something he couldn't help in the past. We all have pasts that are less than perfect, but sooner or later we must become responsible for our own acts. There isn't any other way."

She grimaced and made a slight gesture with her fan. "King and Roger were in Korea together and they became good friends. King was with my son in the hospital when he died. Later, when he was free, King came to St. Thomas to see me and tell me all he could about Roger."

The old lady opened her eyes and I saw in them the shine of tears. She blinked a few times before she found her voice again.

"I liked King and he liked me. He had suffered a loss too, since he was devoted to Roger. I invited him to stay with us. Perhaps I even aided and abetted when it came to what followed. Catherine could be enormously beguiling, and he thought of her as Roger's sister, expecting her to be like him. I might have warned him, though I'm not sure he'd have listened. But I saw in him possible salvation for Catherine if she really fell in love. I kept hoping she would change if only she loved someone enough."

The old lady was silent again, her eyes closed.

"There's something I should tell you," I said. "A little while ago I had a talk with Mr. Stair. Like everyone else he thinks there's nothing I can do for Leila in this situation. He—he told me a little about the past."

She opened her eyes at once. "Such as?"

Again I held back the information Aunt Janet had given me, since it seemed purposeless to pain her further.

"He said you were afraid history might repeat itself."

"Did he give you the details?"

I shook my head and she relaxed a little. "Good! We needn't go back to that unhappy affair. But Alex is more right about history repeating itself than he knows. That's why I feel so strongly about this—because I've been through it before. Oh, Leila isn't her mother and she would never do what Catherine did. But the fault was mine in sending Catherine out of my reach and care. And now Catherine is trying to use Leila against King in just the way her own father used Catherine against me."

I wanted to stop her from telling me more. Since I had no intention of staying, it was not right to permit her this humiliation.

"Please don't go on," I begged. "There's no way in which I can help you here. I'll stay out my week, if you wish, but Mrs. Stair is right—I'm too weak a straw for anyone to grasp right now."

Maud's fine eyes flashed me a look of reproach. "Nonsense! Do you think I can't read through the story Janet gave me? Do you think I can't see what Janet has missed? You had a job on your hands and you did it in the only way possible. Perhaps you had to compromise, as we all must do, but you made a more sensible choice than many people would, and you didn't go under, you didn't lose your courage."

In a sudden gesture she held out her hand to me, and when I gave her my own we smiled at each other in liking.

"Listen to me, my dear," she said. "Just listen."

"I'll listen," I agreed, "but I can't make any promises about the future."

She went on at once. "I haven't told you all this because I am a garrulous old woman. If you're to help Leila you must understand what has gone into her making, and what is being done to her now. My own marriage was an unhappy one. From the moment she was born, Catherine was Roger's favorite child and he saw very quickly that he could use her against me whenever he chose. When I would have disciplined and restrained her, he undermined me and gave her whatever she wanted. Because that was the best way in which to hurt me. The worst of it was that Catherine knew very well—and early—what he was doing, and she played his game. In fact, she carried it further than he intended. I had other things to interest me, and a good part of the time I closed my eyes and let them go their own way. Now I'm paying the penalty for my own mistakes because Catherine is now using Leila to revenge herself upon King."

"Revenge herself?"

"She always wants whatever is denied her," Maud Hampden said. "She wanted King from the first, and men newly home from war have been fooled by attractive women before this. Only she couldn't fool him forever and that's the thing that irks and goads her now. It's wickedly wrong for a child like Leila to be used as a pawn in her game."

"Then why don't you do what Mr. Drew wants and send her to Colorado?" I said. "Isn't that the best way out?"

She sighed heavily. "What do you think will happen if I send her away now? Perhaps I see what King doesn't. The child would hate being sent off—banished. She won't understand why it's being done. If she goes now she'll leave idealizing her mother, and hating her father as she is being taught to hate him. A wholly wrong judgment. That's the heritage she'll grow up with. It will affect her all her life."

I looked at Maud Hampden with increasing respect. I could see very well what she meant, and I knew that she might have put her finger on a basic truth. Perhaps King was too deeply involved to recognize the more deadly, permanent harm that might be done Leila if what Maud claimed was true.

"This is a crucial time," she continued. "Something must break the pattern and free the child from her mother here and now—at home where the damage is being done." She smiled ruefully. "Alex says you can't break the spell of witchcraft by running away. You stay and destroy it with counter magic. But how are we to find counter magic? Unless perhaps you hold it in your hands?"

I could only shake my head futilely. I needed counter magic of my own.

Maud Hampden leaned toward me, her eyes still bright with unshed tears. "I've been ill. I'm getting old. I'm living out the mistakes of the past, and I haven't the strength to fight this battle much longer. That's why I've snatched at you as a last chance. You know young people, you like them. I can see the small ways in which you're already drawing Leila to you. She needs a new idol. Someone unconnected with either her mother or her father. Crushes are easy at her age, and sometimes they're a good thing."

"Me—an idol! Oh, no!" I cried, thoroughly startled. "That would be the blind leading the blind!"

"Who knows better the problems of the blind than another blind person?" Maud demanded. "Can't you see how foolish it is that Leila should be damaged in her self-confidence, in her young pride —when she has so much more of value in her character than her mother has?"

"Of course I can see," I acknowledged.

"Yet you're still living with the same sort of damage in yourself! I never knew your mother, but Janet has told me what she was like, and how superior you are to her in every way."

Without warning the old flare of anger sprang up in me—anger against anyone who attacked Helen. "Aunt Janet never liked her. She never understood her, or knew how much Helen did for my father. It's not fair for you to take her word when—"

Maud Hampden's look, her very stillness stopped me. I let my words fade into shamefaced silence. I was reacting exactly as Leila would react if Catherine were attacked.

"*You* may not be able to change," the old lady said dryly, "but at least you've enough native good sense to recognize what you're still doing to yourself. For that very reason you may be the right person to stop its happening to Leila. Catherine is growing more reckless every day. Now there's this boy to whom she has attached herself over the last year—in order to use him against King, of course. Not that I worry about Steve. He's dazzled at the moment, but he has a hard streak in him that will look after Steve O'Neill. Now, however, the two of them have taken to running over to Caprice when the whim moves Catherine. That's my husband's home in St. Croix."

My attention quickened. Here again was the name that had been used with special meaning between Edith and Catherine on the stairs last night. Indeed, it had been used by Catherine almost as if in threat.

"I suppose you know that she has just returned from a trip around the Caribbean spending money she can't afford," Maud said. "And before we can turn around she'll be off again to San Juan, or somewhere else."

I nodded. Aunt Janet had brought up the matter of Catherine's spending, and so had King.

Maud's feelings were running away with her and she hurried on. "The moment she got home this time she headed for Caprice, and Steve went after her. He was in and out of the place as a sort of errand boy—and goodness knows what else—for the two days she stayed there. The caretaker is my friend, so I get reports from time to time. Ostensibly they're busy finding shells for Alex. This time Catherine came home furious because King has been going over her head in an effort to preserve that beautiful old place by getting it into government hands. We can't afford to keep it up, and this is the only way to save it from the ruin that overtakes so many of these lovely old houses."

"Why should Catherine be against that?" I asked.

Maud drew a deep breath in an effort to quiet her own indignation. "Sometimes I think she's driven solely by her own uncontrolled emotions—except that she can also be shrewdly scheming when she pleases. Caprice belongs entirely to her own emotional world. To her it stands for her father and for a past that would have suited her. Roger—my husband—should have been a plantation owner in St. Croix's early days. Slave days. The life would have suited him—and suited Catherine too. In any event, she has thrown herself into complete opposition to King's plans and keeps talking about restoring Caprice herself. With what I wouldn't know. When she got there this time and found inspectors from the government checking over the place, she nearly went out of her mind. Now she's even more determined to punish King than before. I'm afraid she has a penchant for high places—the cliff's edge, the reckless moment of high speed. She's afraid of pain, but not of danger, and if I'm any judge she's running full speed ahead toward disaster, meaning to bring King down with her."

Exhausted by her flood of words, Maud lay back and once more closed her eyes. The fan hung limply from one hand, and her breathing was quick, her color high.

I felt as weary as Maud looked—as weary as I had felt when I first came to the island. I'd had enough of women who reached out and took what they wanted without regard to the rights of others, without concern for the pain they might inflict. In me there was left only the urge to find a quiet place and loneliness, so that I could be myself—learn how to be myself. All these years, it seemed to me, I had never been alone. I had never been away from the demands of young people, sometimes a little cruel in their urgency because youth is often unable to see anything but its own center of gravity. Nor had I been out of reach of the summons of my mother's voice, making its own demands upon me quite as blindly, quite as self-centeredly.

He's a lovely boy, Jessie. Do bring him around more often. Let's get out the silver tea set and the Souchong. Boys like a touch of graciousness, you know. Of course he'll think me quaint and old-fashioned, but perhaps you two young people will bear with me, for all that.

Of course they thought her nothing of the kind. They said she was too young to be my mother, while I grew older by the moment and did exactly what Leila had done there on the gallery, when Catherine had put on her red dress. No—not ever again! I would not live it again. I too had loved my mother. But sometimes I had hated her as well. Leila had not yet come to that and when she did it might be too late, as it had been for me. I could not involve myself in this emotional morass Maud Hampden had spread before me. I must tell her at once that I would not stay—not even for a week.

But when I tried to put the thought into words I saw Leila again in my mind's eye, whirling in her flame-colored dress, her face bright with happiness, sure for the moment of her own youth and beauty. And I saw her as she looked moments later suffering at Catherine's practiced hands. The words died on my tongue and I could not speak them.

"Will you stay?" Maud asked. "Will you try to help me?"

"For a week," I said feebly. "Only for a week!"—and fled her presence like the rabbit I was, running along the gallery and into the house, into my room to fling myself upon the bed and wait for quiet to come to me. A quiet that I knew would be out of my reach as long as I stayed in this house.

VI

The rest of that morning passed uneventfully. Catherine spirited Leila off right after lunch and again I had no pupil.

During the afternoon Aunt Janet phoned me and I managed to be evasive. There was time enough to tell her my reactions when I ran to her in retreat, and I did not want her arguing with me over the phone. She had, she said, been invited to the buffet party next week, but she was busy at the hotel and probably would not come. By that time I would be free of Hampden House and its problems, and I too would be absent from the party.

Not until the sunset hour just before dinner did the house come to life, with everyone returned and gathered in one place. The little maid, Noreen, summoned me to join the family. I put on a candy-pink cotton that Aunt Janet had bought for me since I'd come to the island, and which I knew my mother would not have liked. I could almost hear her: "Honey, pink is my color—not yours. It fades you out completely. It's not for anyone with your skin and dark hair."

I put it on defiantly and looked in my mirror. There was nothing wrong with the color. If I appeared lackluster, this was not due to the dress—it was due to me, to the confusion and irresolution that stirred through my mind and would not let me be. At least I could brush my thick brown hair to a shine, and I could recall that Leila liked the way I wore it. Who was helping whom? I wondered wryly.

They were all out on the terrace when I joined them, sitting about with tall, cool glasses in their hands, conversing politely. All, that is, except Kingdon Drew, whom I looked for at once. Faintly disappointed yet somehow relieved at his absence, I went to the low retaining wall, built of the local blue stone, and stood with my back to the others, hardly noticed by them.

That lovely pink sheen I had seen before in the sky above St. Thomas shimmered over everything. While the sun set over the western hills of the island, the glow was reflected to this side from puffs of cloud, and the candy pink of sky and water matched my dress. Even the gray stone tower of Bluebeard's Castle, standing out on its own lower hill near the harbor, looked pink under that shimmering sky.

As I stood watching I heard the voices behind me. Alex Stair was asking Leila if she had found what she wanted in the shop today. One of the clerks had told him of the purchase of two red dresses.

Leila answered hesitantly, "I picked the wrong dress. I'm going to change it for something else, if you don't mind."

"Oh, darling!" Catherine's tone was mock-plaintive. "I wanted us to look alike. And that red is such a wonderful color!"

"You're brave to risk that sort of competition, Columbella," Alex said, faintly mocking.

I turned my head in surprise and saw that the others watched him too.

He smiled around at them, clinking the ice in his glass. "Don't you see what's happening in our midst?" He toasted Leila and drank. "We've a beauty growing up among us. Catherine will have to look to her laurels before long."

Leila squirmed uncomfortably and cast an apologetic glance at her mother. "He doesn't mean it, Cathy. He likes to tease me."

"This is not teasing but a matter of obvious fact," Alex said, his voice as cruelly soft as before—a pirate voice, reminding me of Leila's sketch.

Catherine's laughter rang high and light, and I did not like the sound of it. She was dressed decorously enough for dinner in blue silk shantung that changed its shading to green when she moved, and in the rosy glow from the sky she looked smoothly young and vibrant and hardly to be rivaled by an awkward young daughter. Yet Alex had baited her, and I wondered why uneasily. Such tactics —for Leila's sake—were dangerous. I could imagine how much harder Catherine might work to undermine any budding confidence if she saw her daughter as a rival to herself. This too I knew of old and something in me winced in painful anticipation. Once more I could not bear to watch or listen.

Since I was no real part of the group, I slipped away alone. At one side of the terrace a dirt path opened onto the hillside and I followed it idly into the tropical grove I had seen the night before from the gallery. It ran with much twisting through the thick growth that had looked so dark and secret by moonlight. Now, by early evening light, I found it equally ominous. Tall trees shut me away so quickly, and the terrace was so quickly lost to view that I seemed isolated in some faraway place. All about me crowded a tropical jungle—so varied and strange in its assortment of trees and plants that they could only have been set here by deliberate plan.

Much of the growth was unfamiliar to me. There were trees with limbs like twisted lianas, a banyanlike tree with a broad, ridged base, rain trees whose leaves shimmered in the faint pink light that sifted through from above. I saw a few acacias with their spiked tufts of yellow blossom sweetly scented, and there were the usual palms and banana plants.

As I ventured deeper the trees grew taller, meeting thickly overhead, closing me into dark seclusion. The very air seemed quiet within the grove, except for the twittering of birds as they settled themselves for the night. Behind me, the house, the very hillside, had vanished. As the path turned again I rounded the protruding bole of a black wattle tree like one in the garden of Aunt Janet's hotel, and came abruptly upon a small clearing in the tangle.

Here a circle of scrubby grass opened upon the verge of a hill. Across it grew a giant mango tree, perhaps forty or fifty feet high, its slender, dark green leaves spreading thickly to roof a part of this open space. From every branch hung long stems as thick as a finger, suspending clusters of heavy green fruit that would later turn golden.

At the point of lookout above the hillside a rustic wooden railing had been set as a guard, with a low marble bench nearby. I went to the rail and looked out upon the scene. Beginning at a sharp drop immediately below, an enormous spread of stone pitched down the hill. It was almost as large as a city block, and had been entirely paved with great flat slabs of rock. In only two places was the flat expanse broken. About a third of the way down blue-black rocks thrust their heads into two jagged, protruding mounds that stood above the rest. Apparently the builders had decided to let these natural mounds of rock have their way and had built the catchment around them.

That it was a catchment for water, I knew. When I had first arrived in St. Thomas my eye had been continually jarred by the sight of huge bare patches that scarred the hillsides wherever one looked. Aunt Janet had explained that these were a part of the constant effort to preserve every drop of water that fell upon the land. At the foot of each spread—of rock, or cement, or corrugated iron—were underground cisterns into which the rain water poured through gutters and pipes, to be safely held for human usage. St. Thomas houses had no usable basements, since cisterns must be placed beneath every house, with numerous drains to conduct all possible rainfall into them.

I had not been as close as this to a catchment before and I examined it with interest. The rocky expanse looked pink in the sunset glow. I could gaze out over it in every direction, since so wide and clear a sweep of hillside made a perfect spot for a lookout post. The view, the loneliness, began to quiet me, and I rested my hands on the wooden railing, emptying my mind, my very body of its weariness, letting go of futile struggle. To be alone and quiet—that was all I wanted. To have nothing asked of me! This was the nourishment I sought.

I did not have it for long. Because the earth of the path was soft and powdery dry, I did not hear the sound of steps behind me. I did not know anyone was near until Kingdon Drew spoke.

"Good evening, Jessica Abbott."

I swung about, startled, and the moment I faced him all my old alarums began to ring. I was on guard, up in arms, hostile—and more than a little drawn to the very cause of my alarm. I knew very well that I must be wary, that here was a greater threat than Catherine to the peace I wanted so badly. I must post myself in opposition to all that overwhelmed me about this man. It was a ridiculous reaction, yet there I was, tilting my chin, frowning at him, wholly on the defensive. My nerves remembered too well the betraying sympathy, the softness I could feel toward him, and now I had more reason than ever to be on guard against myself.

"So you've found Mrs. Hampden's garden," he said mildly enough. "It didn't originate with Maud, but she continued the planting of it years ago when she used to come here on visits from St. Croix as a young bride. Earlier Hampdens acquired it as a sort of town house close to Charlotte Amalie, and the garden was started by Maud's mother-in-law. Now we think of it as belonging to Maud."

This was a safe enough topic and I looked about with renewed interest.

The man beside me gestured. "That old mango tree you see there was the beginning of the idea. The elder Mrs. Hampden thought it looked lonely and misplaced all by itself, so she started a miniature jungle to keep it company. Since that time Maud has brought in as many tree species from the Caribbean islands as she could gather here, and with the help of a few gardeners over the years, she's managed to make them grow. Lately the place has gone neglected because she hasn't been well. You can see how quickly the wild undergrowth can take over. Still, it's a spot we all enjoy."

The warnings that had begun their ridiculous clamor in me quieted a little at this innocuous opening. Perhaps this was what he intended, sensing in me a tendency to alarm and flight—though that thought did not comfort me either. I fixed my gaze upon the unruly ridge of dark hair above his right temple, not wanting to meet his eyes.

"What a wonderful place to be alone," I said.

He seemed mildly curious. "Do you want so much to be alone?"

That was my affair and I met the question in silence, waiting for him to go on to more dangerous topics, as he was sure to do. I knew why I was uncomfortable with this man. It was because a current seemed to spring into being between us when we were together—a strangely disturbing current composed of a mixture of antagonism and attraction, perhaps in equal parts, so that I did not truly know which force was the stronger.

When he saw that I meant to indulge in no idle conversation, his manner stiffened a little and he gestured me toward the marble bench. "Will you sit down, Miss Abbott? I'd like to talk to you for a moment."

Warily, I seated myself and waited. In a moment I would allay all his fears about me. In a moment I would tell him that I could do nothing for his daughter, that I believed him right in his decision to send her away—and that I myself would like to leave as soon as possible.

"Have you had any further opportunity to be with Leila today?" he asked. "Have you seen enough of the situation to come to the only possible conclusion?"

I spoke quickly, lest I change my mind. "You were right from the first. This is a family matter. There is nothing I can do. I'll leave tomorrow, if you wish."

I could no longer fix my attention safely on that dark ridge of hair, for his look had changed. His eyes studied me intently and his straight, rather harsh mouth smiled a bit grimly.

"You astonish me. I expected more of a fight from you. Certainly you've been arrayed in battle dress against me from the first, and I thought I might have real trouble in persuading you not to stay. Thank you for a pleasant surprise."

"There's no point in attempting the impossible," I told him with as chill an air as I could manage.

"Exactly. And of course you're right. Maud is completely mistaken in her notions. Any young woman with good sense would run after one look at what exists in this house. Your reaction, considering your experience with your own mother, is wholly natural."

My reaction was one of outrage. "My own mother!" I could hear the quiver of indignation in my voice.

He continued to regard me in his cold, judicial way. "It was natural that your aunt should tell Maud about your mother, and of course that Maud in turn should tell me. Rather in detail, you might as well know. She expected this to be a strong selling point on your coming here. I saw it differently."

"Detail? How could anyone possibly know the details of my life?"

"Isn't the parallel pretty evident? Of course, this is why Maud saw in you what she mistakenly thought was rescue. She expected you to be so sympathetic toward Leila's predicament that you'd fly to her aid. I told her you'd be far more likely to fly in the opposite direction and refuse to go through this sort of experience again."

He had understood my reactions so quickly and clearly that I was taken aback. It was one thing for me to see the reason for my running, and quite another for the world to see. For Kingdon Drew to see.

"My mother was nothing like Mrs. Drew," I said heatedly. "She was never a sophisticated woman, but quite innocent and well-meaning about everything she did. Mrs. Drew knows very well what she is doing. Which makes the problem a different, and much more difficult one."

He thrust his fingers into that ruff of thick hair in a gesture that seemed to reveal his anger with his wife. "Yes, she knows what she's doing. She means to make Leila over in her own image. She's doing her damnedest at this. And it's not something I mean to stand by and see happen."

"She's doing more than that," I countered. "She's breaking down Leila's self-respect, her hope for the future, her confidence—and all at the most vulnerable time in a young girl's life."

"That's part of it too," he said. "It's all the more reason for packing Leila off as soon as possible."

Without warning I found myself remembering Maud's shrewd analysis and arguing the other side. "Is that the real solution? Wouldn't it be better if Leila could do her growing up here and now? Better if she could learn something about herself while she's still in contact with her mother—instead of running off to carry all her insecurity and her scars with her? Perhaps Maud is right about that much of it."

When our voices stilled, the evening was quiet. The birds' drowsy twitter had died away and the insects were just beginning to take over. Below us, down the hill, lights were coming on in the town and around the harbor. The pink glow had faded and the blue-gray sky was repeated in dusky water and darkening hills. Kingdon Drew turned his back on me and stood looking out over the scene, while I sat tensely, cooling my wrists against the marble, waiting for him to answer.

"If this is what you think," he said, "then why are you running away from Leila's need?"

I flung out my hands in desperation, hating to be cornered, but no longer able to hold back the words. "Because what you've said about me is true! I have a need too! I've been through all this before. I can't go through it again. All I want is to find myself. I want to be— whatever sort of woman I am! I don't want to be only a teacher. Or only a daughter." Suddenly I was close to tears and hating myself for my own engulfing weakness.

He turned toward me and there was that alarming gentleness about him that I had seen before. Neither his anger nor his impatience frightened me as much as this gentling did. I had grown too long unaccustomed to kindness from men. Particularly kindness that seemed personal and all too understanding. There could be a protective quality about this man. He had a way on occasion of looking at me—not as a teacher for his daughter whom he wanted to be rid of but rather as a woman who interested him and made him curious. Probably he was kind to lame kittens and wounded birds too, I told myself impatiently. Now he was sorry for me—and I stiffened against him.

"I understand how you feel," he said. "I don't blame you in the least, and I'll take you back to your aunt's whenever you want to go. Thank you for coming—even though I'm relieved that you've decided not to stay."

I folded my hands in my lap and stared at them because I could not meet his eyes while so intense an awareness of him filled me. Why couldn't I have met Kingdon Drew under different circumstances so that I need not fight him, need not humiliate myself before him? Why must I feel drawn to a man who was caught in the trap of a hopeless and impossible marriage?

He had not moved from the clearing and I knew he studied me again while I stared at my hands. To what purpose I could not guess.

"When are you going to stop running away?" he said.

I looked at him then—in astonishment. "But you want me gone. You've told me—"

"From here, yes. I'm not talking about that. I mean when are you going to stand still and face the woman you ought to be? Do you know what I see when I look at you?"

My fingers hurt with their twisting. "I don't want to know! I don't care!"

But he was not a man who lacked knowledge of women and there was a brightness in his eyes as he watched me. "Of course you care," he said, his tone roughening a little. "You're a woman bound to the past. A woman without confidence or belief in herself. A woman grown accustomed to running. There's nothing you could possibly do for Leila when you can't act for yourself."

Aunt Janet had told me something of the same thing, but from this man it seemed far more outrageous. There was no chance to answer him, however, even if I'd known what to say. He swung about and went quickly away through the trees, leaving me alone and furious, hurt and frightened. Because if what he said was true, then there was very little hope for me in the future. But I could not accept his words as meekly as he expected. Some inner core of courage in me rejected them.

I had a right to be angry! Lately, it was true, I had been running away from any commitment to life. But I ran as a woman who was drained and weary, who needed to renew herself before she faced the combat of living again. By coming here to Hampden House I had halted my flight from pain. I had made a small beginning. He couldn't know that in my own way I had been a fighter of sorts, even in the past.

While my mother was alive I had worked out a manner of living for myself that had permitted me to care for Helen as no one else would have. Yet I had also had my work and I had done it well. Nor had I been constantly unhappy during those years. I had too much pride for self-pity. What I did now was something else, and certainly no solution for my own problems lay in remaining here as Maud Hampden wished, or in the joining of so futile a battle as the one against Catherine Drew. King himself had not done so well in that fight. And Maud had trapped herself and her granddaughter long ago when she had not been able to keep Roger from destroying Catherine. It might already be too late to help Leila. None of this was my problem.

What Kingdon Drew chose to think of me did not matter. Indeed, getting away from his disturbing presence was one of the first things to be considered in my own battle for life.

I was free now to return to Aunt Janet whenever I liked. As I started back to the house I wished I could feel a greater sense of relief over a fact that should have been very welcome.

The sound of a gong made me quicken my steps. That was undoubtedly the summons to dinner. There was still the ordeal ahead of dining with this ill-matched family. I would not enjoy the meal, but it must be lived through. Tomorrow I would be free of them all.

As I followed the path back toward the terrace, the tropical growth that crowded along my way seemed twisted and strange in the unfamiliar shapes lent by early darkness. Ahead of me a small animal flashed across the path and disappeared into thick underbrush. It was probably no more than a mongoose—those little animals which had long overrun the island. Its darting passage startled me into hurrying further. In this place I no longer had any desire for loneliness.

When I reached the terrace I found that the torches along the outer wall had been lighted, and wavering flames showed the family going up the steps to dinner. Maud saw me and beckoned and I went into the dining room at her side.

The room opened off the great central hall, and was large and high-ceilinged. The walls were paneled in fine walnut, while the table and chairs were massive, old-fashioned mahogany. There were no touches of the modern Scandinavian here. If these pieces were Danish, they were very old. On two sides the room opened upon the circling gallery, so that evening breezes banished the day's warmth. Candles down the center of the table were protected by tall hurricane globes, their flames steady and unblinking, unlike the wind-blown flares on the terrace.

Maud sat at one end of the table, with King at the other, and I was placed on his right, beside Alex. King himself took the trouble to seat me and there was nothing in his manner to remind me of the harsh words he had spoken in the clearing above the catchment. Indeed, he seemed to put himself out to be kind to me, perhaps feeling that it did not matter now that I was leaving.

As a maid placed cups of jellied consommé before us, Catherine leaned toward me from across the table, her green eyes bright with malice.

"So King has shown you our private jungle?" she said. "What do you think of it?"

How closely she must have been watching to know we were there, I thought, but when I expressed my interest in the forest, she was soon bored, her purpose having been fulfilled—to let me know that I had not gone unobserved.

Alex had brought the murex shell to the table with him and he pushed it across to Catherine. "I thought you wanted this," he said. "It seems to have been traveling around the house all day."

Catherine pounced on it with an air of mock delight, and put the black-spined shell to her ear, listening raptly.

"Is the ocean very loud tonight?" Maud's tone was dry.

"It's not the ocean I listen to!" Catherine gave her mother a tantalizing smile. "The voices are there in the shell, talking to me. But they whisper so softly that I can't understand what they're trying to tell me."

"It's just as well." Maud picked up her spoon. "Voices giving advice from seashells are a bit too much at dinnertime."

"A teacup over the ear will do just as well," Edith said. "Catherine is performing again."

"I'm not altogether sure it's nonsense," Alex said.

His pale eyes were alight as though what he had done to Catherine on the terrace still pleased him. The candlelight gave a warm gloss to his beard—a warmth, however, that did not reach his eyes.

"There's a recognized phenomenon called 'shell hearing,' you know," he went on. "I suppose it's akin to automatic writing, or speaking in tongues. Something managed by the subconscious, perhaps—with a touch of self-hypnosis. So perhaps Catherine's voices are not to be sneered at. Perhaps she's telling herself something we ought to know about."

Edith seemed to find it difficult to swallow her consommé. She bent her head over the soup cup and even by candlelight her off-red hair lacked life and sheen. Maud made an effort to turn the talk onto safer ground by launching into a discussion of plans for next week's buffet supper to be held at Hampden House.

Apparently old friends were coming from the States to move into one of the new houses King had built in St. Thomas. So this was to be a party of welcome for them. Ostensibly. But I quickly sensed familiar strains running beneath the surface, tensions that were common to this family, whether one understood the cause or not.

I ate my cold consommé in silence, hardly relishing its flavor. With one part of me I listened and watched, while another part, perhaps as astral as the voices in Catherine's shell, distracted me, whispering unhappy accusations in my ear; accusations that were an echo of words so recently hurled at me: "A woman bound to the past . . . a woman accustomed to running . . . without confidence in herself."

King's voice, breaking through, caught my attention.

"I thought we'd agreed to hold no more such entertainments for a while," he said abruptly.

"It's *my* parties you don't like," Catherine reminded him, slyly. "This is Edith's affair—so you can't object to that."

"I fancy it's Edith's affair because Catherine has been twisting my wife's arm," Alex put in. There was a good deal of malice in the man, I thought, and it seemed to be directed at Catherine as often as not.

A dark flush came into Edith's face, making her hair look an uglier color than ever. She threw her sister a quick glance that hinted more of fright than anything else.

"Of course it's my affair. We owe invitations to everyone—everyone!" she protested, and dropped her soup spoon on the floor. "We can't go into retirement and never invite anyone over."

"Of course not," Catherine agreed, still slyly sweet. "Especially when it's just that King thinks I spend too much money."

Maud seemed to lack all energy tonight, but she made an effort to stop her two daughters.

"This party is not to get out of hand. It's to be a small, informal affair—let's keep it that way."

"Besides," said Alex, "we need a bit of divertissement, don't you think? Providing it doesn't go too far. I believe Catherine has given her promise to behave this time, and not indulge in whimsical games."

Catherine laughed softly, and Leila, who had been watching as uncomfortably as her grandmother, suddenly held out her hand.

"Let me listen to your shell, Cathy. Perhaps your voices will talk to me."

The distraction served momentarily. Catherine pushed the spiked shell toward her daughter and Leila picked it up, her rapt expression duplicating Catherine's as she held the prickly thing to her ear. After a moment she shook her head regretfully.

"All I hear is the sea, as usual. Rushing in and rushing out."

"Let's not have that shell with dinner again," King said, his voice taut.

Again Catherine's disturbing laughter rang out. "Besides, there's no point in worrying about money spent on a party when I'm really going to splurge pretty soon. I'm going to start fixing up Caprice. Have I told you about that? I'm going to buy new furniture and stop the leaks and mend the stonework, and the woodwork where termites have got in. Perhaps I'll even live there when I'm through, and give all the parties I like for as many people as I like. Wouldn't you enjoy living there, King? After all, you admire the house so much! You have to admit that it's handsomer than anything you've been able to build."

King said nothing, but I saw the pulse in his temple, the tightness of his mouth. She was pushing him too far.

"That's enough, Catherine," Maud said. "This is something to discuss at another time. We have a guest—"

The flush in Edith's cheeks had darkened painfully, replacing with anger the almost fearful look she had earlier given Catherine. Without warning she leaned across the table and clasped her sister by the wrist.

"Where did you go last night? Why did you go outside so late?"

Once more Maud made an effort. "Please, Edith dear—let's not —at dinner—"

But it was too late. Everything was out of hand. In these civilized surroundings the veneer was cracking badly. Catherine drew away in distaste from her sister's touch.

"Why shouldn't I go out? I was lonely. I have a husband who stays away all hours, so I got up to look for company."

"Did you find it?" Edith's face seemed to be breaking up, shattering like a cracked cup along minute trembling lines—a dreadful thing to see.

"Why not?" said Catherine lightly. "Don't I always?"

King stood up, flinging down his napkin, and strode from the room. I wished with all my heart that I could go with him. It was appalling to glimpse the savagery beneath what was happening, with Catherine always the catalyst deliberately stirring passions to the seething point. She was a dangerous woman, I thought, and evil— evil!

Maud's voice was stronger as her own indignation restored flagging energy. She spoke not to Edith, or to Catherine, but to me.

"I apologize for the shocking behavior of my family, Jessica. Please believe that we're not always like this. Such an outburst—of which I am soundly ashamed—is hardly our common pattern."

Alex came to her support, his faintly malevolent gaze missing nothing. "I agree, Maud dear. At least at mealtime we can be light and superficial. We can avoid subjects that bring on indigestion."

Catherine put the shell to her ear and murmured that there was nothing wrong with her indigestion—it was Edith who did all the suffering. Edith and King.

Maud and Alex ignored her and for the rest of the meal they engaged each other and the rest of us in forced conversation. All except Edith, who sat at her place eating little, looking pale and shaken, as though she would have liked to follow King's example if she dared. I did my best to help Maud Hampden in her effort to restore peace to the meal, answering casual questions that were asked me about my home-town suburb on Lake Michigan, about my impressions of St. Thomas, and other innocuous topics. As I talked Catherine began to watch me, and I soon became aware of her fixed attention, of the way she hung on my every word in a manner calculated to make me feel self-conscious and ill at ease.

Eventually Maud brought up the subject of Leila's lessons, which must surely start tomorrow, and at once Leila began to protest.

"I don't want to spend the summer on lessons! I want to be outdoors. I want to swim and go out in Steve's boat, and have fun in my own way. Cathy, will you take me along the next time he runs you over to Caprice? I don't want more lessons when school is out. It's silly!"

"And you needn't have them, darling, if you don't wish it," Catherine said with a glance at me. "We all know that Miss Jessica Abbott is here to keep you away from my dreadful influence, but perhaps I'll have something to say about that. As for Caprice, we'll see. That depends on how I feel when the time comes."

"Why not give Miss Abbott a chance?" Alex put in. "Perhaps she'll provide Leila with something more interesting than she expects. Surely you aren't afraid of her good works, Catherine?"

Catherine touched her chin where the pin scratch showed, watching him. "I'm not afraid of Miss Abbott or anyone else," she said. "If she wants to start these silly lessons, let her go ahead. They won't last very long."

Maud said, "Thank you, Alex. Tomorrow you can get started, Jessica."

I withdrew into myself for the rest of the meal, venturing no further remarks. I did not care for the steady scrutiny of those faintly tilted, greenish eyes. Catherine's look was venomous and I wanted to attract her attention no more than I could help. Yet the occasion of this already uncomfortable meal did not offer the proper time to make the announcement that I was leaving.

We finished our dessert, a crisp native pastry filled with coconut, and it was a relief to get away from the table. As soon as I could, I left the others to return to the sweetly scented evening air of the terrace. Once more I needed desperately to quiet the turmoil of my own nerves. I must talk to Maud soon and tell her of my decision. She must not be allowed to count on me, or believe futilely that she had found a solution to her impossible problem.

As I stood there, trying to form in my mind the words that I must speak to her, and finding them difficult to express, someone touched me lightly on the arm. I turned to find that Leila had come to stand beside me.

She smiled at me shyly, seeming unsure of herself. "I'm sorry," she said, doing a complete about-face. "It's not your fault that you haven't been able to get on with those lessons. I shouldn't have said what I did at dinner. What I find to do around the island is just the same old thing, and it isn't all that interesting. It's only visitors who can keep busy every minute. Sometimes I'm dreadfully bored. I won't mind working for a few hours every day. But if I promise to help you get started with what you're here for, will you do something for me?"

Considering the trend of my own thoughts, I hardly knew how to answer her. It would be cruel to reject her advance by announcing flatly that there would be no lessons tomorrow because I would not be here. I postponed the difficult moment and took a side road.

"What would you like me to do for you?"

She turned her head, not meeting my eyes, and the light from a nearby torch touched golden highlights into her smooth brown cap of hair.

"It's about that red dress. Uncle Alex says I can take it back and get something else. Will you help me pick out something that will look nice for the party?"

In spite of myself, I was touched. It was so small a thing that she asked of me. Perhaps I could help her find something meant for her, instead of for Catherine. This was the least I could do before I left tomorrow. It would not be the first time I had helped a young girl to choose a dress. In fact, it was easier to help others than to help myself, since my mother's voice was less apt to get in the way when others consulted me.

"Of course I will," I said. "I'll try to help, if you think I can."

She looked more pleased than seemed right under the circumstances, betraying all the more evidence of her need.

"Oh, I know you can!" she said eagerly. "I love that pink dress you're wearing. Sometimes"—she cast a quick, uncertain look about the terrace—"sometimes I think Cathy chooses things that are a little too dramatic. Of course I'd never say that to her. She gets her feelings hurt so easily."

Yet with so little compunction about hurting others, I thought. At least what Leila had just said was heartening. Once more I had the feeling that her apparent adulation of her mother was cracking a little around the edges. Given time and opportunity, the right person might be able to help her change directions. But that right person was not me.

Noreen, the little maid with the merry dark eyes and exuberant manner, came toward us across the terrace. Mr. Drew would like to see me, she said. Now, if I would please come. He was in his "office room" at the front of the house. I said I would come at once, and started to follow her, but Leila put a quick hand on my arm and I paused. Her words—meant, I suppose, to be encouraging— took me by surprise.

"If Dad tries to scold you, don't pay any attention," she said lightly. "None of us do, you know. Cathy says he was born to be a feudal lord and he's out of place in the twentieth century. So he shows his bad temper by jumping up from the table—all that sort of thing. He's a bit silly sometimes. So never mind what he says."

My reaction was so quick and indignant that it took me unaware and I did not try to suppress my immediate upsurge of impatience. Leila was showing the common insensitivity of the young, with not the least notion of what she meant to her father, or what he might be suffering because of her. I couldn't see Kingdon Drew throwing his own life aside simply because Leila was young.

"Do you suppose it's possible that you haven't given much time to appreciating either your father or his position?" I asked her coolly.

I saw the sudden change in her face, caught her stricken look, but I did not soften. Let her be stricken. It was time for her to do a little soul-searching that would lead her outside the charmed circle of herself and her mother. This, too, was a basic part of education— and since I had come here as a teacher, I could leave her with this at least.

"Think about that," I said, and walked across the terrace and into the house without another glance in her direction. At that moment I had no idea what I meant to do. When I went toward King's office I believed I was thinking only of Leila's heartlessness toward her father. But whoever I really was, that inner woman whose acquaintance I was trying to make must have taken a firm hold as I walked briskly into the room. The callous brutality of Leila's words were an echo of Catherine and they forced me to the action I had been so reluctant to take.

I sailed into the room where King awaited me, a bit breathless, yet somehow eager for this confrontation.

VII

Kingdon Drew sat at his big steel-gray desk with plans and blue-prints scattered before him. Though he held a pencil in his hand, he did not seem to be working. The suddenness of my arrival brought him to his feet.

"Something has upset you?"

"Something has upset me," I agreed.

He misunderstood. "I don't blame you. We all behaved atrociously at dinner. Certainly I shouldn't have left the table as I did. I wanted to tell you that I'm sorry that had to happen while you were here. We might have waited till we were alone to indulge our antagonisms. I'm sorry too for anything I said earlier that may have hurt your feelings. I had no business speaking to you like that. Perhaps it will be easier for you if you pack your things now and let me take you back to your aunt's this evening. There's no need for you to endure us for another night."

His face still seemed drawn and tight, as if he held himself sternly in check. Yet there was kindness in his eyes when he looked at me. He truly did not want me embroiled in the troubles of this house. I tried to order the impulses that drove me, tried to find reasonable words to explain my stand. Instead, I spoke tersely, hiding all feeling.

"I've changed my mind," I told him. "I've decided to stay."

At once there was withdrawal in him. Where he had seemed ready to be kind a moment before, he regarded me coolly now.

"May I ask why you've done this sudden turnabout?"

There were waves of unfamiliar emotion surging up in me, striving for release. I wanted to say, I'm on your side, even if you don't want me there! I think your daughter can be a brat at times and someone ought to take hold and counteract her mother's influence! I said nothing of the sort. I held back this alarming tendency to let my emotions go—I who had been so quiet and controlled for so many years!—and spoke with restraint. I told him that Leila had come to me, asking for my help, and I felt I could not let her down.

If she could make this gesture in my direction, then I had to stay. Even if I failed, I had to try.

"Perhaps you were right and it will be good for me to stay and fight for something," I told him. "Perhaps I've never tried what you would regard as fighting. Not when I was as young as Leila. Or even when I was older. Not for myself. I suppose I can't just keep on running."

His look softened in the way I was coming to know and dread a little because it weakened my resistance to him.

"By fighting, I meant for yourself—and not here. You'd be doomed to defeat here, as we all are." He sounded fatalistic, a man without hope, but before I could protest, he went on: "In the past you let that young man of yours go because you weren't tough enough to stand up to your mother. Do you think you can possibly be tough enough for the far worse situation you'd have to face here?"

So Aunt Janet had betrayed me by talking about Paul too! And she was wrong—they were all wrong!

"That's Aunt Janet's sentimental notion," I told him hotly. "I suppose you got it from her, via Mrs. Hampden. I suppose it's what a lot of people who knew me thought at the time. But it isn't the truth."

He stood behind his desk, waiting. I caught my breath and went on more quietly.

"I let Paul go because I didn't want him any more. I couldn't bear to marry someone who was more in love with my mother than he was with me."

Kingdon Drew reached out to the model of a small house on his desk—part of a miniature neighborhood with yards, sidewalks, trees. Absently he followed the path to a front door with one finger.

"Do you suppose that idea might have been jealousy on your part? The young don't always see things clearly."

Perhaps he was remembering his own young marriage to Catherine, I thought, though I could not believe he had ever been as young as I, or as young as Leila. I did not need to defend myself, however, or explain about my mother. He had only to look at Catherine. After a moment the straight, grim line of his mouth softened and he glanced up from the model.

"There must have been other men coming along to interest you," he said more gently. "There must have been someone worth fighting for."

Suddenly it seemed terribly important to make him understand what I had never tried to explain to anyone else. "After Paul, I was careful. I watched myself. You see, it had happened before, when I didn't care as much. I couldn't blame Helen—my mother. She could be very dear and charming, and she never admitted to herself what she was doing."

Not like Catherine, I thought, feeling again the contrary pang of missing Helen. Surely she had never been like Catherine.

I went on, trying to make clear what was not wholly clear to me. "After Paul I didn't want to find myself involved. It's true that I didn't want to be hurt again. So I've been a teacher and a daughter. For a good many women such substitutes have to be enough, and what I've done has counted for something, I think—self-respect, if nothing else. That matters to me."

The room was quiet. When King tossed his pencil down it made a clatter in the silence. "You really didn't fight, did you?" he said.

My mind felt suddenly clear of a great deal of rubbish. It was as if by taking a stand I had opened a door that led through to a place of clear, truthful light.

"Perhaps you don't know me very well," I told him. "Perhaps there's a different kind of fighting—a woman's kind. It's true that I've been running away ever since I came to St. Thomas. But I don't believe I've always been the coward you think. I had to work this out my own way. Anyway, there's a job to be done here. Not only for Leila, but for me as well. Because otherwise I can't live with myself ever again."

In a way, I would be taking a stand for King, too, I thought, though I couldn't tell him that. He could not possibly guess how I had been lining myself up on his side, a single faltering step at a time, ever since I had come to this house. Now I had taken a longer, more irrevocable step. Oh, I knew I would be unsure of myself again. I would be seized with qualms and doubts and fears—what woman wouldn't be in a situation so grave? But now I would run for no warren like the rabbit I thought I'd become.

He studied me with a thoughtful air, almost an air of discovery. "When we talked earlier I didn't really believe what you were telling me. I didn't believe that you'd walk out on Leila. I was right. I've sensed something in you from the first—a quality that I haven't seen much of lately. Call it decency, honesty, if you like. Old-fashioned terms, perhaps, but you've brought a rush of fresh air into this house."

His words warmed me, drew me to him more than ever in liking and loyalty. Yet I wasn't convinced that I deserved them.

"I'm not sure I succeed in being honest," I said.

He smiled, his eyes lighting. "Whoever does when it comes to judging himself? But it's something to try. Don't belittle yourself, Jessica Abbott. Maybe you're a bigger person than you think."

An unfamiliar wave of sensation washed through me—a mingling of relief and gratitude, even a new sense of courage, all because Kingdon Drew did not think me wholly a coward. If we could fight this battle together—but he dashed any such feeling at once.

"Don't misunderstand me," he warned. "Personally, I'm applauding your determination. But I still mean to send Leila away as soon as it can be managed without upsetting Maud and the child herself too badly. Unless you can convince me that keeping Leila here will be wiser than sending her away, I'll oppose you at every turn. I respect your decision, but I won't let that stop me."

I swallowed hard to down the dismay which so quickly replaced that brief sense of well-being I'd felt. I should have expected this. He was fair—he would give credit where it was due, but he had not swerved an inch from his original stand.

"I'll do my best to make you change your mind," I said.

"I'm afraid it's not so much what you may do that determines my stand. Here—look at this!" He picked up a newspaper, folded to an inner page, and handed it to me.

These were no longer headline stories, I saw. One was of a much hashed-over crime of passion that had occurred some weeks before in St. Croix. Another the continued account of jewel thieves preying on wealthy women in luxury hotels around the Caribbean. And then the story he meant me to see.

The column was one of faintly malicious gossip and it asked rather pointed questions about a married woman of good family who chose to cavort about island beaches after dark in the company of a man much younger than herself. Did the lady's husband have no care for her reputation, even if she had none for herself?

Sickened, I gave the paper back to him. There was nothing to say.

"You'd better go tell Maud of your decision," he suggested grimly. "She'll be grateful. But tell her what I've said too—that I mean to play the heavy-handed father at the first misstep and send Leila off to Denver."

I turned away and as I did so I saw again the framed photograph of high, snow-capped peaks where it hung upon the wall.

"Do you ever miss the cold in your sunny islands?" I asked. "Do you ever get tired of the tropics?"

He answered readily. "Sometimes. I'm an exile here, just as you will be if you stay—even though it's by choice. There are days when

I'd give anything to head into a good stinging blizzard and feel snow crunching under my feet."

This was something we shared that the island-bred would never understand, I thought a bit wistfully—and laughed at myself at once.

"I'd rather not fight you," he told me more gently. "I'd rather have you on my side."

I turned away from the picture. "I am on your side," I said, and went quickly out of the room.

Upstairs Maud was lying on her bed, and Edith was with her, putting cold cloths on her head. I think Edith did not want me to intrude, but Maud saw me in a mirror and gestured her elder daughter aside. I went to stand at the foot of the handsome pineapple four-poster bed and looked down at the old woman.

"I've come to tell you that I'll stay as long as you want me to," I said. "I've just said as much to Mr. Drew. He doesn't approve and he promises that he'll oppose us both."

Maud sat up and tossed the wet cloth from her head. "Good girl! I knew you had it in you the first minute I laid eyes on you. Run along, Edith. And put that ice pack on your own head."

I saw Edith's face as she turned away, and was startled by the intensity of resentment it revealed—whether directed against her mother or against me I could not tell. She said nothing, however, and when she had gone sulkily from the room, Maud got off the bed and took my hand.

"Thank you, my dear," she said. "The child already likes you. Make her love you. Win her."

Her warm approval was something I needed, knowing as I did that I could count on no help from King. I was on Maud's side too, finding myself increasingly fond of this woman who fought against the odds of age and flagging strength to take a stand for the sake of what she believed was good and right. She and King—and now I—were all engaged in a struggle for the same thing. It was just that our choice of solutions differed. In fact, my solution might not be entirely Maud's. I was still undecided and feeling my way.

Mrs. Hampden walked briskly to the door with me, and into the hall, as though, having won me over, she was more than anxious to show affectionate approval.

As we neared my room I saw that Noreen must have forgotten her housekeeping duties, for a broom stood propped on its handle beside my door, ill balanced with the bristles pointing up. I offered to take it downstairs, but Maud stopped me with surprising vehemence.

"No—don't touch it! Let it alone." She went to the bannister and called down the stairs.

Noreen answered and came running up. Maud pointed at the broom and the girl halted abruptly, no longer smiling.

"What it is?" she asked uneasily, using the island transposition of words.

"It's a broom, as you can see," Maud told her. "Did you put it there?"

"No, missy!" Noreen said emphatically. "I didn' put it there. Jus' me and myself be up here today. And I didn' see no broom."

Maud sighed. "Well—never mind. You can take it downstairs now and put it where it belongs. Tell whoever it was not to do that again. You understand, Noreen?"

For a moment I thought the girl would refuse to touch the broom. But as Maud waited she picked it up in a cautious hand and hurried downstairs, holding it away from her as though it were something alive.

"What was all that about?" I asked.

"Nothing—just carelessness," Maud said.

I knew something had upset her, but she chose not to explain. She stayed only to thank me again and left me at my door.

For the rest of the evening I stayed alone in my room. Tomorrow my duties would start in earnest with the almost impossible task ahead of me. I must find my course of action. Not merely that endurance which had seemed necessary in the past, and which, as I'd told King, had been a kind of fighting in itself—but now something far more decisive and challenging than I had ever faced before. I felt a certain exhilaration at the very thought of flinging myself into a real struggle against a woman who meant only to destroy.

Tomorrow there would be a start in my tutoring efforts with Leila and we must begin to be friends. Perhaps we would exchange the red dress, and that too would serve as a positive step in the campaign I must wage against her mother. Because that was what all this must add up to—preventive measures against Catherine. I would move quietly at first, managing a little at a time. Nothing could be done all at once.

Yet, in spite of my eagerness to begin, to take action, to prove myself—the penalties for failure never completely left my mind. Failure might mean permanent damage to Leila. It could mean injury and hurt to Maud and King. And for me—disaster, for reasons I did not dare look at too closely. I knew that I could not afford to lose. In a sense, my life hung in the balance.

When I had faced all this I sat for a time listening idly to the small radio I had brought with me, attending the storm warnings that were common to the area at this time of year. A hurricane was boiling up out in the Atlantic, but its progress seemed northward, so it would miss the Caribbean, and there was nothing to worry about at present. A real hurricane had not struck the Virgin Islands for a good many years, and while everyone battened down for a blow several times a season, there had been no disastrous damage to St. Thomas for a very long while.

I went to bed earlier than usual. Having made my decision, taken my stand, I would surely sleep tonight. If there were scenes in the hall outside my door, I would not get up to investigate. I must think of Leila now, and of how I might best begin with her.

I fell asleep thinking of her father.

Nothing reached me for hours. I must hardly have stirred. When I awakened suddenly I had a sense of the time being well after midnight. It was no sound that had brought me awake, but a scent—the odor of cigarette smoke close at hand.

At the realization, I came wide awake, holding myself tense in the hushed gloom as I sniffed the acrid odor. Tonight I had been less nervous about going to bed, and I had left the bamboo-decorated draperies open to the air from one of the gallery doors. There was moonlight outside and the mass of the open doorway was lighted from without. Inside the room darkness lay thick, permeated by that eerie odor which told me someone was here, perhaps only a few feet from my bed, smoking a cigarette. As quietly as I could I raised my head from the pillow and caught the gleam and movement of the tip burning in the dark.

"Who is it? Who's there?" I demanded.

"I thought you'd never wake up," said Catherine Drew softly.

The glowing tip of the cigarette drew an arc in the air as she rose from her place. A moment later she had switched on a lamp and turned to face me. She wore a mauve-colored nightgown and filmy negligee of the same tint, and her long blond hair lay loose about her shoulders, with a gold ribbon tying it back from her face.

I sat up in my pajamas, grasping at that teacher's authority which I'd learned to put around me like a garment when I had to face some difficult situation.

"Do you often prowl the house at night and come into guests' rooms without permission?" I asked tartly.

One slender finger drew a line down the pin scratch on her chin.

"Night hours are always best. Then we drop our daytime masks and let our feelings come through."

I was reminded of some feline creature—though nothing so tame as a cat. A beautiful panther, perhaps, poised and ready to pounce. I had not noticed that she hid her feelings by day, and I waited for her to tell me the reason for this intrusion.

She scattered ash carelessly and gave me her sly smile. It never seemed that she smiled with anyone, but rather that she smiled to herself and for herself, so that only she knew why her lips curled in secret amusement.

Without warning she came to the point. "King says you've decided to stay. I've come to tell you I don't want you here. There's nothing you can give my daughter that she needs from you. I want you to leave tomorrow morning."

I pulled up my knees and clasped my fingers about them, feeling the need to do something strength-testing with my hands.

"I've already told your mother that I mean to stay."

She could move like a panther. She left her chair, sinuous in her quick motion, and came to sit on the foot of my bed. Now the smell of her cigarette did not cover the sweetish scent of water lily as she bent toward me. It cost me an effort not to shrink away.

"I don't like meddling and interfering," she said. "It will be better for you if you leave at once."

She spoke with the assurance of a child long accustomed to her own way—a spoiled child who would not grow up. And she was dangerous in a child's way, with the ready cruelty of the child, ungoverned by those restraints which an adult learns with the passing years. Yet she was cleverer than a child, and with an adult's strength—a strength I must somehow oppose.

"Why must I leave?" I asked.

She seemed faintly surprised that I should question her wishes. "I can make things unpleasant for you if you stay here. Do you doubt that?"

The pattern that had created Catherine Drew was increasingly plain: Roger, her father, indulging her, encouraging her to have her own reckless way; Maud struggling, opposing, but often taking the wrong course and going down repeatedly to defeat; King raging and storming off, trying to fight her with anger and physical strength. Perhaps there was a flaw to start with and in the face of this twist in her nature no one had ever taken a sound enough stand to teach her what she needed to learn. Now it was too late. Teaching her was not up to me, even if I had known how to go about it. I could only try for my own course and play whatever cards came to hand. I played one now.

"Is it because I saw you on the beach at Water Island a week or two ago that you want me to leave?"

Her greenish eyes seemed to flicker. "I thought you'd recognized me. Just as I recognized you the moment I saw you on the terrace last night."

"Listen to me," I said, playing the teacher again. "What you do is your own affair. It's no concern of mine who you meet, or where. My work lies with Leila."

"Don't be silly!" She waved her cigarette scornfully. "Of course you'll make what I do your business—if it's to your interest. I would myself."

"I don't think we're much alike, Mrs. Drew. My concern is with Leila. I would hate to see her hurt."

"Do you expect me to believe that? I've seen the way you look at him. King is already your concern."

An alarm rang through me, setting every nerve alert and on guard. Here was the essence of her enmity toward me—and if I was to be honest with myself, there was justification. I could not help my own feelings, but I must do better about hiding them if I was to stay in this house.

"Your husband wants me to leave," I reminded her. "He wants to send Leila away."

"But you'd like to show him you can win my daughter over, wouldn't you? Oh, I'm sure you're filled with all sorts of noble, teacherish purposes. But you're a woman—even though you've managed to cheat yourself of being one. Don't you think I know the signs when his attraction is working?"

"What good will it do if I go away?" I asked, ignoring her words. "The moment I'm gone Mr. Drew will send Leila to his sister. Then you'll lose her anyway."

The secret, unnerving little smile touched her lips. "I won't lose her. There's still time to make sure of that. Perhaps it will be good for her to go away for a while. Perhaps I've been wrong in opposing that."

I knew what she meant. Alex Stair had given her a glimpse of what it might mean to have Leila growing up here on the island— young and increasingly beautiful as she matured, while Catherine grew older and faded in contrast. No, of course she would not mind sending Leila away. She wanted no worshiper who might also prove to be a rival. She might permit her daughter to be sent off to Denver, no matter what pretense she made with the girl herself. But she did not want her to leave before she had made sure of a final smashup between Leila and her father. Then Leila would go away broken-hearted over leaving her mother, with the pattern frozen in resentment and dislike of her father—just as Maud Hampden feared it might be.

"We still have a little time," Catherine repeated, sounding pleased with her secret plans. "After you leave I will manage."

I had to make a beginning. I had to meet attack with attack.

"Not if I can help it," I said quietly.

She looked at me from her perch at the foot of my bed as if I were some odd species of creature with which she was unfamiliar. Her eyes were very bright.

"If you must be so stupid as to stay," she said, "I will have to take steps. And I can promise you they won't be pleasant ones. I never bother with half measures. If you stay I'll make you very sorry indeed."

There was a long moment while we stared at each other and antagonism quivered in the air between us. In spite of the fact that I had managed to oppose her with words, she frightened me not a little. With her ungoverned impulses, I had no idea how I could defend myself against whatever she might try. But something stubborn had awakened in me and would not be beaten down. I said nothing and my lack of an answer was my reply.

She shrugged and slipped from the bed. Moving with smooth grace she ran barefooted across the room, a rippling of mauve floating about her. With no by-your-leave she drew out the green negligee from the closet and searched its pockets.

"If you're looking for your gold locket and chain," I said, "it's not there. Your sister found it in your robe when she brought me here last night. She said you were sometimes careless with your possessions, and took it away."

"Careless! I've always kept personal things in this room. I had no idea they were going to put you here and move my things out until it was done! Maud loves to spite me, and so does Edith. But I'll pay them off, never fear."

She flung the green negligee toward a chair, from which it slipped to the floor, and gave me a last careless look of warning before she went out of the room.

When I left my bed I found I was trembling in reaction. At least I had stood up to the woman—I had begun my struggle. Perhaps

I could learn a more direct kind of fighting. Perhaps it was not too late.

When I listened at the door all seemed quiet in the hall beyond. The odor of cigarette smoke and the scent of water lily mingled pungently in my room and I flung both gallery doors wide to let clean sea winds sweep away such tangible reminders of Catherine Drew. Then I went back to bed and, strangely enough, fell soundly asleep, free for a little while of the threat that had hung over me ever since my arrival. I knew its source now, but I did not think that Catherine Drew would return to disturb me for a second time in one night.

VIII

No one called me the next morning, nor was I coddled with the arrival of a breakfast tray. When I went downstairs it was still early, but the lower house seemed empty and it was Noreen who served me something to eat in the dining room. I talked to her a little, fascinated by her swift Calypso speech—which she made an effort to clarify so that I could understand her. There was a slurring and transposing of English words, and accents fell on different syllables, so that the very tune was different. Sometimes the stranger was left as baffled as though he heard a foreign tongue.

Noreen had come here from Guadeloupe—a bonded servant, as were most of the domestics who worked in St. Thomas, remaining here only while they were in service, with their employers wholly responsible for them.

After breakfast I went looking for Leila with the firm intent of capturing her and at least talking over her studies. I must put Catherine's threats out of my mind and try for a fresh, productive start. I must not think of King at all, except in helping to solve the problem of his daughter. As always, night phantoms seemed much less real by day. I was ready to get started.

I found the girl on the terrace, standing at the stone wall studying the harbor through a pair of binoculars. This morning she wore a cool white blouse and a bright skirt patterned with swimming fish. On the gallery Alex Stair sat in a cane chair watching her, once more fingering the brown cone shell I had seen in his hands yesterday. He did not see me as I came to the door, and I heard his faintly challenging words to Leila.

"What do you see out there that you haven't seen before?"

She answered evasively, without lowering the glasses. "Nothing much, I guess."

Her uncle's bearded face had a gloomy cast this morning. It appeared that the watcher at the play was not amused, I thought wryly.

"You're wasting your time." His tone was dry. "They left an hour ago."

Still Leila did not turn, but there seemed a dejection in the very set of her shoulders that told me something was seriously wrong.

Alex saw me then and nodded with no great cordiality. "Good morning, Miss Abbott. Do you propose to start your classes today?"

Before I could answer, Leila swung away from the wall, paying no attention to me, all her interest upon her uncle.

"I knew Cathy was going out," she told him, clearly on the defensive. "They've gone to hunt for shells. Cathy said yesterday that they might."

"They're overdoing it, don't you think?" Alex asked. "Edith has more than she can handle now. That last stuff they brought in was trash."

He looked sour and disgruntled and I did not like the way he seemed to be baiting Leila. She came purposefully toward him up the steps.

"You've said yourself that no shells are worthless these days, providing they're not chipped or broken. I heard you telling Steve that there's a decorating craze for shells. They're used for jewelry besides, and goodness knows what else."

"Don't get excited," said Alex dryly. "I think you know I'm not interested in getting into a mass market for shells. It's the rare varieties that most interest me."

Leila turned from him impatiently and seemed to notice me for the first time. I said, "Good morning," and she smiled with a certain bravado, as if she still defied not Alex's words but his thoughts.

"Let's get started," she said, taking me by surprise. She set the binoculars down on a table with a thump and went past me into the house.

For a moment I waited, watching Alex. Though he spoke to me, he did not glance up from the shell he fondled in long, sensitive fingers. "You'd better take your pupil while she's willing. It's probable that her mother won't bother you for the rest of the day."

That he was morose over whatever Catherine had done was clear, but I knew I would learn nothing from him in this guarded mood, and I followed Leila inside to the coolness of the study.

Her books and papers waited for us on the long worktable, but the girl avoided them, moving restlessly about the room, poking with no particular interest at a shell here and there, ignoring me as though it had not been by her invitation that I was there.

I drew out a chair and sat down at the table, waiting for her to join me. Evidently my silent waiting began at last to disturb her, for suddenly she came across the room, moving with that unconscious, youthful grace that was natural to her when her mother was not about, and perched herself on a far corner of the table. It was clear that she was keyed up and ready for dispute. I had seen girls look this way before—girls who were spoiling for trouble.

Nevertheless, the subject she broached astonished me.

"You found a broom beside your door yesterday, didn't you, Miss Abbott? Do you know why it was there?"

"I'm afraid I don't," I admitted. "Your grandmother seemed upset when she saw it and she called Noreen to come and take it away. Did it mean something special? Something I ought to know about?"

"It doesn't matter whether you know or not," Leila said. "You won't be able to stop it anyway."

"Stop what? Suppose you tell me what you're talking about."

She flicked a finger at a bright red fish swimming down her skirt. "No one can ever stop obeah. That's what it is, you know. Put a broom upside down by a door and you hurry the departure of an unwanted guest. You'd better look for spilled salt on the doorsill next."

I gaped at her. "But who would do anything so foolish?"

She gave me a slanted look that reminded me of Catherine. "It's not foolish. Obeah's supposed to be against the law in the Virgin Islands, but it hangs over from the old days, and it comes in from other places. There's a lot of it in Guadeloupe, where Noreen comes from. Are you afraid, Jessica Abbott?"

"Not of that sort of thing," I said.

"Maybe you should be. If Cathy's got it in for you, she'll try anything. She came to your room last night, didn't she? She told me she sat in your chair and watched you till you woke up. Did she frighten you badly?"

Clearly the girl had set herself to torment me, baiting me as her uncle had baited her. I moved with caution in the face of this effort to antagonize.

"I suppose she wanted to frighten me," I said calmly. "She told me she wanted me to leave, but I let her know I planned to stay."

Leila leaned toward me from her perch on the table. "Why? Why should you want to stay when she wants you gone? Don't you know it isn't wise to cross her? It might even be—dangerous."

" 'Dangerous' is a very large word. I'm here because your grandmother thinks I may be of use in helping you with your studies. If you don't take advantage of what I can offer, then you'll probably be sent to a stateside school in the fall, whether you like it or not."

"School!" She was scornful. "That's the least of my worries. If it wasn't for you, Cathy might have taken me along this morning when she and Steve went out in his boat. Uncle Alex doesn't know where they've gone—but I know. If Dad guessed, he'd have a fit."

She crossed her legs and clasped her hands about one knee, rocking back and forth on the table's edge, still watching me in bright defiance. My attention had quickened. I'd better find out about this —though I could never manage it directly with the girl in this mood. With King's threat about missteps hanging over my head, I did not dare to lose so much as a skirmish.

Pushing back my chair, I left the table and went to the iron-bound pirate chest Alex had showed me the day before. Without a further glance at Leila, I took the big key boldly from its hook and slipped it into the lock. In a moment she was off the table and across the room to snatch at my hand.

"What are you doing? What's in that chest is mine! You've no right to go snooping!"

Quietly I drew my hand from her grasp and turned the key in the lock, half braced for some rough move on her part. With the example set by Catherine, there was no telling what her daughter might do. But she surprised me by stepping back with an air of puzzlement.

"You really aren't afraid, are you?" she said.

"I suppose I've had to work around some fairly immature antics in my time," I said dryly, and reached into the chest to bring out the stack of drawings. "These interest me. Whatever it is that prompted you to work on them interests me. All your talk of danger and native magic really doesn't, and I hate to waste time on subjects that bore me."

That I should be bored by anything instigated by her mother seemed to give Leila unexpected food for thought.

I carried the pictures to the table, leaving her to follow or not as she pleased. She came after me, caught in spite of herself, and curious to see what I would do next. Besides, if she possessed anything of an artist's pride, she would want to know what I thought of her work. With the stack before me, I sat at the table and started to sort through the drawings.

At once she leaned over and placed a hand on the stack. "Wait, Miss Abbott! Please!"

I smiled at her. "If you really don't want me to look at your work, I won't."

She shook her head in denial. "It's just that this morning I put in a couple of new pictures. I haven't shown them to anyone yet, and I'm not sure I want to."

"Why don't you pull them out then?" I said, relinquishing the stack. "I'll look at the ones you don't mind my seeing."

Swiftly she paged through the drawings and drew out two sheets. Then she stood back from the table to study them, apparently uncertain. I paid no attention but began to look through the sketches and tempera paintings of shells that Alex had shown me. When I came to the one that reminded me of Georgia O'Keeffe's work, I laid it aside.

"This is my favorite," I said. "You've caught the texture of that dun-colored background. And the rosy color of that big shell among the cream-colored ones is effective."

Leila dropped into a chair beside me, leaning across my arm to look at the painting with a rapt air, the two drawings she had withdrawn turned face down in her lap.

"Do you really think so? Do you really like it?"

"Very much," I said matter-of-factly and went on turning the sheets.

Her attention was given wholeheartedly now, and the very fact told me how much this talent meant to Leila Drew. Here was something I could use to move toward friendship with her, perhaps toward her greater confidence in me. Now and then I commented appreciatively on a drawing, but without flattery, and she hung on my words with touching attention.

"This is a talent you must go on developing," I told her, when we had looked at every picture in the stack. "You'll need to be ready for a university with a good art department when the time comes."

Perhaps I had gone too far, for she drew back from me, a question in her eyes. "How do you know? What subject do you teach, Miss Abbott? No one has told me that."

"It's a good question," I agreed. "Art certainly isn't my subject. I teach what they call social studies—ancient history, historical geography, current events—the whole tie-in between history past and history in the making today."

Again she challenged me. "How can any one person know all that? How can you possibly teach such a huge subject?"

I laughed. "How right you are! Most of the time ancient history stays put—though I suppose we're always finding new interpretations for what has happened a long time ago. But when it comes to what's happening right now, my students are often a jump ahead of me, and that's fine. If I can get them to think for themselves and discuss these things intelligently, listen to all sides and not try for pat solutions, or ape the opinions of others, that's my purpose. Often I learn from them."

Leila considered this for several moments. When she spoke she did not look at me. "Cathy thinks my drawing is a silly waste of time."

Without warning I was stricken again, pierced by the old hurt that could spring at me suddenly out of ambush. I was remembering something I'd nearly forgotten because I wanted to forget. I could hear Helen saying, "Why should you sit at a desk writing those silly stories, Jessie? You'll never do anything with them. Come and talk to me." And I had put aside the stories she ridiculed and talked to her. This must not happen to Leila.

"You have a gift," I said, "but that's only the beginning. Now you have to do something with it for yourself, and you never will if you accept the words of anyone who tries to discourage you. Criticism can be useful to you, but not discouragement. You asked me a sensible question a few minutes ago. It's true that I know nothing about art as an artist. But I love to visit art galleries and museums and we have some very good ones in Chicago. Art is part of history —modern as well as ancient—so I have to know a little about it, even though I'm only a spectator."

Something of her tension had lessened and so had the resemblance to Catherine. She made a quick gesture, drawing the two sheets of paper from her lap, placing one of them away from her, face down on the table. The other she turned upward before me.

"You can look if you like," she said almost shyly.

Once more she had turned to caricature. In a sense this was a sister sketch to the one she had done of Alex. The face in this picture was, however, more than an exaggeration of Catherine's features—it mocked a little as well. The hair was black, instead of fair, and Leila had drawn it witch-straight. The eyes were atilt, the cat face even more feline than reality in its small triangle. Catherine's daughter had created a picture of a rather disturbing young witch —not an altogether pretty witch.

"Cathy hasn't seen it yet," Leila said, biting her lower lip critically as she studied her work. "I'm not sure how she'll take it."

I was more than pleased. Here again was evidence that the girl did not always regard her mother with blind adoration, but was capable of an objective look now and then.

"I think I drew it to be mean," she confessed. "I—I don't like some of the things Cathy says and does. And I suppose I hate the way she brushes my drawings aside as if they didn't matter. Though I know that isn't fair of me. Cathy happens to like action things—swimming, boating, dancing. *Doing* things. She doesn't understand how anyone can sit still and make silly marks on paper. She can't help that and I really ought to forgive her, since there are so many other things she does for me."

I loved the child for her generosity and intelligence, but I had seen little evidence that Catherine Drew gave anything selflessly away.

"Like helping you choose your clothes?" I asked, a little sly myself.

Leila did not miss my meaning and she would allow no one else to criticize Catherine.

"If you mean the red dress, I'll probably keep it. Cathy knows much more than I do about clothes, and she thinks it will be fun if we look alike for the party."

I said nothing, and perhaps my very silence implied criticism, for Leila took back the witch picture and hid it in the center of the pile of drawings. Then she reached for the second sketch and turned it face up on the table.

"Look at this," she said. "This is one of the things Cathy is doing for me."

The new sketch was very different from the others I had seen. It was a pencil drawing done with a delicacy and pictorial grace that seemed less modern than her shell drawings, though it suited her subject perfectly. The drawing was of a house built in the gracious architectural style of an older day—an English manor house, built in the form of a bracket, with a spacious, recessed entrance and long, shuttered windows on either side. This was a different view of the same house King had shown me in a photograph.

"Lovely," I said, wondering why she had hesitated to show it to me earlier. "This is Caprice, isn't it?"

"How did you know?" she asked in astonishment.

"Your father showed me a photograph of it yesterday. But I like your drawing better. What a beautiful house it must be."

Leila leaned so close beside me that her soft breath touched my cheek. "Yes—it is beautiful. It will be mine someday. Cathy says she'll see to that. She's going to restore it—make it just the way it was in my grandfather's time."

I thought of what King and Maud had said about preserving this house, and knew that we ventured upon uneasy ground. This time it was I who withdrew a little, though I tried not to let her see.

"Won't that take an enormous amount of money?" I asked. "More than is reasonable to spend for a private home that no one lives in any more?"

"Sometimes Cathy lives there," Leila said. "Sometimes she goes over and stays for days at a time. I wish she would take me with her, but there's no use coaxing with Cathy. She hates me if I beg."

I noted the pronoun Leila used. She had not said that her mother hated *it* if she begged, but that she hated *her*.

"Perhaps what your grandmother and your father want most for the house is to preserve it for the future," I said gently. "These old houses are sometimes safer in public hands. That way generations to come can enjoy them."

"What do Cathy and I care about generations to come?" She snatched the picture away from me impatiently. "You sound exactly like Dad and Gran. I'm sorry I showed you. Cathy has gone to Caprice today, and I wish I'd gone with her. Steve took her to St. Croix in his boat, and if Dad knew he'd be wild."

A certain wariness must have shown in my face, for when I made no comment Leila drew abruptly away.

"I knew it!" she cried. "I never should have trusted you. You're on Dad's side, of course, and you're against Cathy—just as she said you would be. No one understands how cruel he has been to her, or the way he treats her. Oh, the things she has told me about him!"

Her attack had come so suddenly that I was unprepared. Almost anything I might say could be wrong, and as I sought for some answer she rushed on.

"There's no use in your denying anything. Cathy told me you'd defend Dad right down the line—because silly females like you can never resist him!"

The look of her mother was upon her again, frighteningly. It was almost as if, for this instant, she had become her mother. And Catherine was someone with whom I did not know how to deal.

"Perhaps we can talk about this when you're not so upset," I said.

But she would not listen. She wanted only to repudiate and reject, and she stayed for no more, but picked up her drawing of the house and ran toward the door. Alex stood in the opening, barring her way.

"They went to Caprice, didn't they?" he said and I felt again the malevolence that could drive this man.

Leila looked suddenly frightened. "I don't know. I don't know for sure!"

"Your father told her she wasn't to go there again with Steve," Alex said. "Don't you think he'd better be told what she's up to?"

"No—no, please, Uncle Alex! If he finds them there, Dad might —he might—"

"He might hurt someone badly—is that what you mean?" Her uncle's tone was caustic, the note of spite all the more evident.

The girl nodded, her eyes like those of a young animal—driven.

"Which might be a very good thing for—someone." Alex spoke gently, but there was no gentleness in his intent. "As it happens, I'm on my way downtown now. I believe I'll stop in at your father's office."

He turned from the doorway, and Leila let him go. In a gesture painfully desperate in its appeal, she flung out her hands to me.

"Please go with him! I—I'm afraid of what Dad may do when he hears. Uncle Alex wants to punish Catherine for—oh, I don't know for what! He wants to make Dad angry with her. If you're there, perhaps you can say something to stop my father from doing any-thing wild. He mustn't hurt Catherine—or Steve either. But he'd never listen to me."

Her alarm had infected me. King was no more likely to listen to me than to anyone else, but I knew I had to go with Alex, if he would take me. I must try, and not only for Leila's sake. I touched her arm lightly in encouragement and hurried after Alex, catching him as he reached the front door.

"Will you take me down the hill with you? Let me get my bag and I'll be right with you."

Leila was already running up the stairs with the drawing of Caprice in her hands and Alex looked up at her sardonically.

"So she's frightened you, has she?" He shrugged. "I'll wait for you outside."

I hurried upstairs for my handbag and as I stepped through the door of my room I felt a gritty substance on the doorsill. I dropped to one knee to touch it with a fingertip—and found that it was salt. Salt!—the old, old magic that had belonged to the Caribbean from the days when the first captives had been brought here from Africa. I suppressed a tendency to shiver. Catherine wanted to terrify me —so I must not be terrified.

When I went downstairs I found Edith Stair standing in the door-way, watching while her husband got out the car. At my step she turned, her hands plucking at each other, betraying her lack of ease.

"King mustn't go to Caprice," she said at once. "Alex will want him to—but you must stop him if you can."

My surprise must have been evident, for she made an impatient sound. "I've been in the dining room, polishing silver. And you were all speaking loudly enough. I suppose it's silly to ask you to help. I suppose there's nothing you can do."

I wondered why she did not try to dissuade her husband from going to King in the first place, but before I could suggest this, she moved away from me down the room. When I looked back from the doorway she was picking up the telephone. Always her actions seemed futile, ineffectual, and I forgot her as I went outdoors.

Alex was waiting for me in his car and as we started along the hilltop drive I saw no point in mentioning Edith's words.

Following the pavement toward the downhill turnoff, we passed a low house built of redwood, set on a level of hillside below the road. It looked like the one King had shown me in a picture.

Alex gestured as he went by. "That's one of the Drew houses. King built it for himself and so far he hasn't sold it to anyone. You must ask him to let you see it sometime."

There seemed some hidden mockery in his words, but I had no time to give it thought. My mind was already busy with this situation into which I was so suddenly plunging myself. What was I to do if King threatened angry action once he knew Catherine and Steve had gone to Caprice? Leila's fear had been very real, born, undoubtedly, of experience with her father's temper, and Edith had been frightened too. What was I—a stranger, an intruder—doing in this affair? But whether I wanted it or not, King was no stranger to me and I could not be indifferent to what might happen.

In spite of my fearful concerns, my spirits seemed to rise in reverse order to our descent. In brilliant sunlight I could see more of our way than on my first journey up after dark and the scenes on every side held and entranced me. The zigzag road from the drive slanted beneath that great stone catchment dropping downward from Maud's tropical forest, and when I looked up I could see the thick growth of trees above, not so great in its spread as it had seemed yesterday when I was within its dark midst.

With an exhilarating rush of color, red and white and yellow roofs came up to meet us, and before long we were following Charlotte Amalie's steep, narrow streets. Often there were stone enclosures on one hand surrounding fine old homes, while on the other rose flimsy board shacks in which a family could live, at least without weather discomfort in the tropics. Yet the two seemed to mingle in a not unneighborly fashion, with a friendly enough acceptance of one by the other.

"You're quiet this morning," Alex said.

His words gave me an opening. "Why were you so unpleasant to Leila? Why must you stir everything up like this?"

The slight smile he turned upon me had a bitter twist. "What woman ever understands male pride? Do you think a man like Kingdon Drew will stand still forever while the woman who carries his name behaves as Catherine does? Sooner or later she has to be brought to heel, and King is the one to do it."

It seemed that Alex's pride, too, was involved, though Catherine was not his wife.

"Do you think angry explosions ever solve anything?" I asked.

His slanted look was sardonic. "Sometimes they do. It depends on what one is trying to solve."

My distrust of the man was increasing and I said no more.

We had slowed to a crawl, since pedestrians on these hills appeared to regard the roads as theirs, and often strolled across the pavement with careless heed for automobiles. Now and then Alex touched the horn lightly, but there seemed no impatience in him to reach our destination. It was as if he moved slowly and confidently toward a sure and expected outcome.

In the downtown area Alex found a parking place not far from the post office, where Dronningens Gade began. We walked together down the old Danish main street of the town—King Street, if one translated. By now I had learned to pronounce it "Gah-da" like everyone else. Here there were narrow sidewalks on either hand, with just enough width between for the one-way stream of motor traffic down the center.

King's office was in the old Pissarro house—where the artist had been born—and we wove our way toward it without hurry through the throng of tourists. Visitors to St. Thomas could be easily recognized, looking as they did like exotic tropical birds set down among the more sensibly feathered chickens that were the island residents.

The house, its upper half painted white, rose flush with the sidewalk. The lower façade boasted a series of stone arches, with long green shutters secured back against the walls. Downstairs there were shops, while from upstairs came a clatter of office typewriters. Alex led the way through a narrow passage to an inner courtyard that reminded me of some New Orleans scene. Here, though there was stone underfoot, I had a sense of tropical growth, with potted plants everywhere, fringing the courtyard and the curve of stairs that led to the office floor above.

We climbed to an upper hallway and went through swinging doors set at eye level. The pretty girl who worked at a typewriter had glossy black hair and a skin the shade of pale caramel. She greeted Alex and smiled at me, showing us at once through a second pair of swinging doors into an office less spacious than the one at Hampden House. An old-fashioned electric fan vibrated from the ceiling to keep the air moving, while behind King's wooden desk double windows opened on the sunny street. Clearly Madison Avenue with its plush decor and air-conditioning had not yet reached St. Thomas to any great degree, and I had a sense of stepping back into the days of a century that seemed to fit this house.

"Mr. Drew will be back in a moment," the girl said and waved us into straight-backed chairs. I sat down, but Alex went to the window and stood looking down upon the street. My feeling of freedom over escaping the oppression of Hampden House had faded and the alarm with which Leila had filled me was returning. Something very unpleasant was about to happen, and I had no knowledge of how to meet any dangerous crisis.

In a few minutes King came through the swinging doors to greet us dubiously, as though he knew we could not bring good news. I found myself once more studying the details of his face, as if to check my own remembrance of him, and oddly enough, he looked at me in very much the same way.

All too aware of Alex watching us, I began to chatter. "What a fascinating house for your office! I suppose the old rooms have all been partitioned off, but I can still catch something of the flavor—such high old ceilings—"

I was grateful to Alex for stopping this idiotic outburst. "This isn't a social visit," he said. "Catherine left for Caprice with Steve early this morning, King. I thought you'd better know. Miss Abbott wanted to come with me, though I'm not sure why. I'll leave her to her own explaining. If you'll excuse me—"

As abruptly as that he was gone, not caring to stay and watch the effect of the words he had dropped. King stared after him blankly and I saw the dark flush rise in his face, saw the tightening of his jaw. Then, without another look for me, he strode to the window and stood there, his back to the room, though I think he saw nothing of the street below. His hands were clenched behind his back in a gesture of violence barely restrained.

I glanced about the small room as if for help, searching for something of quiet to offer him—something to guard against the coming explosion. Strangely, I found it. On the wall across from where I sat hung another mountain picture, but of a very different subject from that range of majestic peaks in the scene at Hampden House. This was the photograph of a high mountain meadow, sloping gently downward from below timberline, with only the tops of two or three peaks as a backdrop. Diagonally across the picture tumbled a mountain stream, rushing over wet black rocks. The meadow itself was a mass of blooming wild flowers scattered thickly through the grass, and where grass and flowers had been pressed down in the foreground the shadow of an indentation lay across them—where a man might have lain dreaming in that peaceful place.

"What a lovely spot," I said softly.

He looked around at me, startled. "What? Oh, that! We had a cabin near there when I was a boy. But it's a spot I can never go back to. I know. I tried to go back when I took that picture on a visit a few summers ago. It seems to have changed, the way I've changed."

I studied the scene of that high mountain meadow where a small boy must once have roamed and played. It was as though the picture had something to tell me, to offer me.

King looked at his watch. "There's just time to make the plane," he said. "I'd better leave for St. Croix at once."

I turned from the picture. "Take me with you."

For a moment he stared at me as though he had never seen me before, as though he could not remember my identity. All the rage that had risen so visibly in him was directed toward that distant place on the island of St. Croix, where his wife had gone against his wishes. There was nothing left of him here.

I went to him and put my hand on his arm, gripped it almost impatiently, calling him back to the present while there was still time for the present to change the future.

"Leila asked me to come," I told him. "Please take me with you."

Slowly, almost painfully, he returned from his place of anger, from his projection into a violent future that was rushing upon him. There was a strange, quiet moment in which we looked at each other and a bond between us seemed to strengthen. For the first time in my life I stood my ground. I did not step back from what I saw in his eyes. I took the risk that involved me in living instead of in running. All reason warned me against such a stand, but I let my heart rule.

The thing that leaped between us was no more than a flash, a kindling, that died almost at once, but I think we both knew it had happened.

"You should never have come to Hampden House," King said.

"You were made for a different sort of life. You don't know the first thing about dealing with evil. I hope you never need to learn."

Abruptly he left me and went to speak to the girl in the next office, waiting by her desk while she made a phone call. When he returned he moved quickly.

"There's a seaplane leaving in ten minutes. It will get me to St. Croix in half an hour, and I can take a taxi to Caprice. I've reserved seats for two. You can come if you want."

At least he had not made me stay behind. Before I followed him out of the office I cast a backward look at the photograph on the wall. There was the key to something in that picture—in the reason that lay behind his hanging it there where his glance would fall upon it every day.

We went downstairs and crossed to a side street that led to the waterfront. We walked together through one of those pirate alleys that led us to the broad waterfront street which followed the curve of the harbor.

Along its cement walk men from a fishing boat had spread out their catch and as we came along one of them put a huge conch shell to his lips, to blow a blast that could be heard all over town, notifying householders that fresh fish had been brought ashore for their purchase.

We threaded our way among boxes of fruit and vegetables and huge stalks of bananas that had been unloaded from a craft with furled sail moored alongside, and reached the place where a motorboat waited to take us to the seaplane. Along with two or three other passengers for St. Croix, the boat ran us out to where the small plane floated on calm waters, and King helped me up the ladder and seated me beside a window inside. As he took the opposite seat across the aisle from me he could hardly have looked more grim and I knew that all the anger which had driven him for so long would not be held back much longer.

In a few moments the seaplane was skating across the harbor on tilted pontoons, running toward the tip of Hassel Island on our way to the open sea. In moments it lifted from the water and I could look down at the orange-red bricks of old Fort Christian, and at Bluebeard's Castle, and the aerial tramway up Flag Hill. Then St. Thomas was falling away behind as we flew out over the Caribbean toward the southernmost island of the Virgins.

We made no attempt to talk across the aisle above the noise of the engines. Below us the sea rippled with tiny whitecaps, and here and there the long wake of a boat carved a widening wedge on its surface. I thought of Catherine and Steve going out across that sea early this morning, on a trip that would take much longer than this one. Nevertheless, they would be there well ahead of us.

I did not want to think of that. I did not want to face what might happen when King found Catherine at Caprice. I could live only a single moment at a time and my one solacing thought was of that calm mountain meadow and the foreground shadow a man's body had made, pressing into the grass. That picture told me a great deal. It showed me a man who longed for peace.

IX

As our cab left Christiansted and we drove out through open country I became quickly aware that St. Croix was a very different island from St. Thomas. While there were mountainous areas, much of this larger island was made up of great flat expanses which had led to an agricultural economy. There were still occasional fields of sugar cane and pineapple, though the great plantations were long gone.

We followed good roads on which there was little traffic, and King seemed to relax a little, as if he too postponed the moment of confrontation that lay ahead, and ceased trying to live it ahead of time. He spoke to me quietly of the island and its history—a dark and restless history that made St. Thomas' seaport days seem tame by comparison. Pirates might have visited St. Thomas and dipped into its tills on occasion, but the Negroes there had been made freedmen early and they had become the businessmen, tradesmen, professional men that their descendants were today.

In St. Croix the story was a different one. Great plantations had required slaves and freedom had come later than in St. Thomas. Thus there had been uprisings of the same sort that had swept bloodily across many a Caribbean island, and there were old resentments that still smoldered. The St. Thomian was a happy, democratic fellow. In St. Thomas everyone was color-blind. There might be prejudices, but they were more apt to be of a geographic nature, with the native islander looking down his nose at the continental, of whatever race. In St. Croix a white skin might still be met with faint distrust.

It seemed as I listened to him talk that King was deliberately avoiding what lay ahead at Caprice, and I dared ask no questions. His mood seemed quieter, but since he often masked emotion, I couldn't be sure how long such calm would last.

The taxi turned off the highway down a side road and King spoke to the driver. "Stop at the gate, please."

When we were out of the car and he had paid the fare, King led the way toward two high stone portals with double iron gates sagging half closed between them.

"The first caprice," he said and gestured toward a stone post.

On top of the right-hand post the dancing figure of a unicorn had been carved in stone, forefeet pawing the air, horn jauntily atilt. There had been little wearing away of the stone and the figure was nearly intact, observing the visitor with an eerie mockery that seemed to evoke the past and scorn the present. On the opposite post, however, the partner unicorn had fared much worse. Its head was gone, and one pawing forefoot had been broken off, so that only its body and the hind legs on which it danced were clearly defined.

"That fellow was smashed during a slave uprising long ago," King said as he pushed the rusting gates further ajar to let us through. "They tried to burn the house, but it was saved by workers loyal to the Hampdens. Until young Roger died in Korea, the house has always come to a male descendant."

Rain fell more often in St. Croix than in drought-ridden St. Thomas, and it must have rained some hours before, for the earth of the sandy driveway was damp in places and reddish in color wherever water stood. We followed as it curved between what must once have been a double row of fine mahogany trees, many of which had been cut down, so that only a few giants were left to lend dignity and beauty to the approach to the house. King moved without hurry, as though we had all the time in the world, with no disastrous meeting threatening when we reached the house.

We could see the ruins of the mill off to our right, roofless, but with its great stone chimney intact. Its arches and peaked walls, its hollow windows overlooked a considerable area, and within the shelter made by its wings grew a garden of tropical plants and trees. Beyond, unprotected, offering a naked windbreak against the gales that blew out of the Caribbean, ran a hedge of such giant philodendron as I had never seen, thrusting upward in a rugged tangle, for all that some of its leaves were blackened and curled where the salt blasts funneled in from the sea to shrivel them.

As we rounded a sudden turn King put a hand upon my arm to halt me. My breath caught in alarm, but no green-eyed woman stood at the end of the drive—it was Caprice itself he wanted me to see.

Not any photograph, not even Leila's sensitive drawing, could have done justice to this lovely old house. It had been built of stone and ballast brick brought over in the holds of sailing ships during another century. Its walls had been painted over and over in the past until they now boasted an ingrained rosy color that would be impossible to imitate. The style was Georgian, with a recessed, white-columned doorway and ornamental white fan above. Brick steps made a half circle at the entrance and the even rows of windows on either side were closed by long white shutters—except for a single upstairs room in one of the wings of a bracket, where a window stood open. As my eyes noted the fact, King saw it too and stiffened at my side. Was someone watching us from up there? Had I caught a flicker of movement?

His hand tightened upon my arm. "Come—we'll go in. If we meet anyone, you're here because I offered to show you the house."

I had sensed before this how very close to the surface his rage against Catherine simmered, and suddenly I was afraid of the house.

"Wait," I said. "Before we go in, there's something I've wanted to say. You told me something back at your office that I couldn't accept."

"Yes?" he said, impatient now, wanting to get on with what he had come here for.

"That photograph of a mountain meadow and a stream, with the peaks behind—you said you couldn't go back there. I have a place like that too."

He was looking at me in surprise and I made myself go on.

"Mine is a place beside Lake Michigan where I used to play as a little girl. Not as beautiful a place as yours, but a quiet place that still helps me sometimes. I can close my eyes and cut myself off from everything else. I can go there and sit in a spot I know where trees run down to the lake and water laps over a pebbly beach. It doesn't exist any more. Not really. There's a motel there now. But no one will ever take it away from me. When things are very bad I can go there and think. Afterward, it seems as though I can handle everything a little better."

My words came haltingly, awkwardly. They were difficult to speak because I was afraid he might think me silly and naïve, perhaps a little maudlin, afraid he might laugh at me. There was no easy way to tell such things to another person. I stared at Caprice and did not meet his eyes.

He was silent for what seemed a very long while. Then he said, "Thank you for telling me that."

I could look at him then, and he was not laughing. There was only kindness in his eyes—a wondering, tender sort of kindness that seemed rather grave and did not mock me at all.

He held out his hand and I put my own into it easily, feeling the way his fingers closed over mine in a light clasp. Together we crossed the broad carriageway and approached the fan of brick steps.

"A second caprice," he said and gestured to the right of the door.

A plaque of white stone had been set against the brick and there, carved in bas relief, appeared the same dancing unicorn that graced the outer portal.

"The Hampdens were addicted to unicorns," King said, and added wryly, "Catherine likes them too."

Of course she would, I thought—since the unicorn was a magical beast and Catherine fancied herself as something of a witch.

At the top of the steps the door stood ajar, and King went ahead, as if to meet first whatever awaited us inside. But the great house was silent and the gloom seemed deep after brilliant sunlight, the air gratefully cool. I stood blinking for a moment in a small antehall before King led the way over a raised doorsill into an enormous central room that ignored the square outlines of the house and formed itself about us in the shape of a lozenge. I was beginning to understand why the house had been given its name, for it must have taken a good deal of architectural caprice to achieve this room.

Toward the rear the shutters on a single tall window had been opened and enough light penetrated the gloom to let me view the enormously high ceiling with its intricate plaster decorations, and the beautiful crystal chandelier which hung from its center. King stepped to the wall and touched a button so that the chandelier came brilliantly to life with an electric fire that struck rainbow colors from every tiered branch and glass teardrop.

"We've kept our electricity," King said. "And the place has a telephone, so it's not isolated. There's a caretaker, but he doesn't seem to be about at the moment."

No one seemed to be about and I began to breathe more easily.

"How beautiful it is." I spoke in a hushed voice.

King nodded. "It is beautiful—almost perfect of its kind. What I wouldn't give to have a hand in the building of a house like this. But it belongs to the past."

He moved around the room as he spoke, circling the bare floor, studying sheet-shrouded furniture as if he searched for some special sign. Of Catherine's presence? I wondered.

"This morning," I told him, "Leila assured me that Caprice would belong to her someday—that her mother had promised her that."

"More mischief-making!" King said. "Promising the child what can't be fulfilled."

"Leila said her mother was going to restore the house just as it used to be."

"Absurd!" He flicked a sheet back from a lovely rosewood sofa, its gold damask upholstery faded and shabby, then turned it back again. "The house has become a white elephant. There's no money for its upkeep."

"I told Leila that the best way to preserve the house for the future might be in the way you suggest. But she was angry with me. I'm afraid this is the second time I've made her angry."

"And when was the first?" he asked, still moving about the room, noting its details.

"The first was yesterday when I asked if she had ever really considered your viewpoint or your feeling toward her."

He was bending over a cabriole desk, but his head came up at my words. "You said that to her?"

I nodded. "Yes. I wanted her to grow up a little and begin to think of someone besides herself and her mother."

His eyes were shadowed in the dim room. "Thank you," he said. "I didn't know you were on my side."

"I think I've always been on your side, really," I told him. "It's just that we want the same thing in different ways."

He turned from me almost abruptly and moved toward the stairs. Though our footsteps echoed on bare floors, the house was still quiet about us, and no one came to offer us either welcome or objection to our presence.

"There's a room upstairs from which I can see the beach," King said, moving ahead to lead the way.

The stairway with its polished mahogany rail curved gracefully upward in an oval curve to complement the room below, satisfying the eye in a way that modern angles never seemed to do. Upstairs the house was more conventional in shape, with a long central hall that turned at either end into the two ells of the bracket in which the house was built.

Our footsteps roused echoes along the bare hall as we moved away from illumination cast upward by the stairwell and toward the gloom of the far ell. There King went to a room on the seaview side and opened a door upon darkness. Here there were no shrouded shapes to bar our way, and King went quickly to a window and flung the shutters wide, admitting a cool breeze from the sea, as well as a bright shaft of sunlight that set dust motes dancing visibly.

Caprice had been built on somewhat higher ground than the rest of the area, and as I stood at the window beside King I could see out over the barrier of the philodendron hedge, and beyond it to a sandy ridge where sea grapes grew. A portion of this weedy growth had been cut away and through the gap we had a clear view of a stretch of sand rimming the green waters of a cove.

"The beach belongs to Caprice," King said. "There's good swimming here, though only a little way on the coast turns rocky and there's no place for a boat to put in."

"Do you suppose Steve's boat is down there now?" I asked uneasily.

"If they came here, it's got to be," he said. "But the sea grapes hide most of the beach, so we can't tell."

As we studied the brief stretch of white sand a man wearing swim trunks ran suddenly into view, his wet, tanned body glistening in the sun. Though he was too far distant to be recognized, I guessed that it must be Steve O'Neill and I felt King tense beside me. The figure paused and raised an arm, as if beckoning to someone out of sight—Catherine, undoubtedly. I did not want to see her run into view. I could not bear to watch. King, too, turned from the window.

"I'm going down there," he said roughly.

I touched his arm. "Please—oh, please be careful!"

"Careful! The time for being careful is past."

All his anger was coming to the surface. All that he had held in check for so long was ready for violent release. I understood Leila's fear, for now it was my own.

"Not while you're in a rage!" I begged him. "You can lose everything—everything! No matter what she has done—"

He flung off my hand. "I suppose I'm to go sit in your quiet place and meditate while Catherine pulls everything down around our ears?"

I stood my ground. "You could do worse. If you harm her, if you harm that boy—it's Leila you'll damage. Can't you wait until you get yourself in hand?"

"This isn't your affair," he said. "Don't try to come with me. Amuse yourself—explore the house. The caretaker's name is Henry. If he shows up, tell him I'll be back shortly."

I went with him out of the room and down the hall. At the top of the stairs he paused, softening toward me a little.

"Don't worry so much. There's a good walk ahead of me to the beach. Maybe it will calm me down. I'd like to wring her neck, but maybe I won't. Not yet."

His feet struck an echo from uncarpeted stairs as he disappeared from sight and I heard the creak of the front door. I had no desire to return to the room from which we had viewed the beach. Whatever might happen now, I did not want to witness it, even from a distance.

I wandered along the hallways of the second story, opening one door and then another, seeking to occupy and distract myself. This was no time for frantic worrying. In one room I found a candle and matches, and with the aid of this illumination I could better find my way through shuttered dimness. In rooms where the furniture stood shrouded, I now and then lifted a sheet to glimpse a lovely chaise longue of faded pink satin, a lady's powder table of inlaid wood, a Queen Anne wing chair.

As I moved in flickering shadow from room to room the ghosts began to move with me in a house no longer quiet. As long as King was there the place had seemed utterly still. What sounds there were, we had made. But now it whispered as old houses do, creaking and sighing. Footsteps crept about in empty rooms, to fall silent when I opened a door.

What had those long-ago Hampdens who had lived here been like? Had there been an ancestress of Catherine Drew from whom she had inherited her strange, warped nature? This notion of presences everywhere began to oppress me and the house seemed too full of sound to be truly empty. Once I went into the hall and called Henry's name—but the ringing echoes that crashed through the upper house were more disturbing than the whispers and since there was no answer, I did not call him again.

Only a few rooms in the opposite ell from the sea remained and I opened one of these doors idly, meaning to end my exploring and return downstairs. But I met with surprise. This was a large room, occupying the entire front of the ell, and it was a room presently lived in. My candle flame leaped in the wind and I blew it out. Here shutters were open and I saw that this was the room I had noted from the steps. Though fresh breezes had cleared away all mustiness and banished stale air, there was a slightly odd smell in the room that I could not at once place.

More curious than I wanted to admit, I went a little way in, leaving the door ajar behind me. There was no shrouded furniture here —everything was in use. Standing out from one wall, dominating the room, stood a great fourposter bed with a high mattress and a mosquito-net canopy. The bed was made up, its pillows plumped and ready for use, while across it clothing had been carelessly strewn —items of lingerie, a blouse, and the green capri pants I had seen Catherine wear. A brown leather belt with a brass buckle coiled toward the floor, and leather sandals had been dropped where the edge of the counterpane nearly touched the floor.

So this was where Catherine lived when she stayed here overnight. Curiosity held me, and my glance went on about the room—to dressing table, desk, comfortable chairs, all of which had been refurbished. Here was none of the shabbiness of old wear. Even the wallpaper was clean, bright, fresh—and completely arresting. Three sides of the room were done in pale gray, while one end wall had been dramatized with figured paper—paper that had very likely been designed for this room. The background was pale rose, and against it an assortment of the stone-white unicorns of Caprice danced among tiny golden shells. This indeed was a room for Columbella!

From open windows a breeze stirred the mosquito netting looped above the bed and creaked the open doors of a wardrobe cabinet. I started at the sound and looked toward the huge old-fashioned armoire of heavily carved mahogany, to see its massive double doors move gently as air touched them. A few garments hung within—and there was something else.

All that concerned Catherine now concerned me, and I went without hesitation to the wardrobe and pulled the doors wide by their brass claw handles.

Thrust beneath the clothes that hung there were three boxes. One seemed to be a tool kit of some sort—containing pliers, small monkey wrenches, a hammer. The other two were cardboard cartons, the first of which was filled with damp sand that looked as though it might have been collected from a beach that morning. The second was a carton of seashells, and as I bent toward it I realized that it was from this that the slight odor I'd noticed emanated—that fishy odor which sometimes clings to seashells.

Why anyone should place a box of fishy-smelling shells in a wardrobe closet, I couldn't guess. I knew little about shells, but these looked like the common beach variety and not the rare shells Alex collected. If hurriedly gathered, I suppose they could be used as a cover for possible lovers' meetings at Caprice.

By now I had grown so accustomed to the rustling of Hampden ghosts that a faint creaking of boards in the hall did not startle me. I turned my head casually—to find that Catherine Drew stood in the doorway watching me. I had thought her far away and the sudden sight of her was disturbing.

She was barefooted and wearing the briefest of green bikinis. Her blond hair had been piled on top of her head and a swim cap dangled from one hand. I saw at once the green and spiteful fire in her eyes, and I could have wished myself caught anywhere else than here in her room.

"What are you doing?" she demanded and her look swept past me to the open wardrobe doors, her indignation mounting. "How dare he bring you to my house! How dare you come into my room and touch my things!"

She darted past me to slam the wardrobe doors shut with such force that they promptly bounced open again. I could only watch her in growing alarm. It was true that I had no business in this room, even though I had come upon it innocently, and I could say nothing in the face of her flashing anger.

When she turned, her eyes looked a little wild and my alarm changed to very real fear. The woman was in no rational state and I thought again of a panther, untamed and savage, ready to spring. Warily I began to edge toward the door.

"Edith telephoned me," she said, "so I knew King would come. I was watching at that very window when you came strolling up the drive like a pair of lovers. I suppose that's why he brought you here —to a fine hideaway! Except that this house is mine—and I won't have you in it!"

"If you'll listen for a moment—" I said, and took another step toward the door.

"Listen? I have listened! I hung over the stair rail and listened while you two were downstairs in the drawing room. While you were talking about Leila—and about me! This is my father's house —not King's. The only thing of my father's that I have left."

My fear of her did not lessen as her words poured out uncontrolled, turbulent, and all the while her glance darted about the room, seeking, searching—I couldn't tell for what. Once more I edged toward the door. King would be well out of hearing on his way to the beach by now and I knew it might be dangerous to stay alone with this frantic, half-demented woman.

Before I could reach the doorway and make my escape, however, she found what she sought—something on the bed—and sprang toward it, caught it up, turning to face me with the leather belt in her hands. She looked triumphant now, as though the belt she slapped back and forth across her palm gave her confidence and a power over me as she moved to block my way to the door.

I stood facing her, listening to the repeated slap of the belt, catching the gleam of that sharp brass buckle, knowing that she might strike out at me with it at any moment.

"I warned you last night!" she shrilled. "I told you something unpleasant would happen if you didn't leave. Now you're going to find out what I mean!"

If I ran for the door, she would be upon me and at my back. It was better to face her, to wait for a chance to grasp the belt as she flailed out at me. I braced myself for the opportunity, though I had never been so frightened.

At that instant we both heard a sound on the stairs—there was nothing ghostly about the thud of running feet. Catherine whirled away from me, the belt in her hands and sudden terror in her eyes. But it was Steve O'Neill who appeared in the door—to take in the scene with quick understanding. He saw the brass-buckled weapon in Catherine's hands and at once he crossed the room to twist it from her grasp and fling it to the floor.

"Have you gone completely nuts?" he demanded. "Do you know that King is here? He's down on the beach talking to Mike by this time. Let's get going before he comes back."

Once she saw that it was Steve, Catherine had relaxed visibly. "Why should I—" she began, but Steve went to the bed and scooped up her clothes, then bent to retrieve her sandals from the floor.

"Come along." He spoke more quietly now. "If he finds you here with me there'll be the dickens to pay. You're not ready for that kind of blow-up yet—are you? And even if you are, I'm not."

His words seemed to dash cold water over the heat of her rage, though she did not give up at once. "What good will it do to run? He'll know we've been here."

Steve ignored that. He looked about the room and saw the open doors of the wardrobe. "Shall we take the sand and the shells with us—for Alex?"

Catherine seemed to pull herself together as she gave Steve a look. "There's no use in that. Edith is still working on the last batch. They'll be all right here. No one ever touches this room except me. Go along. I'll come with you in a minute."

Steve threw me a doubtful glance and went into the hall.

"There will be another time," Catherine said to me, and I knew she made me a promise. "You'd better leave Hampden House while you have the chance, Miss Jessica Abbott. Right now you can get out of my room. And stay out!"

I hated to pass her so closely in the doorway, but she did not touch me, though I was near enough to feel the warmth of her bare flesh. When I was out of the room she slammed the door and ran barefooted after Steve. I heard the light sound as she ran down the stairs —and was gone.

There seemed nothing more important to me at the moment than to sit down and still the trembling that had come over me. I turned my back on that room with its odor of shells and its ghostly unicorns. The stale, shut-in air of the hallway seemed a relief after that fishy scent. A bit shakily I went to the top step of the stairs and sat down. To quiet my own shivering reaction, I crossed my arms across my body and clasped myself tightly, laid my head upon my knees.

Catherine Drew had set herself to be rid of me, and surely she was on the verge of dangerous madness. My forehead was damp with perspiration as I thought of the dreadful scene which Steve had so luckily interrupted.

I was sitting there on the upper sweep of the stairs, with the glow of illumination flooding upon me from the room below, when King came into the house. As he climbed toward me I raised my head and looked at him.

"She was here?" he said at once, and I nodded mutely. "Did she hurt you—did she try—"

"Steve came in time," I said. "He—he stopped her."

King ran up the remaining steps and stood above me. "There was no one but Mike at the beach. Apparently Mike came along with them today, being half owner of the boat—even though the other two didn't want him. It was Mike who was out of sight when we saw Steve beckoning—not Catherine. As soon as I knew she must be at the house, I hurried back. What happened?"

"She's gone now," I said. "With Steve. Can you just—just let them go?"

He bent toward me. "I know by the way you look that she frightened you. I want to know what she did."

He was in no mood for evasion, though I was afraid to tell him with that intensity of anger burning once more in his eyes.

"She had a leather belt," I said. "But I wouldn't have just stood there. I'd have fought her if I had to. Besides, I don't really know if she was bluffing—or if she meant to use it."

"She'd have tried," he said bitterly, and pulled me almost roughly to my feet.

From the moment on the veranda at Aunt Janet's, when I had first seen him coming toward me, I had known instinctively that we must come to this. Two lonely people with wrecked years behind them, thrown together and drawn as well by that heady attraction that could be the prelude to love. No wonder I had been afraid. But now I had stopped fighting myself, and if there was something here that justified alarm, I thrust it away and leaned against the broad comfort of his chest, knowing this was where I belonged, putting off any moment of sensible reckoning. His cheek was against my hair and I could hear without astonishment the words he was whispering. Soft endearments they were—words like "dearest" and "beloved," while he held and kissed me with rough tenderness.

All around us the Hampden ghosts whispered uneasily, and downstairs the telephone began to ring.

King made an impatient sound as he released me and went to answer the summons. I leaned against the bannister, dreamily bemused, hearing in the distance his conversation with Maud. He was telling her that I was here. Yes, Catherine had been here too, but she was in the company of both Steve *and* Mike. No need to worry. He would bring me home on the afternoon plane.

When he hung up he came only as far as the turn of the stairs and stood looking up at me. For my sake I believe he tried to let me go.

"What an impossible mess to bring you into!" he said wearily. "Now—somehow—I've got to get you out of it."

"I brought myself into it," I told him. "I'm going to stay."

The sound he made was like a groan and it caught at my heart. I knew what lay behind it—that it added up to one name. The name of his wife, Catherine.

"I've got to do something," he said, "Leila or no. I've got to find a way out for myself."

Whatever courage I possessed came sweeping back on a stronger tide than ever before and I agreed with him boldly.

"Yes! You *must* find a way out. When you sacrifice your own life for Leila, you hurt her as well as yourself."

I knew I was right about this. The first rule was to find a way to make life bearable, no matter what the pressures and circumstances. Otherwise we were no good to ourselves or to anyone else. By staying at Hampden House, King was doing himself and his daughter great injury. He had to find himself before he could help anyone else. I ran down to where he stood at the curve of the stairs.

"Go away from St. Thomas," I begged him. "Go home to Denver yourself."

He answered me wearily. "Do you think I haven't tried that before? I had all the evidence in my hands to do what needed to be done, though scandal would never matter to Catherine, or stop her. It mattered to Maud—because of Leila. When I'd been away for a couple of months Maud came after me herself because she saw what Catherine was doing to my daughter, and because of what might be spread across the newspapers and made public knowledge. All this would have damaged Leila mercilessly, since the bond that holds her to her mother is so strong. I knew I couldn't go through with it—not yet."

I would not give up. "It's different now. You needn't cause a scandal. Just go away and stay away. Save yourself. Later perhaps Leila can come to you. For the present Maud and I can work together to keep her out of Catherine's hands. I don't know how—but there's always a way. There has to be!"

I knew I was giving him up for good, giving up even the small comfort the sight and nearness of him could bring me. But I had to be strong enough to fight Catherine Drew—if such an action could save King.

He reached out a forefinger and traced the cleft of my chin, touched my hair lightly. "Do you know what you're coming to mean to me, Jessica? You told me something today about that photograph in my office. I wasn't laughing at your quiet place. Once that mountain meadow was a place like that for me—but it hasn't worked for a long time. Perhaps now I've found a new source of sanity—and honesty and decency. Things I thought I'd lost touch with for good during the last few years. A source that isn't a place, but a person— you."

Tears welled into my eyes, a lump tightened my throat. With all the longing in me I wanted to be in his arms—not to find quiet, because that was no longer what I sought. But I dared not because he *must* go away—and if I held him to me, sheltering myself in his arms, I knew he would not go.

I stepped back from him and started up the stairs. "There's something I want to show you up here."

He came after me along the upper hall, but when I reached Catherine's door and put my hand on the knob he hesitated.

"I never go into that room," he said. "She has a right to her privacy."

"No one told me not to, so I went in," I admitted. "There's something odd here that you'd better see."

The smell seemed even stronger as I opened the door, and the small white unicorns seemed to arrest their dance in the midst of tumbling golden shells. King sniffed questioningly.

"Shells," I said, and went to the wardrobe to open the doors wider. "They're for Alex, I suppose, but why would she put them here in her bedroom?"

He dipped a hand into the carton, to bring up a fistful of shells and pick them over. "These look like the beach variety to me—dead shells —not the sort Alex prefers."

"There's a carton of sand too," I said, and pulled it out for him to see.

King nodded. "That's the way Steve and Mike pack their best finds so the more fragile shells won't be damaged in bringing them home. But why they'd store sand or shells here I wouldn't know. Anyway, Catherine will be out of reach by now. Let's make use of the few hours we have left before we catch the plane for St. Thomas. We can take a cab back to Christiansted and have lunch. Then I'll show you something of the island. I'd like to keep you with me for a little while."

I wanted nothing better and when he held out his hand I gave him mine without hesitation. Downstairs he phoned the nearest town for a cab, and just as he hung up Mike O'Neill came through the front door. The younger boy looked stocky and brown in his swim trunks, his dark hair water-slick, his eyes solemn and worried.

"Where'd they go?" he demanded at once. "They haven't come back to the boat."

"They're around somewhere," King said. "And not far, I should think. Maybe Henry will know."

Mike scowled. "Cathy sent Henry away for the day as soon as we got here. But I know a couple of places to look"—and he went off doggedly on his search.

"I don't want to go with him," King said. "I haven't the heart for any more right now."

Together we walked down the driveway toward the road and stood waiting for our cab. Beside us the undamaged stone unicorn did his endless dance, and I found myself turning to look back along the drive in the direction of Caprice, with its empty rooms, its shrouded furniture—and that one bright room where tiny golden shells tumbled beneath the hoofs of a hundred unicorns.

X

I would never forget the few hours we spent together in St. Croix. They were hours of discovery—of each other, and, for me, a discovery of myself. We did not speak of Hampden House or Catherine, or even of the problem of Leila. We were, I think, wholly lost in a pretense that some future together would be possible for us, though we did not speak of this. For a little while we pushed aside all that separated us and behaved as we might have done under freer, happier circumstances.

As we talked, all that had been tenuous and uncertain began to take stronger, more painful root. We told each other of youthful experiences, and while I began to see Colorado and the Rocky Mountains as King had known them as a boy, he began to glimpse through my eyes the vast expanse of Lake Michigan, the granite towers of Chicago.

But these few hours of pretense had to end. We boarded the seaplane for the flight home, and in St. Thomas, driving back to Hampden House, we hardly spoke. I knew King was as heavy of heart as I. Not until we were almost up the mountain did he put a last warning into words.

"From now on you must be more careful than ever of Catherine. She'll be more cunning the next time she tries to trap you in a vulnerable position. I'd rather have you out of this altogether, but you've given me your answer on that—and I need you here for Leila, whatever I do myself."

I promised to be careful, and that very evening he put a bolt upon the door of my room, and chains on the French windows, so that I might have air and safety at the same time. All that we did appeared a little unreal, and the interlude of the trip to Caprice began to seem like a dream to me, though there was one reality. I remembered King's arms about me, and the longing that had built to an intensity between us at his last kiss. I remembered, too, the sight of a woman slapping a leather belt across her palm, back and forth, again and again. There were moments when this picture had the greatest reality of all.

The days before the buffet supper passed quietly enough, although I knew that Catherine watched me, staring openly at every opportunity, a secret, disturbing smile on her lips. Whatever she might be planning, her silent scrutiny made me increasingly uneasy, though I managed to avoid any clash that could aggravate her.

Fortunately, she was away a good deal of the time. She seldom announced in advance where she was going, but I knew from Leila that she went again to Caprice in Steve's boat. And on the day before the party she flew to San Juan and stayed away overnight. This was not unusual for St. Thomians. Shopping trips to San Juan were almost like going downtown, since that cosmopolitan spot was only a half hour away by plane and there were frequent flights during the day.

On the morning of the buffet supper Leila made a sudden request of me. During the days since she had flounced out of Alex's study with her sketch of Caprice, she had surprised me by coming meekly to discuss her schoolwork with me every morning, and had even started work on some brush-up assignments I had given her. She was guarded and wary, perhaps—not really friendly—but she came, and she did not ask Catherine to aid in her release. Maud, I suspected, had talked to her, but whatever the cause I took advantage of it in every way I could. By now I knew something of where she stood in the private school she attended on the island, and we had begun study in her weakest subjects. She was quick and intelligent—and bored. Deliberately bored, it seemed to me, so that it was almost impossible to gain her interest when we stayed on the subject of schoolwork. There was an inner resistance to me that must have its source in Catherine's influence, and I was unable to break through it, no matter how hard I tried.

On the morning of the party she did not appear at her usual time for our lesson period, and Alex dropped by to tell me that she had gone to the airport in a cab to meet her mother and that I would probably see her later.

I sat in the empty study, waiting for Leila to return, and fell at once into the dreaming state that now came to me so easily. I was like a girl enraptured by first love. Indeed, I suppose that is what I really was. The long-ago feeling I'd had for Paul seemed pale by comparison to my feeling for King. If Helen had been here now, and if she had made so much as a coy gesture in King's direction, I knew I would have proved myself a very different woman from the girl who had watched her flirt with Paul.

I *was* a different woman. And I was faced by far more insurmountable obstacles.

Leila came into the study to find me musing. She looked solemn and worried and did not sit beside me at the table, but roamed the room restlessly, playing with Alex's shells as she often did when something had upset her.

"Did your mother have a good trip?" I asked, trying for an opening.

Only then did she cross the room and drop into a chair beside me. "No—she had a horrid time. Somebody broke into her hotel room last night and stole those darling diamond earrings Grandfather bought her when she was a young girl."

I remembered seeing the lovely stones shining in Catherine's pierced earlobes.

"Of course she reported it to the police," Leila went on, "but I don't suppose she'll ever get them back. There was a lot of red tape, since the thieves got into other rooms too, and she almost missed her plane this morning. I'm glad there's a party tonight to cheer her up. Cathy loves parties."

"You haven't seemed very excited about the party yourself," I commented. "You've been acting as though the whole idea depressed you."

She reached for a piece of notebook paper and picked up a pencil. Absently she began to draw small neat figures across the paper. I looked over her arm to see that she had drawn a shell and a small horned animal. Over and over, with quick expressive lines, the same two figures—a columbella and a dancing unicorn.

"Cathy has invited Steve to the party," she said suddenly, her pencil still.

I understood the connection her mind had made. I took the pencil from her fingers and touched its point, first to the shell, then to the prancing unicorn.

"Catherine—she's the columbella, isn't she? And Steve is the unicorn she dances with? Yes, he might play that role, though I can better imagine him with the pipes of Pan."

She flashed me a look and promptly tore up the paper. I did not mind. Now I was getting close to what troubled her.

"And Mike?" I asked. "Is he coming too?"

"Oh, of course Mike," she said with indifference. "He's supposed to come so there'll be a young person for me. As if I cared!"

"I suppose you and your mother will be wearing your two red dresses tonight?"

She came to life and flung the scraps of paper away from her. "On the way back from the airport Cathy told me about seeing you at Caprice that time last week. She told me she gave you a fright—with that brown leather belt of hers."

"She was upset about finding me in her room," I said. "She was excited and I had no right to be there."

"She might have hurt you. I wouldn't have liked that. I—I don't think she ought to play such tricks." Leila hesitated, then faced me squarely. "I don't want to wear that red dress tonight. Uncle Alex is going downtown in a little while and he says I can exchange it if I like. So will you come with me and help me pick out something else?"

I could not have been more pleased. Catherine's story of the belt had affected Leila in a way she had not foreseen. Besides—there was the matter of a young unicorn who would be coming tonight, and because of whom Leila wanted to look pretty.

"Of course I'll help if I can," I told her warmly.

She jumped up to look out a window. "There's Uncle Alex now, getting his car out. I want to return some library books at the same time. I'll go get the dress and my books and be with you in a minute."

I was dressed suitably enough for town in a blue denim skirt with deep side pockets that I found handy, and a blue cotton overblouse. I had only to get my straw handbag from my room, and I was ready. We met in the upper hall and as we started downstairs together Catherine came in from the terrace with a basket of flowers in one hand. Her quick glance noted the red dress flung over Leila's arm, and she guessed at once what her daughter intended.

"I'll come too," she offered. "If you really don't like the red, darling, I can help you find something else. Though I'm disappointed that we aren't going to look like sisters tonight."

Her words were intended to make Leila feel guilty, but there was no way in which I could prevent Catherine from coming with us if she wished. Leila's resistance was already weakening before her mother's reproach and she flung me a pleading glance. It was Alex Stair, however, who rescued her.

He had come to the front door and was in time to hear Catherine's offer. "Let the child pick out her own clothes once in a while," he said.

Catherine turned angrily away and as she did so a spray of yellow cassia flew out of her basket and dropped to the parquet floor. She did not pause to pick it up, but went swiftly out to the terrace.

Leila looked after her in dismay. "Now her feelings are hurt. Now she'll be even more upset."

"She'll recover," said Alex shortly. He retrieved the spray of flowers from the floor and presented it to me with mock gallantry.

We went outdoors and Leila dropped her books and the red dress in the back seat and got into the car, sitting between Alex and me. He turned out of the driveway quickly, as if he sensed her uncertainty and wanted to prevent any change of mind.

As we started down the hill my fingers moved along the brown stem of the cassia spray and suddenly I held it to Leila's cheek.

"Cassia yellow! Do you have a yellow dress, Leila?"

She shook her head. "Cathy says yellow's wrong for us. It washes us out. It points up yellow tones in the skin."

I sniffed the flowers absently and said nothing, but I was aware of the turning of Alex's head. When I looked at him he gave me a slight nod that Leila did not see, and I knew I would find a yellow dress in her uncle's shop.

As we started the zigzag drive down the mountain Leila tensed beside me and turned her head to look behind.

"Cathy's following us," she said.

Alex flicked a glance at the rear-view mirror. "Yes, I know."

"It's just that she wants me to look right." Leila was too quick, too earnest. "She's always doing things for me, helping me."

I felt a tightness in my throat. Never had I detested anyone as I was coming to detest—and fear—Catherine Drew. She held too great a power in her hands because of Leila—power not only over the child, but over King as well, since, through Leila, she could hurt him so dreadfully. Old doubts engulfed me. What could I do to change any of this? My position was one of no real authority and all the strength of the situation lay against me. Yet I had to try, and the dress was a beginning.

The car behind hooted derisively.

"We'll let her pass," said Alex, and slowed to the side of the road, just as King had done the week before when I had first come up this mountain.

The white car went by with a last toot of the horn and was gone around the next turn.

"She'll break her neck in that car one of these days," Alex said, and I sensed as great a tension in him as in Leila.

At once the girl sprang to her mother's defense. "Oh, no! Cathy's a wonderful driver. She's always in control of her car. The things I've seen her do!"

"The things you haven't seen her do!" Alex snorted, and I glanced at him curiously.

He still puzzled me, leaving me always uncertain as to his true motives and his feeling about Catherine. Often he spoke of her sharply, cuttingly, and yet there had been times when his eyes were upon her, when he thought no one was noticing, and I saw the pirate in them again, covetous, perhaps ready to take—yet vindictive when she held him off? As he had been the day he had sent King off to Caprice? What was the play between these two? And what was Edith's role?

Certainly Edith had hurried to warn her sister that King might be coming to St. Croix, yet there was a conflict between the two women more often than not. Lately Edith had seemed even more on the verge of hysteria than usual. She had been shutting herself into her room for hours on end, coming out only to attend her mother, or to work on her husband's shells. For the rest of the trip to town I puzzled over these matters, while Alex too seemed lost in thought and had little to say.

When he dropped us off in the downtown area Leila picked up her books and the red dress, and we walked along Dronningens Gade, passing perfume and curio shops, stores where African carvings were sold, a place where Brazilian gems were displayed at free-port prices. But it was toward an area of alleyways cutting through to the waterfront that Leila led me.

Here were long stone buildings stretching at right angles to the street—buildings that had been the original warehouses and slave markets of the town when St. Thomas was a thriving gateway to the Caribbean. Now they housed shops and offices in picturesque surroundings, with narrow passageways between, and cross-alleys connecting one with another.

Leila turned through an opening of concrete arches into a long passage shadowed by leaning palm trees, where a cool wind from the sea funneled through. Set upon the cobblestones were small tables and chairs where people sat drinking coffee and eating refreshments brought out from an adjoining restaurant. We walked past a graceful flight of brick stairs, rimmed with handsome iron grillwork, and went on toward Alex's store. Palm Passage, they called this alley now, but once it had been a place familiar to the buccaneer and the old legends came close to one here. Where pink stucco had cracked away, the original foundations could be seen—built of stone and brick ballast brought over in sailing ships, and often put together with molasses for mortar.

We followed the cobblestone walk until Leila turned again through an arched doorway. Apparently Alex's shop ran through to front on Dronningens Gade, but this side entrance let us into the rear section given over to women's dresses. I had been half afraid to find Catherine waiting there, but when I looked down the long aisle she was nowhere in sight.

A pretty young Puerto Rican woman came to wait on us, eager to help as Leila began to slide dresses aimlessly along the nearest rod. I moved to another rack, fingering, searching, discarding. Yellow— I must look for cassia yellow. I still carried the sprig of blossoms and I held it up for comparison whenever yellow appeared in the pattern of a print. But it was not a print I searched for, though apparently visitors to the island indulged recklessly in Caribbean prints.

The frock, when I came upon it, hung so slimly to itself, so well hidden by flashy neighbors on either side, that I almost missed it. A mere pencil line of yellow caught my eye and I pounced and pulled the dress out, holding it up on its hanger.

Leila turned unhappily toward me. "I don't know how to choose. I keep seeing Cathy. I keep picking what would look right on her."

I held up my dream of a yellow frock. "Try this one on, will you?"

She rejected the look of it at once, shaking her head. "Oh, no! Not a babyish thing like that! Besides, it's the wrong size—too big. I take the same size as Cathy. And it's the wrong color too."

I hung it promptly back on the rack. "It's up to you, of course. Pick out whatever you'd like," I said indifferently.

She gave me a doubtful look and chose three dresses almost at random. We went into a dressing cubicle and I sat on a corner stool while she put on one after another. All were obviously wrong. An electric fan buzzed overhead, but it was warm in the small dressing room and I began to feel sleepy. I smothered a yawn and closed my eyes until Leila's voice brought me wide awake.

"I'm sorry if I'm boring you. I should have brought Cathy along! She looks at something and knows in a minute whether it's right or wrong."

"Right or wrong for her," I said. "Like that red dress. Maybe you'd better keep the red."

She almost flung the dresses at the girl. "All right! There's a yellow dress out there. What else can I do but try it?"

The salesgirl had seen me holding it up. She went off at once and brought back the cassia yellow. This time I stood up to help Leila into it.

"You've got more meat on your bones than your mother has," I told her. "The larger size will give you a chance to make the best of what you have. It's not your style to be lean and sinuous."

I opened the back zipper and turned her away from the mirror. When the dress was over her head, had been pulled into shape and rezipped, I pushed her gently toward the glass—and held my breath. I had not known I could pick so well. Somewhere in my memory a voice seemed to whisper, "No, Jessica—no! That's not the right color, dearest," but I found I could turn a deaf ear to the voice and know it was wrong.

There was no sickly yellow in Leila's skin, it was a golden tan that had not darkened and weathered as Catherine's had begun to do. The princess lines of the linen were subtle and set off the rounding of her slim young figure. From a circular neckline the dress curved gently in at the waist and flared to wider gores at the hemline. The yellow was pale as spun gold and here and there throughout the weave yellow petals of the same tone had been embroidered. There was no other decoration.

Leila stared, her lower lip caught between her teeth. "I don't know. I'm not sure. It—it scares me a little."

"That's because you're seeing you, instead of Catherine. Your mother couldn't wear this dress." I didn't say that Catherine would fade in it and look too old.

Leila glanced at me and then back at the mirror. "It's so plain. Cathy will laugh when she sees it. She'll tell me I've gone back to grade school."

I was a little taller than Leila and I stood beside her with my own dark brown head close to her light brown one as brown eyes and gray eyes looked into the mirror together. Cassia yellow was not bad for me either.

"If you don't take it, I will," I said.

Her eyes met mine in the glass, startled, and I laughed. "Wait! We need another judgment on this."

I left her and went to the front of the store looking for Alex Stair. He stood at a counter, arranging a strand of amber beads against saffron-colored Italian silk, his hands moving as though he took a sensuous delight in color and texture.

"Please come," I said. "Come and tell us what you think."

He came without question and I drew Leila out of the cubicle to where big mirrors gave back her reflection in yellow.

Alex regarded her for a moment. With a motion of his fingers he made her turn slowly while he studied her from every angle, his glossy beard slightly atilt. When he nodded I breathed again.

"Yes, it's right. The fit is perfect, the color flattering. But it needs another touch, I think."

He spoke to the Puerto Rican girl and she hurried away, to return in a moment with a string of carved beads and matching earrings of pale coral. When he had clasped the strand around Leila's throat and clipped on the earrings, he nodded again, approvingly.

"A gift—to wear for the party," he said.

Leila touched the coral in delight as she studied a stranger in the mirror. "Thank you, Uncle Alex. But do you really think the dress is right for me?"

He scowled at her fiercely, making a pirate face. "Don't argue with me. And mind you, none of that eye gunk! I don't like to see a masterpiece distorted. Lipstick, but not too much or too dark. No powder, except a touch for shine, and no rouge."

Leila gave him a faintly tremulous smile and went back to the cubicle to change. While the Puerto Rican girl helped her with the dress, I followed Alex toward the front of the shop.

"Thank you," I said. "That was a—a good thing to do."

His rather thin-lipped mouth smiled without amusement. "'Good' is the wrong word. Perhaps 'malicious' is a better one."

He went back to his display, leaving me troubled because I could guess toward whom his malice might be directed, and baiting Catherine was a dangerous game.

The girl was dressed in her blouse and swimming-fish skirt again, waiting for her package, when I rejoined her. For once she seemed her age—a healthy, happy fourteen-year-old who was looking forward to a party and a chance to dress up.

We left the shop, stepping into the windy corridor of the alley, where palm fronds rustled overhead, shading from the sun the little tables down its center. Leila touched my arm, arresting me, and I followed the direction of her glance.

There at a small table, sipping iced coffee through a straw as she watched the door to the shop, sat Catherine Drew.

"So you've found something, have you, darling?" she said at once. "Something even nicer to wear than our red dresses?"

Leila moved hesitantly toward the table. "Miss Jessica—uh—Jessica Abbott—helped me to pick out a different dress. I don't know if you'll like it or not."

I hoped that Leila would not open her parcel then and there, but she dropped into a chair and began fumbling with the string.

"I'm sure Jessica—uh—Jessica knows exactly what is right for you," Catherine said. "She has known you for such a long time."

I could only watch while Leila stubbornly fought the string and took the lid off the box. Tissue paper crackled as she opened it, and the neatly folded front of the cassia-yellow frock was displayed to her mother's view. Catherine stared at it for a moment. Then she caught up the dress from the box and shook it out scornfully. When she had turned it about once or twice in her hands, she flung it indifferently back in the box.

Leila sat in quiet dejection, while yellow linen spilled out of the box and over her hands.

"You don't like it, do you, Cathy?" she said miserably.

Catherine sipped her coffee. "You didn't really expect me to, did you? Yellow! But we mustn't be rude to your captive teacher, must we?"

She threw me an upward glance from beneath thick lashes. It was once more a promising look and I remembered the sound of a belt slapping across the palm of her hand. But there was no reason to fear what she might do here in public in broad daylight.

"You can't judge how Leila will look in the dress until you see her in it," I said, knowing there was too much of an edge to my voice.

"I'm sure she'll look very nice in it, if you say so," Catherine drawled. And then to Leila, "Do put it away for now. The color makes me slightly bilious."

Leila had the petal-soft skin of a young girl, sensitive skin that could flush too easily. It had mottled, and she was breathing quickly, close to tears. I had to stop this cruelty. I had to strike out, somehow, against Catherine Drew.

"We called in a third judgment," I told her. "Mr. Stair came to look when Leila had put the dress on, and he feels it's exactly right for her. He even added a gift of coral earrings and beads. I rather think we can trust Mr. Stair's taste."

There was a ruthlessness in the look Catherine turned on me. She would stop at very little now, but I was beyond caring what I said to her.

"So Mr. Stair approves?" Catherine mused. "Though he really has no business meddling with my plans for Leila, has he? Mr. Stair is—shall we say—in a rather vulnerable position. Perhaps more so than he knows. I believe I'll have to arrange a little talk with Mr. Stair."

She seemed to shrug me off as she turned back to her daughter.

"Never mind. The real test will come tonight, won't it, darling? When I'm in the red and you're in the yellow. But you needn't ask me to switch with you later. I rather think my red will do."

Hurriedly Leila began to cram the dress into its box, forcing on the lid. I took box and dress from her hands and made a neater task of fitting the two together.

Catherine paid for her coffee and then smiled coaxingly at Leila, easily winning her back.

"I've got my car parked not far away. I'll drive you home if you like—you and Miss Jessica-Jessica. But first I have to look up Steve on the waterfront. He has brought over a new batch of shells for Alex, and I'll need to get them to Edith right away."

Leila nodded dispiritedly and an arrangement was made for me to go with her while she returned her library books. Then we would wait for Catherine behind the library on Back Street.

Catherine went off with a light flick of her fingers for her daughter, ignoring me. On the way to Dronningens Gade I carried the dress box, half afraid that Leila might leave it somewhere or do something to damage the yellow frock. We had nothing to say to each other on the way to the library. A cunning and cruel sort of hurt had been done to Leila's pleasure in the dress and I had the feeling that no matter how lovely she might look in it tonight, she would never believe in that fact or have any confidence in her appearance.

More than ever I was coming to understand the anger that churned constantly beneath the surface in Kingdon Drew. He *must* get away —and soon, before something frightful happened. Each new thing Catherine did must feed the fire of the anger that drove him. If she would go to such trouble over so small a matter as Leila's dress, what might she be capable of where she really cared? I could guess by now that Kingdon Drew was one man whom she had never owned, one man who had turned away from her—and that she could not bear. I knew now that she would never stop until she destroyed him completely. Using Leila was her best means, and I could look forward with nothing but dread to the supper party.

XI

Leaving the bustle of Dronningens Gade, we went through a stone
tunnel which opened at the far end upon a large paved courtyard
surrounded by high stone walls. Within the enclosure grew a surprising variety of colorful shrubs, as well as a few flowering trees.
In the Islands even the plants were as bright as flowers, their leaves
streaked and speckled with shadings of brilliant yellow and red.

The building that housed the library was a massive stone structure, very wide and three high-ceilinged floors tall. To my eye it
looked like a public building, but it had once been a rather grand
private residence. Behind it the old part of town went up the steep
hills in tier after tier of small houses, as brightly colored as the
very shrubbery.

Just as Leila and I started toward the flight of stone steps that
led from the courtyard to the second floor, Kingdon Drew came
through a gate from Back Street, intent on business of his own.

We had of course seen each other a good many times since that
day in St. Croix, but always in the company of others. He had carefully avoided any meeting where we might be alone, though I kept
hoping there would be some chance for him to tell me his further
plans for leaving St. Thomas. When this did not happen I began
to be afraid that he had changed his mind. Something in me continued to twist with hurt when I saw him and none of the futile
yearnings that had begun in me had died down in the least.

It was to Leila that he spoke, his eyes avoiding mine. "I phoned
the house and heard that you'd come downtown to get a dress for
tonight. Did you find what you want?"

Leila stared off at some distant place beyond her father's head,
as if she had not heard him speak.

"I think the dress will be fine," I said with too great assurance.

Leila came to life. "Cathy doesn't think so."

"You've seen her downtown?" King's attention was arrested.

"Of course," Leila said. "She's driving us home. We're meeting her in a little while out in back."

King looked as if he wanted to say something more, but I caught his eye and shook my head slightly. He gave me a remote look and went up the broad flight of upper stairs that led to offices on the top floor.

Outside the library I sat on a veranda couch and waited until Leila came to tell me there would be a delay about finding the book her uncle had asked her to look up for him. Would I, she requested, go down to the back gate of the library courtyard and explain to Cathy?

"She hates to be kept waiting," Leila said. "Just tell her I can't help it and I'll be there the minute I can."

Leila's concern for her mother was always too anxious, too intense, but I did not argue. I returned to the warm dazzle of the courtyard and found the stone and iron gateway to the narrow Back Street that had once been more interestingly known as Wimmelskafts Gade.

Here traffic was again one-way, moving in the opposite direction from the parallel of Dronningens Gade. Stone walls and an adjacent building came together in a wedge just out of the direct line of traffic, with a sign on the wall reserving the angled space for library parking. It was empty at the moment and offered a place for me to stand while I waited.

Overhead the usual puffs of cloud sailed across a blue Virgin Islands sky. Sometimes such clouds turned fiercely black and filled with rain, but seldom did they drop their burden on St. Thomas, even in a shower. Although this was the hurricane season, no real storms had blown up since my coming. The weather report on the radio every morning was always the same: "Variable cloudiness and scattered showers." But even when it showered, as I had seen it do furiously once or twice, the rain was quickly over, wet bricks dried in a hurry, and puddles quickly vanished.

Staring at the sky, I tried to relax for this brief, snatched moment. A spurt of traffic went by, leaving the street empty behind except for a white car that turned into view several blocks away. It was Catherine's car, and when I saw that she was driving too fast for this part of town with its busy cross streets, I had my first flash of misgiving. True, this was broad daylight, and I was in a public place—but how would that help me if Catherine took advantage of a chance opportunity? I stepped as far back into my wedge of space as possible, so that my back was against the wall. Here I offered her no safe target, in case her cunning mind seized on the idea.

The car bore down on me so swiftly that I thought for a moment, having seen me alone, she meant to go past without stopping. Then, to my horror, the nose of the car turned deliberately in my direction, coming straight at me. There was no other place for me to move to save myself. I pressed my back flat against the wall and crossed my arms before me in a futile gesture of protection. It wasn't possible that she would take such a chance—but the car hurled itself at me with what seemed full intent to crush and kill, even at the cost of damage to herself.

I could only close my eyes and pray. With a screech of brakes, the white car came to a jarring halt inches away from me, and as I opened my eyes Catherine switched off the motor and slid across to the passenger's side. I saw her smile and the look was as frightening as what had nearly happened to me.

"What's the matter, Jessica-Jessica?" she called. "Did I really give you another fright?"

Through my thin blouse I could feel the hot stones of the wall behind me, burning my skin. My straw handbag lay in the dust where I had dropped it, and the box containing Leila's dress, but I could not move to pick them up. In the distance I heard the sound of someone dashing down a flight of stone stairs, heard running feet across the paved courtyard. A moment later King burst through the gate, flinging it open with a clatter. A quick, searching look seemed to tell him that I was unharmed, and he turned at once to Catherine.

"Get out of the car!" he said. "Get out and into the back seat."

For a moment she stared at him as if she did not mean to obey. He reached toward her in no uncertain manner and she drew swiftly back, clearly afraid of his touch. Moving as slowly as she dared, she got out on the street side and slid into the back seat, her manner insolent, defiant.

King turned back to me. "Are you all right? Did she hurt you, graze you?"

I shook my head. A reaction had set in and I found that I was shaking, that I could not speak. Gently he took my arm, helped me into the front seat, and then retrieved the dress box and my handbag from the dust. All the while I was aware of the bright malevolence of Catherine's unwinking stare.

"I'll drive you home," King said to me. "I was keeping an eye on matters from the top floor back there, and I came down as fast as I could get here."

We went around the car to get into the driver's seat just as Leila hurried through the gate to regard us in surprise.

"What's the matter? You look sort of funny. How come you're driving Cathy's car, Dad?"

"Get in back, if you please, Leila," King directed. "Miss Abbott has just had a fright. Your mother nearly injured her."

Catherine was no longer afraid of his touching her, as she had been a moment before. "Don't be an idiot! You know very well that I can handle this car. I stopped exactly where I meant to stop."

King said nothing. As he turned the wheel and entered the traffic flow along the street, I knew that he was dangerously close to a total loss of control. He moved the wheel too sharply, touching the horn with violence. Once I flicked my gaze toward the rear-view mirror and caught a glimpse of Catherine's face. She looked as if she might be purring.

As we drove up the mountain I closed my eyes to shut out the color and movement beyond the car. I suspected that Catherine would not have been sorry if she had pinned me to the wall. Now I knew the full extent of her malevolent intention to be rid of me, one way or another.

When we reached the house King was the first one out of the car. He paused only to ask if I was all right, and when I nodded mutely he ran up the steps and into the house as if he did not trust himself to speak again to Catherine.

Neither Leila nor her mother paid any attention to me as they got out of the car and I heard their brief interchange.

"I'll carry Steve's box of shells around to Edith's workroom," Catherine said, sounding as calm as though nothing had happened. "If she's there, I'll keep her talking. That will give you a chance to run upstairs to her room and get my columbella locket back. She's had it ever since she carried it off last week. I want it to wear tonight. I've lost my darling diamond earrings, but at least I'll have my locket."

"Why don't you ask her for it yourself?" Leila said. "She won't like it if she catches me in her room."

"She won't catch you. She's hiding it because it was a gift from Alex—and she's jealous. But I want it for tonight."

Leila gave in, though with a slight air of exasperation. "All right, Columbella. Don't worry. I'll get it for you."

As Catherine lifted out the carton filled with shells and wet sand I eyed it intently, but I could not tell whether it was one of the same cartons I had seen at Caprice. Leila watched her mother carry it off around the side of the house, and then turned to where I stood waiting.

"Tell me what really happened," she pleaded.

At least she was not putting the incident entirely aside. I told her exactly what Catherine had done and she listened in growing dismay, so that I began to hope she had been stirred to revulsion, perhaps rebellion. But when she spoke, her words shocked me.

"I've got to stop her," she murmured. "That belt thing—and now this! I've got to stop her before she hurts herself. But what am I to do?"

I wanted to keep her there, talk to her, shake her from so foolish an acceptance of responsibility for her mother's behavior, but I knew this was not the time. I reached into the car and drew out the box containing the yellow dress.

"I'll take this up to your room," I said.

I think she did not hear me. Her preoccupation with Catherine seemed to have shut her off from everything else. When she turned her back on me and ran into the house I followed more slowly, almost as much shaken by Leila's reaction as I had been by the incident itself.

My next thought was to consult with King. When I went to his office I found him there with Maud Hampden. She looked weary and discouraged, and I knew he had given her an account of what had just happened.

She beckoned me in at once. "Do come here, Jessica. I need you on my side. How are you feeling after that dreadful experience?"

"I'm all right," I said. "The car didn't touch me."

King pulled out a chair for me and I sat down.

"She means to destroy us all," Maud said, "in order to destroy King."

This was the thought I'd had—that Catherine wanted King's destruction above anything else, that this was her true, vindictive intent.

"She never forgives anyone who sees through her," Maud went on. "Even now she romanticizes herself—just as she did when she was young. Columbella—delicate and lovely as a shell. At least that's one of her roles. She has others less innocuous. You found her out in all her deceptions and pretenses, King. In your eyes she is scarcely the center of the universe, and she can't endure the injury to her tender ego. Now that Leila is older, Catherine can get at you through her. She's out to smash the mirror you hold up to her—by breaking you. It's as simple as that."

What it cost Maud Hampden to say these things showed in her eyes, in the very slackness of her shoulders. It could not be easy for a mother to face these shattering truths about her child as realistically as Maud had forced herself to do.

King flung out his hands angrily. "I won't have Leila's life ruined as it will be if she isn't sent away. Nor will I stand by and see Jessica hurt because she's trying to help my daughter. For the last few days I've thought of going away myself. But now I know that's out of the question. Whatever my responsibility is, it lies here. No one is safe from Catherine's malice now."

This was the change of course I feared. "But what can you do here?" I pleaded. "It's far better for you to go away!"

He did not look at me. "I can at least see that Catherine harms no one before the time when Leila is sent away. Once the child is gone from the house, Jessica will leave. We can't breathe easily until then."

My outburst had caught Maud's attention and I saw quickened awareness in her eyes. There was very little this woman missed.

"Catherine knows exactly where you're vulnerable," she said to King. "If you send Leila away now, she will still win. She'll write and phone and visit her—so that distance will make everything worse. She may really want her away now, thanks to Alex's needling. But she won't release the child emotionally, even if she's sent away— because Leila is her one best weapon against you."

King did not answer. I think his mind was made up by that time and he would not change it for anyone's argument. He glanced at the clock on his desk and shrugged.

"There's nothing further to be done now. I need to get back to the office."

But before he left he made one last effort with me. "Haven't you had enough by this time, Jessica? Do you begin to see what she is capable of?"

The smile I attempted had a tendency to slip. There was only one answer I could give him, and he seemed to read it in my face. He touched my shoulder lightly, as if in salute, and went out of the room.

Maud Hampden sat where she was, her eyes closed, and there were tears on her cheeks.

"Most small children have barbaric instincts to start with," she said. "Growing up, becoming civilized and educated, means learning how other people feel. But Catherine has a flat side, a blank side, that nothing has ever changed. Leila isn't like her—yet. That's why you're my one hope, Jessica. You may still be able to reach Leila in this really desperate struggle. You can help her to escape. Not physically—from the island—but emotionally from this dependence on someone who will harm her."

"I can only try," I said. "But don't you think King ought to get away?"

She looked at me for a moment and then held out her hand in her generous, affectionate way. When I gave her my own she pressed my fingers lightly.

"You might work on that too, my dear," she said, and drew herself wearily from her chair. It seemed to me that she had aged since the first time I had seen her. When we went to the door together she permitted herself to lean upon my arm.

With so much happening, I had almost forgotten about the supper party tonight. In the big main hall Edith was giving instructions for the placing of buffet tables, the rearrangement of furniture, her gaunt, rather bony person flitting anxiously from table to table. Though she managed efficient enough results, it was always with too much expenditure of nervous effort.

Since Catherine had disappeared and Edith would not stop for food, Maud and Leila and I had a quiet lunch on the gallery fronting the terrace. What Catherine had done that morning went unmentioned between us. Leila seemed remote and thoughtful, and I wondered what success she'd had in recovering the columbella from her aunt's room.

Once she mentioned the theft of her mother's earrings in San Juan. "They would have been mine someday—like Caprice," she told her grandmother. "I would have had my ears pierced to wear them."

Maud roused herself. "I remember when your grandfather bought her those earrings. They're better off lost. They were intended to make amends for Catherine's hurt feelings—when she should have been punished. I hope they'll never be recovered."

"Oh, Gran!" Leila cried. "I know what you mean. Cathy has told me about that bracelet she took at school. That was only a prank —to tease a girl she didn't like. And then everyone made such a fuss, and you came to whisk her home in disgrace."

Maud said nothing for a moment and I could not meet her eyes. When she spoke I heard deep pain in her voice.

"A prank, dear?" she asked softly. "A prank? Like running Jessica down in the car this morning was a prank?"

Leila stared at her grandmother in shock and outrage. Then she jumped up and ran off to her room.

Maud and I had little to say to each other for the rest of the meal. I knew how deeply she was suffering, and I could offer nothing to lessen her pain.

After lunch Edith put Leila to work and Maud stayed downstairs to help supervise arrangements as long as her strength lasted. No one needed me, and Edith clearly did not want me about. I spent most of the afternoon in my room, still trying to quiet my nerves, after the thing that had nearly happened to me at Catherine's hands. But it was hard to be inactive, and at length I went outside to wander for a while in the little tropical forest. There was, however, something about the place that I was beginning to dislike. After a few steps into its maze of paths, I felt suddenly alone and too far from the house, closed in by that dark and sinister-seeming growth. It was not a place where I wanted to meet Catherine alone, and I did not stay there long.

Wandering about closer to the house, I came upon the place where Edith Stair cleaned and prepared seashells for her husband. I had seen the single-roomed stone building she used, but until now I had never gone inside it. I found my way along a path walled by a hibiscus hedge and went to the door. It was unlocked and I pushed it open tentatively. No one was inside and I went in. The building had once been a separate kitchen for the main house and there was a great brick chimney into which a Danish oven had been set. Now it was used for a totally different purpose.

The marble top of what had been a kitchen table, the soapstone slab beside the sink, cupboard shelves, and even the wide stone window ledges were laden with shells in every condition of processing. There were shells in pails of water, probably being kept alive; shells drying in the sun on window ledges, shells ready for final polishing. The stone floor beneath my feet felt gritty with sand, and the same peculiar shellfish smell that I had found in Catherine's room at Caprice tainted the air. Beyond a window ledge, stephanotis bloomed white and waxy, and when I drew the casement open, its jasmine scent lent a grateful fragrance to the room.

All about were the instruments used by Edith in her work. Curved tweezers lay upon the table, and there was an assortment of stiff wire brushes. On a two-burner gas stove a big pot for boiling water waited for its next batch of shells. On a shelf stood bottles of preserving alcohol. I was reminded on every hand not only of the handsome housing a shell could form, but of the slain tenant as well, and I could understand why the fastidious Alex disliked this part of shell collecting.

From a wall hook Edith Stair's brown work smock seemed to watch me with bright yellow sunflower eyes, and I knew I had no business in this place. Yet the feeling that the room had something to tell me persisted, and I moved on in my inspection. Now and then I picked up a shell to examine it carefully, but learned nothing, and went on, still tantalized.

On a worktable stood a carton half filled with sand in which a number of shells remained nested. But if the box Steve had brought this morning contained those carelessly gathered shells from Caprice, there would seem no need to protect them by bedding them in sand. Knowing little of the subject, I could not tell whether the shells in the sandbox were of any value. To my inexpert eye they looked ordinary enough.

As I stood there, wondering idly, I began patting at the sand in the box, playing with it absently as I had played in sand as a child. It was damp enough for the building of a passable castle, though a bit rocky, and not like the fine-grained sand one found at the water's edge. When my castle had taken on bulk and height, and I had built a rampart with serrated walls, I decorated it with bits of shell and stone, hardly attending the work of my hands because of the growing sense of uneasiness that possessed me.

I had felt like this in my room, for all the new locks on the doors, and again in the dark paths of the little forest. Now the feeling had crept upon me once more, and I recognized it as fear, making me jumpy, giving me a tendency to look askance over my shoulder. This was the beginning of terror and I must not give in to it.

Nevertheless, so attuned was I to watchful uneasiness, and so quick to pick up the slightest sound, that once or twice I had the sure feeling of someone looking in at the windows behind my back, watching me build castles in the sand. Each time the sensation came I turned about quickly, and once I even went to look outside, but there was no one in sight. Hibiscus hedge and the very walls of the stone building offered concealment, so I could not be sure whether someone had really looked in on me or if the jumpiness of my nerves had betrayed me.

Since the room and its belongings told me nothing, and since my uneasiness continued to increase, I was about to give up and return to the house when I heard a definite and unconcealed step on the cement walk that led to the door. At once the thought of Catherine, the memory of a stone wall at my back, swept over me, leaving me to stare shakily at the door.

To my relief it was Alex who stepped into the room. He seemed surprised, and not at all pleased to see me.

"I didn't expect to find you here," he said, with a possible challenge beneath his words.

I explained a bit feebly that I had been exploring, that I had found this place and was curious about it. He listened impassively, his fingers at his beard, and I think he did not believe that I had come here idly.

"Edith seems to have disappeared," he said. "I had expected to find her here."

I'm not sure why I had the instinct that he was lying and that it was not Edith he had come looking for.

"I haven't seen her," I told him. "There has been no one else here."

He came to look down at my mounds and walls with their shell trim and shook his head doubtfully. "If I were you I wouldn't let Edith know what you've been up to here. She's jealous of her prerogatives, you know. No one touches her instruments. She doesn't allow the servants to come here to clean, but takes care of the place herself."

"I'm sorry," I said. "The building seemed open and empty—not at all private."

I reached out to flatten my sand castles, but Alex stopped the movement of my hands. "Never mind—let them be!" he said and I heard the whip of some resentment in his voice.

Standing so near, I could look into his eyes at close hand and I noted something a little strange about them—tiny fleckings of yellow in the pale blue of the iris, as though some fire burned behind, offering sly glimpses of flame. It was a strange conceit and I blinked and moved away, wondering if he wanted me to leave the castles so Edith would find out about my meddling and direct her wrath at me instead of at him. I wondered too if he was aware of what Catherine had done this morning, and what his reaction might be —but I had no wish to tell him if he did not know.

I was half turned toward him, with the window on my right, and from the corner of my eye I caught movement there. Something that came into shadowy, unfocused being at the periphery of my vision—and was gone at once. A face? Someone who had stepped to the window to see us there? This time the feeling was even stronger than before.

"I think someone's looking for you," I said. "Perhaps I'd better go."

He seemed to hesitate, then change his mind. "I'll walk to the house with you. Since Edith isn't here."

So much for Catherine, I thought, if it was she who lingered behind the hibiscus hedges, waiting for a chance to see Alex alone. I was glad enough of his company as we went back to the house together.

Just before we reached the door he halted me beside him on the path. "Be a little careful of meddling with what you don't understand," he said in a low voice, and I had again the conceit of hidden flame showing slyly behind pale, opaque eyes.

"What do you mean by that?" I asked. "How have I meddled?"

"How have you not?" His bearded lips smiled not too pleasantly. "You've stepped between Catherine and her daughter and I think you put yourself in a more uncomfortable position than you know."

"But I do know," I said. "This morning Mrs. Drew came very near to running me down with her car."

He met my words impassively, as if such news did not surprise him, but I could not tell whether he had already heard about what had happened. I hurried away from him up the steps and into the house. What Alex Stair was about, I did not know, but I trusted him less than ever. It was, perhaps, not only Catherine whom I needed to be on guard against. The more I thought about it, the more I felt that Alex was all too anxious to see me gone from Hampden House, even though this was something he had disclaimed in the beginning.

XII

When I reached my room I left the door open so that I could hear
Leila when she came up the stairs. By now it was early evening,
though still light, and in an hour or so the first guests would be
arriving. This was the time for bathing and dressing and getting
ready for the supper. I heard Catherine come out of her room to
take over one of the bathrooms. Once when there was a sound on
the stairs, I went to my door in time to glimpse Edith coming up,
with Alex beside her. They were not speaking and I sensed a chill
between them.

When Leila finally appeared she came slowly, reluctantly, as
though every step she took toward her room brought her nearer to
something she dreaded. Near the top she glanced up through the
stair rail and saw me waiting.

I smiled at her, making an effort to be cheerful, casual. "Let me
know when you're ready to be zipped," I said.

She shook her head. "I've changed my mind. I'm not going to
wear that dress tonight."

"Because of what your mother said? But she hasn't seen it on you.
How can she know how well it suits you?"

Leila nodded miserably. "She's seen it. She made me try it on
for her this afternoon. She thinks it's all wrong."

"So what do you plan to wear?"

"Oh—an old thing from last year." She hesitated, then flashed
me an unhappy look. "I wanted something new to wear. I really did!"

I understood very well her eternally feminine reason. She wanted
to look lovely for a man—or perhaps for a mythical unicorn who
existed only in her own imagination. A man who, in real life, would
probably never notice what she wore because he would be dancing
attendance on a woman in a red dress. Nevertheless, I had to use
to advantage Leila's evident longing to look well.

"Wear the yellow anyway," I urged. "You have to choose for
yourself sometime. Even your mother might make a mistake."

She reached the door of her room and pushed it open impatiently. "Cathy doesn't make mistakes of that kind," she said and went inside, closing the door firmly before I could say anything more.

I stared at the blank wood panel that shut me out, and tried to marshal my thoughts for a real attack on the problem that faced me. This was more than the simple matter of wearing or not wearing a new dress. I knew—how well I knew!—how much more was involved.

If Leila wore the dress and looked as lovely in it as I knew she could, it would help enormously in this struggle against Catherine's destructive control. If only I could help turn Leila away from her worshipful concern with a mother who deserved no such love and concern, then she would begin to lead her own life and King might go away and work out something for himself. As always, the thought of his going away made my heart constrict—but this I must live with. A future for the two of us might never be possible, but King and Leila must have their chance. Something mattered to me once more, mattered enormously as it had not mattered for a long time.

Again I waited, this time for King to come upstairs. The moment he appeared I leaned on the rail and spoke to him.

"I need your help," I said.

He looked dispirited and anything but eager for the evening's festivities, but he came with me to my room. I gestured him into a chair, closed the door, and went to sit on the bed. Though he made no move in my direction, his eyes studied me as though he memorized my face. It was a look I could not bear, a fatalistic look that gave up—relinquished. I knew where it could lead because I had been there myself, and I did not want this for Kingdon Drew.

Quickly I told him the story of the yellow dress, and of how Catherine had set out deliberately to destroy Leila's pleasure in it and shake her confidence about wearing it.

"The problem now," I pointed out, "is to get Leila into that dress in spite of herself."

He heard me through in silence and then rejected the idea wearily. "I'm afraid there's nothing to be done."

"There is if you'll help me," I said.

"How?" There was disbelief in the word.

I threw all the eager persuasion I could summon into my answer. "First, be gentle with her. Keep your temper, even if she says outrageous things. Call her by some pet name you used when she was little. Play it by ear. All we want is to have her try on the dress for you—nothing else."

"A dress," he said, "at a time like this."

There was no time for pleading and explanation. "Just trust me. Trust me and help me this one time."

His look gentled. "All right—I will. What do we do first?"

I ran to the door next to mine. He went with me and waited as I knocked upon the panel. Leila answered grumpily, rudely. I saw King's jaw begin to tighten and I touched his arm so that he relaxed and smiled at me ruefully.

"I'm here with your father," I called through the door. "Can you see us for a minute?"

She did not answer right away and I could hear her shuffling about the room. When she came to open the door she had wrapped a flowered muumuu about her and her feet were bare.

"May we come in?" I said.

She looked in guarded surprise from me to her father. "I'm just getting dressed. There isn't much time."

King came to my aid. "I know," he said. "We can be late for the party together."

There was suspicion in her eyes, and I sensed that she knew very well that something was to be asked of her, and was preparing her refusal.

Quickly I glanced about the room. A flowered green and white dress had been flung across the bed and the wardrobe door stood open. I saw the yellow dress hanging inside.

"Your father wants to see you in the dress you bought this morning," I said. "I've been telling him about it."

She started to shake her head, to stick out her lower lip. King ran his hand over the ridge of hair above his right temple as if the gesture relaxed him, and when he spoke his voice sounded as lightly teasing as I could have wished.

"Come on, chicken! Let's see this wonderful dress on you. Then if you want, you can change back to that spinach green."

"Spinach green" struck exactly the right note and I was delighted with him.

A faint quiver touched Leila's lips before she pressed them together, still resisting him with all her might.

"You used to show me your new things—remember?" he coaxed. "It's been a long time. I'd like to see this dress."

She turned resentfully to me. "What are you up to? What do you want?"

"Nothing very terrible," I said. "I'd like to see you look as pretty for the party tonight as you did in your uncle's shop this morning. Your father and I are going back to my room. We'll wait for you there. Come show us when you're ready."

I took care not to catch her eye, but simply got myself and King out of the room as quickly as we could manage it, before any stormy refusal was hurled at us. I hoped Leila's feminine curiosity would come to our aid.

King sat in the chair in my room and regarded me in frank surprise. "I'd never have thought—" he began, and then changed his direction. "I wanted to spank her, but you gave me a look and—"

"And you stopped being an angry father," I said. "Don't scold her so much. It's hard to be fourteen. She's not a child, yet she's not grown up either, though she's trying hard to convince herself that she is. It's a difficult time for parents too. I know that. Perhaps just loving her is the bridge—making her know you're there to be counted on."

He was regarding me with that warmly searching look which always brought too great a response from me, and I was afraid I could not much longer stay as remote as I must.

It was a relief to hear a sound from the next room and a moment later Leila was at my door. When I opened it she stepped shyly into the room, presenting her back for me to zip up the dress. She held the coral beads and earrings in her hands, and as I helped her put them on I saw that she had taken time to brush her shining cap of brown hair and smooth the oblique line of bangs across her forehead. Her lips were touched with coral pink—nothing more—and her eyes were a clear amber brown. As clear as only young eyes can be when unadorned by the artifice of pigment.

Yet I could sense her anxiety, her lack of confidence. If King failed her now, if there was a false note in anything he said, immeasurable harm might be done. But he did not speak—and that was right. His surprise at the sight of her was genuine and could not have been more flattering. There was no need for him to pretend, and I could see her young confidence swelling as she turned before him preening a little—a glowing, charming picture of a young girl ready for a party.

"I wish I could paint," I said. "I'd want to do a portrait of you the way you look right now."

That was the right response too, coming naturally to my lips. She actually smiled and her father whistled softly. There was no need for fumbling praise about a dress. He turned her about and nodded appreciatively, then winked at her in a way I knew must have been a long-ago signal between them. She flung herself suddenly upon him, no longer fourteen but all of ten years old, and they hugged each other warmly in rediscovery. As I watched I knew how much I had come in this short time to love them both.

"Don't cry *now,* chicken!" he said, patting her shoulder affectionately. "You'll mess up your face for the party. I've got to hurry and get dressed myself. But if you'll wait for me I'll be proud to take you downstairs with me. How's that?"

"I accept!" She let him go and turned to me. "You'll be there tonight, won't you? You'll stay with me, Jessica?"

I liked her easy use of my first name, and I understood her need for support, perhaps even protection. Protection from her mother.

"I hadn't meant to go," I said hesitantly. "I really haven't been asked to this supper, and—"

"Of course you've been asked." King sounded a little rough as if he was fighting his own moment of emotion. "We're both counting on you, Jessica."

"I'll be there," I promised them both, and put my heart in it.

Leila flew off to her room to wipe away any trace of tears, and King stayed for a moment after she had gone. I did not want him there—the longing in me was growing too painful.

"Thank you," he said quietly. "If Catherine hurts her tonight I'll—"

Longing faded at once in the face of alarm. "Don't say it and don't let Leila see how you feel. If you say anything against Catherine, you'll simply put your daughter on the defensive."

"I know. I'll be careful," he promised.

When he had gone I took a quick, impulsive whirl about the room, feeling almost as happy as Leila had looked—and with far less reason. I did not think Catherine would retreat easily or accept the defeat we had planned for her. Yet—I was going to a party and I was in love! By now I was more than willing to shut my eyes to danger and the impossible future.

Dressing a bit feverishly, I found myself wishing that *I* had a new dress so that I too could look beautiful for Kingdon Drew. The candy pink would have to do, but we were of an age tonight, Leila and I, and both foolish.

For that brief, hopeful moment I felt younger than I had in my teens when Helen was alive, and what was more, no whispering voice came out of the past to haunt me.

XIII

That was a night of gold and red, with torches flaring on the hilltop, and the lights of Charlotte Amalie fanning out around the harbor far below. A night of water lily and jasmine and sweetly scented cereus. The night of the shell. Columbella!

When I was dressed Leila tapped on my door and her father took us down, one on either arm. My reckless elation was fading and I could now remember Catherine.

All through the main hall a myriad candles glowed in tall hurricane globes. The buffet tables were laden with attractive delicacies, some of which Catherine had ordered flown in from the mainland to supplement what she had purchased yesterday in San Juan. For an informal supper a great deal of money had been spent and I had heard Maud Hampden protesting Catherine's excesses.

As the three of us descended the stairs I saw that women in sleeveless summer dresses, and men in light suits or the madras shorts and jackets that were common wear in the Islands, already moved among the tables or stood about talking. Though I looked for her at once, Catherine was not in sight. We were late, as we expected to be, and Edith noted our appearance in both disapproval and surprise.

Near the foot of the stairs Maud Hampden stood speaking with a dark-skinned couple, whom I knew to be a senator and his wife. Both Maud and Aunt Janet had friends among well-to-do Virgin Islanders, and I was continually impressed by the dignity and quiet reserve of the older women—a dignity in which there was no arrogance.

Maud saw us and turned aside for a moment to compliment Leila and kiss her cheek. For me she had a secret look of congratulation.

While King moved into the crowd to greet friends, as Alex and Edith were doing, Leila and I slipped into the line carrying plates around long tables. In the charming island manner flowers had been strewn down the center of each table. Hibiscus, bougainvillea, the blossoms of the flame tree, all were there in their natural beauty, laid simply upon lacy cloths, more beautiful without formal arranging. One could be profligate with blossoms, starting afresh each day, since they were always so abundantly at hand.

Steve and Mike had come and the look on their faces when they saw Leila spelled success. Since I had caught Leila doodling little figures of unicorns and shells, I had begun to see Steve in a new and rather disturbing role. He was a little too arrestingly good-looking, a little too confident. He pranced too much, always inviting feminine attention. Now he whistled teasingly at Leila, and I was glad of Mike's more frankly astonished grin.

"Hey!" said Mike inadequately. "Well—hey!" And Leila smiled at him with more friendliness than usual, before her heart-in-the-eyes look turned back to Steve.

We filled our plates and were ready to carry them out to the terrace when Catherine made her appearance on the stairs. It was to be expected that she would do just this—make an appearance. The murmur of voices around the tables hushed and it seemed to me that something uneasy ran through the room, resulting in a sudden quiet.

She stood above us on the landing—a column of flame in her red dress. Its straight lines hugged the curves of a body less softly rounded than Leila's, but seductive enough, flaring into that moving, shimmering froth of ruffles at her knees, revealing the perfection of long slim legs as she came down the stairs. Tonight she had piled her fair hair high on her head in an elaborate formation, and below it her triangle of a face seemed exquisitely beautiful. About her neck the gilded shell, the columbella, hung suspended from its chain, bright against the red of her dress.

At once friends were greeting her, catching her up in their circle, and she was lost from our view. I turned to Leila and saw the dazzled look she wore—as though she had stared too long at the sun.

With a hand on her arm, I drew her away from Steve, who now had eyes only for Catherine, and from Mike, who had begun to glower.

"Remember who you are," I said to her softly. "Hold on to that —don't lose it! You're not your mother and you don't have to be like her. You only need to be yourself—your best self."

The dazzle left her eyes and she turned to me breathlessly. "She'll be angry when she sees what I'm wearing."

I had to take the risk of an attack. There were obligations that went with parenthood—obligations Catherine had chosen not to honor.

"You know why she'll be angry, don't you?" I asked coolly.

Leila's eyes avoided mine. "Because she wants me to look my best. Because she doesn't want to be ashamed of me."

"You look just the way you should look and there's nothing to be ashamed of," I told her, thoroughly indignant and letting her see it. "Remember the queen in *Snow White* when you were small? She *had* to be fairest in the land, and if anyone threatened her, there was always the poisoned apple. Words can be poisoned too, and your mother knows how to use them."

Color flared in her cheeks, but I gave her no chance for an answer. "Come outside and we'll find a place where we can sit down and eat."

Mike O'Neill saw what we intended and hurried to join us. As we stepped outside I looked back—at the very moment Catherine saw her daughter. But though her attention was fixed upon Leila, the girl had gone out to the terrace and did not notice. Mike and I exchanged a glance as we went after her. The moment of confrontation had been postponed, and the longer it was held off, the more chance there would be for Leila to get used to her wings and the heady sensation of flying, so that she could not be so easily shot to earth.

On the terrace Leila ignored the round tables placed all about and went straight to the low wall of blue stone. Outdoors there was a wind, though the hibiscus hedges made something of a windbreak— but then, it was always windy in St. Thomas and no one seemed to mind.

Across the flagstones near the opposite curve of the wall, where torchlight made his olive skin look golden, was a man with a guitar. He wore white duck trousers and a white shirt, with a bright red cummerbund about his plump waist, his black head bare. Leila saw him and waved.

"That's Malcolm," she said. "He's one of the best Calypso singers in St. Thomas. I'll bet Cathy got him here. He always makes up special songs for her."

If Leila had resented my words about Catherine, her resentment had faded. I hoped that I had offered a doubt to buttress any loss of confidence when the need arose.

The man with the guitar flashed us a smile and began to strum softly, singing to his own accompaniment. The song was "Island in the Sun"—and as always the background and the singing spread a patina of emotion over the scene. Here on this hilltop the trade winds blew and torches flared and danced, repeating themselves in ghostly duplicate in all the glass doors and windows of the house. When one looked away from the lights, the stars were bright and close, though the moon had not yet risen. All the paraphernalia of a lovely tropic night were present to tug at our feelings. Perhaps the clouds seemed a bit thicker than usual, mounded here and there across the sky, but we did not worry.

Around the terrace, women's dresses added to the color, and their voices were as light and murmurous as the wind in palm fronds. In and out wove the music, haunting, plucking at memory, reminding us of the elusive passing moment, telling us we were here in this island now, with all its insistent beauty around us—almost too much of it for the senses to bear. In a thrice it might vanish for any one of us—and be gone forever. That was a part of the savoring, perhaps.

Malcolm was singing "Kingston Town" plaintively, and the repetition played upon the strings of emotion that hummed among us.

Suddenly King was there beside me, wanting to know if all was well, if I had everything I wanted. Soon I must come and meet some of the guests. I cast a sidelong glance at Leila arguing animatedly with Mike, and shook my head.

"No, I'll stay here, if you don't mind."

He agreed gratefully, and after a word to Leila and Mike he moved away.

When Alex came outside he too came to speak to us, and to compliment Leila. Her moment of doubt when she had seen her mother on the stairs seemed to have faded, and by the time Catherine appeared with her own group of satellites, Steve among them, I felt she might be in a stronger position to resist whatever her mother might say or do.

For a time Catherine did nothing, and we finished our supper in peace. Perhaps she was all the more a center of attention tonight because she had been robbed in San Juan the night before. Jewel thieves who preyed on wealthy women were not uncommon in the luxury hotels of the Caribbean, but to have one of St. Thomas' own figure in such a happening brought the matter close to home and the island was buzzing.

That Catherine was aware of us, I knew, but she stayed on the far side of the terrace and I wondered if she could be a little fearful of any close comparison with her lovely young daughter. That was too much to hope for, however, and eventually she wound her way to the wall where we sat drinking coffee.

I saw her coming and looked about for King. He was across the terrace, beside Maud, and I knew his attention had focused upon that brilliant figure in the red flame of a dress as she came toward us, moving to the music almost as if she danced. Her hands were empty, free. One of them toyed with the gilded shell on its chain and there was something so glowing, so dazzling about her tonight that I knew she had no fear of being eclipsed by her young daughter. Because of that very fact, perhaps she would be satisfied to leave the child alone.

"Hello, darling," she said as she reached Leila. Her eyes noted the yellow dress, but she made no comment. Instead, she looked at me, her smile sly. "Are you feeling better by now, Miss Jessica-Jessica? I'm afraid that was quite a shock you had this morning."

Beside me Leila made a slight sound. For an instant I thought she was about to speak indignantly, but Steve broke in and the chance was lost.

"What do you mean, Cathy? What sort of shock?"

Catherine told him then, in detail. How she had seen me waiting behind the library and had thought it might be fun to give me a bit of a scare.

Steve did not laugh in appreciation of her story as she seemed to expect, but gave her the same look I had seen on his face when he had burst into her room at Caprice in time to take away the belt with which she threatened me.

"Sometimes I think you're asking for a whole lot of trouble," he said and there was cool disapproval in his tone. She flung him a slanted glance that was not entirely amiable. Not until she explained how King had come tearing out of the library and for a minute she hadn't known what he might do to her—all because of his sympathy for poor Jessica-Jessica—did Steve's face darken.

"Did he hurt you?" he asked her. "Did he frighten you?" and I suspected that it was not consideration that prompted him to be critical, but something more wary that might have to do with self-preservation.

At his question, Catherine did a turn that set the band of ruffles at her knees flaring and came back to him mockingly. "Of course he frightened me. But then—I like to be frightened. If it doesn't go too far. I don't like to be hurt, but it's always exciting to be frightened."

Alex had appeared behind her and I knew he had heard her words. He slipped a finger beneath the gold chain at the back of her neck and pulled it with a little jerk so that the shell pressed tightly against her throat. For an instant I saw real fear in her eyes. She swung around, nearly snapping the chain.

"Oh, Alex!" she cried. "You needn't take me so literally. I thought it was King."

He smiled with little mirth and I was reminded of the way he had looked this afternoon when I had noted the flecks of yellow around the iris of his eyes. Across the terrace, King watched us, his face grim in flickering torchlight.

Malcolm strummed a sudden chord on his guitar, arresting attention. As if at a signal Catherine laughed and turned toward him. He continued to play without singing, and it was as if he drew her toward him with the music. She seemed to forget us all, moving like a sleepwalker. Guests stirred out of her way, and I saw the looks that passed between them—knowing looks, as if they had seen this happen before.

The man began to sing as she neared him—words and music which I did not know. Catherine fixed her unwavering gaze upon him and began to dance, only a foot or two away from him, so that her scarlet ruffles brushed his white trousers as she stepped forward and back. He sang on, now and then smiling, moving slightly to the strum of his own time, matching her steps with his own. Catherine seemed unaware of the sudden quiet around her, of people watching. It was island dancing, slow, sinuous, with a beat that got into the blood. She danced almost in one place, yet with all of her body, with supple movements of her shoulders, her head, the long swaying column of her neck. And all the while that golden shell danced upon her breast, shining red as if it too were fired by flame.

I forced myself to look away from the spellbound figure of the dancer, and saw that Steve was watching her with what I was coming to think of as his unicorn look. Leila's lips were raptly parted. The spell had touched her as well and she was breathing quickly—though she seemed a little frightened at the same time, as if she could not altogether lose herself in a magic that was hardly benevolent. To me she resembled a clean shaft of sunlight there on the dark terrace—something healthy that belonged to a sunny daytime world. I wanted to step between her and any sight of the dancer, but I did not move.

Maud Hampden broke the spell—or tried to. She rose from her table and spoke in a voice that could be heard across the terrace.

"Excuse me, please," she said, and walked with dignity toward the house.

She did not so much as glance at Catherine and once more guests moved aside to make a pathway, and there was a murmur, the beginning of talk. King did not go with her, but stayed where he was, his face no less grim and forbidding than before.

Everyone else was watching Catherine again, but I was more interested in Leila. Perspiration beaded her forehead and I could sense her tension as clearly as though I reached out and touched her.

With a quick gesture Catherine raised her hands to the golden coils of her hair. Carelessly, never missing a beat, she plucked out combs and pins and let them drop to the flagstones until her hair came loose and spilled over her hands. She shook it back with a flick of her head and the wind caught the mass of it and whipped it free about her shoulders.

Steve said nothing, but there was excitement in him now, barely held in check.

"Somebody'd better stop her!" Mike said grimly.

The sound of his voice was startling on the quiet terrace. The ring of it cut through the sound of the music. Catherine turned slowly, still without missing a step, and came toward us, her eyes green-gold, her small cat chin tilted. I expected her to say something to Mike, but she paid no attention to him as she held out a hand to Leila.

"Come, darling. Come and dance with me!"

She pulled the girl to her feet, though Leila tried futilely to hold back. "No—no, please, Cathy!" she begged.

I knew what Catherine meant to do. Out there on the terrace Leila's humiliation would be complete. Catherine would know very well how to make her look awkward and foolish—a silly, clumsy child in a butter-yellow dress, a girl who would stumble over her own feet and be as nothing beside this graceful, wrongfully intentioned woman.

I had been there before. I could feel what was happening along my own nerves. It was part of my tissue, my brain, my memory. Leila's terror of such humiliation was mine—to be experienced sickeningly all over again. But I was no longer as young as she. I need not stand by and endure what was about to happen.

I put a firm hand on Leila's arm. "You needn't go out there if you don't want to."

She started as though I had wakened her to resistance, and drew back from Catherine's touch. The woman knew she had lost for the

moment, and she turned her spite upon me. Her hand flashed out
and I felt the pressure of strong, thin fingers about my wrist.

"You come then!" She pulled at my hand. "The music is wonderful. Come, Jessica-Jessica. I'll teach you how we dance here in our
islands."

It was I whom everyone watched now, though I was too angry
to care. Catherine's fingers hurt my wrist, reminding me of a belt, of
a car, but anger sustained me. I spoke softly, so that only she could
hear.

"I'm strong enough to hurt you badly," I said, and I moved my
hand, breaking her hold, fastening my own fingers about her small-
boned wrist.

At once her eyes told me that I had gone too far. There was rising
hysteria in them and her free hand came up to strike at me, the
fingers tipped with sharp red nails. But before she could touch me,
King was across the terrace, swinging her away with a grip that
made her cry out in pain.

"Try anything more and you'll be sorry," he said, his voice low
and deadly, so that only our own small group heard him.

She pulled away and recovered herself, to go dancing back to the
guitar player. Beside me, Leila was trembling, her face turned away
from her father. Mike put an arm about her, steadying her, holding
her tightly. Steve was laughing openly at King, mocking him, I
thought, asking for trouble.

King paid no attention. With a last look for me, he strode across
the terrace to the house and a few moments later when I looked up
I saw him standing at the rail of the gallery upstairs. It was as if
he had found it necessary to put a safe distance between him and
that dancing woman in red.

Catherine's performance was not yet over. There had been a moment during our interchange when an embarrassed rustling and a
murmur of conversation had broken out. Everyone watched, but uncomfortably, as though wishing she would stop. Now, suddenly, it
was quiet and she held them again.

"You promised me a song tonight," she said to Malcolm. "You
promised me a Calypso about Columbella!"

He agreed, white teeth flashing. "Yes—a song for Columbella."
The guitar notes underscored his voice as he began to sing.

> "Columbella, she is not for you,
> Columbella, she is not for true.
> Down in the ocean far and deep
> Columbella she is sure to weep.

Down where the sand has a golden hue,
Columbella's sure to weep for you.
Up on the island, bright in the sun,
Columbella's golden days be done."

The chords died away and the singer was silent, still smiling, waiting, as his audience waited, tension mounting.

The smile had fled from Catherine's face. She cried out suddenly, crossly, like a petulant child. "I don't care for that song! It's a foolish song. Never let me hear you sing it again—do you understand? Columbella's golden days are only just beginning. Sing something else—sing something else quickly!"

He gave her a careless nod and obliged with a song that was safe and familiar. At once Catherine turned toward the watchers. "Someone come dance with me! I want a partner!"

Steve slipped smoothly out upon the terrace to meet her. He danced without self-consciousness, his eyes both mocking and admiring. He did not touch her but danced facing her, matching his steps to hers, matching the movement of neck and shoulder and hip. The golden columbella on its chain danced with them. The shell and the unicorn!

I glanced about at the watchers and saw Alex Stair, his bearded face enigmatic as ever, his eyes betraying nothing of his thoughts. As I puzzled about him he turned to the woman next to him and drew her out upon the terrace. As if at a signal other couples joined them.

The spell was broken. I felt an enormous relief. What might have happened, I did not know, but I had the feeling that a time of danger had been safely passed. Surely nothing else would happen now.

Leila, too, felt release. She covered her face with her hands and Mike patted her shoulder as he might have patted a child. His look met mine over her head.

"What would she have done?" I asked and he knew I meant Catherine.

"Who knows? It's always different. She winds herself up and up—and sometimes somebody gets hurt. I'm glad you stopped her from hurting Leila."

I was still angry. "Why doesn't someone keep it from happening? Why doesn't someone stop it before it begins?"

Mike answered me curtly. "How? What do you do—lock her up?"

Leila turned on him, still shivering. "Don't talk like that! You don't understand. It's just that she's high-spirited. She's not dull like other people. It's fun for her to do dramatic things, and—and—"

"Oh, wake up!" said Mike rudely.

She stared at him for a moment of shock. Then she said, "I'm going inside," and walked away from us.

Mike would have gone after her, but I drew him back. "Let her go. She'll feel better by herself. I'm glad you spoke to her as you did. You're young enough to tell her off."

He grinned at me wryly. "She's only a kid. There's plenty of time for her to grow up and get over her crush on my brother. It's a good thing you've come here, Miss Abbott. Leila likes you."

I wasn't too sure she would continue to like me after tonight. I looked up at the gallery and saw that King was still there. Over the intervening space our glances met and he nodded to me in grim reassurance. He too knew that disaster had been averted. For the moment at least.

Behind us I heard a torch hiss furiously. Sudden drops of rain pelted my cheek, and overhead a patch of clouds had turned black and roiling, though the sky was still clear and starlit elsewhere, with a plump moon rising from the direction of St. John. As we scattered for shelter a gust struck the terrace and the flamboyant thrashed its umbrella top, setting scarlet petals adrift on the wind. Rain came down with tropical force, striking the tiles and spattering back, stinging my ankles as Mike hurried me toward the gallery.

Indoors Malcolm began to sing "Poinciana," the tune weaving hauntingly through the sounds of the downpour outside. Guests had returned to their dancing, moving in the center of the great hall. When Mike left me to look for his brother I turned my back on the scene and stood at one side of the glass doors, peering through at the terrace. A yard boy was extinguishing the hissing torches one by one, but those remaining threw a reflection of flame across wet stones, and all the while the flame tree—the poinciana—bowed to slashing rain, yielding up its blossoms and heavy seed pods. Even as I watched, the downpour lessened. Wind swept away the overhead clouds, and the night was bright again with a rising moon.

I slipped along a wall behind the tables and went upstairs unnoticed.

King stood alone at the open door to the gallery, still watching the scene outdoors as I had watched from downstairs. He turned as I reached the upper hall.

"Leila?" I asked softly.

He came toward me. "She's gone to her room."

I nodded. "That's best for now. I don't think she'll return to the party. What happened has upset her."

"Yes—I saw."

Hesitantly I ventured a question. "Isn't Catherine's behavior too extreme to be normal? Isn't it a—a sickness?"

"Probably. I've talked to a doctor or two about her. Perhaps there's some truth in that old Biblical idea of possession by evil spirits. I suppose we're all so possessed at times. We ask ourselves what got into us. But in a case like this, what can anyone do against the will of the person involved? I can't imagine Catherine in a psychiatrist's office when she thinks herself saner than any of us. She enjoys being the way she is. And until she puts herself across some dangerous line, no one can force her to anything. She's coming close to that now."

I was silent, suffering because he was suffering. From out of doors the rushing sound of the wind reached me, while nearer at hand party sounds drifted up from downstairs. Yet there in the hallway —at the heart of things—it was still and hushed. At the heart of my life.

I went into his arms to offer the only comfort I had to give, and he did not hold me away. For a few seconds time stopped around us and we were aware only of each other. How intensely I wanted the hurting of his arms about me, how willingly I gave my mouth to the hard pressure of his. There was no gentleness in him now.

Somewhere nearby a door opened and then closed softly. King let me go and we stepped apart, never entirely free in our love. The hall was quiet, all the doors tightly closed. I was afraid.

"Who was it?" I whispered.

He shook his head. "I don't know. Better go to your room now, darling. I'll get back to the party."

"When will you leave the house?" I asked him urgently. "Because you must leave soon—you must!"

He turned away from me without answering and I watched him go down the stairs.

A moment later I was in my room, with the door closed and my back against it, waiting for the sickening thud of my heart to quiet, for the heavy beat of my pulses to lessen. This could not go on. Either he must leave or I would have to. I wanted him openly, honorably, without hidden, guilty meetings, and I suspected that he wanted me in the same way. But Catherine stood between, governed by her own hysterical hating, and increasingly dangerous.

Gradually I quieted, gradually the room about me made itself known, so that small matters began to ask for my attention, informing me that all was not as I had left it. Both gallery doors had been closed when I went downstairs. Now one of them stood open, with bamboo-green draperies blowing out. When I went to fasten them back I found the cloth wet, as though they had been caught outside in the rain. The shower had struck this side of the house and while the wet floor of the gallery was already drying in the wind, the storm must have dashed a good deal of water against the house.

Thoughtfully I turned to look about the rest of the room, and found that the bed had been readied for the night by one of the maids. But a maid would not have tampered with the French doors as I had left them. I stepped to the bureau, puzzled, and the glass gave back the look of a woman bemused—gray eyes wide and troubled, lips parted, the wings of brown hair smoothly framing a slender face. As often before, I wondered how others saw me, what they really thought.

My face in the mirror seemed to lose its familiarity as I stared at it—as though it belonged to someone less vulnerable than I. The voice, when I spoke aloud, was mine, yet it was directed toward me from that more critical girl in the mirror.

"Be honest!" she challenged me. "Tell yourself the truth and learn how to accept it. You pulled down all the fences around you when Helen died. You stood out there in the open without protection and you fell in love with the first man who came along and was reasonably kind to you. If you've got any spunk at all you'd better face the fact that this has happened. He's lonely, and he's grateful to you and touched because you've tried to help his daughter. But you—you're in love with him! And there isn't anywhere to go from here. So what do you have to say for yourself now?"

I turned away from the accusation. There seemed no answer for me anywhere.

XIV

That dreadful night!

It was almost dawn and I sat in my room, troubling no longer to lock my doors, struggling to put my thoughts, my emotions, my understanding, into some sort of sensible form.

The sounds of people moving about on their weary duties had died away, though lights still burned across the driveway in the servants' area. There were no longer the sounds of a party—all that was long over, and even the memory of it was fading. In a little while the lights of Charlotte Amalie would dim and sunrise would streak the sky. If I sat here long enough, there would be a new day—with all its new and frightful problems to be faced.

At least I'd had a little sleep at the beginning of the night. Though even that was restless sleep because of what I had discovered there at my bureau when I first came back to my room. I do not mean merely the accusation which my own reflected face directed at me— but the fact that someone had come into my room and carefully searched a small portion of my possessions.

Over those years spent with my mother I had learned orderly habits. When two people live together and one of them drops her possessions carelessly about so that she never knows where anything is to be found, the other one usually becomes methodical to a fault. The weaker perhaps? Or, hopefully, the more considerate? At any rate I had learned to keep each article, not only in its appointed place but often in a certain order.

"Finicky," my mother said. "Old maidish." But these were words she used to protect her own feckless ways.

Tonight the habit served me well. I knew my powder box was not where I had left it. My comb and brush had been moved—though I could not see why, since they hid nothing. A maid might have done these things in dusting, but no one dusted at night, and they were not where I had put them when I went downstairs to the supper.

In the top drawer everything looked neat enough—but there were changes visible to my practiced eye.

The small padded case in which I kept my few pieces of jewelry had been carefully searched, and earrings, pins, and beads put back in a way I did not keep them. My stack of clean handkerchiefs in the top drawer had been looked through one by one, so that the edges were slightly askew, the stack moved slantwise from its corner. So it was through the two top drawers of the bureau. As far as I could tell, the lower two had not been touched. When I undressed and put my lingerie into the mesh bag I kept for laundry, I found the mouth of the bag turned round on its hook.

As I got into my pajamas I tried to figure out the puzzle. As far as I could tell, nothing had been taken—so no one had come to steal. I would have little of value for a thief, in any case. Whoever had gone through my possessions must have been looking for something specific. But what small thing—since it must be small if such places were searched—could I be presumed to have hidden? And why—why?

Perhaps this was another effort to frighten me away. But then it would surely not have been managed in so neat and secretive a manner. I could imagine Catherine coming to my room, hurling everything about vindictively, and leaving the upheaval for me to discover. But I would not expect of her this quiet seeking. A seeking that appeared not to be complete—so that perhaps the seeker would return and try again?

When I was ready for bed I turned off my lamp—and then decided that I did not like the dark. Tonight darkness seemed too lonely. I lit a match and touched it to one of the hurricane candles cupped in heavy glass, and got into bed, pulling up sheet and light blanket to shut out the faint eerie glow. Downstairs the party was still noisy, the music tireless. Malcolm seemed to be repeating his repertoire, but he did not sing again the "Song for Columbella" that had so angered Catherine.

From the next room—Leila's room—I heard no sound and I hoped she was asleep. The young could be hurt so easily. There was no way in which I could convince Leila that her painful feeling for Steve O'Neill would suddenly be gone overnight and she would be wholeheartedly interested in someone new, and perhaps closer to her own age. Change was the proper order of the day for the young. Even Leila's worship of her mother was something she might well throw off, escape from, in the very near future. If only there was time to wait for this and nothing happened in the meantime to damage her beyond repair.

As I lay there my thoughts began to turn from Leila to myself and a strange, drowsy comfort came over me. As sleep began its gentle encroachment and my breathing grew more regular, a sense of warm happiness began to spread through me. Perhaps there was a hint of danger and excitement laced through it, but these were not unpleasant. I slipped into a dream in which I was coasting down a mountainside on a wild toboggan ride—yet I had no fear of the probable crash at the bottom. I knew only that someone sat behind me, guiding and holding me safely, so that I need not be afraid. I had only to relax, to cease the struggling that possessed me when I was wide awake. It was a pleasant way to fall into deep sleep.

My awakening came with a jerking suddenness that was far from pleasant. I sat up and stared at the chair across from the foot of my bed, but no golden-haired woman in a flame-colored dress sat there smoking. The wick burned low in its glass and the room seemed hot and humid.

Somewhere down the hill a dog barked furiously, steadily, and I suppose this was the sound which awakened me. Now that I was fully roused, the feeling that something was amiss—if not in this room then somewhere in the house—was so strong that I knew I would not sleep again until I had tried to determine the source of my uneasiness.

I flung on some clothes, slipped my feet into walking shoes, and went out on the gallery. The garage and driveway areas were dark and quiet. The last car had left the hill long ago and the servants were alseep by now. The moon had begun its downward movement in the sky, but it was still large and full and very bright. Far below, Magens Bay lay like an irregular silver platter, partially rimmed in the wild beauty of its protected park.

Slowly I walked along the side gallery toward the front of the house. Leila's outer door stood ajar and I paused to listen for a moment, but the rushing sound of the wind outside hid anything so soft as a sleeper's breathing. At least her room seemed innocent of restless tossing. Maud's room was dark, with no light to be glimpsed behind shutters, though I knew she sometimes stayed up very late at night reading.

From the front gallery I could stand in the shadow of climbing bougainvillea and look down upon the terrace. There were still patches of wet, as though more showers had fallen during the night. No wavering torch flares lighted the scene; only the moon lent a touch of silver to scattered pools of water. Here and there puffed clouds promised more showers and the wind seemed stronger than before—almost a gale. It tried to blow me along the gallery and I held to the cold iron rail, resisting its thrust.

My sense of something being wrong had not been lessened by rising and moving about. How quiet the night seemed—and how noisy! The trees dripped. Night insects kept up an incessant clamor from every bush and tree, and the wind rustled through branches without cease. Yet there was a void of human sounds. What stars could be seen were very bright. Bright and close—and deadly cold. In the tropic night I shivered and was dreadfully afraid.

Although nothing stirred within my line of vision and though lights were scattered and few in the sleeping town, I had the feeling that *something* was up and about. The moonlight had a wickedly greenish cast to my receptive senses—like the colors of some illustration for a story of dread and mystery.

Fanciful, fanciful! I could almost hear my mother's voice, but the fancy remained. Whatever antennae of perception I possessed were tuned to some quality of the night that I could not see or hear or understand. I told myself that quiet was not ominous, that dreadful deeds were not done in silence. Wicked acts needed movement and sound. Yet only the wind rushed across the island and flung itself out to sea, hurrying, hurrying because there were other islands it must brush in its breathless journey before the night was done and the sun came blazing up from the Caribbean.

The movement I sought became suddenly real and my hands tightened on the rail. Someone burst upon the terrace from the direction of the tropical forest. In the fluid line of Leila's running she betrayed herself—her entire body spoke of the fear and desperation that drove her. She still wore her yellow dress—greenish now in the wet shine of the terrace—as if she had not gone to bed at all, and as I watched she ran into the house, disappearing from view beneath me.

Moving quickly, softly, I ran along the gallery and back to my room. When I went through and opened my hall door I was in time to meet Leila as she came running up the stairs terror-driven. At once she clasped my wrist and pulled me into her room, shutting the door. Outside it began to rain again—another quick, heavy shower, pounding upon roof and gallery, pouring water down the waiting catchments of St. Thomas, to drain into echoing cisterns underground. Inside there was only the sound of a girl gasping out words while I strove frantically to understand what she was trying to tell me.

She had not let go of me, and she almost pummeled me in an astonishing mixture of anger and entreaty.

"It's your fault and you've got to stop him! Dad's down in the lookout clearing with Cathy. They've had a frightful quarrel and I think he's going to kill her."

I was on my way downstairs before she stopped speaking, alarm ringing along every nerve.

The room below was quiet and empty—dark, with the night pressing against glass at either end, the door to the terrace open. I ran the length of the room toward a rack near the door, where raincoats and beach coats were kept, with flashlights on a nearby shelf.

My hands fumbled over the hooks and I felt the coarse material of the enveloping burnoose Catherine liked to wear. It was damp to my touch and my hands snatched up a plastic cape and reached for a flashlight. Putting the cape around me as I ran, I hurried down the terrace steps and toward the path through the woods. Already the last shower had stopped and shrubbery dripped around me as I ran beneath the branches of the flamboyant, catching the spattering of drops on the slick surface of the cape.

Shiny-wet tree boles sprang up about me as I started into the forest. There were patches of mud and in my haste I slipped and nearly fell, catching myself against the rough wet trunk of a tree. Scarcely losing a moment, I went on and my beam of light ran ahead, picking out turns of the path amidst the darkly crowding growth. There was a smell of wet foliage and earth, laced by the penetrating sweetness of jasmine and cereus—a sweetness that brought Catherine's perfume sickeningly to mind.

Still there was no sound anywhere, except the dank dripping of the trees. Ahead of my stumbling feet the black, twisted bole of a tree protruded into my path, its wet bark like glistening black satin in the shine of the torch. In relief, I saw that this was the tree which marked the way to the clearing, and I knew it had taken me only moments to get there. I found my way around the tree, sweeping the light beam ahead, so that the green fruit of the huge mango sprang into vivid color.

The clearing was empty. I had surely taken no more than two or three minutes since Leila's words had sent me on my way, but whoever had been here was gone. How had the quarrel ended?

I stood still to let my thudding heart quiet. The showers had blown away in the sudden island manner, and moonlight shone white on the empty marble bench where I had sat talking to King. Across wet earth and grass the wooden rail guarded the lookout place.

The wooden rail!

My heart lurched again and I stepped closer, sending the flash beam along the barrier. It was not as it had been. A portion of railing had broken through like kindling and hung outward into empty space, the raw ends sharp and jagged. I swung the light down toward the catchment, but in that vast, steep spread the beam was quickly lost and ineffectual. I did not need it, however, for the clouds had moved on and moonlight touched the stone slide, revealing the black humps of rock that protruded part way down. Three black humps. Three!

I remembered only two protrusions of rock interrupting the smooth downward flow of the catchment. Yet now there was a third black huddle, too far away for my flashlight to reach, too undefined to be made out clearly by moonlight alone.

Two people had quarreled here—furiously, according to Leila. Now one was gone, the railing broken through—and something sprawled down there upon the catchment. Which one—Catherine or King?

I called out frantically, but the dark mass upon the stone did not move and there was no answer. I considered kicking off my shoes, letting myself through the broken space, crawling down the steep stone slide. But even if I managed without falling, I would be of no use once I was there and time would be wasted.

I ran from that dreadful place and back toward the house. In spite of slippery spots and sharp turns of the path, I ran. Once or twice I had the horrid feeling that Catherine might step out from the black tangle on either side to catch me by the arm and stop me from getting help. Sometimes it seemed that this had really happened, for the very trees reached rain-laden branches to grasp at me, to catch at my hair and slap wetly across my face and body.

But the beam rushed ahead, showing me the way, and I reached the terrace driven by a terror that winged my heels. On the flagstone my shoes made a noisy clatter, and just as I reached the steps to the gallery a light went on inside and Edith Stair came to look out as she had done on my first arrival at the house. As I ran toward her, out of breath, unable for a moment to speak, I noticed that she too was fully dressed.

She came down the steps and when I would have cried out my alarm she grasped me by the arm. "Hush! Don't waken the house. Just tell me what has happened—what has frightened you?"

Under the pressure of her hand I managed to steady myself, and as I did so the first awareness of a need for caution roused itself in me.

"There's been an—an accident!" I cried. "The railing down at the lookout point has broken through and I—I think someone has fallen down the catchment."

She stared at me, whether in disbelief or challenge I could not tell. Then she said, "I'll call King," and ran inside and up the stairs.

I walked into the big hall where a light now burned, trying hard to get myself in hand. The import of what lay behind that broken rail was beginning to penetrate my sheer fright. It was far less likely that Catherine could have pushed King through the railing than that he might, in his fury, have flung her down from the height. Until I knew what had really happened, I must be careful about what I blurted out.

Absently I noted that down the room near the stairs a line of light shone beneath the door to Alex's study—so he must still be up.

Edith came running downstairs almost at once. "King's not in his room. Nor is Catherine in hers. Their beds haven't been slept in!"

The door where the pencil line of light glowed was pulled open and Alex came out. He wore night clothes and seemed faintly elegant in a dressing gown of maroon silk over gray pajamas.

Edith rushed to him. "Miss Abbott has been in the garden. She says the wooden rail is broken through and someone has fallen down the catchment. Neither King nor Catherine is upstairs."

Alex gave me a sharp look and took the flashlight from my hand. Then he ran across the terrace in the direction of the path. Edith went after him and I followed. Even though my knees had a tendency to buckle, I had to know what was down there.

Alex reached the clearing first and kicked off his slippers before he lowered himself through the opening in the rail, dropping lightly to the top stones of the slide. There he started down backward in his bare feet, clinging to crevices with his fingers, moving surely and quickly. When he neared the mounds that interrupted the smooth flow of stone, he turned the flash beam upon the third dark huddle that lay humped beside the other two. At once a gleam of bright red shocked my vision.

Beside me, Edith drew in her breath in a gasp. "It's Catherine!"

The light moved along the inert shape and I glimpsed the gold of loosened hair fanned out upon wet stone. Alex stayed a few moments, bending above her. Then he extinguished the light and climbed up the steep slope to the top, where Edith helped to pull him through the broken rail to the clearing.

When he stood up I saw how shaken he was, how grim. "She's

dead. I can't bring her up alone. We'll have to get help—call the police."

"The police!" Edith wailed. "Why not the doctor, the hospital?"

"Those also," Alex agreed. "But first the police. We don't know how this happened and it's better to have everything in the clear."

He had turned on the torch again, and I saw by its indirect illumination the look that passed between husband and wife. A look that seemed both searching and defensive, as though each probed what the other might be thinking, yet by mutual agreement did not speak.

Edith reached out almost absently to touch the splintered rail. When she held up her fingers there was a dusting of wood powder upon them.

"The rail was rotten," she said. "There are always termites. Anyone who leaned against it could have gone through."

Alex started for the house and we followed him along the narrow pathway.

Where was King now? I wondered. And what was I to say when someone asked me why I had gone down to the woods? If only Leila would stay in her room, say nothing—at least until I'd had time to talk to Maud. Or to King.

As we reached the terrace and started up the steps Edith suddenly took my arm and I realized that she was trembling in reaction and shock. When we reached the main hall Alex went directly to the phone while Edith stood in the center of the room, plucking at her fingers, a strange look of growing realization in her eyes.

"I can't believe it," she said. "Catherine is dead." And then, as though the truth was at last coming home to her, "My sister Catherine is dead."

I did not like the tinge of yellow in her skin, or the way in which she almost savored the words she spoke. I moved away, looking about the room. Dishes and food had long since been cleared off, but the tables still wore their lace cloths, and down the center of each lay red blossoms, curling at the edges, turning brown—hibiscus, bougainvillea, flamboyant clusters, all wilting and ugly, where they had been so lovely last night.

"Someone must tell Mother," Edith said, making an effort to pull herself together. "And Leila."

I spoke quickly. "Let the child sleep. There will be time enough to break this to her in the morning."

As soon as I could I would get upstairs to Leila, I thought. And then what? The girl would never be silent once she knew what had happened to Catherine. Yet all my guilty thoughts were moving in one direction—blindly to the protection of Kingdon Drew. If he had played any part in this, then he would return and say so. No other action would be possible for a man like King. But if he had indeed flung Catherine to her death—then was I not to blame, as Leila had claimed? Had I not, by my very presence and actions, my response to him, driven King to some final, dreadful action? If that was so, then I must help him in any way I could, until he was ready to speak. He would not run away—this I knew.

Edith put up a finger to still the twitching of her left eyelid. "Very well," she said. "But Mother must be told now. She'll know what to do. She'll take charge. I—I can't cope with anything like this."

At the far end of the hall I could hear Alex on the phone, explaining, giving what details he could, speaking in an even, colorless tone. As I stood listening a phrase began to repeat itself in my mind, and the haunting fragment of a tune.

> Up on the island, bright in the sun,
> Columbella's golden days be done.

They were done indeed, as the song had promised. I looked at brown poinciana petals and shivered. Catherine was gone, but the evil she had created was very much here and present, and we would not, I thought, be free of it—perhaps never in our lives.

XV

Maud Hampden looked white and ill when she came downstairs, but she rallied to meet the demands of the moment, and Edith leaned upon her mother's greater strength. Alex had mixed himself a stiff drink and I sensed that he was keeping himself in hand—and, as always, on guard. How he felt about Catherine I did not know, and behind the screen of his neat, glossy beard he betrayed nothing of whatever emotion he might be feeling.

No one needed me for anything and I pushed a chair into a shadowy corner near the door to the terrace and sat there watching. There had been no sign of Leila, no sound from her room, and I glanced fearfully at the stairs from time to time, ready to move in her direction if she appeared, still postponing the moment when I must go up to her room. Once Leila knew that Catherine was dead, there would be the problem of keeping her quiet until King could appear and speak for himself. Maud, I thought, might help me in this effort—but there was no chance to speak with her alone.

I could do nothing except watch—and wait for King to come home. Someone said that his car was still in the garage. Indeed, all the cars were there. The servants were up and moving about by now, wide-eyed and fearful, whispering among themselves. Maud had a good many orders to give, as though she knew it was best for everyone to be occupied. But she had forgotten me. I was an outsider, and I had nothing to do but think.

The police officer—a Captain Osborn—was a gentle-mannered, courteous, dark-skinned man with an air of quiet authority and a slightly formal way of speaking. Accompanied by the doctor and the ambulance men from the hospital, he went off to the garden.

After a long interval they brought Catherine to the house and laid her upon the couch on the lower gallery. When the doctor had completed his examination she was covered with a sheet and Noreen was left, weeping, to guard her, while the others came inside.

The doctor told Maud and the police officer that Mrs. Drew must have leaned against the rail and gone through to roll down the catchment. She had struck both her face and the back of her head as she fell, and rolled with force against the rock that stopped her full descent to the bottom. Either of these blows might have fractured her skull and killed her. Only an autopsy would tell.

Further arrangements were being made as to where to take her, and Captain Osborn was asking courteous but probing questions in order to reconstruct what had happened. I was almost the first to be questioned—having sounded the alarm—and I was asked how I happened to go down to the clearing at such a time, and while it was raining.

I could only plead the silly whim of a female who was excited after a party and could not sleep. I never minded rain, I told him—which was true enough—and I wanted to see what a tropical island was like after a shower. I managed to keep Leila and King out of my account, and that was all I cared about at the moment. Probably a good many people with much less to conceal than I had silly reasons for silly behavior, and Captain Osborn accepted my explanation gently and went on to the more important matter of King's whereabouts.

It was at this point that King himself walked into the house, to look about in apparent astonishment at the lights and activity, at the group of people gathered in the living area. Once he had stepped into the room, I had eyes for no one else, and I saw the dazed expression he wore when Captain Osborn told him of Catherine's death. It was as if, like Edith, he could not believe in it—and there was something here I could not understand.

Nothing was said of angry voices or a possible quarrel between King and Catherine. If others in the house besides Leila had heard, or if they guessed what had happened, they were not saying. The probing was apparently aimed toward searching out a cause of accident, and everyone lent himself to this theory—Maud, Alex, even Edith in the little she said. The family, I suspected, had closed in a solid front to protect one of their own, if that should be necessary.

About King, I could not tell. I had thought he might well come striding into the house to admit his part in what had happened at once, and explain exactly what had occurred. He had done nothing of the kind—and this I did not understand. Across the room, Alex stood a little apart, watching King with a fixed, conjectural stare that I did not like, and I wished King would see and answer it. But his air of daze and disbelief continued, and he offered nothing.

"Then it is your custom, Mr. Drew," Captain Osborn was saying in his quiet, formal manner, "to take the night air in long walks along the mountaintop after the sun has set? Thus it is natural that you were not about the premises when this sad thing occurred?"

"I walk a lot at night," King said.

Maud came to stand beside him and she put a hand on his arm. "It was an accident, my dear. A dreadful accident. That was Catherine's favorite spot for mooning. We all know she loved to haunt that place at night. The rail had rotted and it broke under her weight. This is a terrible thing and how we are to bear with it I don't know. But we must try. *You* must try."

This seemed a false note and I looked at her in surprise. Maud would be realist enough to know that once the shock of sudden death was over, everyone might come to live quite comfortably without Catherine. Everyone except Leila. I wondered at her words until it came to me that if King had been about to say anything more, Maud had checked him surely and effectively. What she had done reminded me of the look Edith and Alex had exchanged down in the clearing. There seemed indeed a strengthening of family solidarity in evidence. Yet I could not believe that King was the man to lean upon such protection. If Leila had told the truth about what she had seen and heard, then there did not seem any reason for King's dazed disbelief. I was right in keeping still, I thought. I must talk to Leila again, question her more carefully when she was less excited.

The time element seemed to baffle the captain. King had said he did not remember when he had left the house, and I was vague about the hour when I had started my sleepless roaming. In like manner, no one seemed to know when Catherine had gone outside and down through the tropical garden. Her red dress was soaking wet, but there had been several showers, and she might have been outdoors for a time before the accident. One thing seemed certain—she had been found shortly after her death and could not have lain for long on the steep catchment with rain streaming over her, washing away all stains of blood. This I could have corroborated myself. Very few minutes had elapsed from the time when Leila had seen her mother and father quarreling, and the time when I had rushed down to the clearing.

Through all the talk and questioning I continued to sit in my chair near the terrace door, struggling futilely with the puzzle that King's behavior raised in my mind, and wondering with some apprehension what could be keeping Leila so quiet upstairs.

It was there Noreen found me. She appeared suddenly outside

the doorway and cast a frightened look at the group centering about the captain. When she discovered me close at hand she spoke urgently.

"Missy, missy—come to me."

I knew the vernacular by now—"to" for "with"—and her tone of alarm brought me quickly from my chair.

She made a frightened gesture as I hurried out the door and I saw at once what had alarmed her.

Beside the couch where Catherine lay, stood Leila, a cotton plaid robe tied over her night clothes. Apparently she had come down the back stairs. She had flung aside the sheet which covered her mother and was staring down at the slender body in its flame-colored dress, staring at wet, loose-flung hair, and the cruelly bruised face. I noted absently that no golden columbella hung from its chain upon Catherine's breast, and that there was a bruise upon her bare arm, where King had grasped it earlier that evening, to swing her away from me. A bruise that was a precursor of so much worse to come? At the same hands? I wondered miserably.

But it was the girl who held my attention now. Leila stood frozen with shock, and her pain seemed my own. I spoke her name, but though she must have heard me, she did not look away from her mother's face.

"That dog down the hill was barking tonight," she said. "The island people say a dog is a prophet."

Noreen made a soft, frightened moan, and I gestured her to go back to the house and leave us alone. Then I moved quickly to pull the sheet into place, covering that cruelly wounded face from view. I heard my own voice speaking almost without volition, repeating the words I had heard Maud say.

"It was an accident, Leila dear. An accident. She fell through the railing down at the lookout point."

Leila flung me a quick, scornful glance, and then cried out in terror. "Look—look!"

I looked and saw the spreading scarlet stain upon the white sheet, while my own breath almost stopped in horror. Then I understood.

"It's the red dye from her dress," I said. "Those ruffles are staining the sheet."

Leila began to shiver uncontrollably, but when I would have put an arm about her to draw her away, she snatched herself from my grasp.

"It's my fault!" she cried. "It's my fault that Cathy is dead! I should have stopped him. But I ran back to the house—I talked to *you!* How could I have told you, when I know you wanted her dead! I should have known you'd do nothing to help her!"

Her words shocked and alarmed me. I dared not let them pass. There was no time for gentle sympathy now and I took her by the shoulders and shook her as hard as I could.

"Stop it!" I cried. "You've got to come to your senses. You mustn't say such things. Whether you like it or not, you'll have to grow up now and be a woman."

Her brown eyes that I had seen so warmly affectionate, stared at me with hatred, but her body went limp in my hands and something of her reckless fury died away.

"Listen to me," I said. "There's a policeman in the house questioning your father. So far he doesn't know there was a quarrel between your father and mother—*if* there really was. If you rush in there mindlessly without thinking of the consequences, you may do your father irrevocable harm."

She caught at just one word. "A policeman? Then I'll go talk to him now. I'll tell him—"

"Tell him what?" I broke in. "That you saw your father fling Catherine down the catchment? Is that what you saw?"

She stared at me in sudden silence, hating me, fighting me with all her will. Then she turned away, no longer shivering, and walked with quiet dignity through the open door into the big lighted room. I went with her despairingly.

King was the first to see her. He stopped in the middle of whatever he was saying to Captain Osborn, and took a step toward his daughter, put out his hand. She ignored him as if she did not know he was there, and went directly into her grandmother's arms.

"Oh, Gran!" she whispered. "Gran, help me! Help me!"

The old woman held the girl to her, and each seemed to lean upon the other, their cheeks together, their tears mingling. It was the doctor who came to take charge, drawing Leila gently from the old lady's arms.

"Let's get her upstairs," he said to Edith, who came stiffly to help.

Leila reached out to her grandmother. "Gran—I want to talk to you. Please, Gran!"

But Maud Hampden had dropped into a nearby chair, able to bear no more. "Tomorrow, darling," she said weakly, her cheeks still wet with tears she had not shed till now. "Tomorrow we'll talk. This isn't the time now."

Edith took the girl by the arm, and at her aunt's cold touch Leila straightened and walked toward the stairs beside the doctor. She went straight past her father, not looking at him, not speaking.

Maud remembered me then. "Please go with her, Jessica. Help her."

"She doesn't want me now," I said. "It's better if I stay away from her for a little while," and I slipped away to my shadowed chair near the door.

With an effort Maud pulled herself to her feet. "I can't bear any more tragedy tonight. I've used myself up. Captain Osborn, do you mind if I go to my room?"

Clearly the police officer knew Maud Hampden of old and would ask nothing beyond her strength at so difficult a time. He said good night with quiet consideration and let her go.

King had stood watching his daughter go upstairs with Edith and the doctor, the same bewilderment in his eyes that I had seen earlier. Now he too spoke to Catherine's mother, rousing himself.

"I'll see to whatever needs to be done, Maud dear. Don't worry about anything—I'll manage."

Gradually the room emptied. Alex went unobtrusively away. He had said little during the questioning, merely stating that he had remained in his study long after the party was over, and had no idea when Catherine might have come downstairs.

When Catherine's body had been taken away, the doctor left, and so did Captain Osborn, after mentioning something about an inquest to King. At last only King and I were left. I sat in my corner, waiting, though I was not altogether sure for what. I knew only that I could not go back to my room until I had spoken to him.

At length King saw me there and came to draw me to my feet. "Go to bed," he said gently. "There's nothing more to be done now. Tomorrow Leila will need all the help you can give her."

Remembering how thoroughly Leila had blamed and rejected me, I did not know whether this was so. Now I had to seize my chance to speak to King, even though speaking meant to hurt him more where Leila was concerned.

"There's something you have to know," I said hastily, blurting out the words, sparing him nothing. "Leila heard you quarreling with Catherine. She went down to the clearing and saw you with her there. She was frightened and ran away, but she believes that her mother died on the catchment because of—you."

"So that's the reason," he said heavily, and I knew he was remembering how Leila had walked past his outstretched hand, not choosing to see him.

"Tomorrow you can tell her the truth!" Again I was blurting out words. "You can make her understand that it was only a quarrel—that you weren't to blame for Catherine's fall." I waited eagerly for his agreement, longing for reassurance.

His look seemed suddenly cold. "I am probably responsible enough for what happened," he said. "It's quite possible that she died at my hands."

I could only echo his words in bewilderment. " 'Probably responsible'? 'Possible that she died'? What do you mean?"

"I'm not sure what happened," he told me curtly, and went off to the kitchen to give final orders to the servants and send them back to bed.

He would not talk to me now, I knew, and I climbed the stairs slowly, more frightened than before. I had expected him to deny or admit. I had not expected this curious claim that he did not know what had happened.

When I reached my room I found that the hour was past three-thirty. Once more I got ready for bed. But when I went to put my clothes away in the closet I found Catherine's pale green negligee hanging there. I did not need to touch it to catch the odor of water lily, and the very scent made me a little ill. I carried the soft, clinging thing into the hall and left it there, draped over the upper rail of the stairs. I could not bear to sleep with it in my room—if there could possibly be any sleeping left to me in what remained of the dark hours.

As I got into bed I knew that no green-eyed woman would come through my doors to sit smoking and watching me while I slept. Yet there was no reassurance in the thought and I was not even sure that it was true.

The moment I closed my eyes pictures moved behind the lids and would not be still. I could see Catherine on the terrace, scarlet ruffles flaring at her knees, the columbella dancing on her breast. The words of the song which so displeased her ran mockingly, endlessly through my mind.

How surely she must have been moving toward some danger that drew and enticed her—because she liked to be frightened, even while she hated pain? Had she, after all, reached the goal she had been so recklessly seeking? I remembered Maud's words about her liking for high places. In the end the danger had been real, and the fall had been from a very high place.

I could not believe that it was, as Maud claimed, an accident and I wondered if Maud believed that herself. Catherine had engendered too much hate, she had been involved in too much trickery to have escaped violent retribution forever.

But at whose hands had she died? Whose—if King for some strange reason was not sure?

He had been there with her. Yet something had held him back, kept him from going at once to tell Captain Osborn the truth as I had expected him to do. Was he trying to protect Leila from the results of so great a tragedy? Or even to protect me? I rejected the last thought swiftly. There was enough of guilt in this for me without that. I had come to detest Catherine. I had truly wished her out of King's life—and Leila's. So how much of this unexpressed, unaccepted feeling had I managed to convey to him? How close to violence had he been driven because of me?

I tossed in self-torment and could not sleep, while all through my troubled thoughts ran the new, dreadful realization that had come to me about King's daughter. Where Catherine had been the enemy before—now her young daughter might very well have stepped into that same role, holding over her father's head the power of life or death. Tonight she had not spoken out. Perhaps the things I had said to her while she stood beside her mother's body had held her back. But for how long?

Suddenly I remembered something—and understood. King had held me in his arms and kissed me in the hallway last night. Somewhere in the upper part of the house a door had opened and closed softly. Now I knew who had seen us there together—it was Catherine's daughter, Leila.

XVI

In the morning I awakened after an hour or two of sudden, exhausted sleep. It was a strange, slow awakening in which I did not at first know where I was, or scarcely who I was, but lay enveloped without thought in a warm sense of all-pervading joy. I lay quiet and was happy. Though I did not know why until around the bright outer limits of this quiet bliss a darkness began to intrude, curling in from the edges, creeping toward my consciousness until all the dreadful events of the night swept back and I remembered everything.

Catherine was dead. She had been an evil woman who had blighted all that was good and decent around her, yet the cost of a human life was too great a penalty to pay and with full remembrance I could no longer be childishly, senselessly happy.

With full awakening came awareness. Foolish relief gave way to even deeper anxiety. Catherine was gone, it was true, but in many ways everything was worse than before, and not one of us was free of the blight she had set into effect, not only by living, but by her very dying.

Now I remembered all of last night, and I got hastily out of bed. Too many things remained not only unsettled and unsolved, but alive with immediate threat.

When I'd taken a quick shower and dressed I opened my door, meaning to look for Leila. As I did so Edith came out of Leila's room and stood for a moment with the closed door behind her back, unaware of my presence. I could see her face and the sight surprised me. Here was no tense, trembling, frightened woman, but someone bolder than I had dreamed Edith could be. Almost overnight her face seemed to have filled out, its lines lifting into what must pass for her as a semblance of well-being. I understood, since I'd felt the same thing—with the difference that my own relief had not held once I was fully awake. Here, however, was a woman to whom hope had returned.

It seemed indecent to stare and I spoke, asking about Leila. At once her expression grew more guarded, yet relief lingered in her manner and she made fewer nervous movements with her hands and eyes.

"The child is up," she told me curtly. "I just went in to bring her some breakfast, though I don't think she'll eat it."

"I'll look in on her," I said. "How is your mother?"

"Taking charge," Edith said dryly.

She moved toward the stairs, leaving me to my own devices, and I saw her stop beside Catherine's negligee, still lying where I had tossed it over the rail early this morning. She snatched it up with what seemed an air of triumph, to carry it away downstairs, and I had the feeling that the gown would now find its way into the possession of maid or cook.

When Edith had gone I tapped on Leila's door. Without asking who was there, she called, "Come in," listlessly. I opened the door and found her standing with her back to me, looking out upon a morning bright with sunshine and no trace of rain. She wore shorts and a rumpled blouse and Japanese sandals.

"I hope you could sleep a little," I said.

At the sound of my voice she turned and her sorrowful look, the marks of tears on her cheeks, the dark smudges beneath her eyes were painful to see.

"What do you want?" she demanded in a tone that told me at once that her feeling toward me had not eased. My conceit of last night had been true—Leila was now the enemy. Yet to me, a dear enemy, whom I could not turn against or abandon to her own dark thoughts.

"I'd like to talk with you," I said, and moved toward the untouched breakfast tray. "There's enough here for two. May I share it with you?" I was scarcely hungry, but I wanted her to eat.

Without waiting for permission I drew up a chair and sat down, while she watched me in the silence of antagonism.

"What can we possibly say to each other?" she asked at last.

The only approach was a direct one, and I made it. "I'm glad you didn't tell Captain Osborn anything last night that might have made matters more difficult for your father. It was sensible to wait. If there is anything the police should know, your father has the right to tell them himself."

"As if he would!" Leila cried. "My father is a—a—"

I spoke sharply. "Don't say what you're thinking. It isn't true. Don't say anything you'll be sorry for later."

She stood looking at me as I sat before the tray, and I was aware of something subtly changed about her this morning. This was a different girl from the Leila of yesterday, not only because she had suffered the tragic loss of her mother, but in some other, stranger way. I knew I must find my new course with caution.

She came a little closer to me, though warily, like some prowling creature that stalked its prey.

"You don't have to pretend with me," she said. "I know what you want, and you needn't think I'm going to keep quiet forever and help you get it."

The look of her young, ravaged face broke my heart—yet I knew she would accept no gentleness, no sympathy from me. Besides, she spelled danger.

"What do you think I want?" I asked.

She tossed her head and I was reminded faintly of Catherine. "My father, of course! You both wanted to be free of Cathy so you could have each other. Didn't you? Catherine said you were trying to take Dad away from her—and now I know how right she was."

I busied myself buttering a piece of toast and took my time about answering her. There was no answer, really, because there were half truths in what she said—yet, for all our sakes, I had to try.

"Do you think it was possible to take from your mother what she had thrown away a long time before I came here?"

With a grimace of rejection Leila flung herself across the bed. "What I'm going to do now," she told me, "is to see that you and my father never have each other—never!"

"Why don't you talk to your grandmother about all this?" I said. "Tell her whatever it is you think you know, and ask her to help you."

"I tried that last night, but she didn't want to hear me. It's no good anyway. She always thinks of the family first and she'll try to keep everything quiet so as to protect Dad and the family name. I suppose he'll take her protection and—and what happened to Cathy will be passed off as an accident. That is, it will be unless I tell the truth."

"What is the truth?" I persisted.

She sat up on the bed to stare at me. "That Cathy is dead, of course. That my father killed her. Because of you. And that I'm to blame for what happened because I didn't do anything while there was still time."

I could only repeat what I had asked her last night. "Then you saw him fling her down the catchment? You actually saw him do that?"

"I didn't have to see it! It must have happened. They were fighting each other—and now she—she's dead." Leila's voice broke. "So what else could have happened?"

"I don't know," I admitted. "But I saw how your father looked when he came back to the house last night and learned about your mother. And if ever I've seen anyone stunned and shocked—it was he. I think he truly doesn't know what happened. And if that's so, then he can't be wholly to blame."

For an instant hope seemed to flash through her pain and despair, and I pressed my advantage quickly.

"You told me you were outside last night when you heard them quarreling. Did you see anyone else at the time?"

"Only Uncle Alex," she said.

I would have pursued that with eager questioning, but she began to think aloud about what had happened, moving step by step, and I did not want to stop her flow of remembering.

"First Cathy came outside. It was long after the party was over, but she said she couldn't sleep—just as I couldn't sleep. We've always been a night-prowling sort of family, I guess. She wasn't pleased to find me sitting there on the gallery couch, and she tried to send me back to bed. But I had a feeling she had come outside to meet someone, because she was all keyed up. I was curious, so when she went to walk in the woods I stayed where I was."

Leila closed her eyes and I saw her shiver. After a moment she went on.

"That was when Dad came out on the gallery. I could tell by the way he moved that he was still furious over what happened at the party—and about the scare Cathy gave you with the car. I didn't speak to him, and he didn't see me there. He stood on the terrace, staring off toward the lights of the harbor. While he was there Uncle Alex came to the door. I was sitting in the dark and he didn't see me, but he saw Dad. He waited for a few minutes watching him. Then he went back inside the house."

I asked a question. "How was your uncle dressed?"

"Why—in that silky light suit he had on at the party. What difference does it make?"

"Probably none," I said.

She was pondering something, biting her lip. "I think maybe Cathy went down to the clearing to meet Uncle Alex. She said something about teaching Aunt Edith a lesson, and I know she had missed out on catching him alone earlier. When he went to Aunt Edith's workroom in that little cookhouse building, you were there, so she had no chance to talk to him alone. She was mad about that. It was just another thing against you."

I was learning a good deal, and the enigma of Alex Stair seemed more puzzling than ever.

"What did your uncle do when he came outside?" I asked.

"Nothing. He saw Dad on the terrace and I suppose he changed his mind about seeing Cathy. When he went inside I didn't see him again till afterward. Cathy must have got tired of waiting for him because she came back to the terrace and found Dad there. That's when they started quarreling. I couldn't catch the words—just their low, angry voices, as though they were trying not to let the house hear what they said. I think Cathy was taunting him about something, trying to make him wild, the way she liked to do. Finally he reached out and caught her by the arm, but she pulled away and ran back into the woods. She didn't come out again, so she must have gone to the clearing."

"Then you didn't actually see your father with her down there at all?" I said, hope suddenly rising.

"Oh, yes, I did! He must have stayed on the terrace for another ten minutes, smoking and walking up and down as though he was in a rage and trying to get himself in hand. Then he started into the woods after her. I had to see what he meant to do, so I followed through the wet trees all the way to the clearing. When I got there he was shaking her—choking her, maybe. I was horribly frightened. I shouldn't have run away—but I did. I did! And because I did, Cathy is dead."

For all her anguished recital, Leila seemed calmer now, more intently thoughtful. There was no comfort I could offer, either to her or to myself. I set down the glass of orange juice I had picked up, unable to swallow a mouthful.

"I remember how Cathy looked when she came out on the gallery while I was sitting there," Leila said. "I remember everything about her. I remember what she was carrying."

Her own words seemed to remind her of something, for she rolled suddenly off the bed and stood up.

"I'm going outside. There's something I want to look for."

She hardly seemed to notice when I followed her downstairs. When she stepped out upon the lower gallery I was close behind. The couch where Catherine's body had lain was empty now. Red dye had stained its coverings and Leila stood looking down at them for a long moment. Then she bent and touched the red stains with a finger.

"Poor Columbella," she said.

I wanted to draw her away from the sight of that couch with its stained coverings, but I dared make no move, lest she run away from me entirely.

Held there by a terrible fascination, she went on, tormenting herself with memory. "I saw her face last night. Her forehead. Cathy hated to be hurt, and it must have hurt dreadfully when she fell. How awful if she lay out there in the rain suffering and helpless, with no one to save her. Oh, how could he—how could he! He loved her once—I know he did. And she always loved him. That was what made her behave in such an awful way."

Again she was speaking half truths and there was nothing I dared say in answer. I could only attempt distraction.

"Last night when they put her there she was no longer wearing the columbella locket," I said. "I wonder where it is."

My words served better as a distraction than I intended, for she turned upon me in sudden fury. "Yes—where is it? If it's down there lying on the ground, I want it. It belongs to me now. But there's something else I want to find as well. Something Cathy brought with her when she came outside last night. She was holding it in her hands all the time she was talking to Dad. And if—if he took it from her—"

There was a look of such horror in her eyes that I felt the shock of it along my own nerves, even though I did not understand what she meant. Without another word she ran down the steps to the terrace and hurried toward the tropical garden. Again I followed her. There was so little I could do or say to help her—or to help King. I could only *be*. Just be near and wait—and learn whatever I could.

In the sunlight of that hot August morning there seemed nothing ominous about the close-twined little grove. Free of their burden of rain, the trees no longer reached branches toward us as we passed, or snatched at our clothes.

Near the edge of the clearing Leila came to a halt. "He's there," she whispered in the same horror-stricken voice. "My father."

I looked past her to see King kneeling at the edge of the cliff, his back to us as he worked with lumber, putting up a new railing, pounding in the nails with strong, forceful strokes. Beyond, through the open space, I could see the blue and green of harbor and islands, looking as clear and innocent under the brilliant sky as a postcard picture. Violence had no place in that calm scene.

Leila drew me back into the trees. "I don't want to talk to him. So you look for it—will you? I'll wait for you on the terrace."

"Look for what? The columbella?"

She was impatient with me, as though I had not listened. "That black and white murex shell. Cathy had it in her hands when she came outside last night. I asked her about it and she said it told her secrets best at night. But where is it now? It must be there in the clearing. Look for it, Jessica."

"But why? What does it matter?"

"I want it!" She was stubborn, yet not willing to explain. "If you're going to stay around, you might as well help me, as long as I decide to wait."

When she ran off, leaving me there, I stepped uncertainly into the open. King turned and I saw how dreadful he looked, his face drawn by the strain of the night before. He stared at me without welcome —a stranger whom I did not know.

"I—I'm sorry," I faltered, though I was not sure what I was apologizing for. "Leila wanted me to see if I could find that murex shell down here. She has an idea that Catherine carried it with her when she came out last night."

Something flickered in King's eyes—some stirring of wary interest. "What does she care about that shell now?"

"Perhaps it's only a distraction," I said. "But if you don't mind, I'll look around a little."

Without answering he went back to his work. It was as if we meant nothing to each other, as if that day in St. Croix had been only a dream. Perhaps that was the truth of the matter, and Catherine's death was the only reality—that and the fact that Leila believed her father had killed Catherine.

The very vigor of his pounding seemed to give him a release in action that he needed. I watched for a moment, lost in the futility of trying to reach this man I loved. Then I began to look about the clearing, idly poking into brush that had grown up around the base of the big mango tree. I stared at the ground, scuffing at it with my feet, finding nothing, not really expecting to. It was not Leila I thought of now, or her quest for a shell, but of the man behind me and how to break through the wall he had set up against me. Not so that I could assert myself with him, but because I must find a way to help, and I could not help while he held me off.

He spoke to me suddenly, a little roughly, without turning around. "When are you planning to leave?"

"I'm not planning anything right now," I said, "either to leave or to stay."

"I want you away from here as soon as you can pack," he told me, and returned to his pounding.

The shade of the great mango tree lay all about me, shielding me from brilliant sunlight. I looked up into its high, full branches, where irregular green ovals of fruit hung so plentifully. Through them, here and there, I could glimpse the blue skies of St. Thomas.

"Once in this very place," I said, "you told me that I did too much running away. You were right. Now I'm learning not to run."

"There's a time when it's better to run for your life," he said. "For the sake of your own safety and future."

"What do you mean by that?" I demanded, but he only stared at me for a moment without speaking, and then went back to his work.

"Anyway," I said mildly, "I don't have to decide right now."

I had already decided, but I would offer no more fuel to his anger. Whether he had accepted the fact or not, I knew very well that I was part of whatever tragedy had overtaken him, and here I would stay until I was forced to leave.

He gave the last nail a powerful stroke of the hammer—as if he struck out at more than a nail. "Has Leila said anything more to you this morning?"

I knew what he meant and I held nothing back. I told him what Leila had said, what she believed. He listened, his eyes upon the distant mound of Hassel Island where another bare catchment scarred the hillside. When I had finished he drew a deep breath and released it slowly.

"Everything she has told you is true," he agreed. "I was angry enough to kill. When we stood talking on the terrace, I told Catherine that I meant to send Leila home without waiting any longer. I meant to get her out of her mother's hands, no matter what. She laughed at me. She said in that case she would follow wherever Leila went and stay close to her. Then she taunted me about you, and told me how much trouble she would make if you stayed here. When she went off into the woods I tried to give myself time to cool off. But there was more that needed to be said. She's trapped me on every hand for years, and bound me to her emptiness simply because the outcome could be tragic for Leila no matter what action I might take. Last night I meant to smash through and be damned to her."

He pounded one fist into the palm of the other hand.

"Well?" he said. "Do you want to hear more?"

I was suddenly afraid. I no longer wanted to hear, but I stood in the cool shade of the mango and listened, watching him in love and dread from my place of shadow.

"When I saw her standing here in the clearing last night, the words I meant to speak went out of my mind. I wanted nothing except to punish her. I wanted to hurt her physically as she could so easily be hurt. But I don't *think* I meant to kill her. I still had some control over myself and when the feel of her shoulders in my hands got too much for me, I flung her away and got out through the other side of the woods. I climbed to the road and walked to a spot where I could be quiet and think—and come to my senses."

I crossed my hands before my body and held myself tightly, as I had done that day at Caprice after my encounter with Catherine. Held myself because there in the hot morning I was once more shivering.

King dropped his hammer to the ground. "I didn't come here merely to put up a new railing—though that had to be done. I came to see if I could reconstruct what happened. When I stand here remembering, everything I felt last night comes washing through me all over again. I can feel the rough cloth of that beach robe she wore under my hands. I can smell her perfume just as I did last night—and lights begin to explode in my head."

I was sharply aware of the burning thing that consumed him, tearing him apart.

"She's gone," I said. "You have to find the truth about what happened, King. You didn't mean to kill her—you don't *know* that you did."

"You haven't heard me out. I shook her. I could feel the bones of her shoulders in my hands. I knew I was near to killing her. So I flung her away from me. Standing here thinking back, the whole thing is sharp enough in my mind. I flung her against that railing, and I flung her hard."

"But if you didn't intend what happened—if you didn't hear her fall—"

"It was raining hard and I took off as if the devil were after me. I wouldn't have heard an elephant go down that hillside. I never thought about the railing or the cliff. I only wanted to get away so I wouldn't harm her seriously. Which is an ironic joke on me, when you stop to think of it. That's why I was stunned when I came back last night."

"But you don't know!" I cried. "You don't know for sure. What if there was someone else in the clearing?"

He shook his head at me unhappily. "There was no time for anyone else to get there. You've told me that Leila saw me shaking her before I flung her away from me. She tore right back to the house, and you met her and ran down here at once. How long do you think that took?"

"Three or four minutes." I had to admit the truth.

"And the police think Catherine must have been dead only a little while by the time Alex climbed down the catchment after you raised the alarm. So we've got to face reality. Everyone was back at the house—Alex in his study, Maud in bed, Edith somewhere about the house. So who could have been here in three or four minutes' time without being seen by you or Leila? Or by me, for that matter?"

I didn't want to face what he called reality. I meant to blind myself to it with every means in my possession and move in just one direction—to disprove what he was saying.

"You'd better talk to Maud," I suggested.

"I have," he said. "I've told her exactly what I've told you. Her main concern now is to save Leila from further ugliness. The police would charge me at once with Catherine's death and Maud wants to put that off."

"I think she's right," I said staunchly. "Even if Leila believes the worst now, it isn't as bad as vicious publicity would make it—the dredging up of things that might mark her forever. Now there's at least a chance of persuading Leila that you didn't intend what happened. While Catherine was alive you had no trouble deciding that Leila counted for a great deal more than her mother did. Why isn't that still true?"

"Maud made that pretty graphic," he said grimly. "A fine, wrong-headed, female approach to morality! Women always care more about those they love than they do about abstract principles."

I had to admit that in my present state of mind this was true. There was a good deal of what Maud felt in my own reaction. What happened to King and Leila, who were essentially good and decent, mattered to me, and I cared very little about avenging the death of a woman who was basically evil. Reason had nothing to do with this. All my emotions were up in arms in defense of those I loved. Wrongheaded or not, I was on Maud's side. I tried again.

"What if you really weren't responsible—not even accidentally? What if you're so deeply surrounded by trees that you can't see the woods?"

He shook his head. "Don't reach for feeble straws."

I frowned, still impatient with his stubbornness. I had been a feeble straw myself, and now—for the moment at least—I was standing up pretty well.

"What if there's someone else in the picture? Someone who would love to see you blame yourself for what you had no hand in?"

"You're suggesting that some other person came here and pushed Catherine down that catchment last night?"

"Why not? What if she met someone after you left?"

He shook his head. "Catherine would have struggled, fought, screamed. You would have heard her."

"Perhaps not, if it was someone she knew and wasn't afraid of."

He shook his head wearily and I had to give up, hardly convinced by my own words.

"What are you going to do now?" I asked.

"I promised Maud that I'd give Leila a few days to recover from the shock of Catherine's death. But I made no promise not to act soon. The longer I wait, the worse it will be for me."

"There's *got* to be something—some way out." I was the stubborn one now.

His eyes grew kind as he looked at me. "But there isn't any way out. Catherine managed to tie me up in barbed wire while she was alive, and she's done it again in death."

He picked up the hammer he had dropped and turned his back on me to pound in another nail where no nail was needed. Clearly he wanted me gone with my foolish chatter and questionable morality. I walked out into hot sunlight and turned toward the path.

Behind me King spoke. "About that murex shell—I remember Catherine holding it in her hands when we were having an argument earlier on the terrace. I didn't think much about it at the time because she always indulged herself in play-acting fantasies. Later on I didn't notice. It was dark in the woods. I suppose she must have dropped it on the ground. Though it would be big enough to see if it were still around. Unless, of course, somebody kicked it into the underbrush during all the coming and going last night. Anyway, it can hardly matter now."

He had been momentarily puzzled, but had apparently explained everything to his own satisfaction—though not to mine.

I stared at him. "Tell me something else. When you saw her earlier on the terrace, was she wearing that gilded columbella shell on a chain around her neck?"

"I suppose so. Yes—I remember it. The moon was out then and I saw the thing shining."

"But when they brought her up to the house the locket was gone. So there are two things she must have lost here in this place. Why haven't they been found?"

Once more he tired of my questions. "What does it matter?"

I spoke in a rush. "What if there was a struggle? What if someone—"

"You never let go, do you?" he said. "Run along now. At least you've got something to think about, what with strugglings and mysterious assailants."

There was no use fighting him. Walking as slowly as I could I followed the windings of the path toward the terrace. His gibes had not upset me or turned me from my blind course. It was true that he had lost sight of the woods because of his own particular trees. But I was in another part of the forest and the trees I saw were different ones. If what had come into my mind led anywhere at all—then there might very well be a third, shadowy figure yet to be revealed. Someone who had acted against Catherine for a private reason. But if this was possible, it brought to mind a new and alarming element, for this would be a person who was still alive, someone willing to do further violence.

When I emerged from the grove Leila was sitting on the wall waiting for me. Beneath the flamboyant tree lay a circular shadow of red petals, and I turned my back on them, not wanting to remember the wet scarlet of a dress and a life snuffed out. Or to think about a ghost who held in her misty hands a power to destroy that was almost as great as it had been in life.

"You took long enough," Leila said. "What did you find?"

"Nothing," I said. "No murex shell, no columbella."

"Then you didn't look hard enough. They've got to be there."

"Why don't you look yourself?"

"I told you—I don't want to see my father. And anyway, I can't bear to go down there."

"Why are you so anxious to find that shell?"

She shrugged evasively, not looking at me. "I just want it."

I had the feeling that I was getting close to something important. "It's more than that, I think. You'd better tell me."

She flashed me a scornful look. "Cathy said it had—powers. She could hear voices when she listened to it. If I could find it perhaps they'd talk to me now—tell me what I want to know."

"That's pretty silly," I said. "And I think you know it. What's the real reason?"

For a moment longer she hesitated—and then gave in. "Maybe you'll be sorry you asked, but if you must know, it's because I want to see whether that shell could have been used as a—a weapon."

I stared at her, waiting.

"Cathy showed me one time how it would make a dangerous weapon if you slipped your hand inside it. And when they found her, there was that great gash on her forehead."

"Because she fell face downward onto the catchment," I said quickly.

"There was a bruise on the back of her head too—a fracture." Leila's voice began to rise. "So she could have been struck with the shell and fallen backward through the railing. That's why I have to know where the shell is. Perhaps my father hid it somewhere so the police wouldn't find it."

She jumped up from the wall and I put both hands on her shoulders and sat her down again—hard. There was rising hysteria here and it had to be stopped.

"Listen to me! As far as your father is concerned, this is what happened," I said, and told her exactly what he had told me, holding nothing back yet trying to make her understand the big question that remained—the chance that he was not responsible, even accidentally, for her mother's death.

She heard me through quietly enough, and when I finished she thrust my hands from her shoulders. As far as I could see I had made little impression. Her eyes were as sly and suspicious as her mother's might have been.

"You had a lovely visit with my father, didn't you? I suppose you think you've worked everything so as to keep him out of trouble? I suppose you think everything will be easy for the two of you from now on?"

I managed a deep breath before I spoke. "What I think is that it doesn't become you to be cruel and malicious."

A faint, betraying flush touched her cheeks and told me my words had gone home. Yet she did not retreat from her stand.

"All I have to do is go to Captain Osborn. All I have to do is find that shell and show it to him—and the person who killed my mother will be caught and punished." She pushed past me to run across the terrace and up the steps into the house.

I stood for a few moments longer staring out over hillside and town and harbor. On the water far below a long white cruiser was making its way toward the piers at the foot of Flag Hill. The wind was blowing this way and a faint strain of band music reached me. Down there aboard a ship were travelers, perhaps putting into St. Thomas for the first time, bent on gaiety, with no notion of the evil that could lurk in even so lovely a spot.

I turned my back on the sound, wondering if I would ever again feel as carefree as that, and went slowly into the house. There I found myself on the edge of a group that centered around the weeping maid, Noreen.

XVII

Maud and Edith sat together on a sofa, Maud weary and frail-looking, Edith a bit yellow and once more tense. Slightly aloof from what appeared to be a domestic crisis, Alex leaned against a stair post observing the scene with pale, attentive eyes. Leila had thrown herself into a chair to watch what was going on and her cheeks were still flushed, her breathing quick.

"As if we didn't have enough to occupy us right now!" Edith wailed. "Do be a good girl, Noreen, and don't worry us with such nonsense."

Maud Hampden put a hand on her daughter's arm. "Hush. Let the girl talk. We can't have the servants getting stirred up any more than they already are. Though I do think, Noreen, that your imagination is working overtime. No one else has seen jumbies around the house."

The girl dabbed at her eyes, speaking so quickly that I could understand very little.

"Nothing is going to hurt you," Maud said when the torrent stopped. "I'm sure Mrs. Drew's spirit has not appeared on the terrace since her death. You've let those who are ignorant fill you with this jumbie talk, Noreen. If you think anything is wrong, come and tell me at once and we'll talk about it together. However, if you go stirring the others up, I'll have to send you home to Guadeloupe."

The girl managed a shaky smile. As she went off toward the kitchen she threw me a look askance, remembering, perhaps, that I was the one who'd had a broom placed upside down beside my door.

When Noreen had gone, Alex disappeared into his study and Maud pulled herself to her feet. Edith sat where she was, her hands in her lap. The earlier elation I had sensed in her—as though realization of her sister's death had brought her some emotional release—had passed, and she looked stricken and uncertain. When Maud spoke to her she started and put a hand to her lips.

"Stop worrying about everything," Maud said, not unkindly. "Take one thing at a time."

When I asked Maud if there was anything I could do to help, the old lady glanced in Leila's direction and shook her head. I went upstairs to my room, knowing that I had better phone Aunt Janet soon, before she started calling me.

But for the moment I wanted only to sit quietly alone and try to figure out some course of action. What Leila had said about the murex shell might be wholly farfetched, or it might lead somewhere —I didn't know which. The one thing I was sure of was that her wild accusation about King seizing the shell and striking Catherine with it was anything but true. In fact, he had told me her hands were empty when he found her in the clearing.

What was it that kept eluding me? There seemed some discrepancy in these stories that I could not put my finger on, but which kept worrying me.

Then, as I sat there staring about my small room as though it had something to tell me, I felt again the same disturbing awareness of objects misplaced that I had experienced only yesterday.

The closet door was ajar, though I had not left it open. When I looked inside I saw that my suitcase had been moved, and I pulled it out to find that the few things I had left in it had been stirred about. The third drawer of the bureau had been searched as well, just as the top two had been yesterday. This time, however, the searching appeared to have gone more frantically and hurriedly, as though the searcher had grown desperate and taken less care to cover traces. This time it could not have been Catherine.

What could I possibly be suspected of hiding? Why should anyone bother with my possessions?

During the next few days these unanswered questions kept returning to trouble me, even though there was so much else to occupy my attention.

All the immediate aftermath of tragedy had to be lived through— the inquest, with its verdict of accidental death, the funeral and its attendant strains. Hampden and Drew friends rallied around, and I saw again many of the people who had watched Catherine dance on the terrace the night of the party. St. Thomas was a small island and gossip buzzed, as Aunt Janet took pains to tell me. The Hampden and Drew names made headlines throughout the Caribbean as well as locally.

The inquest brought out nothing of note. The wooden rail in the clearing was indeed termite-ridden. Catherine Drew had been known to roam about at night when the mood prompted her. The fact that King too was abroad that night seemed of no significance to the investigators, since he was, presumably, in another place, and there appeared to be no reason to doubt his word. The family showed a solid front and nothing was said of the quarrel which had occurred between King and Catherine immediately before her death.

During the proceedings King was so morose, so short-spoken, that I was afraid he would bring too much attention to himself and arouse antagonisms that could hurt him badly. But he was well liked in the community and everyone seemed willing to consider that he had suffered a tragic loss and must therefore be forgiven his behavior.

At last, quite suddenly, everything was over and we could be quiet again in our own uneasy way, though I felt sure there was no one at Hampden House who believed that trouble was really behind us.

Through those anxious days I was at least able to hold to one comforting thing. Leila did not blurt out her story to anyone who might have used it against King. Perhaps between us, Maud and I had helped to keep her silent, even to arouse some doubts and hesitation in her. But we had only to look at the girl's tragic young face to know how dreadfully torn she was between the anguished loss she felt for her mother, and the old love for her father that she could not quite throw off, even though she might wish to. Her silence could not go on forever—something would crack. And before that time there must be a better answer to give her than the one she believed was the truth. At least she did not need to appear at the inquest, though after it was over she began to show a strange, unstable side that I found alarming. Now and then it reminded me all too vividly of Catherine.

During this time the same questions kept tugging at the edge of my consciousness that had troubled me from the beginning. I kept feeling that there was some one obvious thing that I knew and which would give me a clearer view of the truth, if only I could put my finger on it. But always the thought evaded me and slipped away tantalizingly.

I might not have remained at the house, had it not been for Maud. She still insisted that Leila needed me and I knew that she was right, however much the girl resisted me. Edith wanted me gone, and so did King, who seemed grimly determined that there should be not so much as a look between us. Though I wept at times when I was alone, I knew that he wanted to raise a bulwark against the moment when he would speak out about what had happened the night of Catherine's death—whether or not he was to blame. He was determined to

bring every shred of truth to light where his own actions were concerned and only awaited Leila's recovery from shock, hoping that
he could keep her from permanent hurt and let the wound heal a little
that was now so raw. More than ever he seemed to me a man doomed
—and I could not bear it.

A week after Catherine's death I awakened one morning to hear
hurricane talk coming through on my radio more insistently than
ever. Precedent had it that these islands were no longer on the main
hurricane path, but even the flick of a hurricane's skirts is not to be
trifled with, and Virgin Island radios were tuned to frequent weather
reports during the hurricane season.

The announcement that morning concerned Hurricane Katy, not
too far out in the Atlantic, and moving this way. Warnings were
being flashed that the Virgin Islands were in her uncertain path and
we had better brace ourselves for a blow. *Katy.* I didn't like the name.
It reminded me of Catherine, who had been a dangerous hurricane
in her own right.

When I got up that morning the day was bright blue and gold, with
only the usual puffs of cloud over the green hills of St. Thomas, and
no storm threat on the visible horizon. There was only a stillness in
the air, and a greater sense of heat than was usual on our mountaintop.

For once all the family breakfasted together, although our meals
had become a time of uneasiness and tension. Increasingly I had the
sense of something that moved secretly beneath the surface, worrying, fretting, perhaps eating itself up with fear of the small slip that
could mean quick exposure.

In my mind Helen's voice whispered the old refrain: "Fanciful!"
But I realized with a deepening gratitude to Kingdon Drew how
faint that voice had grown. Certainly it did not make me throw off
my present uneasiness. Every day I grew more sure that fear walked
in our midst, though I had no inkling of where this feeling came from.

At breakfast that morning I played the grim game of trying to
figure out the source of this mounting sense of tension, but since
each one of us had legitimate sources of worry, it seemed hopeless
to seek for hidden causes besides. Maud was concerned lest either
Leila or King should blurt word of the quarrel, of which the police
were still unaware.

In Maud's mind there seemed no longer any sense of the morality
of the situation. She had accepted the fact that Catherine's death
was accidental, and she opposed King's going to the police to stir
everything up, as she said, "needlessly." King and Leila, of course,

had their own obviously sharp anxieties and I shared them almost as intensely. Edith followed her mother's lead and looked anxiously at both King and his daughter, and here I felt was a woman who harbored private dreads of her own. Now and then I caught her looking at Alex almost fearfully, even though Catherine was gone, and his attention could no longer drift in that direction. Alex seemed the least worried of us all, but as always he remained a puzzle to me, and while I felt sure that he had been the man on the beach with Catherine, I still did not know what their relationship had really been. Certainly she had not played up to him as openly as she had to Steve O'Neill.

While we breakfasted that morning I found myself remembering the first time when I had sat at this table with the others, and Catherine had been among us. Now our places had been shifted to omit one plate, but it still seemed that each of us felt her restless presence. That morning I could almost see her lifting the murex shell to her ear, and catch her high, silvery laughter as she pretended to hear voices speaking to her from the shell. So far the murex had not turned up, although I had looked for it more carefully myself. Leila still dreaded the clearing and would not go near it.

And then, quite suddenly, during the meal—as though my inner mind had been pondering the problem and working its way toward a possible answer—I thought of a place where the shell might be hidden.

When breakfast was over and we left the table I lingered downstairs idly, watching where the others of the household went when they left the table. The day was Saturday and King did not leave for his downtown office but retired to the room he used at the house for his work. Leila vanished into Alex's study, where I knew she had been drawing pictures again, though she had not shown me her efforts. Saturday was as good a tourist day as any for Alex's shop, but that morning he did not leave for town but stretched out in a deck chair on the terrace for a smoke. Maud and Edith had gone upstairs together.

Of course I could not know for certain that any of the four would remain where they were, but this was my chance and I took it without hesitation. I let myself unnoticed out the door to the front driveway and slipped behind the hibiscus hedge, following the path to the Danish kitchen which Edith Stair used for the preparation of shells.

The door stood ajar, though a glance through one of the low windows told me no one was there. I went in and stood looking eagerly about. Now I had a theory to go on. If Leila was right and the murex shell had indeed been used as a weapon—though not by King—perhaps the person who had used it in the clearing had spirited it away to place it in the most innocuous place possible: here among the shells where Edith worked.

A quick glance told me that the box of sand in which I had built castles was still here, though it did not seem as deep as it had been, and it was no longer damp. The last box of shells Steve O'Neill had delivered to Catherine was also there, looking rather like the box I had seen at Caprice, though I could not be sure. Edith seemed to have done little work in preparing this batch for shipment, there being undoubtedly too much else on her mind.

The rest of the room, too, seemed the same. Shells lay on the window ledges or waited for sorting and labeling on open shelves. How easy it would be to set the murex among them and remove it from suspicion. But though I searched the shelf of larger shells, where it would be most inconspicuous, I did not find it there. Already I had used up several minutes, and there was no telling when those at the house might leave their posts and wander in this direction—particularly whichever one might have a guilty conscience. I began to move quickly, nervously in my seeking.

For the first time I noticed that on each side of the wide brick chimney that housed the oven, there was a closed door. Storage space, I supposed, and went to one of them and pulled it open to look inside. A closet, large enough to step into, had been fitted into the space. Shelves reached to the ceiling and there was room for tall mops and brooms besides, but the shelves held only bottles of preserving alcohol, brushes, cleaners—the sort of supplies Edith used in her work. There were no shells.

I backed out, shutting the door. As I did so I heard a sound. Startled, I turned my head in time to see the twin door on the other side of the chimney closing by a hair's breadth. Someone was in there! Someone who had peered through the crack, watching me, closing the door as I came out the opposite side. There had been no more than a whisper of sound, the faintest movement, yet I was sure.

My first impulse was to run from the place—to escape while I could. But if I ran I would never know who had hidden in the closet, never know who among us kept a secret that made it necessary to hide.

I looked about for help. On either side of the room sunshine poured through open windows, and the scent of stephanotis was sweet on the air. The house, after all, was very near. Alex was outdoors and would hear me if I shouted. I had only to scream and help would come.

I faced the closed door. "Who's there?" I called, edging nearer the outer door and my own line of escape.

For a long moment nothing happened, and I wondered if my bluff was about to be called. I had no confidence in my ability to walk to that door and pull it open. There was danger here—the very smell of it was in the air.

Before I could take my next step the door of the second closet banged open and an apparition rushed out in my direction. I had only a glimpse of a tall figure completely enveloped in a hooded robe. Then rough hands pushed me out of the way with a force that flung me backward so that I fell, banging my head against the bricks of the oven.

For a few moments I sat on the floor with my head ringing painfully, my vision spinning, and in my ears the sound of footsteps running away. When the spinning stopped, I pulled myself up and stood shakily on my feet. My eyes began to clear and I could see the open door of the second closet—where there had been plenty of room for someone to hide. Gingerly I felt the tender place at the back of my head where I had bumped it, but my hair had protected me and there was only surface soreness.

The room had nothing more to tell me. The shell I'd looked for wasn't here—but now my apprehensions were confirmed. I was on the trail of someone who could not afford discovery. And at the thought a new alarm went through me. The hood of that concealing robe had kept me from glimpsing a face, but could the one who wore it be sure of that? What if there was doubt as to whether I had recognized the wearer?

Shaky though I was, I started back to the house, wanting only to escape this place that now seemed dangerously isolated. This was no longer a fanciful matter. Another person was now obviously involved in our troubles.

As I came from behind the hibiscus hedge I stumbled over the beach robe, which lay on the ground at my feet. Picking it up, I shook it out wonderingly. My assailant had been wrapped in the Arab burnoose that Catherine had affected for beach wear and that King said she had worn that night in the clearing. As I held it in my hands I could catch the faint but still permeating odor of water lily, with which she had liked to saturate her clothes.

At the moment I was hardly able to think in clear, logical terms. I was merely *feeling*. Something had started moving toward the light, and I knew that I held in my hands—in this robe—the answer to something important. An answer, perhaps, to that tantalizing question which had troubled me ever since I had talked to King that morning in the clearing.

I did not want to be seen holding the robe in my hands, and I hurried toward the house, hoping I would meet no one. The living area was empty, but as I walked its length Noreen came down the stairs and saw me. She cried out softly, gesturing toward the robe in my hands, murmuring the word "jumbies."

I stopped to question her. "What do you mean, Noreen? What has this beach robe to do with jumbies?"

Her words came too fast for me to translate, since excitement always sent her into a torrent of Calypso talk, but I managed to catch something about Mrs. Drew appearing on the terrace in this very robe—after her death—and I gathered that in Noreen's eyes some sort of haunting was going on.

When the girl ran off, apparently not wanting to be near the robe, I went to hang it on the rack near the terrace door. There was some answer here, though the pieces would not yet fall into place.

I turned to see Edith coming out of the dining room.

Her gaze rested at once upon the robe in my hands. "What are you doing with that?"

I answered indirectly. "I found it just now outside on the walk. I thought it belonged on the rack here."

"Not any more!" Edith said and came to take it from my hands. "There's no point in keeping Catherine's things around as reminders."

She went toward the stairs with the robe over her arm and I had the feeling that she was the logical person to have hidden it away in her workroom in the first place.

When she had gone I went out to the terrace, to find Alex still in his deck chair, smoking his pipe. He sat up as I appeared.

"I've been wanting to talk to you about Leila," he said.

The lump on the back of my head hurt a little and it was difficult to appear calm and unruffled, but I dropped into a chair and waited for him to continue.

"Have you looked at the sort of thing she has been drawing lately?" he asked.

I shook my head. "She hasn't wanted to show me."

"Then look anyway," he went on. "I don't like this new trend. It's morbid."

More than anything else just then I needed to talk to King, but I did not want to make straight for his office while Alex sat watching me. It was necessary to move with seeming innocence and openness, and not like a woman who had discovered something vital.

"I'll go and look at her drawings now," I said. "Thanks for telling me."

He gave me his usual sardonic smile and I hurried into the house. The study door was ajar and when I looked inside I found Maud Hampden there ahead of me. Leila sat at the worktable, a pencil in her hand, a drawing block before her. This morning she wore tight navy-blue pants that had belonged to Catherine, combined with a white blouse of her own. Somehow I did not like to see her wearing Catherine's clothes.

Her grandmother stood nearby, looking down at Leila's bent head. I had never seen a more sorrowful expression than Maud's in that unguarded moment. When she saw me she gestured silently toward the drawings scattered across the table before Leila.

From a shelf a radio was relating the progress of Hurricane Katy in its continuing southwesterly direction, and the broadcast was the only sound in the room.

Leila must have seen Maud's gesture, for she looked around at me, and at once a look of challenge came into her eyes. "Have you ever been in a hurricane, Jessica?"

I said I had not and she went on.

"We may get a real blow this time. They're on hurricane watch, and that means there'll be once an hour reports until we know what Katy will do. She seems to be heading for Guadeloupe—so maybe we'll catch the edge by tonight. Can you feel how hot it's getting?"

Though I'd had little time to think about it, the heat had indeed grown oppressive, but it was neither heat nor storms that concerned me now, but those drawings toward which Maud had gestured.

As I stepped closer to the table Leila reached out and flipped them quickly face down. Maud brushed a hand across her face, as though she brushed away something she could not bear to witness.

"Why not show Miss Abbott what you've been drawing?" she said.

"Because I can imagine what she would say," Leila answered, her voice a little high. "Do you know what I wish? I wish that hurricane would hit us head on. I wish it would blow Hampden House right into the sea. Hampden House and—and—"

"And everyone in it?" her grandmother asked.

Leila bent her head over her drawing block, looking faintly ashamed of her outburst. "Not you, Gran. You're the only one I can count on any more."

Maud looked at me, and I saw again the grieving in her eyes. But there was nothing tremulous about her voice when she spoke.

"Show Miss Abbott your drawings, dear."

Thus commanded, Leila shrugged and pushed them toward me. One by one I picked up the sketches to study them, increasingly disturbed by what I saw. Each pencil sketch concerned itself with the subject of death. One showed a grave in a churchyard, with willow trees drooping above a flower-strewn mound. The next sketch was of a cypress-lined path winding through the white stones of a cemetery, a small church in the background. The third was more distressing —a woman's figure floating face down on the surface of a pond, with water lilies drifting about her. All the sketches seemed rather cool, pretty pictures in spite of their subject matter, and lacking in reality.

I set the drawings aside and leaned over the pad on which Leila was completing another sketch, aware of how anxiously Maud Hampden watched me. This time the drawing showed Juliet on her bier—looking a little like Catherine, with long hair flowing, and lighted candles burning at either end of the bier, lighting the dark crypt.

Leila was watching me too, and when I met her eyes she laughed as though my expression pleased her.

"You're shocked, aren't you? You think I'm being morbid—just as Gran does. And Uncle Alex."

Silently I agreed, but I would not let her know that. Besides—morbid though they were, there was something about these pictures that made me think we need not be too seriously disturbed by them.

"Your grandmother and your uncle are probably right," I said. "Though I don't think they need be upset, since the drawings show so little real feeling."

Leila stared at me for a moment and then startled me by flinging down her pencil. "You've seen through them! They're only doodling, really—like drawing unicorns and columbellas. Death isn't like this. Death is ugly, horrible. My mother hated pain—but I saw that dreadful wound on her forehead. Made by some wicked person who hated her."

I pressed my hands upon Leila's shoulders as she would have risen, excitedly, and held her in her chair. I heard Maud's soft intake of breath and when I looked at her I saw her eyes had clouded with tears.

"The young can be cruel," I said to Leila. "It's time you began to think of someone else's pain besides your own."

Leila had not looked at her grandmother. "Whose pain? Whose? No one cares but me!"

Maud had started toward the door, tears wet on her cheeks, but she paused to speak to her granddaughter. "Miss Abbott is quite right. I think you forget that Catherine was once my little daughter."

With quiet dignity she moved to the door and went out it and up the stairs without a backward look. Leila looked after her, stricken, and it was at that moment that Noreen came to the study to summon her.

At once Leila flung off her concern and sprang to her feet. "That's Steve! I phoned him to come!"

She ran out of the study and I followed in dismay. Steve O'Neill was the last person Leila should be seeing now.

Dressed for a swim in trunks and sweat shirt, he lounged near the front door, though for all his jaunty manner he did not look comfortable. Just behind him stood his brother, Mike, even less at ease.

"I thought you wanted to go swimming." Steve spoke to Leila impatiently. "You don't look ready to me."

"Wait," Leila said. "I'll get into my suit and be with you in a minute."

None of us noticed that King had come out of his office until he spoke. His voice stopped Leila as she started toward the stairs, and I knew that trouble was coming.

"No trips to the beach today," he told her curtly.

Mike nudged his brother. "Let's get out of here."

But when Steve would have moved toward the door Leila flung herself upon him, clasping his arm. "No—don't go! Wait for me, please. He can't stop me. He can't lock me up!"

I saw what was about to happen and I stepped into King's path as he started across the room.

"Let's make it a swim party," I pleaded, and over my shoulder I called to Steve and Mike. "Wait for us outside, will you, boys?"

King had come to a halt and I went to put my hands on Leila's defiant shoulders.

"You can't go alone this time, dear."

She pulled away and ran upstairs, leaving me to face her father.

"Please come with us," I said. "I know I've interfered and that you don't like it. But this is important. Besides—I've got to talk to you. At the beach there may be a chance."

I could see that he wanted to hear nothing I might say, that he was bitterly opposed to going anywhere with Steve O'Neill—or with me, for that matter.

I tried again. "It will be worse if she goes off alone with him. Between us, we can at least prevent that. If only you'd move gently with her, King—she's having a bad time."

He was still holding me off, but though his look was cold, he gave in. "Get into your suit," he told me. "I'll wait for you in the car."

Somewhere upstairs a radio was blatting about gale-force winds due in the Virgin Islands before nightfall, but I paid no attention. We had our own gale to weather first. By the time I'd struggled into my suit and flung a beach coat around me, I was damp with perspiration and fully aware of the humid heat of the morning.

Leila was ready ahead of me, clad in the terry-cloth jacket that left her long brown legs bare. When I overtook her on the stairs I stopped her for a question.

"Why did you ask Steve to come here when you know how your father feels about him?"

"He wanted to come. He keeps phoning me and asking if he can come up here to see me. Poor Steve."

I suppose I looked blank for she flung impatient words at me.

"Oh, don't you see! Now we have something to pull us together, Steve and I. We've both lost someone we loved. So I told him he could come and take me swimming the way he used to do with Catherine."

She pulled away and I followed her down the stairs, my concern growing.

When we went outside we found the two boys waiting in the red convertible, and King, already in bathing trunks, sitting in his own car. I put my fingers on Leila's arm with just enough pressure to urge her toward her father's car. She gave me a troubling glance that I could not read, though she offered no resistance, getting into the front seat, while I sat beside her.

King spoke only once on the drive down to Magens Bay. "I'm sorry," he told Leila. "I didn't mean to blow my top like that. But I think you know why I don't want you out with Steve O'Neill. So don't push me too far, will you, chicken?"

His gentler manner seemed to make no impression on Leila. When I glanced at her I saw the closed, resentful look she wore. Clearly, she meant to accept no softening on his part.

XVIII

The road curled downward through the forest preserve that had been given in perpetuity to the people of St. Thomas, along with the lovely, deep indentation of the bay. Here no hotels could be built, no fences raised to keep anyone out. The place waited for us in its wild, natural beauty.

Few swimmers were about, and when King had parked his car behind the boys' convertible and we had found our way through the clusters of sea grapes that rimmed the sand, Steve and Mike O'Neill were already at the water's edge.

I had left my beach coat in the car, but Leila had kept her terry-cloth jacket clutched around her until she was out on the sand. Now she shed it, letting it fall behind her as she ran with long-legged grace toward the boys. I heard King's sharp intake of breath and saw that Leila had put on Catherine's scant green bikini. The brief bands of cloth set off her rounded, tanned young body, and I heard King swear softly as he came to a halt beside me. Young girls in bikinis were no unfamiliar sight at a beach these days—but Leila deliberately flaunting herself in this suit of Catherine's was somehow wrong.

As we stood watching she ran between the two boys, splashing into the water. In a moment she was swimming, her cap of brown hair wet and sleek about her head—all that was to be seen of her now.

King and I moved more slowly toward the water, as Leila and the two boys swam and tumbled and played. Or at least Steve and Leila played, teasing each other, splashing—seemingly a harmless enough rough and tumble spectacle, and not the sort of play Catherine would have indulged in. Nearby, Mike was treading water, his dark head and glowering expression visible at wave level. He was undoubtedly as uneasy as King and I—and as helpless.

Suddenly King left me to stride into the water alone, swimming out past the gamboling young people with strokes that carried him strongly into deep water. I waded in, keeping to myself, and swam parallel with the beach. The sea felt wonderfully buoyant to my fresh-water-accustomed body, and the sky was blue and serene, with no hint of a hurricane moving closer.

When I looked toward the others I saw that King was a considerable distance out and that the young people had waded in to lie on the sand. Steve had stretched out on his stomach, watching Leila, talking to her, with Mike flat on his back a little way off. Leila sat on the sand with her legs straight out, apparently listening to Steve. I swam in to shallow water and went toward them up the beach, the sun blazing hot on my wet shoulders. As I neared them I heard Steve's words.

"You're crazy if you think anything else, kid. I've been sure all along, but there's got to be some way to prove it. That's why I've been wanting to get up to the house. To—to just look around."

She was pleading with him now. "Please—can't you just let it alone? What good will it do? Nothing will bring her back, and—"

He saw me then and reached out across the sand to clasp Leila by the ankle. "Hush up—here comes Teacher."

Leila looked up at me, her eyes hostile. "Do go away, Jessica-Jessica. You never seem to know when you're not wanted."

"It's no use," Steve said, jumping to his feet. "There's no more to say. Any time you like I'll drive you home."

"Wait!" Leila called and as he turned about a subtle change came over her. She stood before him, lithe and brown, her body provocative in those scant strips of green. Sand clung to her tanned skin and she brushed it off carelessly as she took a few steps toward Steve. With every movement of her body, with all her firm young flesh, she was vividly like her mother as she assumed her role.

Steve came to a halt, and I saw his startled look as she came toward him with the same sinuous dancing steps that Catherine had used that night on the terrace. Before he could know what she was about, Leila was close, marching her two forefingers up his bare chest in a gesture I had seen Catherine make. The mimicry was so convincing that it was almost as though we watched Catherine herself. Steve laughed and reached out boldly to pull her to him, but she broke away and turned to run.

King had come out of the water, and as Leila sprang away from Steve and ran across wet sand he moved toward her and I saw the sick shock in his eyes. As she neared he stepped into her path and caught her, his hands on her arms.

"We're going back to the house," he said.

She stood before him almost as I had seen Catherine stand, looking up at him with a mocking glance that was eerily Catherine's. He held her firmly yet not ungently, and there was a deep sorrow in him.

The mockery went out of her and she began to struggle against his restraint with the uncontrolled anger of a child. "Go ahead, why don't you?" she cried. "Kill me the way you killed Cathy that night! Take me out in the water and drown me, if you like. I don't care. I know what you are! I know the name for you!"

He held her in silence, until her struggling ceased and tears began to roll down her face. Only then did he let her go and she ran away from him toward the rim of sea grapes above the beach, where Steve stood watching, his face masked and bitter. King might have followed, if it hadn't been for Mike.

"Let her go, Mr. Drew," the younger boy said. "I'll take her home. You can count on me to get her to her grandmother."

King nodded wordlessly. He watched as Mike loped up the beach after Leila and his brother, and I waited beside him, shaken and miserable, aware of the depth of his hurt. A sand fly stung my leg—the quiet air before the storm had brought them in—and I slapped at it absently. From beyond the sea grapes we heard the sound of an engine starting, heard the boys' car climbing the hill.

"So that's the way it's going to be," he said in a strangely calm voice.

He walked away from me toward the car and I ran after him, got into the car beside him in my wet suit. When he reached for the ignition I put my hand over his.

"Wait—please wait! I have to talk to you. There's something I need to tell you. Something that may help."

"How can anything help against the facts?" he asked, still quiet and grim.

"But there *is* something. You remember that Arab beach robe Catherine used to wear—you know the one I mean?"

"What about it?"

"You told me you remembered the feel of the stuff in your hands when you took hold of her in the clearing that night. What happened to it afterward?"

"I suppose someone found it on the catchment. Or in the clearing, and brought it to the house."

I shook my head. "No! Because before I came outdoors I looked on that rack near the terrace door for something to put on against the rain. The burnoose was hanging there then. I'm sure of it. I put my hands on it and found it damp, so I took something else. Then I forgot about it, until—until something that happened a little while ago. Don't you see? This means that after you left Catherine someone must have picked up that robe, carried it back to the house, and hung it on the rack. Someone who was with her after you left."

King started the car decisively. "I know a place where we can talk —a place I've wanted to show you. There's something I have to tell you too—about what I plan to do."

He started the car and we drove up the north face of the mountain to the skyline road and followed it past Hampden House. Here and there, high in trees along the road, hung the huge termite nests one saw everywhere in the Islands. From now on the sight of one would make me think of rotten wood, and I would shiver, remembering.

When we reached the low redwood house King had built, we turned into a descending driveway. The house was set into the steep hillside below the level of the road, with a cleared area beside it, where the drive ended.

"It's not Caprice," King said. "But it's the sort of thing I like to build in this setting and for this time."

I had put on my beach coat as we drove, and I slipped my feet into slippers as I left the car. King came as he was, barefooted and with a shirt pulled over his trunks.

The house was unoccupied. There were no curtains, no draperies, no air of a place lived in. The usual hibiscus hedge gave it privacy from the road, but there were no outdoor chairs about, no evidence of everyday living. We went up a few steps to the low deck that ran along the rear of the structure, where the overhang of the roof offered shelter. King unlocked a door of dark, oiled redwood and we stepped into cool shade.

The house stood empty, unfurnished, and I looked around with warm interest as he led me through, feeling somehow closer to this house than I ever could to Caprice. Here King's own vision had been turned into a form of wood and stone, beautifully simple and clean of line. On every hand, use had been made of the contrasts of textured wood and the island blue stone. The outdoor surroundings, the very hillside itself, seemed a part of the whole, blending as though the house could belong nowhere else but here.

Great sliding doors faced the east, framing the next hilltop, with the beginnings of a patio garden planted beyond, so that when one stepped into the living room, garden and hillside and sky were part of the room. He led me onto a wide veranda cantilevered over the steeply pitched hillside, though I had no sense of dizzying space because poincianas spread their flaming tops at our feet, like a carpet that might be walked upon. Beyond, far down the steep hill, lay Charlotte Amalie and the harbor—a strangely empty harbor. Even the yacht basin had few boats in it.

"The ships are gone," I said.

King nodded. "The big ones are getting out of Katy's way. The smaller craft go over to Hurricane Hole in St. John to ride out the storm."

I glanced at the sky and saw that a gray-white haze was spreading up from the southeast, though all was serenely blue overhead. Now and again the still air stirred in a puff of wind.

I looked again at the house—which told me so much more about King than I had known before.

"Why is it empty? How can you bear not to live in it yourself?"

He stared off toward the rounded point of Flag Hill where the lines that marked the aerial tramway were just visible, and his expression was guarded.

"Once I meant to live here. The house has been finished for nearly a year. I wanted to move away from Maud's place, after Edith came to look after her mother. I thought it might be good for Catherine to have a change from the environment in which she grew up, perhaps even adapt herself to something different. Most of all, I wanted Leila to have the feeling of a new background and new responsibilities to live with. It didn't work out that way, and perhaps that was my fault. But while I was planning and building, and while Leila was taking an interest in what I was doing, I felt hopeful about what the house might accomplish. Of course it's always a mistake to expect things to change people. Human problems go deeper than that."

"Catherine wouldn't make the move?" I asked.

His hands tightened on the redwood rail of the veranda. "She was playing out the line, letting the fish run. She seemed to promise, to encourage, to take an interest. And when I had put a great deal of myself into the place and it was built, she laughed at me and said I was an idiot if I thought she would ever move away from her real home."

I ached for him, understanding how it must have been. "Did it hurt Leila—the disappointment over not moving here?"

"Not really. Catherine took care to break down her excitement over the house and spoil her pleasure in it. What Maud says is true. All Catherine wanted was to destroy me."

I could only agree. "If you couldn't tolerate her behavior, how could you love her? And being the way she was, if she couldn't hold you, she had to hurt you, injure you."

He regarded me with the same strange calm with which he had met Leila's attack—a calm I had never seen in him before. "Perhaps I allowed Catherine to do all she did. Because it was easier to go my own way than to fight her. Perhaps that's how we've managed to destroy each other."

"No!" I cried. "You *aren't* destroyed. It mustn't be that way."

He echoed my words. "It mustn't be that way? I wonder. Certainly I didn't mean her to fall through that railing. I don't think I'm the murdering sort. Nevertheless I gave in to my own anger and frustration as I've done too often, and I flung her so she fell against the rotten wood. It's time I faced that fact. I know of nothing else that could have happened. Isn't this what Leila saw?"

I shook my head. "She saw you shaking her mother, and she ran away. But there's still the matter of the burnoose. If Catherine fell through the railing when you pushed her away from you, she would have gone down that stone slide wearing the robe. Yet neither Alex nor anyone else brought it up to the house after she was found. Because they couldn't—it wasn't there. As I've told you, I saw it hanging on the rack near the door—at a time when she was already dead. That means the real attack upon her must have come after she had taken off the robe. Her attacker could have carried it back to the house and hung it secretly on the rack where I came upon it."

"In three or four minutes' time—without meeting you?" He listened to me gravely, but without belief. "Why?" he added. "Can you tell me why the robe should matter that much?"

"Someone must have worried about the burnoose. Otherwise why would it have been hidden away in a cupboard in Edith's workroom? There's something important here. I know there is!"

"What do you mean—hidden in Edith's workroom? What are you talking about?"

I told him then what had happened to me that morning when someone had put on Catherine's robe to conceal himself, and come hurtling out of a closet to push me down and get away without being identified.

King heard me through as gravely as before, and then took a turn up and down the long veranda before he went inside through sliding doors. I followed him in silence, knowing he needed time to consider the question I had flung at him.

"All the more reason for what I must do," he said at last. "I've wanted to clear things up as soon as Leila had recovered a little.

Now, recovery or no, I've got to act. If other disturbing factors have come to light since Catherine's death, we must have police help in a real investigation. We've just discovered—Maud and I—that Catherine has been opening bank accounts in her own name in a number of places away from home—and depositing fairly large sums of money in them. That's why she could talk of restoring Caprice. And of course she was still spending in her usual wild way. Maud and I told her more than a year ago that we'd pay no more of her debts, that the allowance we had both given her would be stopped. Apparently she managed to find a new source of income. We've kept quiet about too much for too long."

I listened in growing dread of what he meant to do.

Again he turned away to roam the room, and as he did so an object on the floor caught his eye. He went to pick something up, and when he held out his hand I saw the two cigarette butts in the palm. Brown scars remained on the hardwood floor where the stubs had burned themselves out.

"This one is Catherine's brand," he said. "I don't know about the other. I know she came here at times. She used to throw the fact in my face to spite me. She wouldn't live here, but she wouldn't leave it inviolate for me, either. There was no keeping her out and I didn't like broken windows, so I let her have a key."

The cruel mockery of insult behind burns on that beautiful floor was plain—the deliberate defacing of something built with care and love.

"Is this where you came the night she died—when they couldn't find you?" I asked.

He took the cigarette stubs to the door and flung them outside. "Yes. I'd come so near to killing her that I wanted to get off by myself where I could cool down and think things through. I've been in the habit of coming here ever since the house was finished. I keep a folding table and chairs in a closet so I can work here sometimes during the day. Not at night, since there's no electricity. Catherine used to make her visits nocturnal—I've found her candle stubs around."

He spoke in the strangely calm way that I had begun to find disturbing. He had always seemed a man of vibrant vitality—a man with a drive that kept him forever fighting the circumstances of his life. Fighting against Catherine, sometimes against Maud, and often against Leila—trying to bend, to storm his way through. And now there was this unexpected stillness about him—as though he had somehow come to rest.

"I want to talk to you," he said quietly. "This is as good a time as any, and perhaps my last chance for a while. This is a place where we can be alone. Wait a moment. I'll get something to sit on."

He went to open the sliding doors of a large storage closet built into one end of the room, and brought out two folding deck chairs. When he had opened one for me and set it upon the bare floor of the living room, he opened another for himself and sat down facing me. I had a feeling that something grim and devastating was coming, and I wanted to hold it off, to prevent him from speaking. But there could be no more postponement.

He reached out across the space between us and took my hand to hold it gently in both of his own, and his eyes were warm upon me. "What you don't understand, Jessica, is that you are the one who has made me try to learn a new lesson about living. I haven't succeeded at it yet—but at least I'm giving it a try."

I could only stare at him in bewilderment. "How could I teach you anything? You said I ran away. You told me—"

"I said a lot of idiotic things. I criticized you because you didn't stand and fight. Lately I've been looking at myself, as well as at you. I went out for a swim today and had a further look. Maybe the sort of fighting that counts can't be done by bulldozing everything out of the way in order to get things running to my own liking. Nor does it do any good for me to butt my head against an impossible situation and drive myself crazy because there's no solution. I expect I've been doing both those things."

There was nothing I could say. I loved him very much and I listened.

"What I've begun to understand about you," he went on, "is that the situation which was thrust upon you as a young girl was no less frustrating and impossible than my own. You hadn't asked for it, but it was there, and yet you worked out a way to live with it as best you could—and productively too. I've done a little of that in my work, but mostly I've chained myself to frustration by fighting all sorts of things that couldn't be fought with the methods I was using."

I had to come to his defense. "You were never free to act—"

"Who is ever completely free?" he challenged. "We all have limits within which we have to operate. You accepted the limitations around you with courage and you pushed them back a little in whatever direction you could. So I'll not laugh at you or tease you any more, my darling. The trouble you were having came after you were free of a situation that had bound you for so long. The unhappiness and the fears you were suffering when you came here grew out of the fact that while you were free of the situation that had hemmed you in, you weren't free of the past. You weren't able to throw off the long damage that had been done to your own confidence and in your ability to move outside old barriers."

"You helped me," I said gratefully. "You made me see."

"And if I hadn't you'd eventually have helped yourself. That's the thing I like most about you. No matter how scared you are, once you take a thing on, you plug away at all obstacles. Now it's my turn. I've no intention of drifting in this new position the way Maud wants me to do. I'm afraid Maud is tied to her own frustrations. Her own life took a stranglehold on her so long ago that it's probably too late for her to be free. So now I must hurt her as well. That's the thing that so often ties our hands—the fear of hurting other people. It tied yours and made you compromise. Now you're moving in new circumstances, with new limitations—and I can almost see the wheels go round as you try to figure a way to make these new circumstances work. But I must choose my own way, with a different sort of action than you want me to take. You'd like to believe that I didn't cause Catherine's death. I think it's very likely that I did."

I knew what he meant to do—and I could not be calm and sensible and courageous now. Not when the outcome meant King's life and happiness.

"But don't you see the injustice that may be done if you go to the police?" I cried. "What do you think they'll make of a misplaced beach robe, a missing seashell? All they'll care about is the quarrel you had with Catherine before she died, and what happened down there in the clearing. And because you've held this back, it will be as you've said—all the worse for you now."

"But not as bad as it will be if I wait still longer. Or if Leila should decide to talk to Captain Osborn before I do. If that happened it might be pretty shattering for us all."

I could not keep away from him a moment more. When he rose to put the chairs away I went to him and pressed my cheek to his. His arms came about me with love and tenderness.

"One of the things that helps me most in all this is that I know now what you're like," he said. "You'll make your life work out somehow—no matter what."

I didn't want to make it work without him. I had no use now for words like courage and good sense. I clung to him and wept. When he had kissed me gently he put me out of his arms and went to pick up the chairs and return them to the cupboard. I watched him bleakly—and saw something that startled me.

There on the bottom shelf of the cupboard rested a large cardboard carton filled with sand.

"What's that for?" I asked.

King glanced indifferently at the box of sand. "I don't know. I've never seen it before. Some whim of Catherine's, I suppose. She carted shells for Alex around in sand to keep them from breaking. But why she brought it here I wouldn't know. Come along, darling—we've got to get back to the house. There's supposed to be a hurricane heading this way and I'll have to get busy battening things down. First at home, then here. If this storm hits us it may be bad."

I forgot the box of sand as we went out to the car. "Just promise me one thing," I begged. "Don't do anything right away. Wait just a little while longer."

"I'll have to wait if there's a hurricane coming. The whole island will be home putting up shutters and barricades. And if it hits none of us will be going down the hill to town until it's over."

All the way back in the car my thoughts were furiously busy, trying to find a way out of this new trap that King was building around himself. With my mind I admitted that he had every right to build it—that he must do what was sound for him. But with my heart, my emotions, I was twisting and turning, looking for loopholes —something that would present facts to Captain Osborn and spare us all the dreadful time that lay ahead.

I had to begin somewhere, and when we were home, and I had gone up to my room and dressed, I came downstairs to start with the first person who came to mind. Not with anyone in the family—but with the little maid, Noreen.

I found her in the dining room polishing the big mahogany table. She hummed a song to herself as she moved in slow rhythm and I caught the words as I came through the door: "I work so slow, I work . . . so . . . slow."

"Hello, Noreen," I said, and she smiled at me with ready island friendliness. She was not worrying about jumbies at the moment, but it was necessary to upset her all over again.

I launched into my subject quickly, giving her no chance to escape. "I think you may be right that something queer has been happening in this house. But I don't think spirits have any part in it. Noreen, will you tell me when it was you thought you saw Mrs. Drew wearing that robe on the terrace after she must have been dead? Perhaps we can clear this up if we think about it."

Her dark eyes widened and I thought for a moment that she would run off in fright.

"You're doing a lovely job on the table top," I said. "That's a beautiful shine."

She nodded, pleased, and leaned into a few more slow strokes. As her cloth swept the glossy surface she answered me softly. "I stay up late dat night. When I see young missy Leila come runnin' up fum de garden, she don' see me. She run right upstairs. Right after come her mama and she walkin' wavy, like she got too much drink. I run away fas' so she not be mad to me."

"Noreen," I said, "do you remember how Mrs. Drew was dressed when she came back to the house?"

The girl cast a fearful look in the direction of the terrace before she answered, then nodded vigorously.

"She all dress' up in dat big coat t'ing."

This was the answer I'd hoped for. "You mean the robe she used to wear to the beach? The one I brought back to the house a while ago?"

Again Noreen nodded.

"Did you go to bed after that? Or did you watch what she did?"

Noreen had not gone to bed, but neither had she stayed on the gallery to follow Catherine's immediate actions after she crossed the terrace. Later, when Catherine was found, Noreen was certain she must have seen a jumbie earlier. Catherine's body might be down on the catchment, but her spirit had come weaving up to the house, and Noreen was very sure of this.

I told the girl that I did not think it could have happened like that. I pointed out that since she had not stayed to see what Mrs. Drew did when she came to the house, it was possible that Catherine had slipped out of the robe, left it on the rack, and for some reason of her own had gone back to the clearing. Only then could she have fallen down the catchment—without the burnoose. Because I had seen the robe here at the house with my own eyes. I had touched it—probably only a few moments after it had been left on the rack —and had found it damp.

Noreen seemed vaguely soothed by my confidently concocted story, and I left her polishing and went outside to be alone where I could think. All the movements had been very close that night, with each of us stepping almost on the other's heels. There seemed no space of time for what I wanted to believe had happened. Leila had come running upstairs and I had spent only a few minutes to find out what was the matter, and then get down to the clearing.

Could there have been time for Catherine to come to the house, leave the robe behind, and return to the clearing where her assailant had waited for her? The thing must have happened just before I reached the lookout point and discovered that third shadow sprawled upon the catchment. It was even possible that whoever had flung Catherine down the hill had stood hidden among the trees when I reached the place, watching my every move.

The thought was terrifying, even so long after the fact, and as I hurried toward the path that led to the clearing, retracing the steps I had taken that night against the handicaps of darkness and the slippery path, the sense of terror that had driven me then seemed to rise in me once more. Like Leila, I had begun to dread both forest and clearing. Yet I must test the way once more, if only to learn how long it had taken me. At least it was broad daylight and the day was bright and calm, instead of dark and rainy—yet the sun-dappled forest seemed again an ominous place.

Thrusting back senseless fear, I retraced my steps as closely as I could. So absorbed was I in what I was doing that it was a shock to round the last protruding black tree bole and find that someone was ahead of me.

A man knelt beside a clump of underbrush with his back to me. He heard the crackle of a twig beneath my foot and looked around. It was Steve O'Neill. The hard appraisal he turned upon me, the grim set of his mouth were anything but reassuring. There was nothing now of that lighthearted unicorn gaiety that had seemed to mark him in the past. He was clearly bent on some secret business of his own, and my sudden appearance in this place did not please him in the least.

Watching me warily over his shoulder, he slipped something into a pocket before he rose to face me, looking in this small place a far bigger man than he had on the beach.

XIX

Where sunlight struck through the branches of the mango tree
Steve's hair seemed like bright gold, and his face had the smooth,
unlined look of a boy, but he was not a boy and I did not like the
warning in his eyes. It was as if he said openly, "Take care. Mind
your own business."

I had no intention of minding my own business. In spite of the
fact that the nameless fear I'd experienced on my way to this place
now had a real object, I had to stand my ground—even to bluff, if
necessary. I had to know what it was he had found in the underbrush
of the clearing.

I held out my hand. "Give it to me. Whatever it is, you'd better
give it to me."

He tried to recover his easy manner, but his eyes retained their
warning and I distrusted him increasingly.

"It isn't anything much, Miss Jessica-Jessica," he mocked.
"Though maybe you'd like to come and take whatever it is away
from me?"

"I won't need to do that," I said. "Because if you don't give it
to me, you must account for it to Mr. Drew. I don't think you want
that."

"You're a spunky sort, aren't you?" he said, ignoring my reference to King. "Always turning up in places where you don't belong.
There was a time when I thought you might stand up to Cathy once
too often."

"Instead of which it was she who tormented someone once too
often? Is that it?"

For an instant I thought he would reach for me in anger. Then
he relaxed with the semblance of a grin, dug into his pocket, and
held up his hand. In his fingers dangled a broken length of chain
from which Catherine's columbella hung by its central loop of gold.
I snatched chain and shell from him and he made no effort to take

them back, but stood smiling at me—a smile without friendliness or amusement in it.

"Did you come here to look for this?" I asked.

"Not that in particular," he said. "But I got the idea I might find something if I looked around here a bit more carefully. That broken chain tells a lot, doesn't it? It bears out what Leila said to her father down at Magens Bay this morning."

It was becoming clear that this young man might prove dangerous to King, and I said nothing.

"The chain must have snapped when Catherine fought for her life. Don't you think that's possible?" he went on. "And in that case you know who it was she had to fight. You know better than anyone else."

I had to answer him boldly then. "If you're thinking of Kingdon Drew, you're completely wrong. He has told us all exactly what happened that night—and it wasn't he who flung Catherine down the catchment."

"Leila saw him," Steve said triumphantly. "She told me so."

He was altogether too pleased with himself, too sure of himself, and I wondered how much he had to hide of his own activities that night. How well might it serve him to have King suspected of causing Catherine's death? He had been an adoring follower of a comet, yes, but there had been times when I'd heard him speak sharply, warningly to her. His motive in coming here to search was not altogether open and clear.

"I'll take this back to the house," I said, slipping the columbella into the side pocket of my skirt.

He stood watching me with that bright, dangerous look and I knew very well that it would not take much more provocation for him to take the columbella from me. Though it cost me an effort I turned my back on him with a pretense of calm and started along the path to the terrace. I walked boldly, letting twigs crackle beneath my feet—walked a few yards until the turn of the path took me out of his sight. Then I stopped and retraced my steps softly until I could glimpse the clearing through thick growth that hid me from him.

Steve was nowhere in sight. I stepped into the open and saw that he had gone over the new railing King had put up, and dropped to the top of the catchment. I ran to the railing and saw that he was climbing down, catlike in his sneakers, moving quickly toward the two humps of black rock that protruded a third of the way down the catchment.

What he was looking for I did not know, but I didn't want to let him out of my sight. I had to know what he was doing and why he was here. He had given up the columbella too lightly for it to be of much importance. There was something else he searched for and I wanted to know what it was.

I found the pathway that led out of the clearing in the opposite direction from the house—the path King had taken along the hillside the night Catherine had died—and ran along it, seeking for a way down the hill. There was an opening a little way along onto a steeper path. I took it, slipping and sliding until I was out upon the open hillside.

Steve had reached the humps of rock on the catchment and he seemed to be searching all around them, but as far as I could tell he had found nothing. He had not seen me yet and I left the path and started down through rough guinea grass that covered the hillside, scrambling and slipping until I was even with the foot of the catchment. If he had the idea that something was still to be found, it might very well lie at the bottom.

The slope was not as steep at the place where the catchment would pour its burden of water into a mesh-covered gutter stretching across the foot. Here I found I could easily climb upon the stones and by walking carefully I could follow the edge of the gutter.

Above, still two thirds of the way up, Steve had seen me and propped himself against a protruding rock to watch what I was doing. I fixed my attention on the stretch of wire mesh. Debris—stones, leaves, twigs—had washed down to be caught there, and I kicked at the rubbish with the toe of one shoe as I made my way along.

A sound high above told me that Steve was coming down, and I hurried, kicking out repeatedly with my foot. Suddenly my toe struck something hard that rolled and clattered. I bent to see what I had kicked and there was no mistaking the object. Dwarfed though it was by this huge expanse of rock, the look and shape of the black and white murex shell were unmistakable.

I picked it from the wire mesh and glanced upward. Steve had nearly reached the bottom ledge and was edging purposefully toward me along the base of the catchment, his fair head bright in the sun, his eyes sharp with intent. I knew at once that it was this shell he searched for and that he meant to have it, if he had to take it from me. Below the catchment the grassy hillside dropped to the edge of the road that zigzagged toward the houses of Charlotte Amalie and the pavement stretched empty of cars or help—my only line of escape. A wind had begun to blow, dispersing the hot, calm air, and I felt the pressure of it against my body as I jumped to the grass and let myself go hurtling down the steep bank toward the road, the shell held tightly in my hands. There were sounds behind me. Steve had leaped from the catchment in pursuit, and now I ran in terror. Without any doubt, I knew the truth—Steve was a desperate man. This shell meant something to him—though what I could not guess.

From the slant of the upper zigzag I heard the sound of a car coming down and I dashed out upon the pavement where it must pass. Just as I reached the road Steve caught me and whirled me about. I screamed and struck out at him with the shell in my hand. He dodged the blow and sprang back, suddenly wary of the mailed thing I held.

"So you'd try that?" he said, and it was not until later that I puzzled over his words.

The shell was of no use to me now, because I could not again take him by surprise, but it had given me a moment's respite. I ran up the road toward the descending car. It braked to a halt, barely missing me as the driver swung the wheel.

Alex Stair leaned out to regard me in surprise. "Are you all right? What's happened to frighten you?"

"Steve!" I cried, clinging to the car door with one hand and clutching the shell with the other.

Steve had halted at the edge of the road and when I looked around I saw he was jaunty again, and laughing.

Able to get no sense from me, Alex spoke to him. "What's so funny? Why is she frightened?"

Steve sauntered toward the car and I pulled open the door and got in beside Alex.

"I think she's gone nuts," Steve said, but though his usual smile was in place, his eyes were still wary. "All I did was come down to see what she'd found on the catchment and she took off screeching and running. Maybe you can make out what's the matter with her."

The unicorn mask was in place—he was all the bantering, casual young man—and I did not trust him at all, or know how to convince Alex that a few moments ago Steve had been someone very different.

"Just take me back to the house, please," I said to Alex. "I don't want to talk to him. No matter what he says, he meant to frighten me—maybe even to hurt me."

Alex regarded Steve with cool dislike, and I wondered if the old rivalry still rankled between these two because of Catherine. He did not speak to Steve again, but turned the car around on the pavement and started uphill toward Hampden House. When I looked behind, Steve was climbing the hillside in a diagonal that led away from the catchment and the house.

"You came just in time," I said, still out of breath.

Alex spoke a bit grimly. "So I gather. The hurricane warnings are getting worse and I want to get downtown while I can and see that the shop is boarded up. Everything stops when there's a hurricane threat. But I'll take you back to the house first. Do you care to tell me what all that to-do with Steve was about?"

I held up the murex. "I found this at the foot of the catchment. Steve meant to take it away from me."

"Why would he want the thing?"

"I don't know." I could not tell him what was in my mind.

Alex said nothing more until we reached the driveway of Hampden House. Then, when I would have left the car, he reached out to take the big shell from my hands. Slowly he turned it about, tapping away bits of leaf and earth that clung to the spiky surface and were caught inside the shell. For the first time I saw the damage that had been done when the shell had bounced the length of the catchment from the top where Catherine must have held it in her hands. Several black spines were broken, and I could see a crack running toward the flared tail. The tail itself was damaged and the tiny pink nose of the shell had been split off in its bounding fall.

Alex shook his head as though he saw only the damage done to what had been a fine shell specimen.

"What a shame," he said carelessly, and gave the murex back, his face expressionless, though his lips had a tight set in their fringe of beard.

I watched him, suddenly interested in his reaction. "Leila has been looking for this shell. She has the notion that it might have been used to strike Catherine with."

Alex grimaced. "That's on a par with the pictures she's been drawing. I suggest you forget the idea and keep the shell out of Leila's sight. If you like, I'll dispose of it for you. It has no value any more."

"I'll keep it for now," I told him and got out of the car, leaving him to return down the hill.

As I neared the steps a figure darted out from behind a hedge and Mike O'Neill came toward me.

"Have you seen Steve?" He sounded anxious. "I can't find him anywhere."

"He was down on the hillside near the catchment," I told him, wondering at the boy's evident anxiety. "The last I saw, he was leaving in that direction." I pointed.

"Thanks," he said and started around the house. Just as I reached the door he turned back. "I got Leila home all right," he assured me. "I got her away from Steve."

We understood each other very well. "Thank *you*," I said, and went inside.

Back in my room I set the murex upon my bureau. By its broken chain I drew the columbella from my pocket and placed it beside the larger shell. Then I lay down on my bed to close my eyes, trying to figure something out.

When the luncheon gong sounded I did not stir. I wanted nothing to eat. I was conscious mainly of time running out, bringing us all inexorably to the moment when King would go to the police and all would be taken out of our hands. There must be something—something!—that would put off that moment.

But only the hurricane offered a chance of postponement. I reached out to turn on my radio. The voice was quietly insistent, warning St. Thomas to get ready for gale-force winds. Hopefully, rampaging Katy would pass well to the south of St. Croix, and thus even farther from St. Thomas, but we must be prepared. Guadeloupe was already on a hurricane alert and real trouble was expected there. "Hurricane watch" had been changed to "Hurricane warning" for the Virgin Islands, since the storm was picking up speed and the course might veer at any time. It looked as though we might be hit by the edge of the storm earlier than had been expected. Sirens would be sounded shortly to warn all islanders to prepare for the worst—though "Take cover" was still scheduled for afternoon.

I must have lain on the bed with my thoughts turning in futile circles for an hour or more. The house was anything but quiet. Loud bangings and poundings told me that hurricane shutters were going up downstairs. In the big hotels, I knew that the help would be pasting miles of adhesive-paper strips over the great areas of sheer glass, crisscrossing each window to prevent a scattering of glass if the wind blew it in. This putting up and taking down of shutters occurred five or six times during the season and the whole island would be buzzing with hurricane talk and preparations. Warning flags would be up and the waterfront would tie itself down and pray.

Undoubtedly the streets were emptying by now, and those hotels on high ground would be turning themselves into emergency centers —just in case. Aunt Janet had told me all of this. But here on our mountaintop we were, as always, isolated from the town—and it seemed a different world. One more exposed and vulnerable than the town itself.

Thinking about hurricanes was getting me nowhere. I rose and picked up the murex shell to have another look at it. The moment I took it in my hand the experiment was irresistible. When I had struck out at Steve earlier I had simply grasped the shell around its spikes, which had given me no great hold on it. Now I slipped my fingers deep into the white hollow that was as smooth to my touch and as slick as the inside of a china cup. There was plenty of room and my four fingers slipped into it easily, except where some tiny excrescence rubbed against my middle finger. With my fingers curled within the shell, gripping it, my hand became a mailed fist. In spite of broken and blunted spikes, the thing was like the knobbed head of a mace, and as dangerous. If used as a weapon it could inflict a crushing, murderous blow. Struck with such a weapon, Catherine would have gone backward through the railing without being able to save herself. A single blow could have stunned her, perhaps killed her. But never, never would Kingdon Drew have struck out with such a thing. It would be completely out of character for him. But even as I reassured myself I remembered that I, who was hardly a vicious woman, had struck unthinkingly at Steve with this same shell—meaning only to ward him off. And he had leaped away from me the moment I'd raised it, however clumsily. He had said, "So you'd try that?"—as though he knew very well what it might accomplish.

I drew my fingers in distaste from the ugly thing, and the bit of shell or rock that clung to the interior came away and skittered across the floor to lose itself in some crack.

Outdoors the wind had begun to howl over our mountain ridge and I could feel the house shudder against the buffeting. Yet the sun still shone, for all the encroaching haze, and since my doors had not yet been barricaded, light glared in from the gallery to strike a dazzle from something in the straw rug at my feet. Since it was easier to think about spots of sunlight than to solve impossible problems, I gave the glint my attention. Some bit of glass seemed to be embedded in the rug, caught in the deep, lacy pattern of straw.

This must be the stone I had just dislodged from inside the shell when I drew out my hand. Curiosity grew. From a bureau drawer

I brought a nail file and knelt to pry a twinkling piece of green glass out of the rug. It came loose easily and I stood up with the small, hard fragment on my palm, my attention thoroughly caught. This was no glass. It was exquisite, perfectly faceted—a green gem stone that looked as though it must once have belonged in a ring. It was undoubtedly an emerald.

As I turned it over I saw something grayish stuck to the surface, something rough to my touch as I ran my finger over the spot—like a speck of household cement. I picked up the shell and curved a finger into the deeply convoluted lip. Yes, there was still a faintly rough place well within the hidden curve and when I picked at it with a fingernail, specks of dry cement came away. The small green stone I held in my hand must have been cemented to the hidden interior of the shell. By Edith, I wondered, working in the seclusion of her workroom? Or by Catherine herself—since she had taken such an interest in the finding and transporting of shells? If there was one jewel in the shell, could there be others? Remembrance of that talk of jewel thieves around the Caribbean, talk I had heard ever since coming here, flashed through my mind.

The murex had a deep, hidden interior, and I could find nothing more until I probed with a curved pair of tweezers. At the first pinch they brought away a speck of cotton, and I thrust them in more deeply, deaf now to the pounding that went on around the house, to the buffeting of the wind outdoors.

In the depths of the shell the tweezers took something in their grasp and I brought out a small rolled twist of dirty white cotton. Picking it away, I found that I held twin diamond earrings in my fingers. These were tiny things, set with fine gold wire and intended for pierced ears.

I was excited now, and on my way to something important, but I needed help on the objects I had found. I had to know whether they could be identified by someone in the house.

Catching up both the murex and the columbella, hiding the emerald and the earrings in my other hand, I went to rap on Leila's door. For a moment there was silence; then she came to open it a crack and peer out at me.

"What do you want?" she asked, her tone hostile.

"I need your help. I want to show you what I've found. You may know something about these things."

Reluctantly she backed from the door, and when I stepped into the room and closed it behind me I saw that she had changed from bikini to her own rumpled shorts and blouse. Her hair was untidy, her cheeks streaked from weeping, and I wanted to put my arms about her, hold her comfortingly, but I put the impulse firmly aside. She would welcome no comfort from me, and the accusations she had hurled at her father could not help but stand between us.

Not until I was well into the room did I see the bed and what she was doing. Across the spread were heaped piles of clothes. Some of the dresses I recognized. These were things that had belonged to Catherine. Leila appeared to be sorting through them, and I knew why she wept. The very touch of such garments must make her loss all the more painfully acute, and I wondered who had permitted her this self-torture.

She looked at me defiantly. "Aunt Edith was going to give everything of Cathy's away, and I couldn't bear that. I want to keep some of these things myself."

I set the murex and the columbella on a table. At once Leila pounced upon the gilded shell with its broken chain.

"Steve found it in the clearing near the lookout point," I said. "The murex was at the foot of the catchment."

She stared at me, pressing her lips together so they would not quiver.

"Do you know anything about these?" I asked, holding out the gems on the palm of my hand.

For a moment she said nothing, her surprise evident. Then she touched the twin diamonds, turning them over on my palm.

"These are Cathy's. They're the earrings that were stolen from her the last time she was in San Juan. Where did you find them?"

"And the emerald? Have you seen that before?"

She was watching me, her eyes troubled. "I don't think it belongs to anyone here. I know all Gran's jewels because she's shown them to me often. And Aunt Edith has nothing like that."

"It wasn't your mother's then?"

She shook her head. "Of course not. What are you getting at?"

"Both the earrings and the stone were hidden inside that murex shell before it rolled down the catchment," I said bluntly.

Leila sat up on the bed among her mother's clothes, the columbella held tightly in her fingers, her eyes closed. When she spoke it was not about shells or jewels and her voice took on a trancelike quality.

"Cathy used to scuba dive a lot. Once she had a terrible experience. She was out in the Atlantic, well off from land, and she'd swum under water away from the boat that brought her out. She surfaced and saw a fin sticking up out of the water some distance away.

Then another and another popped up and they began to circle around her, coming between her and the boat, circling in a little closer all the time. She said it was exciting and dreadful—and she was terribly frightened. She couldn't even move in the water because she kept thinking it would be such a painful way to die, and that paralyzed her. But the people in the boat saw what was happening and they came through the line of fins and pulled her to safety."

I waited, not sure why she had told me this chilling story. Then she opened her eyes and looked at me quite clearly and calmly.

"Perhaps that's the way it is now," she said. "Perhaps the fins are circling around and coming in closer to me all the time. Nearer and nearer and nearer until something dreadful happens!"

My fingers closed about the green stone and the earrings as I stood there trying to put from my mind the eerie picture Leila had painted, seeking an answer to what was happening now. Once we knew who had hidden these things inside the murex shell, a great deal might be explained.

"I know what you're trying to do!" Leila cried, suddenly defiant. "You're trying to find some way to make everything look bad for Cathy. So you can help my father escape what he's done. But you won't get away with it, you know. If that black shell rolled to the foot of the catchment—that's the answer. It's just as I told you— Dad used it when he struck her."

Dealing with her in this distraught state seemed hopeless, but I managed to speak quietly. "You can't have lived with your father all these years and not know him better than that."

Tears glittered in her eyes. "Who was it then? Tell me that—who struck Cathy with the shell if it wasn't Dad?"

"I'm not sure anyone did, but if you must believe that—what about Steve O'Neill?"

She snorted her scorn for my words. "Steve was crazy about her! He'd never have hurt her in any way!"

"Just the same, he knew the shell might have been used as a weapon. He jumped away when I waved it at him quite feebly."

"Of course he knew. I told him myself. But it's no use your trying to play that sort of game—blaming everyone else. You're the one who ought to be punished. You're the one who caused all this. If you hadn't come here and made Dad fall for you—"

She had picked up one of Catherine's dresses, but now she flung it from her violently and pushed past me to open the door and run downstairs as if she were pursued. A voice I had not listened to for some time whispered in my mind: "You're out of your depth,

Jessie dear. You're not clever enough to handle anything as big as this."

I slammed the door on such thoughts and turned my back on Helen. This was *now*. This was reality. There was no one left but me to fight for King—since I did not think he was going to fight for himself. No matter how stumbling and foolish my efforts, I had to keep trying to prove what perhaps could not be proved.

Leaving the shells behind but keeping the gems in my hand, I went back to my room. Edith Stair stood in the middle of the floor, looking around. She had come in through the open French doors to the gallery and she regarded me with a dour expression and no surprise.

I held out my hand, showing her the earrings and the emerald. "Are these what you've been searching my room for?"

She made no effort to deny or defend, but stared at the articles on my palm.

"So you did take the emerald! I knew it all along, though I couldn't find where you'd hidden it."

"Take it?" I echoed. "Take it from where?"

Her gaze flicked scornfully to my face and then back to the gems on my hand. Before I could draw my hand away, her fingers darted out suddenly to snatch the jewels into her own possession.

"Don't pretend such innocence with me! Catherine said all along that you took something from my workroom that afternoon you were there. But where did you find my sister's earrings? She told me they were in a safe place where they'd never be discovered."

I did not like the woman's feverish expression, and I was glad of the open door behind me. Yet I had to stay and coax from her whatever I could learn that might help King.

"I found them just now in that murex shell," I told her. "Leila believes the shell was used to strike her mother down. I found it lying at the foot of the catchment."

Edith's eyes had turned a little glassy, and one lid twitched out of control. She grasped a corner of the bureau to support herself. My thoughts were running ahead, adding things up, giving me answers that raised more questions. That day when I had built sand castles in Edith's workroom she had been terribly angry. Because the emerald had been hidden in the sand? There had been a box of sand at Caprice—and another at the redwood house. Perhaps the same box. Harmless seeming enough, but always put in a place where tampering was unlikely—if it had not been for me.

Edith recovered herself sufficiently to stand free of the bureau.

"You'd better keep quiet about this if you want to save King. You'd better say nothing to anyone!"

She looked quite dreadful and I backed toward the door. I would not bargain with her, nor would I stand there and let her come closer. I could think of only one thing—that sandbox at King's house. I had to get to it—quickly.

The moment the door was closed behind me I fled down the stairs, not looking back to see if she followed. The downstairs area was lost in shadows because of hurricane shutters across the terrace doors. The garden boy was there working on the barricades. Apparently the electric power had already failed, for Noreen moved about the room, lighting the candles that stood everywhere in their hurricane globes. King was nowhere in sight, but Leila was coming toward the foot of the stairs, and in the pale candle gloom I saw tears running down her cheeks. As we met she paused, bearing herself with a certain erect dignity that reminded me of her grandmother.

"I've just telephoned Captain Osborn," she told me. "I've let him know that Cathy's death was—murder. And that Dad was responsible. The captain is coming right up to the house, if he can make it before the storm gets too bad."

Somehow it hurt me to breathe because of the pain around my heart. There was nothing I could say to her, and there were only two things left to be done. I had to get to that box of sand before anyone else did. And I had to find King.

A choking sound from the top of the stairs made me look up to see Edith at the turn, her face yellow-pale. She had heard Leila.

For a moment I thought she might faint, but she clung to the bannister, her lips moving. "Alex!" she whispered. "Where is Alex?"

"He's gone downtown," I told her, and then spoke to Leila. "You'd better look after your aunt."

I ran across the room to Noreen. The little maid had heard and her eyes were wide with fright, the hand that lit the tapers shaking. But she managed to answer my demand and tell me that King had gone to board up the redwood house.

I waited for no more. Now both my goals were the same.

XX

I ran through the aisle of royal palms to the road, finding that I had to fight the wind. The sun had disappeared and the sky was a glittery gray. Each moment the wind seemed to grow stronger, and overhead the racing clouds had a ragged look, running together across the sky like clouds at home racing ahead of a storm. From the road I could now and then glimpse the harbor far below, alive with whitecaps and with that strangely empty look about it. In the waters between Frenchtown and Hassel Island a few medium-sized craft had taken shelter, but there were no other boats to be seen.

The wind tore at my hair, my clothes. The distance to the house was no more than a ten-minute walk, but it took me at least twenty in my struggle against the wind. When I started down the paved drive that led off the highway, I glimpsed King's car parked beside the house, and saw that the door stood open. Eagerly I ran toward steps to the little deck that rimmed this side of the house, and as I ran I saw that someone had carried the box of sand outside, to set it not far from the top of the steps.

I called out to King as I went up the steps, and then dropped to my knees beside the box, dipping both hands into loose dry sand. As I had noticed before, there was a roughness to it. I brought up a handful and let it trickle through my fingers, leaving behind something that winked blue in the fading light. It looked like a sapphire. The next cupped handful netted two large diamonds. When I had put the stones down beside me, I dusted my hands free of sand and sat back on my heels, abruptly aware that King had not answered my call. I was about to stand up and shout for him again, to start searching for him through a house which seemed strangely quiet. But before I could move, I heard a step behind me and looked around.

Steve O'Neill stood in the doorway balancing a heavy flashlight in his hands. This was the same grim young man I had seen searching the catchment—and I was afraid. My interest in the sandbox was clear to him, for my little cache of jewels lay upon the boards of the deck beside me.

"So what are you going to do now?" he asked, his voice deceptively calm.

At least I could get to my feet, my concern for King the main worry in my mind. "You made a good combination, didn't you—you and Catherine?" I said. "Using Caprice and Edith's workroom for your business—whatever it was."

"And you've meant trouble ever since you came here," he said.

I tried to keep him talking, so King would surely hear us and come to my aid. "It was you in Edith's workroom closet this morning, wasn't it? You put on that beach robe and dashed out when I'd have opened the door."

Cold spite looked out of his eyes. "You're pretty smart, aren't you, Miss Jessica-Jessica? But you were getting too snoopy, and I had to move that box of sand up here before you caught on. Now I think we'll put a stop to your snooping."

I saw the gleam of the flashlight in his hands, but before he could move I whirled away from him, running along the deck to the front of the house and the cantilevered veranda. I rounded the corner into the wind, seeking for an open door. I had to get inside now. I had to find King.

There was no open door. Here hurricane shutters were already up and the whole stretch of glass was barricaded. Ahead, the veranda ended in a rail above the cliff cutting off my escape. I had run into a cul-de-sac.

Steve caught me before I reached the veranda's end, and I cried out in desperation, bracing myself, expecting a blow from his torch, but he laughed and dropped it to the floor, swung me about to face him. He could be as cruel as Catherine. The long rail was behind me, pressing hurtfully against my back, and he had me by the shoulders, forcing me over it. Below me lay the sea of flamboyants, thrashing wildly in the wind, their petals flying. Below and through them lay the drop-off to the cliff. I struggled in his grasp, fighting the force that bent me backward over the rail so that at any moment gravity would win and I would go plunging down from the heights.

"Do you think this was how Cathy felt?" he cried, his hands cruel on my shoulders as he pressed me down. "Do you think this was the way she struggled when she knew she must go through that railing?" He was whispering now, close to my ear.

And then, from the corner of my eye I caught movement—the flash of something black in the air—and heard the thud of a blow.

Astonishingly, Steve's hands loosened from my shoulders, slipping away as he went down upon the floor of the veranda. I sprang back from the rail to stare in amazement at Mike O'Neill, who stood looking down at his brother, the flashlight in his hand.

"You all right?" Mike asked, his young face dark and angry.

"King?" I gasped. "Is he—"

"Inside," Mike said, and knelt beside his brother.

I ran along the veranda and around the corner to the open front door. Inside the shuttered house the air was hot and still and the rooms were dark after that bright gray glitter outdoors. In the gloom I found him, face down where he had fallen. My heart nearly stopped as I ran to where he lay and dropped to my knees beside him, touching his shoulder gently, calling his name. He groaned, moved, and my heart began to beat again.

Mike came into the room to dump his brother unceremoniously on the floor not far from King. "What do we do now?" he asked me soberly.

I waved a hand at King and Mike managed a reassuring grin. "I think he'll be all right in a few minutes. I had a look earlier. There—he's coming to now. And so is my brother. I'd better take a hand with him."

Steve was trying to sit up and Mike pushed him back. "Take it easy, pal—if you don't want another conk on the head. You've been playing too rough around here."

King groaned and sat up, feeling the back of his head, wincing as he found the lump where the torch had struck him. Then he looked blankly at me. "How did you get here? I had a feeling somebody was around while I was putting up the shutters, but I never saw what hit me. How about telling me what happened?"

My words came hurriedly, without order. "Steve hit you with a flashlight. He's been mixed up in some kind of jewel-stealing scheme with Catherine. That box of sand outside is a way station to wherever the things were going."

The sound of my voice seemed to wake Steve up and this time he managed to get to his feet in spite of Mike. But while he looked grim, he was still too shaken to be a threat.

"You'd better start talking," King said. "Keep an eye on him, Mike."

Mike stepped closer to his brother, though he did not touch him again. Outside the wind hurled itself at the house, shaking its very timbers.

"Why don't you ask her to talk?" Steve said, nodding at me. "She knows so much. Or thinks she does."

"I know you tried to push me over the veranda railing just now!" I cried. "Perhaps in the same way you pushed Catherine through the railing above the catchment."

"I wouldn't have pushed you over," Steve said in disgust. "I only wanted to give you a scare."

King got up and took a step toward him and Steve edged warily back.

"Watch yourself," Steve said. "You make trouble for me, and I'll go to the police with what happened that night. I'll tell them what all of you at Hampden House are trying to hush up—that Catherine's husband fell for a schoolteacher and found a way to get rid of his wife."

"As it happens I'm going to the police myself," King said evenly. "And when I do you're coming with me."

This time Steve moved suddenly, unexpectedly. He shoved his brother off balance and dashed for the door before anyone could stop him. Mike made no effort at pursuit, and when King would have gone after him Mike held him back apologetically.

"Let him go, Mr. Drew. He won't get far. His car won't start. I found it down the road and yanked out the distributor head. Even if he gets away, this is an island—and there's a hurricane stirring up the Caribbean. He can't even use a boat."

I heard despair in Mike's voice and knew he could not hate his brother, that he was suffering because of what Steve had done.

We went outside to the rear deck and looked over thrashing shrubbery. The wind had an ugly whine to it now. Steve was nowhere in sight. I bent to pick up the gems that lay beside the sandbox.

"Let's go back to the house," I said. "We'd better take this box with us. It's something to show Captain Osborn."

"Show him?" King said.

I met his eyes unhappily. "That's what I came here to tell you. Leila has phoned him to come up to the house."

Mike said, "Poor kid—she's going to hate herself."

King braced his shoulders, as if to recover from a blow. "I'd like to have handled this myself. Come along—we'd better get going. Too bad Steve got away. We might have used him."

"I can tell you some of it," Mike offered quickly. "I've been getting suspicious, and lately I've followed Steve around. He got away from me today when I took Leila to her grandmother. But I've been putting things together."

King locked up the house and we went out to his car. It had begun to rain and the wind was howling over the mountain ridge in a steady gale. King drove slowly, hardly able to see for the downpour, and as we crawled along Mike told us what little he had put together. He had kept still because of his brother, and because he did not have enough information to go on. Besides, after Catherine's death he had expected everything to stop. But Steve had been determined to salvage the last batch of gems Catherine had apparently brought home from San Juan.

King kept his hands tightly on the wheel and his knuckles had whitened. "So that's how she was getting money," he said.

Mike nodded angrily. "I wasn't sure until lately. I guess she found it easy enough to pick up jewels belonging to her wealthy friends when she visited swank hotels away from St. Thomas. Since everybody thought the Hampden wealth was behind her, she could get away with it. Even when it came to bringing the stuff through customs—who was going to search every inch of her luggage? I guess wherever there are rich, careless women, there are thieves operating —so professionals got blamed. She even managed to make it look as though she'd been robbed herself a few times. I heard her laughing about it with Steve a few weeks ago."

The diamond earrings, I thought. No wonder Catherine had not wanted them found to give her away.

"Then she must have used Caprice for a hiding place for whatever she took," King said, swinging the wheel to miss a burro that had stumbled across the road in wind and rain.

"In those boxes of sand," I said, and remembered something else. "There was a tool kit in Catherine's bedroom closet at Caprice. I suppose they took the stuff there and broke it up into separate stones so it couldn't be identified. But then what?"

Mike shook his head. "I don't know. I think the shells had something to do with it."

"I'm sure they did," I said, and told them about the emerald I'd found cemented into the murex, and about the earrings Catherine had hidden in the same shell.

"That's a strange thing," King pondered. "Catherine brought that shell outdoors while I was on the terrace that night. Why? Who did she mean to show it to?"

Alex? I wondered. Leila had said she went out there first to meet Alex.

We had reached the house and King turned into the driveway.
A police car was already pulled up before the door. The worst had
happened.

Mike got out at once and dashed through the rain to the front
door, while King held me beside him for a moment.

"This may be the showdown," he said. "Take care of yourself,
darling. And stay out of it if you can."

I kissed him a little desperately and stepped into wind and driving rain. King came around the car and took my arm to brace me
against the cold pelting as we ran to the shelter of the house.

The door stood open upon the storm, to reduce the pressure indoors, though from this angle no rain came in. As we stepped into
the room, stepped out of wild sound into a hush, I knew I would
never forget the very look and quiet of the scene that greeted us.
So high were the ceilings, so distant the roof, that the roaring noises
of the storm were far away, and by contrast to the out-of-doors
the room seemed as still as the eye of a hurricane. All the strain
and ferment within was in our hearts.

The long main hall was shadowy with candlelight, its myriad
flames burning high and still behind the protection of glass. Across
the far end of the room the terrace had vanished and draperies were
drawn across to hide the blank wall of hurricane shutters. Black
draperies, they were, with clusters of scarlet flamboyant flaring
across them to make a scenic backdrop for the room.

Maud Hampden sat regally against the cushions of a sofa, with
Captain Osborn in a chair nearby. His expression as he leaned toward her seemed gentle, his manner considerate. Leila was nowhere
to be seen.

As we came in out of the storm the captain rose and bowed as
courteously as if this were no more than a social call. Maud watched
him, her face set in a tragic mask, then rose a little stiffly and came
to meet King. He hurried to her and put his arms about her, held
her affectionately for a moment. She would not accept his support
for long, however, but rested her hands on his arms and looked
sorrowfully into his face.

"Our little girl has taken a foolish and reckless step," Maud said.
"But perhaps it is best to postpone no longer. If we talk to Captain
Osborn now, we can finish this thing as soon as possible."

"I am ready to listen to whatever you may tell me," the captain
said in his quiet, formal manner.

"I'm sorry my daughter got to you first," King said. "I have waited
only because she has been through a time of shock and distress.

Now I would like her present while I tell you whatever I know about the night her mother died."

Maud looked up at him in pleading. "No, King—please. She will suffer enough as it is in her own self-reproach, without having her hear what must be said."

King shook his head gently. "We've tried to protect her too long, Maud dear. She isn't the child we've thought her. Jessica, will you bring Leila here, please?"

He was right, I knew. Whatever the outcome, Leila must now be present so that she could learn all the circumstances that surrounded her mother's death, and bear as well the consequences of her own hasty action. I went toward the stairs and saw Mike O'Neill standing near the door where we had forgotten him.

"Go sit down," I said. "You're a part of this now. Perhaps you can help Leila a little."

He gave me a grateful look and found a chair well away from the others.

As I started up the stairs Alex came abruptly out of his study and I paused in surprise with my hand on the bannister. Never had I seen the man with his emotions out of hand before. He looked angry and at the same time like a man seeking escape, a man fleeing an accuser.

Before he had taken three steps, his wife was on his heels, and she, clearly, had gone to pieces.

"It was your fault! Always your fault!" she shrilled at him. "How could I stop when I knew what the outcome would be?"

Maud spoke without raising her voice, but her tone penetrated both distant storm sounds and Edith's frantic tone, arresting her daughter.

"Edith! Come here and sit down at once. There is no use trying to blame Alex or anyone else for your own weakness. The captain must hear everything you have to tell him. This is the time to prove you have a spine."

Edith crumpled into the place beside her mother, giving no evidence of anything resembling Maud Hampden's spine. Alex uttered a sound that seemed a total rejection of his wife and strode to the terrace end of the room, where he stood with the black and scarlet draperies behind him. Maud's look followed him, as challenging and accusing as Edith's, in spite of her words. King watched all three in bewilderment.

I dared wait no longer, but fled upstairs to Leila's room. The door was closed and no sound reached me from inside, except the noises of the storm. I tapped and called her name, but there was no answer.

"Your father wants you to come downstairs," I said more loudly.

Without warning the door was pulled open in my face and all the crashing fury of this storm that was only a hurricane's edge seemed to rush toward me out of that small room. Leila's gallery door had been shuttered, but the rain was beating across it as though it played on a drum and the room danced with shadow as air stirred the candle stubs burning in shallow glasses.

"I'll come in a moment," she said above the noise, and turned back to her dressing table.

She had put on a straight sheath dress that had been a favorite of Catherine's—a shining white printed frivolously with green palm fronds. As the girl stood before the glass she picked something up, fastening its clasp about her neck before she turned. I saw that she wore the columbella on its golden chain. The break in the links had been mended with a tiny gold pin, and the shell gleamed in the candlelight, lifting on her breast with the quickness of her breathing. The evoking of everything that was Catherine was deliberate and clear.

This was no time for play acting, and I had to be brutal. "Don't go downstairs looking like that. You will hurt everyone, including yourself."

She had brushed her bangs back from her forehead, combing her hair in a more sophisticated style that made her look older. Strain had set her face into angles I had never seen before, so that all the roundness of young girlhood seemed to have been wiped away.

"No one cares anything about Cathy except me!" she cried, her voice too thin, too silvery high, too much like Catherine's. "I *am* going downstairs like this. I'm going to make them remember!"

Again I tried. "Do you know that the police captain is here and your grandmother has been talking to him? Your father wants to tell him what he can, and he wants you to be there to listen."

Her lips moved in a smile that was faintly malicious, and her eyes were sly in that way I hated to see.

"We'll both be there to listen," she said, and touched the shell on her breast. "Columbella and I!"

She went past me into the hall, and I had to hurry as she ran lightly, almost triumphantly, down the stairs.

The men rose as we appeared. There was shock in the look King turned upon his daughter. Edith sobbed aloud too dramatically and covered her face with her hands. Though he could not have understood all we felt, the captain lowered his eyes discreetly. Alex turned away to stir the black and scarlet draperies as if he wanted to look out upon the storm-ridden terrace. Beyond him the thick hangings muffled the drumbeat of rain upon the barricades that blocked his view.

It was Maud who spoke, silencing anything Leila might have been about to say.

"It would have been wiser to consult me before you acted, Grand-daughter. Since you did not, you will now sit down and be quiet while we try to work out what remains to be done. You've proved yourself a child today."

As quickly as that was Leila stripped of her pretending, and I saw her crumple into the young girl she really was, so that neither dress nor columbella suited her. Maud's strong words had been needed to return her to reality.

Mike brought the girl a chair, placing it where she could sit in a kindly area of shadow. I found my old place near the now hidden door to the terrace—where I had sat that night watching the start of this tragedy.

King began to tell Maud and the captain of what Catherine and Steve had been doing, but Maud stopped him at once.

"Edith has confided in me," she said quietly. "I think we must hear what she has to say before we come to other matters."

Edith sat with her head bowed, still weeping into her cupped hands. Alex, recovering from a fury that had held him silent, whipped cold words across the room toward his wife's bowed head.

"I would like to be given some of this confidence myself! Perhaps my wife will explain exactly how she happens to consider so many matters my fault?"

Edith raised her shattered face and stared resentfully at her husband. "It was your fault because you were willing to play Catherine's game! I knew how you felt about her, but she never really wanted you. She wanted no one but King—and because she'd lost him she had to destroy him. But she knew she could call you her way with a flick of her fingers and she knew—as I did—that you'd be weak enough to follow. Oh, you'd take sharp little revenges on her with words at times, but you'd have danced to her tune if she'd have had you. So I had to do what she wanted in order to keep her away from you. She needed me for the cover behind which she could send the jewels she stole into the States, where she could get good prices for them."

I glanced at Leila, sitting well back in the shadow on the opposite side of the room, and saw that Mike had reached out to hold her hand, though I doubt if she knew he had touched her. All her attention was riveted on Edith and the story she was telling. Alex listened too, his mask once more in place, his eyes so chill that I feared for Edith, whatever the outcome.

She did not look at her husband as she stumbled on. "It was Catherine's idea to hide the gems in shells she and Steve collected for Alex. They didn't have to be live shells, or valuable shells—any shells would do if the aperture was large enough. They kept a supply of them at Caprice for immediate use. They would hide the gems in a box of sand in Catherine's bedroom—where no one would ever look. Then, when they were ready, they'd bring them here with a few shells strewn about on top to fool everyone. It was up to me to sift the sand and find the jewels. Then I'd cement each gem to the inside of a shell and ship the collection off to Catherine's contact in the States —a man who posed as a legitimate shell buyer. I didn't take anything for what I did. All I wanted was to have my sister stay away from Alex. Of course Steve would do anything for her, but he was looking out for himself too, and she had to share with him. After—after what happened on the catchment, he wanted what jewels were left for himself. I didn't want to touch them, but he told me he'd go to the police if I didn't give them to him. Especially that valuable emerald that had disappeared. I know now that Catherine took it herself—though she tried to make me think Miss Abbott found it in the sand and hid it in her room."

Leila made a choked sound and snatched her hand away from Mike. "I don't believe what you're saying! It's all lies. Cathy wasn't a thief—or Steve either!"

Mike took back the hand she had snatched from him. "Hush now. It's all true and you've got to face it. We caught Steve this afternoon with the rest of the jewels. You'll have to toughen up, kid, and find out what's real and important—and what isn't."

Leila made a soft moaning sound and pulled away from him, repudiating him, repudiating us all. Her fingers played nervously with the columbella on her breast.

King spoke to Mike. "Come here and tell the captain what you know. It's a piece of the same picture."

Captain Osborn nodded. "Yes—it all appears to be the same picture. It seems that there was reason for Mrs. Drew to be in trouble with many people. But in the end all roads must lead to the one who did indeed strike her in the face with a large shell, so that she fell backward down the catchment."

King contradicted him at once. "That's not what happened!"

"No?" There was a slightly steely ring behind the courtesy now. "But Mrs. Hampden tells me she believes this is what happened."

I could feel pain constricting my heart again, so that it was difficult to breathe. In my mind was that chill vision Leila had planted there—of fins circling, circling, drawing always closer to the lone swimmer who would eventually be torn to bits and devoured by the predators. It was dreadful to stand helplessly by, treading water, unable to effect a rescue.

At King's bidding Mike left his chair and went dejectedly to explain to the captain what he knew of his brother's actions. He told how he had searched for Steve until he found him at the redwood house, though he had not been in time to prevent the attack upon Kingdon Drew, or the threat to me.

Listening there in that well-enclosed room, we were nevertheless a part of the storm with each high gust that slapped the building, flinging rain against panes and shutters in what had grown to a steady, muffled pounding. Once a snapped branch struck hard against the hurricane barrier on the terrace side with a boom like a jungle drum, and Edith gasped in fright.

Leila spoke into the sudden hush that followed, her voice high and tense. "Can you hear it? Can you hear the water pouring down the catchment, just the way it did—that night!"

We all turned uneasily in her direction, but it was Maud who silenced the note of rising hysteria in her granddaughter's voice.

"There was very little water rushing down the catchment that night. There were a few showers but it didn't rain the way it's raining now. I know because I was there in the clearing."

No one moved or spoke, though she held the attention of every one of us.

"I was there," she repeated quietly. "I saw exactly what happened. I know the truth about the shell."

Shock was almost tangible in the room, though not, I thought, for all of us. I swallowed hard and stole a glance at the others—at Edith's terrified look. At Alex, alert and on guard. At King, puzzled and alarmed. At Mike watching Leila, and at Leila, sitting on the edge of her chair, staring at her grandmother.

Captain Osborn's manner was no less mild than before as he spoke. "In that case it is time for you to tell us whatever you may know, Mrs. Hampden."

Maud Hampden nodded at him. "Yes, Captain, it is time for me to tell you what I know."

XXI

I think we hardly breathed, for fear of what we might hear, yet also for fear of missing a word. I think not one of us shifted our gaze from Maud Hampden's face as the old lady commenced her story with quiet dignity—though the sense of horror grew among us.

"Edith had already come to me with the truth about the gem stealing," Maud began. "Of course I made her understand that it must stop—at once, and without scandal. She repeated my orders to Catherine, and Catherine used the weapon she held over her sister. She tried to see Alex alone in Edith's workroom while everyone was busy preparing for the buffet supper. But Jessica was there that afternoon, so she proposed another rendezvous—to meet him in the clearing after the party. She warned Edith that she was going to expose her actions to Alex and tell him everything. Catherine had no fear that he would give her away, since Alex would want no exposure of his wife or any scandal that would reflect on the family. When Edith knew what her sister planned, she came to me, and it was I who went to the clearing to wait for Catherine. Apparently Alex changed his mind and did not keep the rendezvous after all."

Maud turned slightly to look at Alex Stair as he stood beside the wall of draperies that closed off the terrace. The man had lost his suavity.

"King was outside," he muttered. "Besides, I didn't care for the idea of this meeting with her. I didn't know what Catherine was up to. I never went near the clearing that night."

Maud nodded gravely and went on.

"Catherine met King on the terrace and they had a heated argument before she reached the woods. I could hear the angry sound of their voices while I waited for her under the mango tree. When she found me there she was furious. She was playing her dangerous high-wire game—risking a fall because danger always fascinated her. She'd brought the murex shell with her—to show Alex proof of the operation she directed. But when she found me there, she showed it to me instead. She gave it to me defiantly to examine. I told her I knew what was going on and that the whole thing must stop at once or I would not hesitate to turn her over to the police. She laughed at me. All her life she had been treated too leniently, protected when she should have been made to answer for the consequences of her action. Perhaps I have been most of all to blame for that."

Maud Hampden's voice faltered and her hands clasped each other so tightly that blue ridges of vein stood out upon them. Leila left her chair and started toward her grandmother, but Maud stopped her with a glance, as autocratic as ever.

"Sit down, dear. I haven't finished. When I heard someone coming along the woods path I thought it might be Alex, after all. I stepped back into the trees out of sight, though Catherine stayed to meet him. It was not Alex, however, but King—and this time he wasted no words. He took her by the shoulders and shook her angrily, flung her away from him so that she fell against the barrier above the catchment. I could have touched him as he brushed past me when he rushed away, out the other side of the woods, but he didn't see me at all. I went back to confront Catherine and finish what I had to say to her. She had torn off the burnoose she was wearing in order to examine her bruised shoulders for the hurt King had done her. Pain could make her lose her head and when she saw me she tried to punish me for what King had done, for what her own folly had driven her into. She sprang at me like a wild thing in an attack I didn't expect and tried to fasten her fingers about my throat. That was when I struck out at her with the shell I held in my hands."

For the first time Maud's voice broke completely. Her fine clear eyes—the feature I had first noted about her—searched the faces around the room, almost as though she asked for mercy. Edith moaned and Leila made a fumbling gesture of hand to mouth. No one else moved or uttered a sound. Captain Osborn stared at the toes of his shoes.

Recovering herself, Maud went on. "When I struck her she went backward through the rotting rail and rolled down the catchment."

Still no one spoke. We could not think, for shock and pain. Then Leila jumped up and rushed to her grandmother, dropping to her knees beside the old woman, flinging her arms about Maud's thin body.

"Oh, Gran, Gran!" she wailed. "You couldn't have—you couldn't!"

Almost absently Maud smoothed Leila's fine soft hair. "I'm sorry, darling. I was the one who most wanted not to injure you."

Leila sobbed and at the sound her grandmother stiffened, as if resistant to the one thing that could weaken her utterly.

"I was left there with the shell in my hands and the burnoose on the ground, stunned by what had happened. I called down the catchment and there was no answer. I had to think about the living and I flung the murex shell away from me, hoping it would never be found. I didn't know that the gold chain about Catherine's neck had snapped as we struggled and the columbella had rolled away into the brush. I picked up the burnoose and wrapped it around me, pulling the hood over my head. I had a vague notion that anyone who saw me returning to the house might take me for Catherine. The one thought in my mind was to get away from that place and let everyone think Catherine's fall had been an accident. Because of the dreadful scandal that would result, with its damage to everyone, and especially to Leila, I felt I had to keep silent."

Leila hid her face against her grandmother's breast. "You couldn't hurt anyone! You're good and brave and wise!"

Maud soothed her quietly. She bent her head and kissed her granddaughter lightly on the cheek.

"I am neither good nor wise and I have managed to build up a pattern of harm to others through most of the years of my life. Not maliciously, but foolishly, because I took pride in too many of the wrong things—among them what I considered my own superior judgment." Her eyes seemed to plead with King. "I didn't see Leila when she came upon her mother and father in the clearing and ran away. Things happened in such quick sequence that I must have gone back to the house almost upon Leila's heels. Noreen was the only one who saw me, and she thought I was Catherine. I hung the damp burnoose on the rack, and later I had Edith remove it to a cabinet in her workroom, so it might be forgotten. But when I hung it there that night, I went upstairs to my room to collect myself and think of a way to raise the alarm. There was no need. Catherine was discovered almost immediately."

Kneeling beside her, Leila pulled away from her garndmother and looked up into her face. All the love and loyalty she felt were revealed in her own.

"It wasn't your fault, Gran. You were fighting for your life. You wouldn't have harmed her deliberately. I know you didn't mean to hurt her."

Maud put a hand against Leila's cheek and held it there. "I don't know what I meant," she said. "I don't really know."

She freed herself gently from Leila's restraining arms and stood up to face Captain Osborn.

"There will be certain formalities you will be responsible for, Captain. As soon as the storm lessens I will go with you and do whatever you wish."

King went to her quickly and put a supporting arm about her shoulders. His face was working and he could not speak.

Captain Osborn did a strangely touching thing. He rose in almost military fashion and made a slight bow, a bending of his body that was somehow a salute.

"Madam," he said, "I am very sorry to find myself in this position. I must say, Madam, that I find you a most gallant lady."

She held out her hand to him and he took it.

"There are extenuating circumstances, Mrs. Hampden," he went on. "This matter will undoubtedly work itself out, though I am afraid unpleasantness cannot be avoided."

"There are no extenuating circumstances," Maud told him with calm dignity. "Nevertheless, perhaps certain unpleasantnesses may be avoided."

He looked doubtful and she smiled at him.

"You will see what I mean, Captain. Now there are a few things I would like to do. If you will permit me—before the storm ends?"

"Of course," he said and stood aside to let her pass.

King held her close to him for a moment, and I saw Maud's shoulders droop, saw a quiver touch them before she pulled away from him.

"You have always been a wonderful son to me," she said so softly that I barely caught the words. "I couldn't foresee that you were going to take this blame upon yourself. Will you forgive me for not telling the truth sooner? I'm not so brave as Leila thinks."

"There's nothing to forgive, Maud dear," King said, and kissed her tenderly.

My throat was tight as I watched, my vision blurred with tears. Leila had fled to the door, where she stood looking out a little wildly upon the storm. Beyond, the rain swept horizontally past across the drive, with the fury of the wind still behind it. Maud started toward her down the length of the room and I followed, more than a little worried now about Leila and how she would react to this new set of circumstances. Matters were moving too fast for our emotions to catch up with us.

"A breath of air—" Maud said and went to stand beside the girl.

I paused, not wanting to intrude upon this necessary time between Maud and her granddaughter. When I glanced back at the room I saw that King was speaking to Captain Osborn, while Alex stared coldly at his weeping wife. Edith had known. Edith had known about her mother's action all along. For the first time I felt real pity for her. All her life she had been the weak victim of her sister's scheming.

When I turned hesitantly toward the door again I found Leila gone and Maud nowhere in sight. The entryway stood empty—alarmingly so—and outside there was only that wildly blowing, stormy gray murk. Shock held me motionless for a moment. Then I shouted a warning to the others and acted purely on instinct. Leila had gone out into the storm—and perhaps Maud had too. They must be found and brought back at once.

The moment I stepped outside, the blast struck me, drenching me, hurling me halfway across the drive. I fought my way back to the wall of the house and was in time to see the white flash of Leila's dress from the direction of the terrace. The wall offered some protection against the wind, but I was already wet to the skin, and water streamed from my hair so that I had to shake limp strands from before my face.

Given the strength of desperation, I was moving faster than I had ever moved in my life. By the time I reached the exposed terrace, the will-o'-the-wisp of Leila's dress had disappeared into the grove of storm-tossed trees, and I ran into the woods after her. There was no sign of Maud.

Behind me I heard someone shout, but I was ahead and I ran on. The trees offered scant protection from wind and rain. The air was filled with debris—wet leaves and flying twigs, even branches that sailed past my head to crash somewhere behind me. I fought my way, while on ahead the white dress flickered, vanished, and reappeared as the pathway twisted and turned.

Then, somehow, I had reached the edge of the clearing. Leila was there—but she was not alone. Two figures struggled together, as if joined in some dreadful dance. One appeared to be straining toward the catchment, while the other strove to hold her back. But with all the noise and movement and confusion I could not tell which of the two was in danger.

Before I could move to stop this appalling struggle, I heard a sudden tremendous cracking sound overhead. In horror I looked up— and saw what was happening.

The storm had split the great mango tree. With an air of slow motion the huge trunk with all its heavy, fruit-laden branches had begun to descend from the heights. I screamed out to the two clasped together in the full path of the tree, but the sound of my voice was wrenched away on the wind as if I had not uttered a sound.

Nevertheless, something must have warned Maud. She looked up at the toppling branches still high overhead, and with a desperate strength she thrust the girl away from her. Leila stumbled backward and I caught her in my arms and pulled her from the path of descending death.

"Run!" I screamed to Maud. "Run!"—and it was as if I spoke in a whisper.

She did not run. She stood looking upward at the ancient tree, its branches tortured by the wind and spilling a torrent of water as they descended. The whole thing took no more than seconds, yet the tree seemed to come down with the slow dignity of a giant felled—first staggering, hesitant, then with its speed increasing on the great descent. King and Mike reached me as the tree crashed down with a boom far louder than the noises of the storm, thundering to the ground across the clearing—crushing the marble bench, smashing through the new railing King had built at the lookout point, settling at last with a trembling that made the earth shudder and left the head of the giant extending into the air far out over the catchment. Rain and wind tossed the great branches, beat at them wildly, and Leila ceased to struggle in my arms.

For minutes after the settling the earth seemed to shake, and while the branches still quivered from the force of the fall, Leila pulled herself free and thrashed her way through quivering leaves and rolling green fruit to reach the place where Maud lay pinned beneath the wreckage. King and Mike were beside her at once but Leila was closest to her grandmother, bending her head to catch her words.

Maud lay on her back, her body covered by green branches, one hand outflung. I saw its brief convulsive movement as Leila knelt beside her. Then the hand lay quiet on the muddy earth of the clearing.

Around us the storm howled. Rain bruised us with a slanting force, churning up the earth, slashing at still-quivering branches, beating down upon an upturned face. King raised his daughter to her feet and Mike brought her back to me. Laboriously, frantically, King strove to extricate Maud from the wreckage, but even with Mike to help him, there was no way to move the tree. Nothing could be done until the storm was over and we could get help. No further harm could reach Maud Hampden. She was beyond our aid.

The four of us stumbled blindly back to the house with the rain at our backs, the wind beating and thrusting us along. Leila gave herself to Mike's helping hands. King's arm was about me, and I leaned on his strength, intent for the moment upon getting back to the house and away from the hurtful, punishing wind.

Captain Osborn met us at the door, with Alex beside him. Across the room Edith still sat weeping, as if she knew very well that only tragic news could be expected. We were all shivering and wet, but we had no wish to hurry off and change our clothes. As King told the captain what had happened Alex, too, listened without surprise. Leila stood between her father and Mike O'Neill, her wet dress mud-spattered and plastered against her body, her hair slick with water, as though she had been swimming. The wildness and strain were still evident in her face.

Sadly the captain heard King through his account. "It was to be expected," he said when the story had been told. "She was indeed a gallant lady. I would have disliked very much to arrest her."

Suddenly I understood why he had not followed us into the storm to help, why he had waited quietly at the house for whatever news we might bring him.

"But why—why?" Leila began. "Gran wasn't to blame!"

With all the kindliness he might have shown his own daughter, the captain answered her. "In her heart the lady took the blame. She acted in order to destroy an evil and save others from the result of wickedness. But the woman she killed was also her child, whom she had once loved dearly—whom she could not wholly hate. I think she could not continue living without making reparation of a personal payment which the law might not have asked of her. The storm offered the lady her chance."

Leila's gaze did not waver from his face. "Gran said something to me down there just before she died. I didn't understand—but you've helped me to, a little."

"Perhaps the tree was the better way," he said gently. "Perhaps it was an act of God. Who is to say what led the lady to the clearing at that fateful moment?"

"Thank you, Captain Osborn," Leila said and turned toward her father. "Dad—" Her voice broke.

King held out his arms and she went into them, clinging to him, perhaps finding him again truly, for the first time since she had been a little girl. From his arms she turned her head to smile at me warmly, and at Mike, who stood a little apart, wet and woebegone, but cheering faintly at her smile.

We were shivering, the four of us who had gone to the clearing, but before I could move toward the stairs Alex spoke to the captain, his voice flat, devoid of feeling.

"What happens to us now?"

Delicately the captain shrugged. "There will be unpleasantness, I fear. Jewels have been stolen. A thief is abroad in the storm and must be picked up."

Edith broke in, her hands flung out in frantic pleading. "There's money in all Catherine's accounts. Some reparation can be made for the things she took. Won't that help a little?"

"Many things will be taken into consideration, I am sure," Captain Osborn said. "The pressures and coercion put upon yourself will not go unnoted—though naturally nothing can be promised."

"And what else?" Alex demanded. "What other unpleasantness?"

For a long moment the captain's gentle brown eyes held the challenge of Alex's pale ones.

"There have been two extremely sad accidents at Hampden House," he said at last. "Our island will grieve for a bereft family which has lost a mother in a tragic fall, and a grandmother felled by a tree in this storm."

The sound of the breath Alex released was audible across the room. He went abruptly to sit beside his wife, and I had the instinct that Alex Stair would always land on his feet, that he would overcome his fury and disgust and do whatever now needed to be done for Edith.

I held out my hand to Leila. "Come along," I said. "If you're as cold as I am, I think we'd better get into some dry clothes. Perhaps your father can find something for Mike."

She came to me and we went upstairs together.

The distant center of Hurricane Katy had moved on at last. Surprisingly, it was still afternoon and the sky grew lighter by the moment as clouds rolled away. The telephone was still in order and Captain Osborn had been able to make the necessary calls to town. He was now waiting for help to come up the mountain with the abating of the storm. Already the servants were taking down hurricane barriers all around the house.

When I went out upon the rain-drenched terrace I found Leila and King there ahead of me. I was still dazed by what had happened.

Events had moved almost faster than time, and it would take a little while to accept and understand.

King spoke to me and I went to join them. Leila stood near him, with one hand through the crook of his arm, as if she needed to stay very close to him. Her other hand was clasped upon something she held in her fingers.

Her face brightened in welcome when she saw me. "I want you to hear too, Jessica. I want to tell you both what Gran said to me, though her words were very strange."

She was silent for a moment, doubtful.

"Tell us now," said King gently.

Leila faced us with a certain young-womanly dignity that became her. "First Gran said, 'Thank you darling.' Then she had to fight for her breath before she could manage the rest. I could just make out her words. She said, 'Now you owe me your life.' I'm not sure what she meant by that."

King answered her soberly. "It's your future life you owe her, honey. What you do from now on. How you grow. How you work things out so you don't let her down. But not just because of her. She would never mean that. It's what we all owe ourselves that matters most. Not selfishly—but to do a little better with whatever we started out with."

Leila nodded solemnly and opened her fingers. I saw the gleam of the columbella shell upon her palm. Then she drew back her arm and hurled the shell away from her high into the air so that it sailed in a far, gleaming arc, to fall at last into brush and guinea grass on the hillside below the terrace wall. She was crying when she turned back to us, but these were not little-girl tears. This was a woman's suffering, and she would rise to it.

"That's for Gran," she said. "My first payment. But maybe I owe a lot of people my life. You, Dad. And—Jessica."

She turned to me and I pressed her hands in both of mine and let her go. She ran up the steps and into the house, out of our sight.

King drew me to him, his cheek against my hair. The barriers would be pushed back now. We would be patient and wait.

When he went into the house in response to Captain Osborn's call, I stood alone for a while, looking out over the hillside where a small gilded shell had fallen out of sight. If Maud knew, she would be pleased. How gratefully she would accept that large payment from Leila of a shell tossed upon a hillside.

Perhaps someday a stranger would come upon it lying there. By that time sun and rain would have worn away the gilt and it would

be no more than a small, creamy-white seashell. The finder would
never guess the story of what lay behind a shell fallen on a hillside
far away from any beach. It would tell him nothing, for the voices
were silent now—my own as well as Leila's—and it was better for us
not to remember too often a woman who danced in a red dress
with a golden columbella on her breast.

DATE DUE